BALTHAZAR'S BANE

KAT ROSS

ISBN: 978-1-7346184-0-2

CHAPTER 1

EGYPT, NEW YEAR'S EVE, 1889

Once upon a time, when only the royal family and its retinue were permitted within Cairo's fortified walls, there was a grand mausoleum known as the Turbat az-Za'faraan. Eleven generations of caliphs rested peacefully in the Saffron Tomb – until the first Mamluk sultan came along and decided it would make a splendid bazaar.

He tossed the royal bones onto a trash heap outside the city, knocked down a few walls and built the bustling souk called the Khan al-Khalili, a warren of shops and cafés and caravanserai. The market would prove a more durable institution than the rulers who preceded it. Centuries later, after the Turks replaced the sultans, the Khan al-Khalili remained Cairo's beating heart, a place where you could haggle for incense and silk, spices and gold.

A place of twisting alleys and shadowed courtyards.

A place where you could knife someone and vanish without a trace.

John Mortlake, blissfully ignorant of the fact that he had minutes to live, wandered through the bazaar, pausing to finger the fringe of a carpet or raise a silver tea set up to the light. The merchants who knew him averted their gazes.

Others approached with welcoming smiles that faltered when they met his cold eyes, and left them muttering thanks to Allah when he moved on.

As Mortlake passed the El Fishawy Café, where men in long white shawbs and turbans drank coffee from battered copper pots, the mirrors covering the far wall caught his reflection: tall and heavy across the shoulders, with a bushy black beard and overcoat dusty from travel. Beneath the coat, he kept a pistol holstered in his belt. The beaten leather satchel over one shoulder held a set of coiled necromantic chains.

Since Mortlake first entered the souk from Qasaba Street, he had the unsettled feeling he was being followed. By long habit, he scanned his surroundings but saw nothing out of the ordinary. It was early evening and the khan hummed with voices: bartering and begging, boasting and arguing. A hundred smells drifted through the air. A hundred colors dazzled the eye. Lamplight gleamed on delicate globes of blown glass and exquisitely adorned silver dallah, those ubiquitous coffee urns that resembled the lush curves of a woman's body.

Mortlake slowed before a shop selling hookahs and waited until he felt satisfied the shadow was a figment of his imagination. He still had a day until the payment was due, time enough to salvage what he could and run. Mortlake knew he was reckless — losing half a million pounds playing whist at the Saint James's Club certainly qualified — but he wasn't stupid. A stupid man would not have lived as long as he had. He would find the money (robbing and murdering someone rich being at the top of his list) and he would give it to Taj.

As soon as feasible.

But first he had to get rid of the girl.

Mortlake wound deeper into the labyrinth, striding through medieval stone archways, up and down flights of worn steps, into the oldest part of the Khan e-Khalili, whose foundations had once sat within the caliphate's eastern palace. The intricate tilework and vaulted ceilings threw back the echoes of his footsteps. There were few browsers and no tourists. The shops grew darker and shabbier. The merchandise on display was peculiar and often macabre; withered paws and yellowing skulls, murky bottles and half-moon daggers whose edges glimmered with fey blue light.

He'd nearly reached his destination when a man stepped from the alley ahead.

Mortlake halted and glanced back. Two more blocked his retreat. All wore flowing robes with black shemagh*s* that exposed only their blue eyes. The men's hands were empty, but their kind had little need for mortal weapons. Frost glistened where their bare feet touched the ground.

For a minute, the only sound was that of shutters quietly closing as the nearest merchants decided it would be prudent to go home early.

"Mortlake," the first one said. "We didn't expect you in Cairo until tomorrow." His breath formed shards of ice that tinkled as they struck the tiled floor.

John Mortlake donned a mask of indifference, turning sideways so he could keep all three in view. "I have other business to attend to. It's none of your concern."

"No," the creature said. "As long as you brought my master's money."

Mortlake licked his lips. "You'll have it when we agreed. Tomorrow."

The aquamarine stare grew colder. "Why don't you pay us now? Since chance brought us together. We have much to do. It would save time."

"I'm waiting for the bank wire to come through this afternoon." Mortlake's voice hardened. "Do you doubt me? I've always delivered."

The two others stepped forward and Mortlake readied himself to run. Then the first flicked a finger and they halted.

"Of course. Besides which, we both know there are other ways of paying debts." Amusement entered its voice. "Our master always has room for another pretty girl."

Mortlake suppressed a growl. "Tomorrow," he said through gritted teeth. "I'll have the money tomorrow."

"See that you do. And our master expects you to pick up the new shipment. He wishes to see you in person."

"I have no objection," Mortlake said, hiding his relief. "We will meet at the arranged time."

The three robed figures faded to shadows and flitted into cracks in the stone wall. Mortlake stood still for a moment, then cursed under his breath. At least they had swallowed the lie. He knew they would be busy recruiting for the Trials. Concubines and would-be heroes.

Mortlake wasn't sure which he pitied more.

After ensuring the agents were truly gone, he continued onward until he reached a dingy shop crammed with oddities of every description. At the sound of his footsteps, a young woman emerged from the rear. When she saw him, she locked the door without a word. Then she turned and unhooked one side of her veil, regarding him warily with large, almond-shaped eyes.

"I can't stay long," he said gruffly, dropping the satchel on a bit of open counter space.

Her gaze followed the bag with undisguised revulsion. Mortlake knew she sensed the necromantic chains coiled within. He had concealed his true nature as long as possible, but once her gift manifested it became impossible.

He opened the satchel and took out several small carvings, six rings and a jade necklace. She examined them one at a time, touching each item with a dreamy expression. Then she divided the contents into two piles, one much larger than the other.

"These are the talismans," she said, indicating the smaller pile.

4

He frowned. "So few?"

"Do you wish to know their purposes?"

"Not now." He gave a bleak smile. "Unless there's one that can be used to capture a jinn."

"I'm afraid not." She studied his face. "You lost the money, didn't you?"

He forced himself to meet her resigned gaze, though he felt the familiar shame. It wasn't the first time his gambling habit had left them deep in debt – though not to Taj.

Never to Taj.

"All of it?" she persisted when he didn't reply.

Mortlake nodded. "Taj's recruiters are here. But they don't know. Not yet."

She waited in silence.

"I managed to buy us another day, but we can't stay in Cairo."

"How much do you owe?"

"Half a million pounds."

She closed her eyes, gripping the counter.

"I'll get the damned money," he snapped. "But it'll take more than a day. Close up the shop and take a train to Alexandria, then a steamer for London. Can you afford a ticket?"

"I . . . I don't think so. I just paid the rent. There's only a few pounds left."

Mortlake fished in his pocket and handed her some bills. "This will cover your passage." He hesitated, then took out a small key. He pressed it into her hand. "There's a safety deposit box at Drummond's Bank in Charing Cross. You'll find more money there. It isn't much, but it will cover a hotel. Be sure to use one of your aliases."

She nodded. "What about you?"

"I'm the only one they want," he lied. "You're safer on your own."

Mortlake swept the trinkets into the satchel and slung it

over his shoulder. He strode to the door and glanced through the dirty window at the alley outside. It was empty. He left without saying goodbye or looking back, though he felt her watching.

Taj would hunt him down eventually, but his agents would be too busy to do it now. He'd get a head start. Plenty of time to make amends somehow.

He strode through the deserted bazaar, lost in dark thoughts, when a frail cry came from the shadows. "As salaam alaikum, sahib!"

Mortlake frowned and peered at the bundle of rags sprawled on the ground.

"Baksheesh," the crooked figure implored, holding out a hand. Glittering black eyes took in Mortlake's pale skin and European clothing. "You are English, sahib. Very good! God bless the Queen. Spare a piaster for a blind old—"

Mortlake kicked the hand away and the beggar groaned, throwing up an arm to shield his face from further blows. The necromancer strode off without a backward glance. The Khan e-Khalili was going downhill if the police permitted such scum within the walls. Perhaps the British would do something about it now that their soldiers occupied half the country. He hurried back toward the busier areas, keeping a sharp eye out for his foes, though he had a feeling it was simply bad luck that he had run into them in the first place.

Taj was his most valued customer. It had taken decades to cultivate the relationship, one that Mortlake had pissed away in a single foolish evening. Taj would never let the debt go — it was a matter of reputation – but if Mortlake paid him a princely sum in interest, he might be persuaded to offer a second chance. It would present no great difficulty to rob a few wealthy victims, though he would need to be cautious. Mortlake had his own reputation to consider. His principal buyers would be off-limits.

6

I'll never gamble again, he vowed, aware it was not the first time he had made such a promise.

Mortlake resolved to catch a night train to Port Said and take a ship from there. His steps slowed as he pondered his route out of the souk. He knew the mazelike passages as well as his own face and didn't want to risk running into Taj's jinn again. A back way out would be best, he thought, turning into a section of the market recently ravaged by fire.

The blaze had spared a popular café but everything beyond was still being rebuilt. The smell of old smoke lingered in the air as he made for a courtyard leading out to al-Muizz Street. Mortlake raised a hand to tug at his bushy beard and it was all that saved him from the garrote that slipped around his neck.

The wire caught his wrist, snagging on bone. He gasped and clawed at his throat. Adrenaline coursed through his veins. Mortlake staggered backwards and slammed his assailant into the wall. He heard a grunt, but the garrote kept tightening. The pain was nearly unbearable. He dug his feet in and slammed the attacker against the wall twice more. The wire fell away.

Mortlake spun and stared into a pair of burning black eyes. It was the beggar. Up close, Mortlake realized he knew the man and cursed himself for not paying closer attention.

"Balthazar," he grated.

They grappled silently, just thirty feet from the busy café where men sipped coffee and puffed on water pipes. Mortlake's right hand burned like hellfire, but he managed to shove Balthazar away long enough to snatch his necromantic chains from the leather bag. He snapped the shackle around his own wrist and felt strength surge into him. He gripped Balthazar by the throat and lifted him off the ground, pinning him to the wall. Black lightning flickered along the chains, but Mortlake held it in check.

"Why?" he spat. "Who sent you?"

"No one," Balthazar croaked.

Mortlake regarded him with narrowed eyes. "The rumors are true then. You stand against us."

The reply was barely audible, his foe fighting for each breath. "I've always . . . stood . . . against you."

Mortlake tightened his grip, the dark magic of the chains aching for release. He could char Balthazar to a husk. Sear him to ash. He felt the power build . . . and some instinct made him glance at the end of the alley. A veiled figure stood in the shadows, her eyes wide and terrified.

Mortlake grunted in pain as a knife flew through the air. He clutched his chest. Blood bloomed between his fingers. He saw Balthazar scrambling for the garrote where it had fallen on the ground. The heart wound was agony, but not a killing blow. Not for a necromancer.

It wasn't too late. He could still unleash the black lightning.

John Mortlake hesitated.

An instant later, the wire loop closed around his neck and he thought no more.

CHAPTER 2

The beggar yanked the shawb over his head. Beneath it, he wore a white linen shirt creased with sweat. The chain of a gold watch dangled from a tailored waistcoat.

"That was a bit close," Balthazar muttered, his throat still raw from the necromancer's grip.

Like Mortlake, he had thick black hair and black eyes, but the resemblance ended there. He was just as tall but leanly built, with a wolfish elegance. Balthazar looked like a man in the prime of life, but he was already old when the Romans built their first outpost along the Nile.

He kicked the filthy shawb away as a second man – the one who had thrown the knife – emerged from the shadows of a burnt-out shop. He was in his late twenties, with a bowler hat and a mustache that he wore waxed to little points. He glanced down at Mortlake's severed head, the eyes already glazing with death.

"I warned you he wouldn't be easy, my lord," Lucas Devereaux replied with a hint of reproach, handing Balthazar a charcoal-grey coat and silk top hat.

"I never said he'd be *easy*." Balthazar smoothed his raven hair and adjusted the hat. He put on the coat and did up the silver buttons. "But it was better you stayed back to keep watch. We can't have witnesses raising the alarm. I'm too well-known around here."

The alley was still deserted, but it wouldn't be long before someone passed by. He bent down and pressed a hidden catch on the chains, removing them from the dead man's wrist. Balthazar stuffed them into the satchel along with the blood-soaked shawb. He rolled up the wire garrote and tossed that into the satchel, too.

Balthazar glanced at his watch with a frown. "Three minutes. Where the devil is it? I'd hate to miss supper on the terrace—" A crack began to widen in the stone between his legs. He stepped away and turned to Lucas. "Would you mind? It's my last clean shirt until the laundry service comes back."

"Not at all, my lord," Lucas replied, the words infused with a soft French accent.

The smaller man drew a short sword and gripped it with two hands, peering down into the crack. A menacing growl came from the darkness below. Lucas waited. A minute later, a head and leather-clad shoulders emerged. The head had long silver hair, caked with dark gore. The eyes were also silver, reflecting Lucas's own face like dull mirrors. Raw-knuckled fingers curled around the hilt of a broadsword, also streaked with old gore.

Lips curled back from rotten teeth. Lucas judged the angle and took its head off with one clean blow. The revenant slipped soundlessly back into the crack.

The creatures were summoned by the death of a necromancer. No one knew why — only that they invariably showed up and it was far easier to put them down *before* they emerged from the crevice.

Lucas gazed at the blade with distaste. "Give me that robe again, would you?"

Balthazar thrust the satchel at him. Lucas cleaned his blade and returned it to the sheath.

"What about him?" he asked, looking at Mortlake.

Balthazar shrugged. "I don't care who finds him once we're gone." His gaze turned to the darkest corner of the alley. "Over there."

Mortlake was a large man and it took both of them to drag him behind some charred barrels. This task accomplished, Lucas grabbed the satchel and they hurried out of the bazaar, emerging across the street from the Al-Azhar Mosque in time for the evening call to prayer. It echoed from minarets across the city, summoning the faithful who streamed through the great doors.

The mosque dated back to the Fatimid dynasty nine hundred years before. It was finally being renovated after decades of neglect by Mohamed Tewfik Pasha, the young khedive of Egypt and Sudan. The pair skirted a flimsy scaffold and strode to a carriage waiting at the end of the street next to rubble from the new construction.

"Lord Koháry." The driver ducked his head, which was topped with a tall red fez. "Did you enjoy the market?"

"Very much," Balthazar said with a smile. "Take us back to Shepheard's."

They climbed in, heading west toward the Nile Corniche. A thousand points of light shone from the mosques, which had oil lamps in glass holders suspended from the domes by chains. Balthazar watched the narrow, crooked streets roll by in silence while Lucas searched Mortlake's satchel.

"There's some jewelry," Lucas said. "Likely talismanic."

"We'll throw it all in the vault," Balthazar said with a sigh. "There's still room at the house on Lake Baikal."

Lucas cast him an inquiring glance. "I thought you'd be pleased."

"I am."

"No, you're brooding, my lord."

Balthazar fell silent for a long minute. "By all rights, I should be dead," he said at last.

Lucas made a small noise of assent. "It's hardly the first time."

"Mortlake got his hand up just as the garrote fell around his neck. When he locked his chains on, I thought it was over. The black lightning was at his fingertips." Balthazar ran a thumb over the glass face of his pocket watch. The ticking of its little clockwork heart usually soothed him. "You must have seen, Lucas. He never used it."

Lucas's brown eyes narrowed in thought. "That *is* rather interesting."

Balthazar shot him a wry look. "*Interesting?* I nearly ended in a scorch mark."

"But you didn't, my lord. And need I remind you—"

"That you warned me not to take him alone?" Balthazar interrupted. "No, you needn't. You've already reminded me several times."

"So what's your point?"

"I want to know why." He tapped an index finger on the watch, which read six thirty-nine. "Tell me again what you know about John Mortlake. Everything."

"According to my sources in London, he comes to Cairo every year between Christmas and New Year's. Clearly some longstanding business arrangement, although he's fanatically secretive about it. He deals in ancient artifacts, many of them talismans, but he's not a collector himself, merely a middleman. He has a nose for valuable objects and an impressive roster of buyers, but he can barely hold onto a shilling of what he earns in commissions."

"The gambling habit."

Lucas nodded. "It's gotten worse in recent years."

"They tend to do that." Balthazar paused. "The obvious reason Mortlake refrained from using black lightning is that he didn't want to risk killing his own kin. If there's someone he cares about—"

Lucas gave a mirthless laugh. "He was a necromancer. By definition, they care for no one but themselves."

When Lucas was a young child, he had lost his entire family to a necromancer. More than twenty years had passed, but Balthazar knew the wound would never heal completely.

"Mortlake is still a man," Balthazar said carefully. "He might not be immune to emotion."

Lucas looked skeptical. "I researched him thoroughly. He's a lone wolf."

"Then how do you explain his hesitation?"

"Does it really matter?" Lucas sighed. "Mortlake is dead."

"I thought you despised unanswered questions."

"I do. But . . . ."

"What?"

"I'm almost out of digestives." This was spoken defiantly.

"My God." Balthazar gazed at him fondly. "Surely we can find you some biscuits. This place is crawling with your countrymen." He arched an eyebrow. "But I must insist that you eat some real food at supper tonight. You can't live on those things. You'll end up with scurvy."

"Better scurvy than an intestinal parasite," Lucas muttered darkly.

Balthazar rolled his eyes. "Anything else about Mortlake?"

"Not really. He was a member of the Duzakh, of course, but he kept to himself. I don't know the exact year he turned, but I gather he'd been a necromancer for less than three centuries."

"A swaddling babe," Balthazar said dryly.

"He claimed he killed the last necromancer who owned the chains. Said he was attacked and got lucky with a sword. I have no reason to doubt it."

"It's rare, but it does happen," Balthazar agreed.

Lucas paused. "There are whispers he had a contact in

Arabia. Someone who provided him with a large number of very valuable talismans. But it was only that — a rumor." He gazed at Balthazar. "You should let it go, my lord."

Balthazar sighed. "Fine."

"And no taking them alone anymore. It's too risky."

"Whatever you say."

Balthazar signaled the driver to stop at the new Kasr-en-Nile Bridge. He and Lucas strolled past the pair of enormous stone lions on pedestals guarding the entrance and walked to the center of the iron span. A man on a bicycle rode past, but the bridge was otherwise empty. Balthazar opened the leather satchel and tossed the bloody robe into the river, where it was swallowed up by sluggish brown water.

"How many of the Duzakh are left?" he asked quietly.

"I'm not sure of the exact number." Lucas paused. "But it's quite a few."

"That's good. I wouldn't know what to do with myself if we ran out of necromancers."

"You'd think of something, my lord."

Balthazar smiled faintly, his teeth white in the darkness. "Well, I would, but I doubt you'd approve of it."

As they returned to the carriage, a group of street urchins ran up with grubby hands extended, begging for *baksheesh*. Lucas dug into his pocket and handed out peppermint sticks. Wherever they happened to be, he always kept candy for the children.

"They'll never leave you alone if you keep feeding them," Balthazar remarked, eying the ragged group with distaste.

Lucas made a noncommittal sound. He'd donned a scarf and gloves even though the temperature was in the mid-sixties.

"Do you really think you can find some digestives?" he asked hopefully. "I know we're leaving tomorrow, but I'd like some for the journey."

"I'll ask the desk clerk at Shepheard's. I've known him for years. He can get anything within reason."

The hotel on Ibrahim Pasha Street was famed for its opulent décor, with lush gardens and huge granite pillars resembling those of the ancient Egyptian temples. The terrace was crowded with the usual assortment of expatriates – French and British army officers, invalids and crocodile hunters, special correspondents and mummy collectors, along with sunburnt tourists in ridiculous pith helmets.

Holiday decorations adorned the date palms. The mood was festive as Balthazar and Lucas made their way to the American Bar. Lucas ordered hot water with lemon and honey, Balthazar a brandy.

"Another year gone," he said, raising his glass with a touch of weariness. "To 1890."

"To 1890, my lord."

They clinked glasses. The thrill of killing Mortlake had already worn off and Balthazar felt boredom setting in. His vocation might be a righteous one, but he was no hero. Far from it.

"I'll put the chains in the safe with those papyri from the Valley of the Kings," Lucas said.

"Do we have all the export permits from the Antiquities Department?"

"It was expensive, but yes. There shouldn't be any problem at customs." Lucas took out two passports stamped with Turkish visas and a train timetable. "Our documents are all in order, my lord. There are a few trains departing on New Year's Day. If you have no objection, I'd like to take the early one. It gets us to Alexandria by four in the afternoon."

"How early?"

"Ten o'clock."

Balthazar frowned. "I suppose I can manage it."

He surveyed the lobby. A few women caught his eye and he gave them idle smiles. With any luck, he'd find a willing partner to warm his bed. It *was* New Year's Eve, after all. He drained the last of his brandy and set the glass down. When they reached London, he would add Mortlake's necromantic chains to a growing collection. Talismans couldn't be destroyed – not by him at least – but he could keep them from falling into the wrong hands.

Once it had been enough. He'd relished the hunt and taken satisfaction from ridding the world of predators who murdered the innocent. But lately Balthazar had felt . . . unmoored. Not even his brush with death seemed to matter. He wasn't suicidal, but nor did he care much about living. And that troubled him far more than Mortlake's hesitation.

Lucas was the one bright spot. Resourceful and dedicated to the cause, he was also inherently decent despite being raised by the worst rake in Britain. Balthazar was still amazed at how well his protégé had turned out.

Waiters were busy rearranging the furniture in the dining room for the party that night, clearing space for a temporary bar and carrying in crates of champagne. Through a fog of listlessness, Balthazar tried to remember where he had been last December 31st. Some party no doubt, although they all ran together after a while. Something to do with a museum . . . . New York? Or was that the year before?

Male heads turned in unison as a woman entered the hotel reception area through the glass doors. Her plain white dress was long and high-necked, but Balthazar's expert eye detected the voluptuous form underneath. His fingers tightened on the edge of the bar. A wide-brimmed hat covered most of her face, but he saw a pair of lush red lips, slightly parted. Strands of dark hair had come loose from their bindings, adhering damply to her nape.

"Dear God," he murmured. "Her cup overfloweth."

Lucas looked up from the train schedule. "Pardon, my lord?"

"Never mind." Balthazar's gaze lingered as she paused to

speak to the desk clerk, then strode purposefully toward the terrace.

"Excuse me for a moment," he said to Lucas, making a beeline for reception. The clerk straightened at his approach. Balthazar always tipped well, even if his requests were occasionally peculiar.

"Lord Koháry," he said with a smile. "How may I assist you this evening?"

"That woman you just spoke to. Is she staying here?"

The clerk gave a knowing smile. "Not that I'm aware of, my lord."

"Have you seen her before?"

"No, my lord."

"What did she want?"

The clerk leaned forward and lowered his voice. "She asked about the Thomas Cook tours." He pointed at a stack of brochures.

Balthazar slid a pound note across the desk. "Let me know if you see her again."

"Of course," the clerk murmured, smoothly pocketing the money.

"What was that about?" Lucas asked as Balthazar slid onto his barstool. "My digestives?"

The hope in his voice brought a stab of guilt.

"I thought I saw someone I knew." He smiled weakly. "I promise I'll ask, though."

Lucas gazed at him with a hint of reproach. "I suppose you're going to the party tonight."

"Naturally. Aren't you?"

"I don't think so."

"Come now, it's New Year's Eve."

"I prefer a hot bath and a tonic of Epsom salts. We have an early start tomorrow." Lucas looked pointedly at Balthazar. "Don't drink too much."

"Have you ever seen me intoxicated?"

"No," Lucas conceded. "But that's only because you have the tolerance of an elephant."

Balthazar stared at the doors to the terrace where his prey had gone to ground.

"Don't worry," he said. "I'll find something to entertain myself."

They retired to adjoining suites on the fourth floor. Balthazar soaked in a hot bath, shaved and donned his black tie. It was after ten o'clock by the time he made his way downstairs. The party was in full swing. The women wore glittering gowns, their husbands in the usual somber suits with starched white shirts. The dining room had been turned into a ballroom with an orchestra. Uniformed waiters moved among the crowd with trays of sweets and glasses of champagne.

Balthazar usually adored parties. He liked to flirt and dazzle, but tonight he was on edge. Perhaps it was a residue of his uncertainty about Mortlake, or just the prospect of facing another year, another decade, another century. He'd only been half joking on the bridge. Balthazar had no idea what he would do when he ran out of necromancers to kill, and he was far from sure he deserved to live long enough to find out.

He looked around the room, but the enchanting creature from the lobby was not there. The party suddenly seemed insufferably dull. He saw a number of attractive women, yet he lacked any desire to approach them. It came as a relief when he heard his name being called.

"Count Koháry!"

The eminent Egyptologist Flinders Petrie and his patron, Kennard Haworth, waved him over.

"What brings you to Cairo?" Petrie asked. In his late thirties, he was ruggedly handsome with intense dark eyes and a beard just starting to show threads of grey. "Sponsoring a new excavation?"

"Just a buying trip. Some papyrus scrolls and a collection

of canopic jars. I plan to donate them to the British Museum."

Should Petrie make inquires, he would find that Balthazar spoke the truth. They knew him as a rich collector from Hungary who always traveled with his secretary. Chasing antiquities provided an ideal cover for his travels, as well as his extensive knowledge — much of which was firsthand. "And you?"

"We've been at Medinet el-Fayum and Hawara for the last year."

"Hawara," Balthazar said, lifting a glass of champagne from the tray of a passing waiter. "Late Middle Kingdom?"

Petrie nodded. "Twelfth dynasty. A pyramid and mortuary complex we're calling the Labyrinth. Both built by Amen-emhat III and dating from about 1700 B.C. to the Roman period."

Balthazar's interest stirred. "Didn't Herodotus mention something about that?"

"Indeed. In Book Two of the *Histories*, he described it as situated a little above the lake of Moiris and nearly opposite the City of Crocodiles. Lepsius began some investigations there in '43."

"What did you find?"

Petrie's dark eyes gleamed. "Among other things, a scroll that contains the first two books of *The Iliad*."

"Well done," Balthazar said with a warm smile.

"The labyrinth itself was demolished, I'm afraid," Haworth added. "Probably by Ptolemy. But we found the mortuary temple intact." He glanced at Petrie. "As well as the tomb of Amenemhat's daughter. It was secured by several nasty concealed trapdoors weighing about twenty tons each. They were undisturbed."

"And what are your plans for next year?"

"I mean to go to the Holy Land, a site called Tell el-Hesi. The dig will be backed by the Palestine Exploration Fund."

They talked shop for a while. Balthazar discreetly withdrew his watch and saw it was still half an hour to midnight. He suppressed a yawn. When had he become the sort of person who preferred bed over revelry? As he looked around at the flushed faces, he found he had no interest in talking to any of them.

But he refused to leave until the clock chimed midnight at least. It was a matter of pride.

Balthazar slipped the watch back into his pocket.

And then he saw her.

The loose white gown had been exchanged for clinging silver lame. Masses of dark hair piled loosely atop her head, revealing a long, slender neck. Her bare arms were rounded but strong-looking.

His companions' words sank to a buzz as he watched her cross the room. The bodice looked like it might split down the seams if she coughed.

Adrenaline flooded his veins. Balthazar's pupils dilated.

"Count Koháry?" Petrie asked.

"Pardon?" he murmured.

"How long will you be staying?"

Balthazar tore his eyes away from the rapturous vision. "I leave tomorrow. Would you excuse me?"

The men exchanged startled glances at his abrupt departure, but Balthazar barely noticed. He strode through the crowd, trying to keep her in view. She wore a solemn, inward expression. Balthazar lost her for a moment as she passed the dance floor and orchestra. He paused, heart pounding, and caught a brief flash of silver leaving through the French doors. Balthazar pushed through the dense knot of people around the bar, ignoring mutters of protest, and stepped out to the terrace.

She stood alone at the far end, gloved hands braced on the balustrade. A few people occupied the outdoor tables, but the evening was cool and most had stayed inside. Balthazar stopped in the shadow of a potted date palm and studied her for a moment. She had an aura of melancholy that only increased his ardor – and curiosity. Why had she come here tonight if not to celebrate?

When she withdrew a packet of cigarettes from her hand-bag, he saw his opening. Balthazar strolled down the terrace and stopped next to her. They were almost the same height.

"Good evening," he said politely.

She turned and met his gaze with a directness that was rare for an upper-class woman of this time and place. Balthazar withdrew a box of matches from his pocket.

"May I?"

He leaned in and lit her cigarette. She wore a hint of some musky perfume. Blood pounded in his ears.

"Thank you," she murmured, exhaling a stream of smoke.

Up close, she was not what the English would call beauti-ful. Her features were too strong, her eyebrows too thick, her nose too bold, her skin a shade too olive. Her accent was clipped British, but with a faint trace of the East. And her voice was a lovely alto, just a bit husky. His infatuation deepened.

Balthazar bowed at the waist. "I am Count Habsburg-Koháry." He smiled. "The title is nominal, but I still exploit it shamelessly."

She held out a hand. He raised the gloved fingers to his lips.

"Mrs. Fitzwalter. Do you smoke?"

She offered him the packet of Kyriazi Freres, an Egyptian brand. Balthazar rarely indulged, but accepted so he had an excuse to linger. She studied him frankly as he cupped the flame. She was older than he'd first thought, early thirties. *Perfect.*

"I saw you looking at the travel brochures," he said.

She turned away and gazed out at the gardens. "My husband booked a Nile cruise with Thomas Cook."

"You don't seem enthusiastic."

Mrs. Fitzwalter gave him a forced smile. "I'm sure it will be very charming."

Balthazar leaned against the balustrade. "I collect antiquities myself. Fund a few digs here and there."

Interest sparked in her eyes. "Where?"

"Alexandria was the last one. We found a trove of items belonging to Ptolemy. Are you interested in archaeology?"

"My father is a history professor at Oxford," she said. "Greece and Rome are his primary interests. I suppose his love of the ancients rubbed off on me. I visited the museum in Giza yesterday." She smiled. "Of course, the most valuable relics are all in England now. Are you one of those who come to plunder our heritage, Count Koháry?"

"I donate to museums all over the world, provided they have the proper facilities to preserve the artifacts." He glanced at her. "So you are Egyptian?'

"Half. On my mother's side. We left when I was a child."

"Do you come back often?"

She shook her head. "Sadly, no. The holiday was my husband's idea."

She glanced past his shoulder down the length of the terrace. It was the third time in the last five minutes.

"Are you expecting someone?" he asked. "I don't wish to intrude."

The thought that she might be meeting a lover inspired a twinge of jealousy.

"No, but my husband dislikes it when I speak to strange men," she said frankly. "Especially when they are young and fair."

Well, *that* pleased him, although the word "fair" made him think of a buxom milkmaid.

"Husbands generally do," Balthazar replied with a lazy smile.

She didn't smile back. Her eyes were wary.

"What's the matter?" he asked with a frown.

She shook her head. "It's nothing—"

"No." He ground his unsmoked cigarette into the sand of an ashtray. "You look afraid."

She didn't reply, but he heard her breath hitch.

"You can trust me," he said gently. "Perhaps I can help."

"We've only just met," she said with an edge of amusement.

She'd rallied. Not a shrinking violet, though he didn't imagine she would be.

"Sometimes it's easier to talk to a stranger," he said. "I can assure you, my intentions are entirely honorable." The lie spilled smoothly from his tongue.

Mrs. Fitzwalter hesitated. Then she laid a hand on his sleeve and drew him over to the French doors. They were concealed by a date palm, but had a view through the fronds into the party. She scanned the crowd.

"That's him."

She tilted her chin at a group of British officers gathered near the bar. They were in dress uniform, crimson coats with silver braid and high collars. Most wore bushy side whiskers and they looked deep into their cups.

"Which one?"

"Far left," she replied glumly. "White hair and a red nose."

"Ah."

The man was old enough to be her grandfather. Balthazar felt pity for her.

"Not a love match, I take it," he said dryly.

She finished her cigarette in silence.

"I know the question is rather forward—" he began.

"It's all right." Mrs. Fitzwalter jabbed the smoldering stub into the ashtray and turned to face him. "I was born in Alexandria. My father taught at university there. My mother and I were very happy, but my father wanted to return to

England. We emigrated when I was twelve. After I'd finished my schooling, I resisted marriage for as long as possible."

Her jaw set. "None of the suitors were to my taste. It made my father very angry. When I turned twenty-eight, he said he would not allow me to remain a burdensome spinster. Within a month, they'd married me off to that old goat."

"Forcibly?"

"More or less. I was given the choice of wedding Colonel Fitzwalter or entering a nunnery."

Balthazar suppressed a shudder at the idea of this spirited woman cloistered away in a convent. She belonged in his bed, naked, hair fanned out across a silken pillow—

"That was three years ago." She sighed. "I could tolerate it if he was a kind man. But he isn't, Lord Koháry. He keeps me isolated in the countryside. I have no friends. No one to confide in."

Balthazar turned to face her. "If I might be so forward," he murmured, "you have a friend now."

She smiled sadly. "That's sweet of you. But I don't see what you can do about my situation."

"Jealous husbands don't scare me."

"Yes, well, you don't have to sleep with them every night, do you?"

Deep bitterness tinged her voice. "Does he hurt you?" Balthazar asked quietly.

She didn't answer.

He felt a surge of outrage. There was little in the world he despised more than men who bullied women. "Times are changing. You can demand a divorce. To hell with your father—"

"Stop," she said firmly. "I've gone too far. This is an entirely inappropriate conversation. The fault for that is mine. Please forgive me. But I think you must go now."

He gazed down at her — though not by much. She was unusually tall for a woman. No, he amended, not just tall . . .

Amazonian. It was a wonder she didn't beat the old man senseless.

"There is no fault," he said at last. "And nothing to forgive."

She nodded. A delicate pink flush crested her cheeks. "Thank you."

"But it's an odd coincidence that you plan to journey up the Nile. I've always wanted to make the trip myself."

She froze. Worry flashed across her features. "Oh, you mustn't."

"Why not?"

"Because . . . because he'll kill me if he knows we've spoken!"

"Why would he know if no one tells him?"

She drew herself up. Her black eyes narrowed with sudden anger. "I'm grateful for your sympathy, but I can take care of myself."

"No one said you couldn't."

They stood very close. Her chest swelled as she struggled to breathe through the tight bodice of her gown.

"Tell me your name," he said raggedly. "Not *his* name. *Your* name."

She tugged a glove off and touched his lips with bare fingers. Balthazar's throat went dry.

Beyond the glass doors, the crowd started chanting the ten-second countdown to midnight.

Balthazar seized her hand and pressed her wrist to his mouth. He felt her pulse beat against his lips. It was strong and fierce. Bursting with life. Their eyes locked. His knees weakened with a wave of desire unlike anything he'd experienced in . . . oh, *centuries.*

"Goodbye, Count Koháry," she whispered.

Mrs. Fitzwalter tore her hand away and vanished through the French doors in a swirl of silver lamé.

"*Happy New Year!*"

Merry cheers erupted from inside. Horns tooted. Glasses clinked.

Balthazar simply stood there, gobsmacked.

He didn't try to pursue. It would be madness with her husband inside. But he had to save her. And after he saved her, he would seduce her.

Or possibly before.

But he knew one thing for certain.

He absolutely could not go back to England and forget about her.

He laughed like a madman, loud enough to draw curious stares from the revelers on the terrace. Balthazar strode inside. He seized a glass of champagne from a startled gentleman in a tuxedo and tossed it back in one gulp.

"To 1890!" he cried.

The fellow grinned amiably. "Hear, hear!"

His friends raised their glasses and bellowed a drunken toast.

Balthazar clapped the man on the shoulder and strode through the ballroom, making for the front desk.

"Abdul!" he bellowed.

The sleepy clerk looked up with alarm. "My lord?"

"Book a passage on that Cook cruise, will you?" Balthazar dropped a wad of bills on the desk. "Two cabins, first class."

Abdul blinked. "Certainly, my lord."

"And give me one of those brochures."

He leafed through it as he paced to the lift with a new spring in his step.

CHAPTER 3

Lucas Devereaux was having the most pleasant dream. He was home in London making tea in the kitchen. The account books waited on the table with three freshly sharpened pencils. Fog pressed against the windows, but he was stocked up on digestive biscuits and Balthazar was still sleeping off the party he'd gone to the night before.

In short, all was right with the world.

Lucas started pouring the perfectly brewed tea into his favorite cup when a gust of wind guttered the candle. He frowned. The door banged open—

Wakefulness came instantly. Lucas shot to his feet, eyes wild and sword ready. He always kept it near to hand, a habit that had saved his life on more than one occasion. It wasn't yet dawn and his bleary eyes saw only a shadow-cloaked figure looming at the foot of the bed.

"Thank you," Balthazar said, easing the tip of Lucas's sword from his throat with two fingers. "But I already shaved today."

Lucas scowled and lowered his blade. "My lord. What on earth are you doing up? Or I suppose you haven't slept yet."

"The second." Balthazar smiled. "And yet I'm fresh as a

daisy." He lit the oil lamp and sank into a chair. Lucas regarded him suspiciously.

"You *have* shaved. And you're wearing a morning coat."

"Is that so shocking?"

"If the hour is before eleven, which it clearly is, then yes."

Rousing Balthazar from his sheets was a lengthy, complicated process that involved escalating threats and several cups of strong coffee. Lucas certainly didn't expect him to be up at the crack of dawn on New Year's Day. Such an event was improbable to say the least.

Which meant trouble.

"There's been a slight change of plans," Balthazar said.

Lucas suppressed a groan. "How slight?"

Balthazar waved a hand. "A minor detour. We're taking a steamer up the Nile. Trust me, you'll love it."

Lucas stared at him. "It's that woman, isn't it?"

"What woman?"

"The one from the lobby yesterday."

Balthazar frowned into the middle distance. "I'm not sure I recall—"

"Spare me the dissembling." Lucas stepped into his slippers, which were arranged at a precise distance from the edge of the bed. "I know you, so let's just get it over with."

Balthazar sighed. "We'll only go as far as the Karnak Hotel in Luxor." He held out a brochure. "Take a look. They have English doctors and a resident clergyman of the Church of England. I'm certain we can get you some digestives."

Lucas eyed the brochure like it was a live cobra. Balthazar sighed again, deeper this time.

"Have you no interest in culture?"

This hardly merited a response and Lucas did not give him one. There was an awkward silence.

"Been going to the gymnasium, have you?" Balthazar asked in an admiring tone.

Lucas wore a short nightshirt that revealed deathly pale if impressively muscular legs.

"I ride my bicycle to that tea shop in Kensington every afternoon," he replied tartly, yanking on a pair of trousers with excessive force. "How long?"

"What?"

"How long is the tour?"

"Er, about two weeks. Round trip," Balthazar added.

Lucas dampened a comb, parted his brown hair severely on the right and began to plaster it down.

"The first cataract isn't until Aswan so we'll have clear sailing to Luxor," Balthazar said cheerfully, scanning the brochure. "By this afternoon we'll be riding donkeys to the pyramids at Giza."

Lucas slid the straps of his suspenders over a clean shirt and began doing up the buttons.

"Seen them already."

"Some sun will do you good."

"Don't like the sun."

Balthazar rolled his eyes. "How very English of you. Well, if you're truly suffering, I'll buy you a turban."

Lucas jammed the bowler hat on his head. "No, thank you, my lord. What about our luggage?"

"I've already made the arrangements." Balthazar sprang to his feet. "Shall I help you pack? I'm all ready to go myself."

Lucas glanced at him in the mirror. Balthazar actually looked *happy* for the first time in ages. In truth, Lucas had been a bit worried. He knew his master better than anyone and had sensed something amiss. But the black mood seemed to have lifted. Lucas found himself relenting.

"I can manage. Do we at least have time for breakfast first?"

Balthazar smiled. "I'll meet you downstairs."

EAGER TOURISTS CROWDED THE RAILS AS THE STEAMER PULLED away from its berth near the Kasr-en-Nile Bridge where they had tossed the bloody robes into the river the previous evening. It was named *Rameses the Great* and had two tiers with eighty cabins for both first and third class passengers.

The first-class suites were on the upper level, with a long shaded balcony connecting them. Resigned to his fate, Lucas pored over the brochure. Balthazar scanned the other passengers, but saw no sign of Mrs. Fitzwalter. He did, however, spot her husband. The colonel was chatting with a group of elderly sightseers. Balthazar's eyes narrowed, his heart pounding with unfamiliar feelings of jealousy and loathing.

"It's a lovely morning," Lucas remarked.

Balthazar gave a noncommittal grunt.

"I'm rather looking forward to the Temple of Denderah. It's not until the seventh day though."

"See?" Balthazar's gaze roved restlessly over the passengers. "I told you it would be fun."

Lucas sighed.

They'd taken the Aida and Queen Victoria suites, which nestled in the gentle curves of the stern. Both rooms were large and lavishly appointed. Once the luggage was stowed, the first-class passengers gathered on the large open foredeck, where the captain stood with their tour guide.

"Gather round, everyone!" the guide called out merrily.

He repeated their itinerary for the day. Lucas's hand shot up.

"Will there be lunch?"

"Naturally," the guide said with a smile. "A picnic at the Great Pyramid."

Lucas handed him a list. "These are the foods I'm allergic to. Can you please convey it to the chef?"

The guide blinked as he saw the paper, penned in a tiny, cramped hand. "I'd be happy to, Mr. Devereaux."

"I assume we'll have shade," Lucas added. "I burn easily."

After receiving adequate assurances, they retired to their balcony with cups of hibiscus punch.

"If she beds you before Aswan, can we go home early?" Lucas wondered.

"Don't be crass," Balthazar replied with a frown. "I haven't even seen the lady today."

The steamer passed the minarets and Roman fortress of Old Cairo, and then the island of Roda with its groves and gardens.

"It says that's where Moses was found in the rushes by the Pharaoh's daughter," Lucas observed.

"Fascinating."

"I thought you were interested in culture," Lucas said innocently.

Balthazar gave him a level look. He pointed. "Do you see that dome on the south end of the island? It holds the famed Nilometer. A column that marks the annual rise of the river. First built in A.D. 715 and destroyed by a flood, ironically enough. Rebuilt by the astronomer Alfraganus in approximately 870 A.D. Blown up by the French in 1825. Rebuilt yet again as you see it now."

"Ah."

"The sixteenth cubit is called the Sultan's Water. The land tax isn't levied until that level has been reached. Do you want to know more? I can bore you for hours."

"Actually, I find it interesting," Lucas said stubbornly.

"I'm glad one of us does." Balthazar finished his punch. "Excuse me, won't you?"

"Of course."

He prowled along the balcony. Colonel Fitzwalter sat at a table four cabins down, fanning himself with his hat. He looked up at Balthazar's approach.

"Good afternoon!" he boomed. "Foreigner, are you?"

"Hungarian," Balthazar replied, forcing a smile. "Count Habsburg-Koháry. And you are?"

"Fitzwalter," he replied, rising ponderously to grasp Balthazar's hand. "Alastair Fitzwalter."

"What do you think of the scenery?"

The steamer was just passing the lofty Citadel of Cairo, the white dome of its mosque visible in the distance.

The colonel shrugged. "I'm more interested in the tombs."

"Of course. Are you traveling with acquaintances?"

"Friends from my old regiment. And my wife, although she's not feeling well. I doubt she'll accompany me today."

Balthazar raised a hand to his forehead. "Yes, I fear I overindulged at the party last night. I think I'll rest in my room. Enjoy the pyramids!"

The colonel nodded uncertainly. "I shall. I hope you feel—"

Balthazar hurried back to Lucas.

"Who was that?"

"The lady's husband."

"Ah."

"She's pretending to be ill," he said gleefully.

"I take it you won't be riding a donkey this afternoon?"

"I'm afraid you're on your own. But you can keep an eye on the colonel for me."

Lucas sighed. "Not a military man. They're often armed, you know."

"Just watch him."

"For what?"

"Make sure he doesn't come back early."

"And how am I supposed to stop him?"

"You'll think of something."

Lucas adopted a long-suffering expression. "Naturally, my lord."

The pyramids of Giza, Sakkarah and Dashoor appeared on the western shore, as well as the immense quarries where the stone had been excavated. A few minutes later, the steamer anchored in the shallows. Those who planned to sightsee disembarked. Balthazar watched the colonel trot off on a donkey.

He sat on the balcony and waited for the door to the Fitzwalters' cabin to swing wide.

Balthazar felt a touch restless, but the anticipation was a pleasure in itself. He moved his chair into the sun, letting it warm his face. The top deck had emptied. Most of the crew were ashore replenishing provisions. If she was in a bold mood, they might even make good use of the deck chairs. He could think of several promising configurations with very little effort.

Balthazar sighed. He cracked an eye. No sign of movement, but she was probably waiting until her husband was well gone.

An hour passed. Then two. He considered knocking, but discarded the idea. Seduction was a fine art. It wouldn't do to appear desperate. He checked his watch again. Poured a cup of punch and downed it.

Perhaps he had misinterpreted the situation. What if the brute had done something to her?

The tour group returned at sunset. Lucas looked distinctly pink, but he seemed in good spirits.

"Well?" he asked.

"Well, nothing," Balthazar snapped.

"You should have come along. The picnic lunch was lovely!"

Balthazar listened to Lucas describe the day's activities in excruciating detail.

". . . and we visited the Serapeum, that's the burial ground of the Divine Bulls of Apis. There's lots of spooky subterranean vaults under the chapel at Sakkarah. Mariette excavated the complex in '50, but it's mostly covered with sand again. Oh, and they took our pictures next to the Sphinx! I bought one for a souvenir. They'll mail the photograph when it's ready." Lucas paused for breath. "How was your day?"

"I drank all the hibiscus punch. And I saw a crocodile."

"A big one?"

"Medium to smallish."

"That sounds . . . fun." Lucas opened the door to the Aida suite. "I'll just wash up." His voice lowered. "I didn't like the donkey part. They shed."

Balthazar dressed in his finest, but Mrs. Fitzwalter failed to appear for supper in the dining room. The colonel was there, though, laughing and drinking with his companions. Balthazar paused at their table and made small talk long enough to insert a polite inquiry about Mrs. Fitzwalter's delicate health.

"Taking supper in her room," the colonel boomed. "Kind of you to ask. I'm about to join her for a sherry."

"We're all going to play some whist together," one of the ladies put in. "She's quite the card sharp!" The other wives tittered at that, and Balthazar felt reassured that she wasn't in mortal danger.

Just avoiding him, apparently.

He retired early to soak in a hot bath, his head tipped back against the rim, one hand loosely clasping the talisman that hung on a chain around his neck. The pendant was in the shape of a snake biting its own tail. A symbol for eternity.

Which was what this voyage was starting to feel like.

A single glimpse and he would have been satisfied. But she had denied him even that.

Well, they had six more days to Luxor. There was always a possibility she wasn't interested, but he remembered the smoldering look in her eye when she'd peeled the glove off and pressed her fingers to his mouth.

Balthazar slid lower in the steaming bath, letting his imagination run wild. By the end, he was forced to sit, shivering, in tepid water for a full half an hour before there was any chance of sleep.

She'd thrown down a gantlet.

Balthazar smiled. He'd just have to rise to the challenge.

———

THE NEXT DAY, HE WAITED UNTIL THE LAST MOMENT TO STAY behind, thinking she might suddenly emerge. This miracle did not occur, so he again feigned a headache. Balthazar expected bitter complaints, but Lucas gamely trundled off to visit the Dwarf Pyramid of Maydoom, the village of Wasta and a sugar manufactory billed as having chimneys two hundred feet high.

"They're lit by gas," Lucas reported afterwards when the steamer anchored at Maghaga. "The sugar season begins this month. The guide said they make several thousand gallons of rum, though they're not supposed to under Mohammedan law."

"I don't care," Balthazar growled.

He had spent the afternoon in another solitary vigil with nothing to show for it but a faint hangover from the hibiscus punch.

"Not turning out as you planned, my lord?" Lucas asked, his face carefully neutral.

"Something is wrong."

"Because she won't come out?"

"Her husband is a scoundrel," Balthazar muttered darkly.

Lucas frowned. "He seems pleasant enough to me."

"Because you're not his *wife*."

"I heard the group talking about their card game last night. Mrs. Fitzwalter was mentioned—"

Balthazar resisted the impulse to seize Lucas by the lapels. "What did they say?"

"She partnered with Mrs. Halloway. They trounced the men. Mr. Halloway was complaining that she had the Devil's own luck—"

"I don't care about the game," Balthazar groaned. "What did they say about *her*? Is she well?"

"I certainly got that impression." He gave his master a pitying look. "Maybe she's seasick."

"During the day only?" He gripped the rail. "Besides which, the current is only three miles an hour! It's perfectly flat."

Balthazar gazed at the far bank, which had a little clustered village and mosque shaded by date trees. Creaking oxen-turned sakies moved in the fields beyond.

"I'm sure she'll come out eventually," Lucas replied in a soothing tone. "And you look very handsome. The shirt sets off your tan nicely. I've no doubt she'll swoon at your feet."

"Don't try to butter me up," Balthazar muttered.

He barely touched his food at dinner, flinching each time the colonel's loud laughter erupted from the next table. Balthazar didn't understand it. He usually had infinite reserves of discipline. Time meant nothing to him. He'd once spent six years courting the particularly alluring wife of one of Venice's doges. Their single afternoon together had been well worth it, though he was forced to flee the city afterwards.

He wondered why he felt so impatient now. So desperate just to hear her voice.

It must be because he hadn't bedded a woman since leaving England three weeks before. The first signs of weakness would come soon. The cravings.

Surely that was the only reason.

The alternative – that she had awakened genuine feelings in him – was absurd.

Part of him wanted to call the whole thing off, return to Cairo, and pounce on the first woman who accepted his advances. Yet he wasn't ready to admit defeat. He realized with mounting horror that any woman would no longer do. It had to be *her*.

After another sleepless night of twisting in his sheets, Balthazar was at wits' end.

So when on the morning of the third day, he glanced down from his balcony and saw Mrs. Fitzwalter, it was as if the clouds of doom had parted and a ray of pure golden light poured down upon him.

CHAPTER 4

Balthazar hurried to join the crowd on the lower deck.

"Over there is the convent of Gebel-el-Tayr," the guide was saying, pointing to a stone structure high on the opposite cliffs. "The monks used to swim out and beg passing boats for baksheesh, but the Coptic Patriarch put a stop to this annoying practice a few years ago."

He droned on, but Balthazar had stopped listening. She stood alone at the rail, slightly apart from the others. She wore the same white dress and broad-brimmed hat, but he knew that height, those sturdy curves. He'd seen them in his dreams for the last three nights.

To his delight, the colonel was nowhere in evidence.

The steamer passed a lavish palace belonging to the Viceroy and moored at Beni-Hassan, where donkeys lined up to carry them to the Rock Tombs. As the group mounted, she looked over and caught him staring. Her eyes widened a fraction and she quickly turned away.

But Balthazar thought she was not entirely displeased to see him. Hope bloomed anew. If he could only get her alone for a few minutes . . . .

The chattering group passed through the ruins of Beni-Hassan, which, the guide blandly informed them, was destroyed on the orders of Mohammad Ali because of the villagers' thieving propensities. At last they reached the first tomb of Speos Artemedos, hewn into the rock cliff on the eastern side of the Nile. Everyone dismounted and followed the guide inside.

There were several galleries and the sightseers soon dispersed, poking into dusty corners and making inane comments. Lucas joined one of the other groups (he'd apparently made friends on the previous outings), leaving Balthazar to observe Mrs. Fitzwalter from a distance. She strolled at a leisurely pace, not speaking to anyone, and within a few minutes the main tour had moved ahead.

At last, she paused and lifted her skirts in consternation.

Balthazar stepped out of the shadows and feigned surprise. "Mrs. Fitzwalter," he said with a bow.

"My lord." She swallowed. "Are you enjoying the tour?"

"Oh, yes." He smiled. "Though the guide has most of it wrong."

She took her hat off and fanned herself. Beads of perspiration dampened the curls at her brow.

"How so?" she asked.

"This was originally a temple of Hatshepsut, but when Seti became Pharaoh he erased her name, replacing it with his own. He even altered the depictions of the queen and recarved them with his face."

She smiled. "Ancient vandalism."

"Yes." He glanced down. "Your shoe's come untied."

"I know." She laid a hand on her waist. "My corset is very tight," she said apologetically. "I'm afraid ladies' fashions are not made for bending over."

The phrase conjured a host of delightful images.

"Allow me." Before she could protest, he sank to one knee and lifted her foot, bracing it on his thigh.

"Oh." She flushed and looked around. "You really mustn't—"

"Nonsense. We can't have you tripping over an errant shoelace." The boot was quite short. Balthazar cupped her ankle, reveling in the sensation of a silk stocking.

"My lord," she began in a stern voice that sent a tingle down his spine.

Balthazar swiftly tied her shoe and set it down. He rose to his feet. "There you are. Good as new."

Her dark eyes held a hint of laughter. "Thank you."

He drew a deep breath. "Come, I'll show you Ameni Amenamah and Knum Hotep. There are fifteen tombs altogether, all generals and officers, but those are the only ones of interest."

Balthazar offered his arm. Mrs. Fitzwalter hesitated.

"If someone sees . . ."

"They won't."

She laid a hand on his sleeve. Her voice lowered. "I think you're a wicked man."

Balthazar's pulse raced like the Nile in flood. "Not half as wicked as I'd like to be," he murmured.

She laughed. "That's what I'm afraid of."

They walked through a narrow passageway into the next tomb. Balthazar pointed to an inscription on the doorjamb. "Prayers to Anubis, god of the afterlife."

"And patron of lost souls," she murmured. "Some scholars believe he is a later incarnation of Wepwawet, the ancient jackal deity of Lycopolis."

"The City of Wolves." Balthazar smiled. "Perhaps you should be leading the tour."

She shrugged. "It is my own culture, after all. I may live in England now, but my heart will always remain in Egypt." She said this with a trace of sadness.

"Is that why you've been hiding?" he asked lightly. "A bout of homesickness?"

She cast him a sharp look. "Not at all. I merely felt tired."

"But you're better now."

She looked away, the delicious flush rising in her cheeks again. "Yes."

"I see your husband remained on the boat today."

"He has gout in his leg. It flared up from all the rich food and drink, no doubt." She paused at the south wall of the tomb and ran a fingertip over one of the hieroglyphs. "This is Knum Hotep's wife, Kheti."

They spent a few minutes discussing the inscriptions. She had extensive knowledge that rivaled Balthazar's own. An extraordinary woman, and not only were her gifts wasted, but she was trapped in a loveless union with a crass old man. It saddened him.

"Rameses the Great had many wives, but Nefertari was his one true love," Mrs. Fitzwalter remarked. "He wrote poetry on the walls of her tomb. I would like to see that when we reach Luxor."

"*My love is unique,*" Balthazar murmured. "*No one can rival her, for she is the most beautiful woman alive. Just by passing, she has stolen away my heart.*"

She looked startled. "You know it?"

"Fragments only. Their story is famous. The statues he built of her were the same size as his own. Unheard of for a king in those days." He smiled. "Or even these days."

She smiled back. "I love the old stories. They are my solace."

"What are your favorites?" he asked, desperate for any crumbs.

"Oh, there are many. Do you know the tale of Rhodopis?"

Balthazar shook his head.

"She was a Greek slave girl. One day, when she was bathing in the river, an eagle flew down and snatched up one of her sandals. The bird carried it to Memphis, where the king was passing judgments in an open courtyard. The eagle dropped the sandal straight into his lap."

Her voice was low and musical, her gestures animated. She relished telling the tale and Balthazar found himself hopelessly charmed.

"The king's heart was stirred both by the beautiful shape of the sandal and the peculiar manner in which it had come into his possession. He grew obsessed with finding its owner. So he sent men to every corner of his realm to search for the foot that fit the sandal."

"Like Cinderella."

Her dark eyes glinted with amusement. "Yes, but this story is *much* older. He finally found Rhodopis in the city of Naucratis. The king freed her and brought her to Memphis, where they married to great celebration. And that is how a humble slave girl became a queen."

"I like that. Tell me another," he urged.

"Do you know the one about the Princess in a Suit of Leather?"

"No."

She told him stories as they strolled through the tomb of Ameni Amenamah, and made him laugh harder than he had in years. Most were folktales with magical beasts and vengeful, meddling deities, but it was her delight in telling them that brought him the greatest pleasure.

"Will you be at dinner tonight?" he asked. The shadows were lengthening.

A dark look crossed her face. "I don't know. My husband is angry with me. He's had food brought to the room."

"You said you were tired."

"I . . . Never mind." Her carefree mood evaporated. "We should go back."

"Why is he angry?" Balthazar persisted.

"Why do you think?" she snapped.

Before he could speak, she was striding for the exit.

The rest of the group was already assembled outside. They rode back to the steamer and she vanished before he could speak to her again.

"Progress, my lord?" Lucas asked as they climbed the stairs to the upper deck.

"It seemed so at first." He frowned, his gaze distant. "But the situation is more complicated than I thought."

"Well, I'll leave you on your own tonight." Lucas winked. "Perhaps your luck will change."

Balthazar dressed for dinner, so tense it took him four tries to fasten his cufflinks. He sat at the captain's table but made such poor conversation his companions finally gave up and ignored him. As usual, Mrs. Fitzwalter did not appear. He watched the colonel guzzle wine and shovel food into his maw with mounting violence.

"And how is your wife tonight?" he asked, pausing on his way out of the dining room.

"Not well, I'm afraid," the colonel replied, oblivious to Balthazar's chill tone. "The sun's too much for the poor thing. She's not very hale."

Lying bastard, Balthazar thought savagely. She could probably throw you over one shoulder and run a marathon.

He strode to the Aida suite before he ended up reducing the man's table to splinters. Balthazar knocked sharply on the door.

"Come in!"

Balthazar entered and flung himself into a chair.

"What is it?" Lucas asked with a frown.

"I need your opinion." He sighed. "Fitzwalter is keeping his wife as a virtual prisoner. She only came out today because he had an attack of gout. She probably snuck off while he was sleeping. But she told me he mistreats her often. It's disgusting!"

Lucas's face hardened. "Should we teach him a lesson, my lord? Toss him overboard?"

"It's tempting to intervene." His jaw clenched. "With force. But that must be a last resort. She's strong-willed, intelligent. She should stand up to him. The woman is clearly miserable."

"So what will you do?"

"I don't know. Speak to her again, if I ever get the chance. If I don't . . ." His gaze narrowed. "Then I'll have a little chat with the colonel myself. We still have Mortlake's chains, don't we?"

Lucas inhaled sharply. "You can't. Not that."

Balthazar realized he was clutching the arms of the chair hard enough to gouge the wood. He forced his hands to relax. "Perhaps that *would* be excessive. But I'm sure he can be persuaded to relinquish his claim on her."

Lucas studied him. "Pardon the honesty, but you look terrible, my lord. Like you haven't slept in days. I'd advise waiting until the morning to do anything. Then I'll do whatever you ask. You can count on me."

Balthazar looked up at him. "I know I can," he said quietly. "Thank you."

He returned to his cabin and poured a stiff brandy. Balthazar didn't bother undressing. He knew he wouldn't sleep. He suddenly felt terribly old and alone – but also more *alive* than he'd been in ages. Settling old scores and bedding an endless string of strangers was hardly an existence. He'd believed his soul was leached of any substance, but Mrs. Fitzwalter had proven this wrong.

Shortly before midnight, he went out to the balcony, unable to bear the confines of his cabin a minute longer. The waters of the Nile were smooth, reflecting a crescent moon. He drew a deep breath. Four more days and they would reach Luxor.

If he and Lucas had chosen different seats at the American Bar, he never would have seen her walk through the lobby. It all began in that instant, didn't it? A chance encounter. And now he was utterly—

His head turned at the sound of a faint, muffled sob.

Balthazar strode down the deck to the stern rail, where a figure huddled in the corner. It was Mrs. Fitzwalter, her lashes wet with tears. She flung out a hand as he approached, as though to ward off a blow.

"Leave me alone!" she cried hoarsely.

Balthazar ignored her protests, his heart hammering. "What has he done to you?"

She turned her face away. "Nothing," she whispered.

He gently lifted her chin. A bruise marred the fragile skin of her collarbone. His eyes darkened.

"I'll kill him," Balthazar said in a low voice.

"No!" She shook her head vehemently. "The law is on his side. You'd be charged with assault."

"I don't care," he grated.

She drew a shuddering breath, composing herself. "I've thought it over. You're right, my lord. When we return to England, I'll . . ." Her voice caught. "I'll file for divorce."

Balthazar gave her an encouraging nod. "Don't worry, I know an excellent solicitor. I'm happy to help you make the arrangements. I have money. You can pay me back later. I'm sure you'll be entitled to a generous settlement."

He took out a handkerchief and she dried her cheeks with a grateful smile.

"We barely know each other," she asked in wonder. "Why do you care what happens to me?"

"Because you deserve better."

"It's that simple?" Her gaze was frank, with no hint of accusation, which only made it worse. "Or perhaps you hope to seduce me yourself?"

"No!" *Yes.* "I . . . It's true what you said. I am a wicked man. But I wouldn't take advantage of your situation." Even as he spoke the words, Balthazar knew he meant them. He suppressed a shudder. What was happening to him?

"That's very honorable of you."

"Let's not go too far," he replied wearily. "But you can take my cabin tonight. I'll sleep on one of the deck chairs. We can find new accommodations for you in the morning."

"Oh no, I couldn't!" She looked scandalized.

"Yes, you could," he replied firmly. "I won't allow you to be mistreated."

"What would people think?"

"I'll wake you early before anyone rises."

She hesitated. "You're very kind, Count Koháry."

He led her to the Queen Victoria suite and opened the door. Balthazar was turning to leave when she laid a hand on his arm.

"I could use a drink. Do you have anything?"

"Just brandy."

"Would you pour me some?"

He hesitated. It was exactly what he had longed for, but it felt wrong. Even for him.

"Please," she said in a low voice, not meeting his eye. "Only for a few minutes. I . . . I don't wish to be alone."

Balthazar had used that same line himself on enough occasions to know what it meant. The tables were turning. He had no objection – quite the contrary – but he found it difficult to reconcile this bold, assertive woman with one who would tolerate an elderly cad laying hands on her for even a single minute.

He almost found the strength to decline. Then she leaned forward and he caught a whiff of her perfume. It had blended with the heat of her skin. The result was intoxicating.

"A few minutes," he agreed, holding the door for her.

She swept inside and looked around, her gaze lingering on the rumpled bed. "This must be their finest suite. It's at least twice as large as ours."

46

Balthazar walked to the sideboard and unstopped a decanter. He poured two glasses and handed one to her, then retreated a safe distance away.

"You never told me your Christian name," he said, feeling oddly unsettled.

She smiled. "It's Zarifa."

Of course it was.

Every syllable had an erotic ring, leaving the lips slightly parted on the final *ahhhh*.

Balthazar leaned back against the sideboard. "That's a lovely name."

She set the glass aside. "I can hardly shame myself more than I already have. If I sleep in my gown, it will be ruined. Perhaps I could borrow one of your shirts."

"Naturally. Do you want the one I'm wearing?"

She blushed. He watched it creep slowly up her neck. But her eyes never left his own.

"I hate to be a bother. Why don't you just give me one you're not using?"

Balthazar exhaled slowly through his nose. He strode to the wardrobe, took out a shirt and tossed it on the bed.

"Turn around," she said.

A smile tugged at the corners of his mouth as he obeyed. He heard cloth rustling.

"Count Koháry?"

"Yes?"

"Might I trouble you to help with my corset?"

A wave of heat rolled through him, straight from toes to crown.

"Oh, you certainly might," he replied.

Balthazar turned around. She stood with her back to him, dress puddled at her feet. Layers of undergarments concealed her from the waist down. But her dark hair was still pinned up and his eyes devoured the clean lines of her back. He walked over and tugged at the laces, loosening the corset but not taking it off. His knuckles brushed bare skin and he heard her sigh.

"Is that better?"

She shivered as his breath stirred the wisps of hair at her nape.

"Yes, thank you."

Balthazar stepped back, curious to see what she'd do next.

"Do you require my services for anything else?" he inquired in a neutral tone.

"I think not. Perhaps you should turn around again."

He held her gaze for a moment in the mirror. "Of course."

He faced the wall.

"It's safe," she said after a minute.

Balthazar turned back around and experienced a stab of arousal so intense it was near to pain.

It wasn't safe at all.

She'd left the top two buttons undone. A small silver crucifix lay in the hollow of her throat. His shirt could hardly contain her and the hem barely reached the middle of her long, powerful thighs.

"Would you drink a toast with me before you leave?" she asked.

He managed a stupefied nod.

"What shall we toast to?" Her forehead creased in a pretty frown. Then she smiled. "I know. To being young!" She raised her glass.

The brandy burned a trail down his throat. He set the glass down. He was extremely aware of the bed between them.

"I'm sure you're tired," he said weakly.

"Not especially." Her dark eyes drank him in. She fanned herself. "I feel peculiar. Did you perchance drug my brandy?"

Balthazar laughed. "Do I look like the kind of man who needs to drug my lovers?"

She lifted her chin. "You presume a great deal, my lord."

"Do I?"

"Yes, you do. Are you saying I'm your lover?"

He shrugged. "Only if you want to be."

Zarifa prowled over and slapped him hard. "How *dare* you?"

Balthazar rubbed his jaw in consternation. She was strong.

Zarifa's black eyes flashed. Then she cupped his face and kissed him.

There was nothing tentative about it. She claimed him like a Viking who had just kicked down the door of a mainland hovel and found naked virgins inside. Through a haze of lust, Balthazar found himself pressed against the wall by those stupendous breasts. She seemed to have grown three more arms and all of them were tearing at his clothes.

Her mouth was a pot of honey he'd gladly drown in. He seized a fistful of his own shirt – how he wanted to tear it to shreds – but then she did something with her feet and he was lying back on the bed with those sturdy thighs straddling his hips.

"Wait a moment, sweetling," he murmured.

She reached up and unpinned her hair. Shining black waves tumbled down to her waist. She leaned over until her lips hovered above his own, tantalizingly close.

"Kiss me again," he whispered, his voice thick and slurred. "Hurry."

The last word came out as *hrrrmnh*.

Onyx eyes regarded him. How long and curling her lashes were, like the spikes of a poisonous night flower.

"It's tempting," she murmured against his mouth. "But I'm afraid we have other business to attend to."

Balthazar dimly heard the rasp of a knife. A blade pressed against his throat. He tried to move, to roll over and pin her to the bed, and found he couldn't lift a finger. His body felt as light and insubstantial as a mote of dust.

"Oh, Balthazar," she said with a soft laugh. "You've been even more fun than I expected."

Zarifa sat up and peered down at him. When he made no attempt to escape, the pressure of the knife eased.

"My father would want me to kill you, but he was a bastard, too. And unlike you, I'm not a murderer." She grinned. "Only a thief."

Balthazar tried to comprehend what was happening. He felt curiously detached. Some primal part of his brain screamed a warning, but it was distant and far too late.

Zarifa unbuttoned his shirt. A chill swept across his bare skin as she spread the starched plackets. Her gaze fell on the ouroboros, a snake eating its own tail nestled in the groove at the center of his chest. She touched the talisman and withdrew her hand with a sharp intake of breath.

"Well, well," she whispered. "You *are* a wicked man."

Balthazar gazed up at her with heavy-lidded eyes.

"So this is how you manage to stay alive. I'd heard rumors, but I didn't think . . . It must be unique." She cradled his limp head and lifted the chain from around his neck. "But unique objects happen to be my specialty."

Zarifa held the talisman up to the light. The snake's jeweled eyes reflected the flame of the candle.

She hung it around her own neck and patted his cheek. "It's been a pleasure doing business with you, Balthazar."

A hand came down, gently closing his eyes, and he slid into darkness.

CHAPTER 5

Zarifa decided to keep Balthazar's shirt. Also his billfold and gold pocket watch.

She left her corset as a little present and quickly searched the room. She'd hoped to find other talismans, but the ouroboros was a greater prize than she dared hope for. How to dispose of it required serious consideration.

She paused at the door and turned back. Balthazar lay sprawled across the bed, shirt open, one arm flung over his head. She gazed at him for a moment. As much as she despised the man, when she'd kissed him . . . well, it hadn't been awful. Perhaps he deserved some compensation.

Zarifa smiled. She opened the billfold and peeled off a single pound note. Then she tucked it into the waist of his trousers.

The deck was deserted as she slipped silently down the stairs to her tiny cabin at the stern. All her belongings fit inside an oilskin bag, which was already packed and waiting.

Two crewman stood watch at the helm, but they didn't turn as she slipped into the warm waters of the Nile. Crocodiles were her greatest fear, but she was a strong swimmer. Two minutes later, she emerged dripping on the bank.

Zarifa changed into dry clothes from the oilskin bag and weighed her options.

Caution dictated running as far and as fast as she could. Balthazar was a dangerous man.

But he wasn't a necromancer. She'd seen Mortlake fight his brethren before. They moved inhumanly fast. Balthazar had nearly died at the bazaar, and Mortlake said he hadn't been seen wearing the chains in centuries.

No, he was something else.

The talisman would fetch a fortune on the open market, but Mortlake had never allowed her to see his client list. It would take time to find the right buyer and she needed money now. Before the marids found her. She knew her father lied when he said Taj wouldn't come after her. He most definitely *would*. When Mortlake didn't appear with the money, they would start searching. And the missed appointment had been days ago.

The other option was riskier but promised the greatest reward and a swift solution to all her problems. Balthazar was rich. No doubt he would pay any price to get the talisman back. And unless he *did* get it back . . . well, Zarifa knew he would hunt her to the ends of the earth. She'd be looking over her shoulder until he finally died and who knew how long that might take? She could sense the talisman's basic purpose, but beyond that she knew nothing about its long-term effects.

Zarifa gazed at the steamer floating at anchor. She'd never shied from risk. Quite the opposite. If the transaction went smoothly, she'd have the money within a day or two. Enough to pay Taj and live comfortably while she decided what to do next.

She approached one of the thatched dwellings, negotiating with the occupants in a rapid exchange of Arabic. A few coins bought a straw pallet and a black abaya, the modest robe worn by local women.

Zarifa sat back and waited for the dawn.

BALTHAZAR WOKE WITH A GROAN. HIS HEAD ACHED LIKE THE devil. Bright sun poured through the windows of the Queen Victoria suite. He flung an arm across his face.

What had happened last night?

He remembered entering his cabin. He remembered unlacing her corset. Everything afterward was a haze. He was still dressed, which wasn't a good sign. And a pound note was stuck to the sweat on his belly.

Balthazar stumbled to the pitcher of water on the sideboard. He drank the whole thing and dropped the empty pitcher to the carpet. His gaze fell on two glasses of brandy, one half empty, one full. Untouched.

Something felt very wrong.

His hand shot to his chest. His fingers closed on nothing.

Balthazar howled. In two seconds, he was out the door and lurching down the balcony. He gave the fourth door a savage kick. It flew open and rebounded against the wall with a crash. He heard a woman scream. Balthazar stormed inside.

The colonel sat up in bed, his white hair sticking up in tufts. "What the devil are you doing?" he roared.

A pale woman in a frilly nightcap lay in bed next to him, her eyes wide.

"Where is she?" Balthazar grated, striding forward.

"Who?"

"Zarifa!"

"You're drunk," the colonel cried. "Get out of my room this instant!"

A glimmer of truth penetrated the fog. Balthazar halted his advance at the foot of the bed.

"Who's that?" He stabbed a finger at the old woman. She pulled the covers up to her chin and gave another little shriek.

"My wife, you dolt!"

Balthazar saw a wheelchair in the corner. For an instant,

he could only tremble, mute. The colonel shrank back. He reached for a cane and brandished it with a shaking hand.

"Help!" he cried. "There's a lunatic in my bedchamber!"

Balthazar sagged against the bedpost.

It was his worst nightmare. He'd grown careless and over-confident. And it had cost him everything.

"Please," the colonel whispered, his eyes watery with fear. "I don't know what you want. But my wife is an invalid. The shock . . . ."

Balthazar rubbed his bloodshot eyes. "I apologize for the intrusion," he muttered.

The door hung a bit askew, but he managed to close it behind him.

A quick search of the cabin revealed that she had also taken his money and watch. The last would have been infuriating on its own, but paled in comparison to the ouroboros. Balthazar stood still for a long minute, despair leaving his mind a perfect blank.

Lies upon lies, and he'd wolfed them down like a starving puppy.

The prospect of revenge finally got him moving again. Facing Lucas would be painful, but he needed a voice of reason. His head still throbbed with the dregs of whatever she'd put in his brandy when he turned around.

Balthazar staggered back out to the balcony and pounded on Lucas's door until it opened.

"You look a fright, my lord," Lucas said, covering a yawn. "I warned you to stay away from that hibiscus punch."

Balthazar entered the Aida suite and shut the door. He sank down on Lucas's bed.

"She took it."

His voice was barely audible.

"What?"

"It's gone."

Lucas's gaze lowered. He took in Balthazar's bare chest. His mouth fell open. "Oh."

"Yes," Balthazar said. "*Oh.*"

"We'll get it back," Lucas said immediately, pulling on a coat and trousers. "She can't have gone far."

"Yes, she can. It's been hours. And I know nothing about her. *Nothing.*"

They both turned at a brisk rap on the door. Balthazar closed his eyes.

"Don't open it," he whispered.

Muffled voices came from outside. "Count Koháry? Are you in there?"

Lucas glanced at him, then strode to the door and yanked it open.

The captain stood there with a grim expression. Colonel Fitzwalter and the first officer hovered behind him.

"I'm told a rather embarrassing incident occurred on board my ship this morning," the captain said, eying Balthazar warily. "Would you care to explain yourself, my lord?"

Balthazar rose to his full height. "An incident?" He gave a strangled laugh. "Yes, I'd say there's been an incident. I was robbed by one of the other passengers! And you're going to tell me everything you know about her. Everything!"

The captain frowned. "Robbed?"

"A woman who claimed to be Mrs. Fitzwalter. Black hair and eyes, exotic-looking but with a crisp Oxford accent. Lucifer in a dress. Sound familiar?"

The captain swallowed. "Yes, I believe I know the one. But she was a third-class passenger. A last-minute ticket, I believe." He turned to his first officer. "Search the boat stem to stern."

Balthazar pushed past them to the deck. "You can try, but I promise she's long gone. It happened last night. She *drugged* me."

The captain blanched. "I'm terribly sorry, my lord. What did she take?"

"Billfold. Watch." His eyes darkened. "Sundry other items."

"We'll make a police report at once. There's a station in the village."

Balthazar gazed at the shore. Young girls filled water jars on the sandbanks, which were thick with waterfowl. Waving fields of corn, sugarcane, golden cotton and tobacco stretched into the distance.

"Where are we?"

"Rodah."

"How far is it from Cairo?"

"About a hundred and eighty miles."

"Is there a train station here?"

The captain nodded. Balthazar swore.

"I'll make the report myself. Get us to shore immediately."

"Of course, my lord."

By the time their luggage was packed, the first mate reported that the woman was nowhere to be found. Her cabin was empty. She'd booked passage under the surname Laverna, which Lucas helpfully pointed out was the Roman goddess of thieves.

"She knew me, though I swear I've never seen her before in my life," Balthazar said quietly as one of the crewmen rowed them to shore. "And she knew exactly what the ouroboros was."

He dredged up everything he could remember, though it was mostly fragments. The brandy. The kiss. The knife at his throat.

"She said her father would want me dead," Balthazar muttered. "But that she wasn't a killer."

"Vengeful father?" Lucas glanced over. "Hmmm. I'm not sure that narrows it down, my lord."

"Probably not," Balthazar agreed with a sigh. He frowned. "You don't think . . . it couldn't be *Mortlake*?"

Lucas shook his head. "He had no children. I'm sure of that."

"He didn't use the black lightning to defend himself," Balthazar said slowly. "If he did have a daughter, it might explain why."

Lucas gave him a flat look. "We're talking about *John Mortlake*. He was incapable of any human emotion save for greed. Even among the Duzakh, the man stood out as a vile specimen."

"Yes," Balthazar said wearily. "I'm sure you're right." His voice hardened. "But she can't have left Egypt yet and I'll make sure she doesn't."

As a respected collector of antiquities, Balthazar knew everyone who mattered. Customs, police, army, black market, criminal underworld. They were all in his pocket. Zarifa might know his name, but she had no clue who she'd just crossed.

"Cable the Consul-General with her description," Balthazar instructed. "Inform Lord Baring that she's stolen an extremely valuable relic. He'll take care of the rest. All the hotels, borders and train stations are to be watched. Make sure he widens the net to the port at Alexandria."

Lucas nodded. "Right away, my lord."

"The odds are good that she's headed for Cairo. Get word to Omar One-Eye. Tell him there's a bounty. A million pounds if he finds the lady and brings her to me intact." Balthazar smiled grimly. "Every cutpurse and lowlife in the city will be hunting her."

They secured their luggage at a dingy hotel run by a Turk who informed them that the next train to Cairo left at 11:04. Lucas headed for the police station to file a report and send telegrams. Balthazar collapsed in a chair at the adjacent coffee house.

He felt horrific.

The Turk brought him a pot of coffee, but just the smell made him ill. Balthazar fought the urge to simply lay his face on the table and whimper. He'd feigned confidence, but the clock was ticking now. Who knew how much time he had left? Balthazar raised a shaking hand to his forehead. He could almost hear it . . . .

"I have a proposition for you," a voice whispered in his ear.

Balthazar looked up with bleary eyes. His jaw knotted as he took in the veiled figure standing over him. She wore shapeless black from head to toe, but he knew that sultry, educated voice.

"Do you want your watch back?" she asked, dangling the gold chain in front of his face. "A small gesture of goodwill—"

Balthazar rose to his feet. The room lurched like the deck of a galleon in a storm. Blood pounded in his ears, but it wasn't lust this time.

"Outside," he snarled, grabbing the watch and shoving it into his trouser pocket.

He followed Zarifa into the alley behind the hotel. The moment they were through the door, he tore the veil away and pressed her against the wall by the throat.

"Where is it?" he demanded.

"Safe."

Balthazar stared at her. Zarifa regarded him with a bored expression.

"Calm yourself," she said. "We're both professionals here—"

He seized a handful of black cloth and yanked the robe up to her chin.

"Hold this," he snarled.

She sighed and gripped the hem as he performed a rough search of her person. She wore knickers and a thin chemise underneath, but there was nothing erotic about it now. Balthazar ran his hands over every inch, methodically searching for hidden pockets sewn into the garments. He even pulled her boots off and shook them.

"Where," he growled, "*is it?*"

"Do you really think I'd be stupid enough to bring it along?" she said. "And if you kill me, you'll never get it back."

"Perhaps I won't kill you." Balthazar gave her a thin smile. "But I'll torture you. Trust me, sweet, I've done it before. More times than you can imagine." He pitched his voice low and menacing. "Pleasure is not my only skill."

Zarifa laughed, which was not the response he'd hoped for. "Really?" She chuckled again. "No, I don't think you will."

He scowled. "How can you be so sure? You've placed yourself at my mercy."

"Oh, Balthazar." She gazed at him. "You like women too much."

"You're not a *woman*," he grated. "You're a harpy from the depths of Hades."

Her eyes went cold. "I've known men who would peel the skin from my body in strips without thinking twice. And it's quite obvious you're not one of them."

Balthazar's brow furrowed. She wasn't joking.

"I agree that you're a rake and a parasite, but you don't frighten me," Zarifa said. "Besides which, I have a partner. If any harm comes to me, they'll take the talisman to Europe and sell it on the open market. So let's just talk business, shall we?"

He crossed his arms, fighting for composure. "What do you want?"

She cleared her throat. "I'm a little short on funds at the moment—"

"This is about money?" He stared at her in surprise.

Zarifa snatched the veil from his hand. "I could make you my slave. Make you do *anything*. You should be grateful."

Balthazar laughed. "Oh, I'll give you the money! Just name your price."

"Good. How fast can you get it?"

"The instant we're in Cairo. I'll draw on a line of credit. How much?"

She eyed him speculatively. "How much do you have?"

"Enough." He studied her. "You're desperate, aren't you?"

"No more than you are."

"Why?"

"The details are not your concern. But know this, Balthazar. You brought it on yourself."

"Does that help you sleep at night?"

Spots of color burned in her cheeks. "Don't you dare judge me. It's because of you that I was left penniless—" She cut off and glanced down the alley. "Oh, damn."

Balthazar turned. Three men approached, faces covered by black shemaghs. All had bright blue eyes and scimitars in their hands.

"I saw them at the bazaar." Balthazar said in a low voice. "Who are they?"

"Agents of the illustrious Taj," the first man said in a jovial tone. "I'm afraid the lady owes our master a substantial debt."

"Well, he can get in line," Balthazar retorted. "She owes me, too."

"I owe you nothing," Zarifa snapped. "You owe *me*."

"This is becoming tedious," the second man said. He looked at Zarifa. "Do you have the money?"

"I will," she said desperately. "You must believe me—"

"Not good enough. We need it now." He strode forward and Balthazar blocked his path. Just the single step brought a fresh wave of nausea.

"Wait," Zarifa pleaded. "I can get it in Cairo—"

"We just came from Cairo. And now we're late, thanks to you. Our venerable master will be most displeased if we return empty-handed."

"Therefore," the third man snarled, "we will not return empty-handed. You will come with us."

"You're not taking her anywhere," Balthazar announced. "Not until I'm finished with her."

"Good sahib." The first man bowed. "We have no quarrel with you. But if you insist on defending her honor—"

"Oh, I'm the last man on earth interested in defending her honor. But she took something from me and I mean to have it back. Until I do, she isn't leaving my sight."

The man nodded. "So be it."

A scimitar appeared in his hand. It carved a whistling figure eight through the air. Zarifa pressed herself against the wall as an icy wind swept the alley. Balthazar frowned, calculating his next moves. It must be the residue of the drug. Surely he was imagining things. He couldn't be seeing the white plume of his own breath.

The alley was too narrow for all three to attack at once. He focused on the one in the lead. Balthazar waited until he was a few feet away, crouching like an animal at bay. As the blade swept around he leapt up and caught hold of the hotel's second-floor balcony. His boots slammed into the man's face with a satisfying crunch. Balthazar caught the sword as it flew through the air. His teeth gritted. The hilt was like a shard of ice.

He dropped down, wrist flicking to slash his opponent's throat, but the man had somehow vanished. Balthazar barely absorbed this improbable development before the other two rushed forward. He parried their attack, spinning to the side with a low cut that sliced through a black robe and drew a trickle of blood.

Dark *blue* blood.

Balthazar shook his head to clear it. Before his eyes, the scattered droplets froze to ice.

Oh, it was all too much! He nearly groaned aloud. Why was this happening *now*? Of all days? Another hour and he would have been on a train to Cairo, halfway to regaining his talisman.

They circled him a few feet away, wary now. But Balthazar knew he'd gotten lucky. He was much too hungover to fend them off for long. And soon enough they would know it, too.

Whatever the hell they were.

Behind the pair, he spotted Zarifa edging along the wall, her gaze fixed on the mouth of the alley. Hot rage bubbled up. All of it was *her* fault.

"Your quarry is escaping," he said with a pointed glance.

One turned and grabbed the back of her robe just as she made a break for it. Zarifa started cursing in a colorful mix of Arabic and French he would have found amusing under different circumstances. Her shouts drew the Turk, who stuck his head out the kitchen door.

"Summon the police!" Balthazar yelled. "These men are thieves!"

The Turk stared at them, open-mouthed. His head disappeared like a gopher into a hole. The door slammed shut.

Balthazar eyed the second man, who glared at him with murderous intent while his companion subdued a wildly thrashing Zarifa. They both had to be disposed of before the first came back. He'd probably gone for reinforcements—

A sudden frigid gust ruffled his hair. Balthazar slowly turned. The blue eyes appeared first, then the black shemagh. He simply materialized out of thin air at Balthazar's shoulder. A hand clamped around his sword arm.

He roared in shock. It was like diving into a mountain lake in the depths of winter. Frost crept up his arm, spreading in a lattice of glittering crystals. He tried to stumble away, but the creature held him fast. His fingers went numb. The sword fell to the ground. He tried to yell for help, but all that came out was a flimsy croak.

Then he was being hauled down the alley like a side of beef. A cart waited at the end. They threw him inside. A whip cracked and the cart lurched forward.

Balthazar wanted to scream, to curse, to fight them. All he

managed was pathetic shivering. The cold wrapped icy fingers around his heart. Each breath came as a labored gasp. A moment later, he felt himself swathed in coarse cloth. Even in his sorry state, he could smell her perfume on the abaya.

"You'll recover," Zarifa whispered. "Just lie still."

He tried to sit. She pushed him down as easily as if he were a child.

"Don't fight. It's useless. You must rest, Balthazar."

He shook his head in protest.

"They could have done worse," she said sternly. "So quiet down and accept your fate like a man."

Quiet down? The only sound was his chattering teeth.

He longed to make a scathing reply, but he was already passing out again. Balthazar fought the lethargy, knowing his best chance was to jump off the cart with Zarifa before they left Rodah. Yet he couldn't make his limbs respond.

With a last muttered curse, he slipped into a grey void.

CHAPTER 6

Balthazar woke to the creak of the cart. The air felt a thousand degrees and dry as a pharaoh's tomb. Sweat stung his eyes as he took in his surroundings. A canvas dome covered the tiny space. It blocked the sun, but also any hint of a breeze.

He hauled himself to sitting. A chain around his leg jerked tight. It ran through a metal ring set into the wooden planks.

The other end was attached to Zarifa. She sat against the opposite side of the cart, watching him with a guarded expression.

Balthazar yanked the flap aside. Four more wagons trundled along behind, along with a train of camels. Golden sands stretched out in every direction. He swore viciously.

A pair of black-robed figures walked at the rear of the caravan. The third must be up front somewhere.

Balthazar scrubbed a hand across his face, wincing at the rough stubble. At least his headache was gone. He flexed his fingers. Whatever they'd done to him, it had worn off without any permanent damage.

"How long was I out?" he demanded.

"About three hours."

"Where are they taking us?" He stared through the gap at his abductors. "And more to the point, what the hell are they?"

Zarifa gave him a stony look. "Marids."

The word rang a bell – and not an encouraging one. "You mean *jinn*?"

"They're a class of jinn, yes. One of the higher echelons."

It had been centuries since Balthazar encountered one. They were native to the Arabian Peninsula and didn't often mingle with mortals. He knew little about them, besides the fact that they were usually servants of something even worse.

"Wonderful," he hissed. "You might have mentioned that before. If I'd known from the start that I was dealing with bloody jinn—"

"Oh, shut up." She drew her knees to her chest and the chain jerked taut again.

Balthazar looked down at his feet. "Where's my other shoe?"

Zarifa shrugged. "I suppose it fell off in the alley."

Balthazar swore again. "Let me guess. They're bringing us to the *illustrious Taj*."

She studied him with disdain. "This is all your fault."

"My fault?" he choked in disbelief.

"Yes, your fault! If you hadn't murdered my father, I would have been on a ship to London by now."

Balthazar mastered himself, if barely. It was all coming together now. The depths of his misjudgment. His utter blindness. "You're talking about Mortlake, aren't you?"

She didn't reply, but her grim face was answer enough.

"Oh, that's perfect." He leaned forward. "Do you have any idea how many people your beloved father drained over the last three hundred years? How many innocents he killed to sustain his own miserable existence? What I did was justice. And long delayed, I might add!"

Zarifa looked away, her jaw tight.

"All right." Balthazar drew a breath. "How many marids are there?"

Her voice was a mere whisper. "Just the three. But there's no chance of escape."

"We'll see about that. Tell me one thing." Balthazar swallowed, his throat suddenly dry. "Is my talisman safe? If your partner sells it—"

"It's safe." She sounded amused. "I promise you that."

"How?" His heart raced. "How do you know?"

"Because I lied about the partner," she admitted. "That was just . . . insurance. In case I was wrong about you. But I know exactly where it is."

"If someone finds it—"

"They won't."

She sounded totally confident. He relaxed a little. "And our bargain stands if I get us out of here?"

Zarifa nodded, though she seemed skeptical.

He settled back against the side of the cart. "So who is this *Taj*?"

"A dealer in talismans, among other things. He did business with Mortlake. I've never met him."

"Where does he live?"

"A place called Al Miraj."

Balthazar frowned. "I've heard of it. It doesn't exist anymore."

"You're wrong. It exists. But my father said it's not easy to find. Only the jinn know where it is."

Balthazar had seen many strange things. He generally kept an open mind. This sounded like one of her wild tales, but it didn't matter. He had no intention of staying long enough to meet the marids' master – who must be scum if he dealt with the likes of John Mortlake.

Zarifa's dark eyes fixed on him. "My father told me all about the Duzakh. He wanted me to know who they were in case any of them came after us."

"I'm not Duzakh," he grated.

"You might as well be," she said scornfully. "You're a predator, just as they are. He made me memorize the descriptions of the most dangerous." She studied his face. "A tall man with a crooked nose accompanied by another man, shorter with a mustache and a scar on his face."

Balthazar frowned and touched his nose. "It isn't *that* crooked. I'd prefer tall, dark and devastatingly handsome—"

"I saw you kill Mortlake at the bazaar. And I knew exactly who you were."

"Well, bravo for you," he said sourly.

"So I followed you back to the hotel. I have a contact there. He told me everything I needed to know." A sudden smile broke across her face. "Including the fact that Colonel Fitzwalter had an invalid wife who never left their room."

"You know I broke down the poor man's door this morning?"

Zarifa cackled and slapped her thigh. "I wish I'd been there to see it."

Balthazar stared at her. "You're insane. I spoke to him at dinner on more than one occasion. It's a miracle you weren't exposed."

She gave a careless shrug. "Well, I wasn't."

"It was a stupid risk. You could have had me the night we met."

"I suppose I could. But where's the fun in that?" She leaned forward. "Besides which, you presented a unique challenge."

Balthazar dragged his eyes away from the soft curves of her mouth. The woman was Mortlake's daughter! A necromancer's progeny. His vile blood ran in her veins. God only knew what she was capable of.

"What are you talking about?" he asked icily.

Zarifa smiled. "A man so jaded he required a special approach. The virgin-whore was too simplistic. No, you needed a woman who was both desperately vulnerable and supremely confident." She shrugged. "It's a variation of the virgin-whore, I'll grant you that, but with my own twist."

She raised a finger instructively. "Thus, a married woman because someone like you would avoid actual virgins like the plague. Too much work and unspeakably boring."

Balthazar stared at her.

"The marriage would be an unhappy one, of course. The moment I saw the colonel, I knew he'd be perfect for the role. A vicious brute to rescue me from." She stuck her lower lip out. "How desperate I must be for your expert attentions. All those long, lonely nights—"

"Spare me the gloating."

She sighed. "To be honest, I was afraid I might have over-done it at the end. I didn't expect chivalry to rear its ugly head. You came near to refusing me, didn't you?"

"Not near enough," Balthazar growled.

"The offer of a solicitor was very kind. I'm serious. I found your concern touching."

"Is that why you left the pound note?" he asked sarcastically.

She grinned. "You earned it, sweetling."

Zarifa scrambled away, laughing, as Balthazar lunged for her throat. The wagon jolted to a sudden stop, sending him sprawling. They shared a quick, wary look. He braced for some fresh atrocity.

A black-turbaned marid opened the flaps. Blue eyes twinkled. "Ah, the lovers are having a spat. But I beg you to keep it civil. My master will be most displeased if there is damage to the merchandise."

"Merchandise?" Balthazar muttered.

The marid opened a latch and the rear of the cart fell open. "It is time to make camp for the night. Come and meet your merry companions."

Balthazar and Zarifa clambered down, keeping as far

apart as the length of chain allowed, which was three paces. The caravan had stopped at an oasis with a watering hole and a few date palms. A dozen men and women were emerging from the other tiny wagons. Balthazar noticed they were all young and of exceptional beauty. None wore chains, but they didn't look exactly *merry*. Their eyes were downcast, their steps dragging.

"What's that smell?" he wondered.

A peculiar aroma filled the air. One moment, he inhaled an earthy whiff of frankincense. The next it changed to the slightly sour, bittersweet odor of saffron. He swallowed as the fetid miasma of an abattoir assailed his senses.

"I am Qadir the Scented," the marid replied. He pointed to another who barked orders at the captives. They scrambled to erect a row of tents. "That is Jabaar the Cruel."

"Ah." Balthazar sighed with relief as the wind shifted.

Qadir indicated the third marid, who had removed his black shemagh. He watched the proceedings with a serene smile. "And Yatha the Harmonious."

Balthazar studied the creature. His face was unremarkable, save for those eerie blue eyes.

Three marids to watch over a dozen captives. He'd been in tighter spots before. A plan began to form in his mind.

"Is it possible to get this off?" Balthazar asked, looking down at the chain. "There isn't anywhere to run."

"For a short while," agreed Qadir the Scented, wiggling a finger. The chain vanished.

"Thank you." Balthazar suppressed a smile. Qadir and Yatha didn't seem so bad. Jabaar, on the other hand . . . he ranted and gesticulated, finding fault with the smallest action. Half the captives were crying. The other half just looked terrified.

"He's the one who killed Mortlake," Zarifa remarked, fanning herself. The sun was sinking, but it was still hot as blazes. "Doesn't that make *him* responsible for the debt?"

Balthazar glanced at her coldly. "Are you really going to listen to a thief? I don't deny killing him. In fact, I'm proud of it. But I have nothing to do with—"

"Now, now," interjected Yatha the Harmonious, appearing without warning at his side. "What's done is done. It is for our wise and magnificent master to decide your fates now. Miss Mortlake, you may save your defense for the audience with the great Taj."

"I'm not Miss *Mortlake*," she snapped. "My surname is Everleigh. I might be his blood, but he was never a father."

Balthazar snorted.

"Miss Everleigh, then," Yatha agreed.

"Thank you. My point is that my father *would* have had your money if this . . . fake Hungarian count hadn't murdered him in the bazaar!"

"Ooooh, you're such a little liar," Balthazar hissed. "You were desperate for cash. And your father's gambling problem is hardly a secret. Taj will never believe for a moment—" He cut off with a silent curse as Jabaar the Cruel strode over.

"Enough of this insolence. You will join the other slaves," he said curtly, pointing at the group erecting tents.

"Brother," Qadir chastened, emitting an overpowering blast of cinnamon that made Zarifa sneeze. "Our fair companions are not *slaves*. The regent would be appalled at such a term." He gazed heavenward. "All know slavery is against the law."

Jabaar growled in disgust.

"So what are they?" Balthazar asked, eying the captives.

"Indentured servants," Yatha replied with a gentle smile. "Their families were paid generous sums of gold. And they will be given an opportunity to work off the debt and purchase their freedom once we reach Al Miraj." He spread his hands. "Our master is a fair man. It's all perfectly legitimate."

"No doubt," Balthazar murmured dryly.

"Get moving," Jabaar snarled, pointing at a pile of black cloth on the ground. "There's work to be done. Shall I inspire you with the lash?"

Yatha and Qadir looked at him with fondness. "You should heed our irascible brother," Yatha said. "It is most unpleasant when his patience runs out."

Balthazar reluctantly joined Zarifa, who shook out the long, narrow rectangle like she knew what she was about.

"It smells like *goats*," Balthazar declared, making a face.

"Oh, do be quiet," she snapped. "Take the center pole and hold it up straight."

"This one?"

"No, the long one. Yes, *that*. Now hunch down . . . . Must you be so bloody tall? Help me throw this bit over the top . . . . No, not like that, you great lummox! There. Now you must draw the ropes tight and pound the pegs in. Oh, for God's sake . . . ."

Balthazar obeyed her terse orders, muttering under his breath, until they'd managed to get all three strips positioned and staked down. She held up a smaller piece of cloth.

"This is the *ruaq*," Zarifa said, speaking slowly. "We attach it to the roof with those pins. That will make the walls."

"How do you know all this?" he demanded.

"I've spent time with the Bedouin." She looked at him with pity. "But honestly, Balthazar, a simpler design is difficult to imagine. It is usually the young girls who are tasked with erecting the tents."

"Well, I am not accustomed to *camping*," he replied coldly. "Are we expected to sleep on the ground?"

"There are usually carpets. I'll go ask." Zarifa headed for the train of camels, who stood placidly chewing grass at the edge of the watering hole.

The sun sank behind the dunes. Yatha clapped his hands. "Gather round, dear friends!" he cried. "We shall break bread together."

The captives trudged over. Qadir the Scented waved a hand and a feast appeared, laid out on carpets. Figs and apricots and olives, fragrant lamb stew, and casks of water and wine glistening with condensation. The others fell on the food with cries of delight, but Balthazar merely folded his arms.

"Sit," Jabaar growled. "Eat what you are given, worm!"

"I'm not hungry," he said, just as his empty stomach growled.

"Does the fare displease you?" asked Yatha the Harmonious.

"It's not real."

"Oh, it is most assuredly real. Can you not smell the delicious aromas?"

"It's a conjuration," Balthazar replied. "Who knows what it will turn into later?"

Jabaar gave an evil laugh. "You are right to be suspicious," he said in a low voice. "Once the food enters your intestines, it will turn into live rats—"

"Pay him no mind." Yatha frowned. "My brother jests. I promise you, the food is real enough."

"Or feel free to starve," Jabaar added. "It matters not to us."

Balthazar sat but stubbornly refused to fill a plate. A short while later, Zarifa returned from her foray to find bedding. She sank gracefully to the carpets without a moment's hesitation. He watched her dig in, licking her fingers and gesturing animatedly as she chatted with the other captives in Arabic.

The sight – and sounds – annoyed him to no end, so he finally turned to the man at his elbow. Older than the rest, mid-forties and bearded, with dark skin and intelligent eyes. He wore a simple white shawb and cheap sandals frayed at the soles.

"*As-salamu alaykum*," the man said politely when Balthazar caught his eye.

"*Wa alaykum as-salam,*" Balthazar replied, giving him a seated bow.

"My name is Khai. This is my brother Mosi."

Mosi also wore a beard, but looked a good ten years younger. Both had powerful builds, though Khai was a head taller. The brothers struck him as different from the rest of the group. Not so timid, and not half as pretty.

"I am Balthazar. Are you caravan guards?" he asked, thinking it would be wise to determine who was who.

Khai chuckled. "No, we mean to contest in the Trials." He eyed Balthazar shrewdly. "I assumed you do as well. You seem like a fighting man."

"Trials?"

Zarifa paused with a fig halfway to her mouth. "He doesn't know."

"Know what?" Balthazar asked.

"It is a strange and tragic tale," she intoned. "One long forgotten by most men." Zarifa pointed dramatically to the crescent moon peeking above the date palms. "But it is remembered in Al Miraj. On the tenth day of Jumada al-awwal, when the new moon rises, the time of the Trials will be upon us."

"What's she going on about?" Balthazar demanded.

"Shall I tell the tale?" Zarifa asked the other captives.

They nodded eagerly.

She rose to stand at the edge of the carpets, a dark silhouette against the western sky. The sands still held some heat, but they were cooling fast now that the sun had set. Past her shoulder, Orion's belt and bow shone brightly above the desert.

"Our story begins on a cold winter's night when the witch Beletsunnu birthed a demon daughter named Fulad-zereh, a hideous horned creature who brought chaos to all she touched. Yet Beletsunnu still loved her. She laid a powerful charm upon the newborn infant. The demon would be impervious to all weapons save for the sword known as the Shamshir-e Zomorrodnegar."

"The Emerald-Studded Blade," Khai murmured, his voice thick with awe and desire.

"The very same," Zarifa agreed solemnly. "Forged by the legendary blacksmith Kave, its existence kept Fulad-zereh in check. She feared the blade, knowing it would someday be the end of her. Long centuries passed. The sword fell into the hands of King Solomon and then to the prince of Al Miraj. But instead of guarding the blade, he used it to force Fulad-zereh to serve him."

Zarifa gazed at the audience, who listened raptly. "She became his greatest general. The city flourished. One by one, the prince's enemies fell to her ruthless campaigns. He grew to trust her. And then one day, Fulad-zereh tricked him and took the Shamshir-e Zomorrodnegar for herself."

"Typical," Balthazar muttered.

Zarifa shot him a sharp look. "She was invincible after that. She carried the prince away to her lair. What became of him, no one knows. But since that day nine hundred years ago, her wicked influence has corrupted the land. The fair realm of Al Miraj lies under her thrall."

There was silence for a long moment. The captives exchanged worried glances.

"Do Hansel and Gretel live there, too?" Balthazar asked. "Or perhaps the demon shares a cave with Ali Baba and the Forty Thieves?"

This drew a few snickers, though not from Khai and Mosi. The brothers frowned at him.

"You don't believe," Zarifa said quietly. "But you will. Once every century, Fulad-zereh offers a mortal champion the chance to win the sword back. It is known as the Trials. Three contests in an arena, each more arduous than the last. Those who prove themselves worthy may enter her lair and hunt for the sword."

"It's why my brother and I are making the journey," Khai said, his teeth gleaming in the darkness. "We shall be heroes!"

"That sounds very exciting. I wish you both luck." Balthazar gave an ostentatious yawn. "But I think it's time for sleep. I'm sure we'll all be rising bright and early." He rose and started walking for the tent.

"You shall take your repose chained to Mortlake's daughter," said Jabbar the Cruel, blocking his path.

"That's entirely unnecessary—"

Jabaar's eyes narrowed. "Or you shall take your repose staked out naked upon yonder anthill."

Balthazar smiled. "I'll take the anthill."

"Very good." Jabaar flicked a finger. The hump of sand boiled with a solid mass of scurrying insects. "They're the biting kind."

Balthazar sighed. "Of course they are."

"So you still choose the anthill?" the marid asked hopefully.

"No," he muttered. "Chain, please."

Darkness fell. Everyone retired to the tents except the three marids, who sat around a brazier near the wagons. Balthazar watched them through a crack in the cloth, weighing his options. He lacked a weapon. His leg was chained to the Mortlake she-devil. The jinn could work magic, and he was still unsure of its limits.

But he'd be damned if he went along like a lamb to the slaughter.

Frustrated energy simmered in his veins. It had built for days and had only one outlet now.

Balthazar wanted to kill something.

To spill blood.

Any color would do.

CHAPTER 7

B althazar waited until the moon had set. Then he rolled over and clamped a hand across Zarifa's mouth. Her eyes flew open.

"Listen closely," he whispered in her ear. "I'm leaving tonight and God help anyone or anything that gets in my way."

She vehemently shook her head.

"But I can't leave without *you*. So you're going to do exactly as I say. We're returning to Rodah, and then to Cairo. You'll give back my talisman and our ways will part forever. Do you understand me?"

Zarifa lightly touched his wrist. Balthazar eased his hand away.

"I fear it is not so simple," she whispered. "Mortlake said only the servants of Taj may travel the road—"

"I don't care," he hissed. "We'll follow the tracks back the way we came."

"But—"

"Do you prefer to wait another day until we are even farther from Rodah? If we leave tonight, we can make the village by daybreak."

"And when they catch us?"

"I've watched them for the last five hours. They haven't moved. They must think we're all too cowed to try anything. At the very least, we'll get a decent head start before they come after us."

Zarifa looked dubious, but she seemed to realize he wouldn't be dissuaded. Balthazar tore strips from his shirt, coughing to cover the sound of tearing cloth. He tied them around the chain to muffle the sound of the links. Then he crawled to the rear of the tent, beckoning Zarifa to follow.

Balthazar peeked outside. The tents had been arranged around the pool of water at the center of the oasis. A galaxy of stars shone overhead. He unpinned the edge of the *ruaq* and crept through the opening. He could see the camels kneeling in a line some distance away.

And the glow of the brazier, with three dark silhouettes sitting around it.

He had marked the direction they travelled in, which was more or less due east. Rodah must lie to the west. Balthazar nodded at Zarifa. Once she emerged, he pinned the wall back in place. They started crawling through the tents. All was quiet save for the occasional snore. Then his knee struck a tent peg that hadn't been pounded down. Balthazar gave a soft grunt. Zarifa froze next to him, the whites of her eyes gleaming in the starlight. They waited for a tense minute, but the figures around the brazier didn't leap up to investigate.

Balthazar gave a slow nod. They began crawling again. Soon the fire dwindled to a speck. When it vanished behind a dune, Balthazar rose to his feet. He could hardly believe it had been so simple. He grinned at Zarifa, who looked equally surprised.

"Let them explain to Taj how they failed to set a guard," he murmured.

"We're not free yet."

"No, but the hard part is over. Now we walk."

Balthazar set a brisk pace and was relieved Zarifa had no trouble keeping up with him. They were forced to match strides, but she had long legs. At first, the deep ruts of the carts were easy to follow in the starlight. The main nuisance was the cold. His coat was still slung over the back of the chair in the coffeehouse.

Then a wind rose. Balthazar paused to untie the strip of cloth from the chain and tie it about his face. Zarifa bowed her head, her long hair torn from its pins. Within minutes, the tracks had been erased.

"Do you the think marids discovered our escape?" she shouted over the roar of the wind.

Balthazar let out a wild laugh. "Let them call a storm! I don't care. We were headed east. We have simply to go west. At worst, we shall adjust our course at daybreak."

They stumbled forward bent into the wind, the chain dragging between them. The gale died shortly after midnight. The temperature grew bitter. He shivered, irritated that Zarifa strode along in stoic silence. They traversed an endless series of slanted dunes, one after the next and the next. Whenever the clouds parted, Balthazar studied the constellations. He knew Orion rose in the east and set in the west.

At last a pink glow appeared behind them. To his delight, they'd been heading in more or less the right direction. There was the matter of thirst. And hunger. But they'd walked all night with one brief stop for rest.

Salvation must be near at hand.

The sun broke the horizon and climbed into the azure sky. Sweat beaded his brow. When Zarifa pulled a peach from her robes, Balthazar nearly moaned. He refused to ask for any, but listening to her chew and slurp made him murderous all over again. How could he have been so unforgivably stupid? Thinking back, he realized he'd never seen her go in or out of the colonel's cabin. He had never seen the two of them together once. The man's description of his wife did not fit

Zarifa by any measure. And yet he'd believed everything she told him without a moment's doubt.

In his weakened state, the thought came – entirely unbidden – that he had done the same to countless women. Pretending to be someone he wasn't. Making promises with no intention of keeping them. Carefully winning their trust, only to shatter it.

The shoe was on the other foot and he didn't like it one bit.

If she'd been a common criminal, he could have forgiven her. Balthazar had been born into poverty and knew what it took to survive. He'd done far worse. And he could hardly blame her for having Mortlake as a father.

But to steal the object that was most precious to him – the only thing he literally couldn't live without – made Balthazar hate her with every fiber of his being. He was not accustomed to being at anyone's mercy. Once he got the ouroboros back, he needed to take precautions to ensure he never found himself in such a position again.

He trudged onward, lost in dark ruminations. The heat went from merely unpleasant to scorching. His shoeless foot sprouted weeping blisters, as did the ankle with the chain. It forced them to walk almost shoulder to shoulder, and to match strides or risk getting yanked off balance.

Hours passed. The horizon ahead remained unchanged, row upon row of golden dunes carved into peaks by the wind. Their tracks were the only sign of life – other than a pair of vultures who rode the thermals overhead.

"How are you faring?" Zarifa asked, breaking a long silence.

"Fine," he growled.

"Would you like a peach?"

He glanced at her. "Is it a *magic* peach?"

"Obviously. I took a few at supper last night. You really should have eaten."

"And you felt no ill effects?"

She shook her head.

He eyed the fruit. "Thank you," Balthazar muttered.

It was delicious. He devoured it and spat the pit to the sand.

"What time is it?" she asked, squinting at the horizon.

He took out his watch. "We've been walking for nine hours. Where's the village?" He paused. "Where's the *Nile*? We can't possibly have missed a huge river!"

Zarifa shrugged. "I told you—"

He flung out a hand. "Don't say it."

They walked for another hour. Then he saw something in the distance. The first thing that wasn't sand. Balthazar broke into a fast stagger, heading for the dark object.

"Wait!" Zarifa cried.

She cursed and lifted her robes to keep up. Balthazar sank to his knees next to a prone figure at the top of a dune. "Lucas," he croaked. His chest swelled with emotion. He might have shed a tear – if he could spare the water.

"My lord?" Lucas whispered, blinking. "Are you real?"

Balthazar seized his shirt and hauled him upright. "How on earth did you get here?"

"The Turk told me you were taken away in a cart. I followed the tracks from the edge of town, but they faded . . . ." Lucas winced. His face was sunburnt, his lips cracked.

"And you've been walking all this time?" Balthazar demanded.

"Without rest. But something is peculiar, my lord. I'm certain I kept to a straight line due east, but twice I crossed my own tracks." He seemed to revive as he noticed Zarifa. "Did you get it back? Why are you chained together?"

"We were attacked by jinn," Balthazar said wearily. "Mortlake owes their master money. They tried to take the daughter as payment. I had no idea what they were until it was too late."

"Daughter?" He looked shocked. "So she really is Mortlake's spawn?"

Zarifa gave Lucas a cold stare. "You both left me in an untenable position. I was merely trying to recoup—"

"Enough," Balthazar snapped. "We have bigger problems to worry about at the moment."

Lucas glanced up at the sky. The pair of circling vultures had multiplied to six.

"We will maintain our eastward course," Balthazar said firmly. "It can't be far. You must have made a miscalculation."

Lucas looked dubious, but he rose to his feet and brushed off the sand.

"How did you escape the jinn?" he asked.

"They failed to set a watch. We crawled out of the camp under cover of darkness."

"And you don't find that excessively lax?" Zarifa asked.

"What's your point?"

"My point is that they weren't worried about escape because it's impossible!"

"Feh," Balthazar muttered. "More children's tales."

"Can someone enlighten me?" Lucas asked, as they started walking again.

"Mortlake said the road to Al Miraj can only be traveled with jinn," Zarifa replied tartly. "He should know, since he's the only one of us who's been there. Every now and then, some fools try to find the city. They wander in circles until they die." Her eyes narrowed at Balthazar. "I never should have listened to you."

He didn't bother responding. On they walked, into the heat of midday. Each time they topped another dune, he expected to see a line of date palms or the thatched huts of the outer settlements that fringed the Nile. But the horizon never altered.

"You didn't bring water?" Lucas groaned.

"I had nothing to put it in. Didn't you?"

"I didn't stop to pack! You'd just been *kidnapped*. I assumed I'd catch up to you within hours."

Zarifa stared straight ahead. She looked aggravated, but even Balthazar was forced to admit she was tougher than either of them. The woman barely even sweated.

Their progress was followed with interest by the vultures, who clearly expected a hearty meal in the near future. The boldest swooped down to study them with a beady eye. Rather than shooing it away, Balthazar felt grateful for the second of shade provided by its ragged black wings.

Then the worst happened. They came across three sets of footprints, along with the distinctive dragging groove from the chain.

Zarifa did not say *I told you so*. She merely stared at him with utter disdain.

"All right," he said, swallowing the last vestige of pride. "Change of plans."

Lucas seemed not to have heard. He slowly sank down and sat with his legs straight out like a child playing in a sandbox.

"Yatha!" Balthazar screamed at the heavens. "Qadir!" He turned in a circle, arms wide. "We give up! You win!"

Two of the vultures alit on a nearby dune, cocking their heads. Zarifa took a threatening step towards them and the chain jerked tight. Balthazar let out a growl. "There goes the last piece of skin on my ankle," he spat.

"Well, poor *you*! All you do is complain. And I'm sure you'll die first, so I'll be chained to a rotting corpse."

"Good! You can fight the buzzards for the choicest bits," he retorted. "I hope they peck your faithless eyes out."

She gave him her back. "At least I wouldn't have to look at your face anymore. That's one bloody consolation!"

The nearest bird flapped its huge wings. Balthazar felt near to madness. They were the most spectacularly ugly things he'd ever seen. Bald and raw-looking on top, with fleshy folds around the thick beak. Balthazar took his shoe off and hurled it at the bird, which merely hopped to the side. He was about to throw his pocket watch when Zarifa seized his wrist. Her eyes were fever bright.

"I wish we'd never left," she whispered.

The desert blurred. Lucas let out a startled yelp. A second later they stood amidst the covered wagons, the train of camels waiting placidly next to the three marids. As much as he loathed them, Balthazar felt a surge of relief. He was at the far edge of his endurance. So was Lucas. Even Zarifa had finally started flagging. Now she flashed a quick satisfied smile. Lucas merely stared in frozen astonishment.

Balthazar faced the marids. They hadn't relented out of mercy, that much was certain. Taj wanted Mortlake's daughter. Of course, they could have taken her and left him and Lucas to die. But they hadn't done so.

Because they were in Cairo with an express purpose. To gather human *merchandise*—

"You could have ridden in comfort," said Yatha the Harmonious, shaking his head.

"But you chose to disobey," Jabaar growled. "I ought to whip you within an inch of your lives."

Lucas reached for the blade at his hip, but it was gone. He took a wary step back, trembling from exhaustion.

"We have no time for that," said Qadir the Scented, emitting a stench of wet dog. "The master awaits."

There was no sign of the oasis, so Balthazar assumed the caravan had been traveling since they abandoned it. He could see the tracks leading west. How far had they come in the last day?

Yatha and Qadir strode for the lead wagon, leaving them with Jabaar. The jinn folded his arms. "You must be thirsty."

Balthazar licked dry lips.

The marid laughed. "Oh, I just remembered. We ran out of water."

Balthazar wanted to punch him in the black shemagh, but couldn't summon the energy.

"You're an awful person," he croaked.

"Thank you," Jabaar replied. "Now scurry along before I change my mind and flog you all the way to Al Miraj."

At that instant, Balthazar saw the flaps twitch on one of the wagons. Khai peeked through and jerked his chin, then let the canvas fall before Jabaar noticed.

"I won't waste any more of your valuable time," Balthazar said quickly, leading Zarifa and Lucas to the wagon. They clambered in and the cart lurched off. The Egyptian brothers moved aside to make room with sympathetic glances. It was stifling inside, but just the shade felt glorious.

"Here," Khai whispered, offering his water skin.

"Have mine as well," Mosi added. He smiled at Zarifa, who gratefully accepted.

Balthazar murmured thanks in Arabic. He gave it to Lucas first, then drank his fill. The water was warm and had a peculiar taste, but he didn't care. His maddening thirst abated. Life flowed back into him and Balthazar found himself deeply touched by the simple act of kindness.

"Where did you disappear to?" Khai asked with a wry smile.

"Nowhere, apparently," Balthazar replied with a sigh. "But if I hadn't tried to escape, I wouldn't have found my traveling companion. This is Lucas. He followed the caravan and nearly died in the desert searching for me."

The men nodded greetings.

"At least you were reunited," Mosi said. "Allah must watch over you both."

Zarifa laughed. "Don't let him fool you. They're both rogues."

"Says the lying thief," Balthazar muttered.

The brothers exchanged a look.

"Never mind," Balthazar said. "Where are we?"

84

"Nearly there," Khai replied. "About three hundred leagues east of Mecca."

Balthazar stared at him in shock. "That's not possible. We never crossed the Red Sea!"

Khai laughed. "There is no sea on this road. But the body of water you speak of lies well behind us now."

"I must return to Cairo," Balthazar growled. "This is all a mistake!"

"I wish I could help you," Khai said regretfully. "But I am sure it will turn out well in the end. Have faith, my friend."

Balthazar was silent for a minute. "What do you know about Taj?"

"Only that his marids approached us in the bazaar. Our uncle has a small shop there. Yatha said his master issued an open call for champions to contest the Trials." Khai's chest swelled with pride. "Our great-grandfather fought in the last one."

"What happened?"

"I don't know. He never returned."

"And you still want to enter?"

The Egyptian shrugged. "Someone has to uphold the family honor. And our prospects were poor. Our own father died deep in debt."

Zarifa glanced at him. "I know how that is," she murmured.

"But if we win the Trials, we will be rich men," Mosi added brightly.

Lucas eyed them with apprehension. "What are the Trials?"

"Ask her," Balthazar said, jerking a thumb at Zarifa.

She sat next to him – the chain left them no choice – while Lucas had squeezed in opposite with Khai and Mosi. Zarifa drew a breath, her dark eyes shining.

"It is a strange and tragic tale," she began. "One forgotten by most men . . . ."

The ordeal of the last day caught up and Balthazar's eyes drifted shut as she reached the part about the sword. He slept deeply. When he awoke, the canvas covering had been rolled back. Lucas was dozing, but the others were awake. Judging by the sun, it was late afternoon.

"Will we be stopping to camp soon?" he asked, scrubbing the grit from his eyes.

Khai grinned with excitement. "They say we are here."

CHAPTER 8

Pink sandstone cliffs rose ahead. The caravan made straight for them and Balthazar wondered if the city lay on the other side, though he could see no way through. Then a chill swept across his skin. It was akin to the sensation of entering the Dominion, that twilight land between the worlds of the living and the dead.

Balthazar gasped and lurched upright, dragging Zarifa with him. She muttered a curse, but fell silent at the sight before them.

The cliffs had vanished. Looming just ahead was a huge wall, fronted with tiers of balconies that looked out over the desert. Through open gates, he saw a city of graceful domes and spires hewn into the rock like a great beehive. Lacy bridges spanned the gaps, with winding staircases leading to higher tiers.

The rose-hued stone glowed in the slanting sunlight, but it was the greenery at every turn that caught the eye. Groves of pine, cypress and olive flanked orchards of pomegranate, pear, quince and fig, all heavy with fruit. Vines with white and red flowers tumbled like waterfalls from the upper stories of the buildings. Even the rooftops were a riot of living color.

Figures paused on the bridges and leaned over the balconies, watching the arrival of the caravan.

"Welcome to the City of Gardens," said Yatha the Harmonious with a dramatic sweep of his arm. "Welcome to Al Miraj."

The captives in the carts oohed and aahed. "It looks very nice," someone said hopefully.

Balthazar snapped out of his trance. "You're *slaves*," he muttered. "Don't get too excited."

"Now, now," Yatha chastised. "I see no slaves here. Only sweet young faces eager to meet their new employer."

Balthazar turned to the marids, who strode along next to the cart. "Well, I'd like to go first, if you don't mind. My business is the most pressing."

"Silence!" Jabaar snapped. "You will do as you're told. Or I will cut off your ears and—"

Balthazar tuned out the rest as they passed through the gates and proceeded down an avenue lined with tamarinds and date palms. All the streets had sinuous, curving lines, making it impossible to see very far ahead, but everything spoke of wealth and prosperity.

"I thought it was supposed to be under the demon's sway," he said to Zarifa. "The fearsome Fulad-Zereh!" Balthazar chuckled. "I'm trembling."

"Keep your voice down," she replied with a frown. "Appearances can be deceiving."

He shot her a look. "Oh, I'm well aware of *that*."

They passed through a much smaller set of gates into a walled garden. Young boys ran out to take charge of the animals.

"You two," Jabaar snapped at the Egyptian brothers. "The journey ends here. You are free to find cheaper lodgings in the city." He eyed their plain robes with disdain. "But I doubt you can afford my master's prices."

"Of course, wise jinn," Khai said agreeably, hopping down from the cart with his brother.

They both gave Balthazar a polite bow, which he returned.

"I'm sure we will see each other again," Khai said. "May Allah protect you."

"And you," Balthazar replied.

He watched them amble off into the city.

"The rest of you scum, *out!*" Jabaar shrieked.

The captives hastily abandoned the carts and followed the three marids down a pebbled pathway to a large rectangular building carved from the same pink sandstone. It rose four stories high, with open terraces stretching along each level to catch the breeze. Bright birds flitted among the acacia trees. It smelled of sunbaked stone and the pink desert roses that grew in a thick carpet to either side of the path.

Runes were etched into the stone above the pillared entryway, though Balthazar couldn't read them.

"What does it say?" he asked Yatha the Harmonious.

"*The Golden Flail,*" the marid replied solemnly. "A most venerable institution. The finest of its kind in all of Al Miraj."

They passed into a tiled antechamber that gave onto a sun-drenched interior courtyard. A fountain babbled in the center. Perched on the rim of the fountain was an assortment of women in gauzy shifts that left little to the imagination. They smiled at Balthazar and he inclined his head, warming somewhat to his new circumstances.

"This way, my sweet young friends," said Qadir the Scented, beckoning to the chattel. "We must make you presentable."

He herded the nervous-looking group away just as a stout woman bustled through an archway. She had long reddish hair with a thick streak of white on the left side. She wore a simple ankle-length grey robe with a heavy ring of keys dangling at her bosom. Her gaze was sharp and assessing, and she gave off an air of authority. Yatha and Jabaar stood a bit straighter at her appearance.

"You were expected two days ago," she said flatly.

"An unavoidable delay," Yatha replied. "I can explain to the master—"

"He will see you at once." She gazed at Balthazar, Lucas and Zarifa. "Who are they?"

"That is what we must explain," Jabaar growled.

She arched a brow, but gave the marids a brief nod. "Come, then."

They all climbed a wide marble staircase to a landing on the second floor. One side opened to the interior courtyard with the fountain. The other had no wall, only a long brocaded curtain of deep maroon.

"You will wait here," Jabaar snapped at Lucas.

Lucas scowled and started to argue, but Balthazar laid a hand on his arm. "It's all right," he said quietly. "Let me talk to him first."

Lucas gave a reluctant nod. Jabaar led the rest of them to the end of the curtain and eased it back, revealing an airy chamber with a frescoed ceiling. Silk cushions were scattered across the thick carpets, along with low tables covered in an assortment of food and drink. A veranda stretched the length of one side, giving a view of date palms swaying in the breeze.

But the main attraction was a sunken pool in the center of the chamber. A wedge of late afternoon sun spilled across the bath, gilding its occupants, who were engaged in activities that would have made a Babylonian whoremaster blush.

"Most illustrious master," Jabaar and Yatha intoned, pressing their foreheads to the carpet.

At first, Balthazar took Taj for one of the concubines. All were beautiful, but the rest paled in comparison to the creature who reclined against the farthest edge, his fingers trailing lazily in the water. Flaxen hair hung over one muscled shoulder in a waist-length plait. He had flawless golden skin, irises an even more vivid blue than the marids, and the face of a Renaissance angel.

Then he flicked a finger and his companions scurried from the bath, dripping a trail of water out the door. His eyes were cold and ageless. When he rose, unconscious of his own nudity, and bent to seize a length of cloth that he wound around his hips, Taj moved with a predatory grace that made Balthazar's hackles rise.

Not a bloody *daēva*.

"Where's Mortlake?" Taj demanded.

"It is a most unfortunate tale, master," said Yatha the Harmonious, wringing his hands. "John Mortlake is dead."

"But we brought you his head," Jabaar the Cruel said quickly, hefting a burlap sack with dark stains.

Taj's lips thinned. "What am I supposed to do with his head? I want my money. And I have talismans for him to sell."

"If I may—" Balthazar ventured.

"Who's he?" Taj demanded.

"The man who killed Mortlake," said Jabaar. "Shall I flog him for your pleasure, master?"

"Not just yet." Taj's perfect features turned icier as he regarded Balthazar. "So you're the reason I'm unable to collect the debt I'm owed."

"I had no idea he owed you anything," Balthazar retorted. "In fact, I was unaware of your existence until your jinn abducted me. But I will happily pay you the entire amount, plus interest." He stabbed a finger at Zarifa. "Just give me *her*."

Yatha pushed Zarifa forward. "This is Mortlake's daughter, O Splendid Master. We thought she could work off the debt if no other solution presents itself."

"Ah." Taj appraised her with an expert eye. "A pleasure to make your acquaintance, Miss Mortlake," he drawled in a warmer tone. "I trust the journey was a pleasant one."

"Indeed. But my name is Zarifa Everleigh." She looked him up and down in a leisurely fashion. "I always imagined

Taj as a hulking, bald-headed brute. I must admit, I'm pleasantly surprised."

Taj smiled.

"Whenever you're done flirting, perhaps we can get down to business," Balthazar said, holding his temper by a thread. "How much did Mortlake owe?"

"Five hundred and twenty thousand pounds," Taj said.

Balthazar didn't blink an eyelash. "Let's make it six hundred for your trouble. As I said, the only condition is that Miss Everleigh is given into my custody."

"Why do you want her so badly?"

Balthazar hesitated. "She stole something from me. The nature of the theft is between me and the lady, but it is an object of great sentimental value—"

"Right," Taj interrupted. He turned back to Zarifa, all business now. "What is it?"

"A talisman that steals the life force from others at the instant of, er . . . release," she said.

Taj frowned.

"Plainly put, he's a sexual vampire."

Balthazar rolled his eyes.

Taj stared at him. "Is this true?"

"She makes it sound so tawdry."

Taj held out a hand. A cup of wine floated over. "What does the talisman do *exactly*?"

"A simple trade. Pleasure for time." Balthazar smiled. "Trust me, no one's been complaining."

The daēva laughed and glanced at Yatha, who clasped his hands and chortled subserviently. "You know, I almost like him."

"I don't," Zarifa said. "He tried to use it on me, but I liberated it before he had the chance."

"*Liberated?*" Balthazar scowled. "And I might have taken it off—"

"Oh, please."

"Don't pretend you have the moral high ground," he growled, and turned back to Taj. "I'm sure you're a busy man. Let me pay this trifling debt, take Mortlake's vile offspring, and be on my way."

Taj nodded slowly. "Of course." He inclined his head. "How do you intend to pay it?"

"I have accounts all over the world. I'll wire the funds to the bank of your choice."

"I don't do business with banks."

"Fine. We'll make it cash."

Taj sipped his wine. "So I'm supposed to let you walk out of here on the promise that you'll return and pay me? I don't think so."

"Do you want to buy his talisman?" Zarifa asked. "I'll sell it to you right now."

Balthazar rounded on her, torn between rage and relief. "So you *do* have it!" He scowled. "But I searched you—"

"Not quite thoroughly enough." She smiled. "I'd hardly allow it to leave my person. What if someone found it?" Her smirk widened. "Come, Balthazar. There's a certain poetic justice, you must admit."

He closed his eyes and pressed a hand to his forehead.

Taj burst out laughing. "Let's have a look." He arched an amused eyebrow. "Is it still . . . ?"

Her cheeks reddened. "No. I have it here." She lifted her robe and pulled the talisman from her boot.

"That's mine," Balthazar growled, stepping forward. Jabaar blocked his way.

"It *was* yours," Zarifa clarified. "Now it's mine." She turned to Taj. "Interested?"

"Very." He held out a hand. Zarifa hesitated.

"I'm not a thief," Taj said in a low, dangerous tone. "I merely wish to examine it."

"Yes," Zarifa said quickly, swallowing. "Of course." She handed him the talisman as Balthazar watched in cold fury.

"An ouroboros," he murmured. "The symbol for eternity." The snake's jeweled eyes gleamed in the sunlight. "A very fine piece of work."

Zarifa beamed. "Then it's settled. When can I leave?"

Taj sighed regretfully. "I'm sorry, pigeon, but I didn't say it would cover the whole debt."

"What?" Her eyes widened in outrage. "That talisman is priceless!"

Taj gave her a thin smile. "Everything has a price." He studied the ouroboros on its silver chain. "It's certainly valuable, but there's only one thing I really want. The Shamshir-e Zomorrodnegar. And it's not in your power to offer me that."

Balthazar stared at him. The Emerald-Studded Blade. So the tale *was* true.

Zarifa bit her lip. "It might be," she ventured.

"How?" Taj demanded.

She looked at Balthazar. "He's a bastard and a scoundrel, but I've heard things."

"Such as?"

She glanced at the sack lying at Jabaar's feet, then tore her gaze away. "I don't mourn my father. He was a scoundrel, too. But he never lied. Not to me, at least. He said Balthazar was the finest swordsman in the world."

Taj laughed. "I've heard that claim before."

"As have I," Zarifa agreed. "But Mortlake wouldn't say such a thing lightly. He told me Balthazar was the most dangerous man he knew." She grimaced. "And my father kept vicious company."

Taj didn't look impressed.

"Make him contest," Zarifa persisted. "If he wins the Trials, you get the sword. Surely that will clear my father's debts and earn Balthazar back the talisman."

"Nobody ever wins," Taj replied flatly. "It's impossible."

"Then you keep the talisman. There are men who'd give their souls for eternal life. Either way, you come out ahead."

Taj looked at Balthazar. "What do you say to this proposal?"

So Zarifa thought to dispose of him in some ritualistic Pagan bloodbath? Balthazar sighed. "I wish the claim were true. But I'm afraid the lady might be exaggerating." He held his fingers an inch apart. "Just a little bit."

"Is she?" Taj said mildly. He turned to the two marids. "What is your opinion? I assume he didn't come along willingly."

"He put up a decent fight," Jabaar said in a grudging tone, "considering he was unarmed. He managed to take Yatha's blade and inflict a little scratch. It was quite tedious. We were pressed for time—"

"So I froze him," Yatha added cheerfully.

Taj looked thoughtful.

"There might have been some luck involved," Balthazar said modestly.

"Perhaps. Let's have a demonstration." Taj gestured at Yatha. "Give him a sword."

Yatha stepped forward.

"Wait!" Balthazar flung out a hand. "Let me take my socks off first."

He wiggled his toes. Then he performed a few squats, breathing hard through his mouth. He bounced on his toes. He stretched to the left. He stretched to the right. Then he gave another sharp exhale and rolled his shoulders. "I'm ready," he announced.

Taj used Air to sweep the tables back and clear a corner of the room. Jabaar clapped his hands. A curved blade appeared in Balthazar's right hand. He gaped in astonishment, then took a few wild swipes. The combatants squared off.

Taj and Zarifa retreated to the cushions. He offered her a candied date, which she gracefully accepted.

"To first blood," Taj said, lounging back on the cushion with one knee bent. "You may proceed."

Balthazar clumsily parried the first blows. He shuffled across the tiles, deploying fancy footwork invented on the spot and which served little purpose but to leave him precariously off-balance. When Yatha swept his scimitar around, he ducked beneath it with a cry of triumph and feinted right, knowing the marid would pick up on the obvious signal of his gaze. Yatha did, and Balthazar froze with the tip of Yatha's sword pressed against his throat. A thin line of blood trickled into his shirt collar.

"Enough," Taj said.

Yatha's blade vanished. Zarifa shook her head in disgust.

"Well, *that* was embarrassing," Balthazar muttered. He unwound the cloth from his head and dipped it in the pool. Then he pressed it to the scratch on his neck. "*Ow.*" He cast the marid an accusing look.

"Here's my counter-offer." Taj gazed at Balthazar. "You killed John Mortlake. Whether or not he deserved it is a debate that doesn't interest me. So here's your choice." He bared perfect white teeth. "We'll start with the more pleasant option. Work for me."

Zarifa burst out laughing. Jabaar scowled and she turned away, pretending to cough, but Balthazar could hear her chuckling.

"Time does not pass here as it does in the outside world. You won't age a single day. Your life will be comfortable. Pampered, even. With your looks and experience, I can charge premium prices for the pleasure of your company."

Balthazar stared at him. "You're serious."

Taj shrugged. "I fail to see how the arrangement would be so different from your former life."

Balthazar opened his mouth, frowned, then closed it again.

"He has a point," Zarifa murmured.

Balthazar shot her a dire look. "How long would this arrangement last?"

"Until the debt is satisfied. Then I'll return the talisman."

Balthazar's dark eyes narrowed. "*How long?*"

Taj sighed. "I'd have to calculate interest into the bargain. I don't run a charity. So . . . ." He looked up at the ceiling, ticking off numbers on his fingers. "Approximately five hundred years."

"Five *hundred* years," Balthazar repeated slowly.

"You wouldn't be a slave. My employees have the right to refuse a client."

"And the other choice?"

"Find the money elsewhere." Taj smiled. "But you can't leave Al Miraj, so your options would be extremely limited. The regent doesn't tolerate thieves. First offense is the left hand. Second offense is the right hand, plus the nose. Third offense is . . . . Well, you wouldn't like it."

"So that's it? Chopped to pieces or eternity in your brothel?"

Taj shrugged. "You shouldn't have killed Mortlake. Truthfully, I doubt you'd have to serve the full five hundred. The magic that conceals us from the world of men is failing. By the time another century rolls around, it will likely be gone altogether. If the sword is not restored to us in these Trials, which I assure you it won't be . . . well, that's it."

Balthazar eyed the wine. "May I?"

"Of course."

He poured a cup, drank it straight down and stared into the dregs. "This contest. Is it really so difficult?"

"No one's ever survived beyond the third round. Not in nine hundred years." Taj gave his head a rueful shake. "Yet when the Trials roll around, all the idiots crawl out of the woodwork thinking they'll be the one to make it this time."

Crawl out of the woodwork? Balthazar thought of the Egyptian brothers, who expected to be heroes and in fact, had been *recruited* by Taj's marids. Clearly, his first guess had been correct. The daēva was scum.

"When do they begin?"

"In two days," Taj replied. "At the new moon."

"I've always wondered," Zarifa said. "Why does Fuladzereh do it? Why even offer a chance?"

"Because she's cruel," Taj replied. "She wants us to think there's hope when there isn't." His handsome face darkened. "Not to mention the fact that she keeps stealing my best whores."

Zarifa looked startled. "She comes here?"

"Oh, yes. Snatches them from their beds whenever the whim strikes." Taj sighed. "She has wings. Flies straight through the window."

"I don't care for either of these choices," Balthazar said.

"You have until tomorrow to decide." He turned to Zarifa. "No one eats for free around here, Miss Everleigh. I'll keep the talisman as collateral, but you must earn the balance."

"I won't work in your brothel," she declared, lifting her chin. "I will not be *owned*."

His expression hardened. "The debts of the fathers pass to the children. Balthazar killed Mortlake, but you're his closest kin."

Zarifa delved into the bowl of candied dates and popped one in her mouth. "Fine. I have something of value to offer. I can sense the purpose of talismans merely by touching them. My father used it to his advantage often." She glanced at Balthazar. "It's how I knew what *his* did."

"I do own objects of unknown provenance," Taj said. "It's dangerous to test them without knowing what they do. We've had some unfortunate accidents." He nodded to himself. "We'll discuss terms later, but I find that arrangement acceptable for now."

Balthazar sensed a dismissal and cleared his throat. "I

have an associate. He followed the caravan. I want to know what will happen to him."

Taj glared at the marids. "He *followed* you?"

"We did not realize until half a day into the journey," Yatha admitted.

"You're slipping," Taj muttered irately. "Very well. Bring him in."

Yatha went to the curtain and drew it aside, beckoning. Lucas Devereaux stepped into the chamber. He looked ragged and sunburned, his brown eyes shadowed with fatigue. A faint crease lined Taj's forehead. He sat up straighter on the cushions.

"Er, hello," Lucas said, glancing at Balthazar. "I couldn't help overhearing and I really must insist—"

"You're French," Taj said with a delighted smile.

"Born in France," Lucas muttered. "Raised in England."

"And what is your . . . relationship to my debtor?"

"I'm his secretary," Lucas replied stonily.

"Ah. You must be quite devoted to follow him into the desert."

Lucas shrugged. "He pays well."

"He must. What's your name?"

"Lucas Devereaux."

"Let us be frank with each other, Mr. Devereaux."

Lucas gazed past his shoulder at the date palms. "I'd rather not."

Taj laughed. "If you were listening, you understand the nature of The Golden Flail. I'm sorry your master dragged you into this predicament, but that's not my fault. You're here now and we might as well make the best of it. Everyone within these walls earns their keep." Taj looked him over while Lucas silently fumed. "I'll be blunt. You're charming in a strait-laced, uptight way. Certain clients would go mad for you."

Balthazar thought Lucas couldn't get any redder, but it seemed he was wrong.

"I . . . ." Lucas stammered. "This is all most—"

"That little mustache," Taj continued relentlessly. "Those melancholy brown eyes. Yes, I definitely see marketable qualities."

Lucas ignored Taj completely. He turned to Balthazar with a withering stare.

"He can fight," Balthazar said quickly. "Better than I can, I promise you."

"I already have marids." The daēva's gaze was all innocence. "Any other special talents?"

Lucas looked around wildly and cleared his throat. "Er, I keep my lord's accounts."

"Oh, he's a *wizard* with numbers!" Balthazar exclaimed. "Mr. Devereaux doubled my fortune in the last ten years. And he actually enjoys it. You should see the books. Not a single digit out of place."

This evoked a spark of interest. "As it happens, one of my agents was stabbed by an ifrit three days ago," Taj said, stroking his jaw. "With the Trials coming up, I could use some extra help overseeing the betting."

Lucas nodded fervently. "I'd be very good at that."

The woman with a streak of white in her hair had waited all this time by the curtain, still as a statue. Now she stepped forward. "Shall I show Miss Everleigh to the Treasury?" she asked.

Taj nodded. He seemed suddenly weary. "Yes. Leave me now. All of you. I have other business to attend to. And, Seneschal?"

She waited expectantly.

"Do not leave Miss Everleigh unattended," he added dryly.

The Seneschal gave a brisk nod. The pair of them

departed together. Lucas and Balthazar hurried to follow suit before Taj changed his mind.

"This way, O Soft-Skinned Concubines," Yatha the Harmonious beckoned.

"I'm not a concubine yet," Balthazar muttered as they slipped into the corridor.

Yatha gave him a gentle smile that said: *You will be.*

CHAPTER 9

The marid led them to the third floor, which he described as the Sleeping Quarters — *sleep* being an obvious euphemism. To the relief of both Balthazar and Lucas, they passed the occupied bedchambers and entered a quieter wing of the Golden Flail. A few servants moved about carrying fresh linen or sprays of flowers, bowing briefly to Yatha as they passed.

"Here we are," he said, sweeping aside a curtain. The adjoining rooms were brothel chic, with yards of purple velvet and tapestries of rutting centaurs that earned a startled blink even from Balthazar. Lucas merely looked resigned.

"You are free to come and go as you please," Yatha said. "Within these walls, all are perfectly safe. No one would dare insult our master by misbehaving. But the city is a lawless place. Be cautious if you choose to explore. And do not waste your time attempting to escape. You would merely wander in circles as you did last time."

"Oh, I'm not going anywhere," Balthazar said firmly. "Not until I recover my property."

"Very good." Yatha bowed and became a stream of smoke that slipped beneath the curtain.

Balthazar sat on the heart-shaped bed. He looked up at Lucas. "I'm sorry."

"I'd say it's not your fault," Lucas replied, "but it actually is." He glanced at the terrace. "At least there's something to jump off. Thoughtful of Taj to give us a high floor."

Balthazar sighed. "I have a fortune kings would envy and no way of getting to it. Bloody *Mortlake*."

Lucas rubbed his forehead. "Maybe we can get the money some other way."

"It's a lot. More than half a million pounds."

Lucas groaned.

"There is a third possibility." Balthazar paused. "The Shamshir-e Zomorrodnegar."

"I'd heard of it before," Lucas replied thoughtfully. "It's mentioned in the Persian tale *Amir Arsalan*. You ought to read books more."

"What do you know of Fulad-zereh?"

"The story says he's a demon who can only be killed by the Emerald-Studded Blade."

"*She*," Balthazar corrected. "And she stole the sword from some Al Miraji prince around the time of William the Conqueror. But if Taj is to be believed – a major *if* – the Trials are impossible to win. And the losers die. Horribly, I assume."

"Then you'd better not."

"That's what I thought, too. But it would be the simplest solution."

"The whole thing sounds shady in the extreme."

"I agree."

"At least you won't age here," Lucas pointed out. "We have time to come up with another plan."

Over the centuries, the talisman had changed Balthazar in some fundamental way. Living on borrowed time carried its own price. Once the process began, it rapidly accelerated. Even if he wanted to, he could no longer simply live out his days as a man.

"If Taj is telling the truth," Balthazar agreed.

"That marid said he's coming back for me in an hour." His face darkened. "And I'd better satisfy Taj's expectations. Because I am not . . . *selling myself* . . . to his clients. I'll enter the Trials myself first!"

"I won't let that happen," Balthazar said firmly. "I swear it."

Lucas gave a curt nod and swept through the curtain to his adjoining chamber.

Balthazar stared unseeing at the lewd tapestries. He needed information, but he was keenly aware of his disheveled, filthy state. A servant directed him to the communal bathhouse, where he performed his ablutions under the curious stares of Taj's harem. Then he returned to the bedchamber and tore apart a cedar chest in search of something suitable, flinging the garments into a heap on the carpet.

They were all flimsy, baggy cotton Balthazar wouldn't be caught dead in. So he dusted off the shirt, waistcoat and trousers he'd ordered from his tailor at Gieves & Hawkes in London. He knotted his cravat, which had a dried splash of blue blood. He combed his hair and tucked the watch in his pocket.

The only thing he lacked was shoes. With a scowl, he slid his feet into a pair of silken slippers.

Then he trotted down the marble staircase and into the courtyard. The sun had descended in the sky, its heat softening to a tolerable level. He strolled through the gardens, his dark eyes drinking in every detail. The pink desert roses had five petals that blushed outward with color at the throat of the bloom. Each specimen was flawless, without a single dead leaf or broken stem. The gleaming stone fountains might have been carved that very morning. It was all too perfect to be anything but magic. Yet when he knelt to touch a flower, the silky petals felt real beneath his fingers.

Balthazar watched warily as a man strolled over, a hand-rolled cigarette in his mouth. He had olive skin and a short dark beard and was handsome enough to belong to Taj, yet he seemed different from the others. Harder around the edges.

"You must be Balthazar," he said. His voice was deep and pleasant, with a Turkish accent.

"And you are?"

"Destan Karatas. Taj asked me to keep an eye out for you."

"I don't require minding."

"Of course not." He shrugged. "I am merely a tour guide. Show you around a little."

"Thanks, but I'll pass. Where's the nearest watering hole?"

"There are many. What kind do you want?"

"The dimly lit, anonymous kind."

Destan laughed. "There are many of *those*. But you'll need currency if you want to drink."

Balthazar reached into the inside pocket of his coat. He'd forgotten the billfold was gone. His jaw clenched.

Zarifa.

He considered hunting her down and demanding it back, but it seemed like a lot of work. At the moment he just wanted to drown his troubles in a sea of alcohol – and figure out who really ran things around here. If it was the demon . . . well, perhaps she'd be open to negotiation.

"Taj owns several such establishments. As his guest, you could run an account." Destan tilted his head. "Come on, I'll show you."

Balthazar hesitated. No doubt Taj had spies everywhere. At least he'd know who it was.

"You're too kind," he murmured.

They passed through the gates and followed a series of winding streets deeper into the city. All the buildings were carved from that radiant pink sandstone, but their facades were different, some pillared and square in the Greco-Roman style, others displaying an Eastern influence with domes and minarets. Few of the walls were solid, favoring scrollwork with a motif of interlacing acanthus leaves and stylized foliage that gave privacy but allowed light and air to penetrate the rooms beyond.

True to its name, the City of Gardens was an oasis. Every balcony and veranda caught the eye with a riot of trailing vines and flowers. Crowds teemed in the sun-baked streets, a motley assortment of human, jinn and daēva, the latter distinguishable by the way they moved, loose-limbed and feline.

Balthazar tensed as a group of men in wide trousers and vests approached from the opposite direction. All were armed to the teeth and rippling with muscle.

"Hopefuls," Destan remarked. "Dumb bastards. But the Trials are very lucrative for my master. Between the whoring, drinking and betting, that demon bitch isn't the only one making a killing."

"I still don't understand." Balthazar caught the eye of the largest one. He was a beast, six and half feet tall with shoulders like cannonballs. The man bared his teeth as he passed. "What's in it for *them?*"

"Besides the glory?" Destan laughed sardonically. "Well, Taj puts up a large purse of prize money. And the winner gets a luxurious suite of rooms at the Golden Flail for life. His or her own personal harem. Jinn to command." He grinned. "Immortality without earning it on your back."

Balthazar didn't laugh. "How long have you been here?"

"Almost four hundred years." He smiled at Balthazar's startled expression. "You wish to hear my story?"

"If you don't mind sharing it."

Destan steered Balthazar up a wide flight of stone stairs. "I was a captain in the Ottoman army. We'd camped in the desert after a great victory over the Mamluk sultan at Ridaniya." He shrugged. "I went to take a piss and never made it back."

Balthazar frowned. "Kidnapped?"

"I wandered over the line." He gave a bitter laugh. "It's invisible, but I guess you know that. Imagine my surprise."

Balthazar recalled their sudden arrival at the city. "Yes, I can."

"I thought I was dreaming. Ended up in the Golden Flail. Had the time of my life. When I woke up the next day, I discovered it wasn't a dream. And I owed a lot of money I didn't have."

Balthazar felt genuine sympathy for the man. "I'm sorry."

Destan flicked his cigarette to the gutter. "Yes, well, that's how it is, eh? I only have two hundred years left. Then Taj says he'll let me go."

They entered a narrow, quiet street of walled courtyards, the din of the lower city fading. Destan approached an unmarked wooden door. A burly marid in the black shemagh stood guard, his arms crossed. Destan nodded a greeting and the marid stepped aside. Inside was a low-ceilinged chamber with cushions and scarred tables. Veiled women writhed to the music of instruments Balthazar hadn't heard in centuries.

"What are you drinking?"

Balthazar looked around. Cats wandered freely among the clientele, grooming themselves on the tables and napping on the cushions. It was like stepping back in time to the ancient world of his youth. That era had its charms, but the quality of the liquor wasn't one of them.

"I suppose they only serve watered wine."

"They serve anything."

He raised an eyebrow. "Absinthe? Cocaine? Opium?"

Destan shrugged. "Anything. Is that what you want?"

"God, no. I was just curious." Balthazar thought for a moment. "I want a Brugerolle. Make it . . . oh, let's say 1795."

"Certainly." Destan gestured to one of the teenaged serving boys and whispered in his ear. He returned a moment later with a bottle and two short-stemmed brandy snifters.

Balthazar examined the label and laughed. "It actually looks authentic."

"Because it is." Destan poured an inch into each glass. "Shall we make a toast?"

Balthazar winced. "I'd rather not." He sniffed the glass. A heady, almost floral aroma met his nose, caramel with hints of orange and apricot. He took a cautious sip, rolling it on his tongue. A gentle sigh escaped his lips. "It's a Brugerolle. I think they even got the year right, not that I'd honestly know the difference." He looked up at Destan suspiciously. "How?"

The Turk jerked his chin at a slender marid who observed the proceedings with a bored expression. His face was bare and he could have been Yatha's twin. "Jinn barkeep." Destan raised his glass. "See, I take you to the best places."

They found cushions in a quiet corner, drinking in companionable silence for a few minutes. The Turk might be Taj's spy, but Balthazar found himself warming to the man. And he seemed willing enough to answer questions.

"So who's in charge around here?" Balthazar asked casually. "Taj mentioned a regent."

Destan swallowed with a happy smile. "This is very good, Balthazar. We must drink together often. Yes, the regent. His name is Mikal."

"So he punishes thieves and bans outright slavery, yet the city is lawless."

"Now it is. But it was not always so. Mikal has turned his back on us."

"Is he a daēva?"

Destan shook his head. "They say he is an archangel."

Balthazar choked on his cognac. "An archangel? *Here?*"

"Once there were four. Mikal, Jibrail, Israfil and Azrael. The Watchtowers. They came when the prince was stolen away by Fulad-zereh. The people thought they would help, but they did nothing."

"Where are the others?"

"No one knows. They left before my time." Destan took another mouthful of cognac. "Mikal hasn't been seen in decades, but Taj claims he remains shut away at the Summer Palace." He leaned forward. "My master is the unofficial mayor, if you will. He keeps things as orderly as possible, but with Fulad-zereh free to do as she pleases . . . Well, his authority is limited."

"Anarchy, in other words."

"More or less," Destan agreed, watching the dancers.

Balthazar considered this. "Power vacuums often give rise to business opportunities. Have you never considered working off your debt another way?"

Destan laughed. "We all survive on the crumbs that fall from Taj's table. He controls the moneylenders, the brothels, the armory . . . the watering holes, as you call them."

"Everything?"

"Everything that counts. What you say is truth. With chaos comes profit. And Taj is the most ruthless of them all." The Turk looked around and lowered his voice. "Plus he has the marids. Yatha and Qadir aren't so bad, but Jabaar . . . Don't get on his bad side."

"Why do they bow and scrape to him?" Balthazar wondered. "Daēvas are powerful, but the jinn can do things I never dreamed of."

"Yatha told me the tale once. Their race was created to serve the angels, but they were too proud and refused. Their name, marid, it means rebellious one. As punishment, the angels bound them to the daēvas instead."

"How wrathful of them," Balthazar said dryly. "So every marid in this city serves a daēva?"

"Mostly Taj, but others as well." Destan glanced meaningfully at a stern-faced man with long dark hair dandling a pretty girl on his knee. "There are many here."

Balthazar knew of three daēvas in Europe, but he hadn't seen another one in more than a thousand years. Now he understood why. They were all in Al Miraj. He would never have believed it.

"Why don't they just take the sword back?" he wondered. "Surely an army of daēvas and jinn could subdue one demon."

"You think they haven't tried? She commands ifrit. The most powerful jinn of all. And she can't be killed without the sword. Which she keeps hidden away."

"Does she live in the city?"

"No. She has her own little realm nearby. She always comes for the Trials though."

The skin between his shoulder-blades prickled. Some dark impulse was stirring and Balthazar didn't trust it. But he had to ask. Maybe the Turk would give him a straight answer. He was on his third glass of the Brugerolle and his eyes were getting glassy.

"What happens in the Trials?"

Destan gazed at him earnestly. "Are you thinking of entering?"

"No." Balthazar smiled. "Just curious about what I'm missing."

"Well, I've seen three now. It's different each time, though the basic idea is the same." He paused to roll a cigarette from a pouch of tobacco at his belt. "The fresh meat is sent into the arena." He made a *poof* gesture with his fingers that nearly toppled the bottle. Balthazar's hand shot out and steadied it. "Sorry, where was I? Ah, yes. Monsters appear out of thin air. The heroes get slaughtered."

Destan struck a match on the sole of his boot and exhaled a stream of clove-laced smoke. "A few always make it to the second round. The ranks are winnowed further. By the time the dust clears from the third, there's nothing left but carrion for the vultures." He gave Balthazar a loopy grin. "So I wouldn't recommend it, my friend."

Balthazar studied his face. A few fine lines creased the corners of his eyes, but he looked no more than thirty.

"Who was your general at Ridaniya?" he asked softly.

"Selim, of course. Do you doubt me?" Destan's gaze hardened. "I was there when we entered the gates of Cairo and routed those Egyptian dogs up the Nile. My company slew the Circassians in their citadel and brought the rest into the fold with fire and steel." He tossed back the last of his cognac. "Those were the days, eh?"

Balthazar frowned. Perhaps Taj had spoken the truth. No one aged within these walls.

And what man wouldn't want to live forever?

"Are you happy?" Balthazar heard himself ask. "Here, in this place?"

"Happy?" Destan looked at him with hollow eyes. "Sure. I eat whatever I want. Drink whatever I want. Fuck whoever I want." He smiled bleakly. "Within reason. I do have a debt to pay off. What's not to be happy about?"

Balthazar glanced around. "Sorry, but it seems a bit like purgatory."

Destan rose unsteadily to his feet. "You get used to it. Look, I'd better be going. That stuff is stronger than I'm used to. I have clients tomorrow. This is our busy season." He waved a hand. "Taj will kill me if I look like shit in the morning."

Balthazar nodded and watched him stagger to the door.

If the magic was truly fading, he might only have to serve a hundred years in this gilded cage before he could leave.

Only a hundred years.

He stared into his empty glass.

If he refused Taj's offer, Balthazar knew he'd be an outcast. Surviving on the fringes, snatching at crumbs. Damn John Mortlake for tangling him up in this mess! And double damn his treacherous daughter.

He looked up as one of the dancers approached. Almond eyes regarded him from above the wispy veil.

"You look lonely," she said in a honeyed tone. "Care for some company?"

Balthazar gazed into her dead, empty eyes.

"I have the pox," he said. "A really virulent strain."

She shrugged. "My master will purge it when you're done." She held out a hand.

He sighed and shook his head. "Perhaps another time."

She drifted away without a backward glance, heading in the direction of a loud group of men with swords and cross-bows. Balthazar was surprised to see they were the last ones drinking. The other patrons had all left. He took out his pocket watch, half expecting it to have stopped, but the second hand still ticked its inexorable circle around the face.

It wasn't yet eight o'clock.

"Not much of a party town," he muttered.

Balthazar eyed the bottle. He wanted more than anything to get rip-roaring drunk, but had a sinking feeling no quantity of liquor would do the trick tonight. Better to return to the Golden Flail and talk to Lucas.

Of course, Taj would charge him for the whole bottle.

Balthazar scowled. By God, he'd finish it — just on princi-ple. Back in his room. Which he'd better find before he forgot the way.

He brushed cat hair from his coat and headed to the door. Lucas would probably combust if he ever brought him here. Cats sent him into fits of sneezing.

"Your friend left you, eh?" the marid called.

Balthazar hefted the bottle with a smile. "Too rich for his blood, I'm afraid."

"Well, be careful." He winked. "It's a little rough after sunset."

Balthazar gave an uncertain nod and stepped outside. Cool night air caressed his face, a welcome respite after the stuffy, smoky chamber. The bouncer was gone. Lights shone down from the highest stories of the adjacent buildings, but all the windows and doors at street level were shut tight.

He turned right, looking for the stairs leading down to the lower city, and nearly tripped over a shattered paving stone. Was he drunker than he imagined?

No, he decided. Not by half. Balthazar uncorked the bottle to take a swig and paused. The whole street was riven with cracks like some ancient ruin. Squinting in the darkness, he examined the buildings to either side. When he passed them with Destan earlier, the walls had been smooth and perfect. Now they were crumbling and off-kilter, ready to collapse at the slightest touch.

His hackles rose. The thin howl of a dog pierced the night.

Balthazar found the top of the staircase and picked his way down, leaping over black gaps in the stone. When he reached the bottom, he recognized a stately mansion with Corinthian columns that marked the next turning. At least the basic layout remained the same. But the farther he went, the more he noticed the differences.

Manicured gardens had erupted into jungles, with creeping vines spilling over the boundaries in a thick carpet that tangled the feet. Everywhere he saw ruin and decay. A crescent moon rode in the sky, and bathed in its pale radiance Al Miraj seemed a most sinister place, as far removed from the bustling city of daylight as a ghoul was from a living person.

"He knew," Bathazar muttered, cold sober now. "And he never warned me."

Nothing else moved in the streets – not openly. But he sensed shadowy presences. Jinn had little need to *slink*. They would simply materialize. Men, perhaps. Or daēvas, though he suspected the lords of the city would be safe behind their walls.

Balthazar found himself grateful for the ridiculous slippers. At least they were quiet.

Unlike the group that was following him.

Every so often, he heard the echo of a footfall. He didn't look back. Let them think he was oblivious.

The furtive noises grew closer. Balthazar ducked into a rubble-strewn alley. He heard them approach, whispering to each other. He looked at the bottle with regret. Then he smashed it against the wall. The loud shatter of glass was followed by perfect silence. He backed a dozen paces down the alley.

A few seconds later, six shadows appeared. They passed through a strip of moonlight. He saw missing hands and noses. The glint of knives.

"Go home," he said.

The group paused to spread out. Their clothes were ragged, though the blades looked sharp enough.

"Come for the Trials?" taunted a man with long, matted hair. He wore a leather vest and loose trousers tucked into short boots. One toe stuck out of a hole. Balthazar almost pitied him. "You can practice with us, if you like."

Balthazar held a palm up. "Look, I've already been robbed of all my valuables. So I'm afraid you're out of luck."

"What about the watch?" He eyed the gold chain dangling from Balthazar's waistcoat.

"That old thing? Family heirloom. Sentimental value but next to worthless."

"Hand it over."

Balthazar surveyed them. "Don't make me kill all of you. It's been a long day." He smiled. "I'm just not in the mood."

"There are six of us and one of you," pointed out a fellow with a hideous scar twisting the center of his face.

"My point exactly," Balthazar said wearily. "Last chance. Go find someone else to rob or die choking on your own blood."

The men snickered.

"Go fuck yourself," someone called out.

Balthazar shrugged. Then he threw himself into the fray. The broken bottle slashed a jugular vein. A moment later, he gripped the dead man's dagger. Rage and frustration erupted in a whirlwind of death. Necks snapped, steel flashed, screams were cut short. The last one tried to run and fell with a knife in his back.

Balthazar braced a bloody hand on the wall, pulse pounding. He only wished there were more to kill. And that he hadn't broken the bottle. He wanted to drink, and then to return to the bar and find that veiled woman—

Slow applause echoed through the alley. Taj stepped from the shadows. His long golden braid hung over one shoulder.

"Nicely done," he said.

Balthazar's eyes narrowed. He adjusted his grip on the knife.

"It was obvious you underrated your skill earlier." Taj halted a dozen paces away. "I was curious by how much. I like to know who I'm dealing with." His cool gaze swept the bodies sprawled across the alley. "You're not half bad."

The sight of the daēva filled him with bloodlust all over again. He ached to lunge at him. To plunge the dagger into his heart—

"Master yourself, Balthazar," Taj said calmly.

Suddenly, he was wrapped in bonds of Air, unable to twitch a finger.

"Or perhaps you'd prefer I left you this way for whatever happens along?" Taj's eyes were wintry. "Things walk the night here. They would enjoy playing with you."

Balthazar stared at him, breathing deeply through his nose. The unholy rage ebbed. Taj watched for a minute, then released him. For an instant, Balthazar saw the strain on his face. A tightness around the eyes.

He's not immune to the magic, but he's learned to control himself — for brief periods at least.

"So you sacrificed those men for a test?" Balthazar demanded.

Taj snapped his fingers and the corpses vanished in puffs of smoke. So did the knife. Balthazar flexed empty fingers in disbelief, then let his hand fall with an irritated laugh.

"They were minor jinn. You didn't actually kill anyone. Disappointed?"

Balthazar loosened his bloodstained tie. "A tad."

"Have you reached a decision?" The daēva gazed at him expectantly, but from the smug look in his eyes, he already knew what the answer would be.

Balthazar felt a wave of loathing. Truth be told, he'd been on the fence. But in that instant, he knew he could never, ever work for this creature. He'd rather die.

"Yes. I'll enter the Trials."

Taj smiled. "Look, I've seen men of equal skill walk into the arena. They never walked out again."

Balthazar said nothing.

"It's always the same. Don't take it personally, but after nine centuries, my expectations are low." His smirk widened. "And I hate to throw you away, Balthazar. You'd be a goldmine."

"I'll take that as a compliment," he replied grimly. "But I still prefer vertical employment."

Taj leaned one shoulder against the wall. "Then it seems we're at an impasse."

"So what was the point of your little test?"

"We'll call it a rite of passage. Perhaps you could be of use to me in other ways." His voice lowered sympathetically. "I'm telling you this for your own good. Don't be stupid."

"If I get the sword, you give me back the talisman," Balthazar said. "Where is it?"

Taj unlaced his shirt. The ouroboros hung on a chain around his neck. It gathered the light, gleaming against the smooth plane of his chest. Balthazar stared at it hungrily. It took all his will not to make a grab for it.

"Tell you what," Taj said lazily. "Best one of my marids and I'll consider it."

Taj laced up his shirt, his eyes never leaving Balthazar's. Something loped past the mouth of the alley behind him. It moved too fast to make out, but Balthazar had a powerful sensation that they were being watched. And not by minor jinn.

"Tell *you* what." Balthazar smiled. "I'll best all three."

CHAPTER 10

A woman studies herself in a dull mirror. She has an aquiline nose and shrewd eyes, framed by finely arched brows. Her flowing gown is secured by a jeweled clasp at one pale shoulder. She slowly unbraids her blonde hair. Then she picks up a silver comb and runs it through the tresses, smiling as the color turns to a rich, gleaming copper. . .

Zarifa set the comb down. The connection broke.

"It alters one's hair color," she said to the Seneschal, who sat across the table with her quill raised expectantly. "Roman era. The origin is likely older, but that's the last time it was used."

The Seneschal nodded and made a notation in her enormous ledger.

Zarifa eyed the comb. It would be a useful item. But the Seneschal had watched her like a hawk for the last four hours. She suppressed a sigh as the woman returned it to a glass cabinet and locked the doors.

"Try this one," the Seneschal said, setting a single pearl earring on the table.

Zarifa had already catalogued dozens of items, ranging from harmless talismans like the comb to a cursed chalice that caused vivid nightmares and a lute that would strike deaf anyone who heard its music. She only saw visions of what they did, but her stomach still tightened every time she touched one. Both the chalice and the lute had been beautifully made, with no outward hint of their true purpose.

"Do you think we might take a break?" Zarifa asked, raising a hand to her forehead. "I get headaches if I use my gift for too long."

In fact, she felt perfectly fine. But she didn't want to catalogue the talismans too quickly. Then she'd be out of a job.

And the alternative was much worse.

She suppressed a grin as she looked around the vast storeroom. If she paced herself, there was little danger of that happening. Despite working for hours, she'd barely made a dent.

Taj's collection was stunning in both sheer size and diversity of objects. Dust cloths covered the larger items – standing mirrors, statues, even an entire marble fountain with a wingèd fish in the middle. He'd arranged it all by type, but Zarifa knew from experience that the form of a talisman didn't necessarily signal its use. Often, the more innocuous or mundane the object seemed, the viler its true purpose. A sinister-looking dagger might bring its owner good health, while a pretty bauble could kill everything in a five-league radius.

She gazed at the dizzying array of weapons in brackets on the far wall. Others held glass cases devoted to household objects, jewelry, and musical instruments. There were chests of clothing and crates of linen-wrapped pottery. The only thing they seemed to have in common was age. All were of ancient vintage.

Zarifa wanted to ask where it had all come from, but the Seneschal's cool manner discouraged questions.

Now the older woman frowned slightly, but laid her pen aside. "You must be hungry. I'll have some supper brought in." She clapped her hands and a marid appeared. As they spoke quietly together, Zarifa stood and rubbed her aching back. Her fingers itched to pocket something, but it was force of habit. Robbing Taj would be a spectacularly bad idea.

Even worse than robbing Balthazar.

Ah, well. She'd gambled and lost. Maybe it ran in her blood.

She still desired her freedom, but part of her – a large part – was wildly in love. Not with the beautiful, treacherous Taj, but with his city. Its graceful bridges, so delicate they seemed to be spun from spider-silk. Its profusion of flowers and fruit trees, each as perfect as a painted still life. The quality of the light when it struck the rose-colored sandstone. The triumphant spires and soaring minarets of pale marble.

But most of all, she was fascinated by the inhabitants.

Her father had never told her Taj was a daēva (most likely at Taj's own insistence), though he'd spoken of their race with fear and awe. They could work the elements – all but fire – and were faster and stronger than humans. But unlike the necromancers, whose power was stolen from others, these gifts were the daēvas' birthright.

Zarifa found them fascinating. So like mortals in appearance and yet so different. So much *more*. The accounts differed, but most agreed that they were neither good nor evil. Merely a unique race thought to be extinct – or nearly so.

Then there were the jinn. Mortlake would banish her to the small bedroom over the shop when the marids came to leave a new shipment of talismans and collect the money from the last one. These visits were invariably brief and uneventful. Until his final catastrophic trip to London, he had been careful in his dealings with Taj.

Mortlake despised them, but Zarifa thought the jinn were marvelous.

She would often sneak down the stairs and peek through the rear curtain at the black-clad figures. She knew her father was a villain and that as his accomplice, she could hardly claim to be much better. But in those moments, the drab, mundane world suddenly seemed full of excitement and danger. Full of magical possibility.

Zarifa had led a hard life with a hard man. But one thing she told Balthazar was true.

She adored a good story.

Tristan and Isolde. Shiva Lingam at Amarnath Cave. The Time Keeper. A Thousand and One Nights. Moon-brow and Auntie Cockroach. The Legend of the White Snake. Father Grumbler. The Kites and the Crows. A hundred others, all of which she could recite by heart.

She was living in one of those stories now, and the timing of their arrival smacked of destiny. The Trials only occurred once a century, but she would be in Al Miraj to see them. Someday, she would tell her children that she had caught a glimpse of the frightful demon Fulad-zereh—

"Your supper is here," the Seneschal called.

Zarifa ate the vegetable stew in silence while the Seneschal scratched away in her ledger. She was starting to feel better about the situation. If there was one thing she was adept at, it was playing a role. With Mortlake, she had been the dutiful daughter. With Taj, she would be the hard, honest worker. She would bide her time until an opportunity presented itself.

And she had not given up on Balthazar. He'd deliberately allowed the marid to best him, but she suspected that in the end he would be too arrogant to accept Taj's terms – which were patently outrageous. Five hundred years in servitude?

Zarifa felt certain he would crumble.

And if he did contest in the Trials . . . perhaps the impossible would happen. Then she'd be free to go wherever she wished. *Be* whoever she wished. It was a heady thought. Zarifa intended to put her talent to use on her own terms. No Mortlake. No Taj. No bloody *men* telling her what to do.

She worked for another hour, then pretended exhaustion. The Seneschal didn't protest.

"Come, child. I'll escort you back to the Golden Flail."

Zarifa started for the doors on the ground floor, but the Seneschal laid a hand on her arm. "Not that way. The streets are unsafe after dark."

They ascended a staircase and stepped outside to one of the bridges. Velvety darkness, heavy with the scent of flowers. A slender curl of moon hung in the sky. Shadows cloaked the city below, though it seemed that shapes moved low to the ground, at the edge of vision. Some appeared to be on two legs, others on four. Zarifa inhaled deeply. She felt . . . peculiar.

The sudden image of Balthazar, sprawled across the bed of the Queen Victoria suite, entered her mind. His shirt parted to reveal smooth skin. Eyes half-open, languid and glazed with lust . . . .

She shook her head, confused and irritated. With effort, she replaced the image with his vicious attack on Mortlake. The blood everywhere. More than she thought a human body could hold. She'd hated her father. Had always known he would die violently someday. But to witness it herself . . . .

I should have slit Balthazar's throat when I had the chance, she thought savagely. I should have—

The Seneschal's cool hand on her arm startled Zarifa from her fantasy of revenge.

"Quickly now, child. We must reach the walls of the Golden Flail." Was that pity in her eyes? "You'll feel better then, I promise."

Zarifa yanked her arm away, but followed the woman as she hurried through the maze of bridges that led down to the lower city. She almost felt drunk, but her mind was clear. Her body tense with the desire to . . . what? Nameless, primitive urges warred inside her. She stumbled and nearly fell, the Seneschal steadying her before she could tumble headlong from the bridge.

"It's worst at the time of change," the Seneschal muttered.

"The first hour or two after sunset. We shouldn't have worked so late. I've grown used to it, but you . . . ." She cast a wary glance at Zarifa.

"What's happening?" she gasped.

"The curse. Just hurry!"

A scream rent the night from somewhere in the city. It wavered for a long moment and cut off. A howl followed, thick with bloodlust. Zarifa's heart pounded. The instinct to run was nearly overpowering, but she knew it would be fatal to abandon her guide.

Fine cracks webbed the next bridge. The balustrades to either side were pocked with jagged gaps. Before her eyes, vines slithered forth, prying into the crevices. Zarifa hesitated, but the Seneschal dragged her across. A flight of steps loomed ahead, and then they were inside the garden walls and passing through one of the rear doors. The moment they entered the inner courtyard, it all just . . . stopped. Zarifa braced a hand on the wall. She was covered in sweat. Shaking.

A group of Taj's whores – male and female – passed by with amused expressions. She dimly heard their laughter.

The Seneschal led her to a small bedchamber on the second floor. Zarifa sank into a chair, her heart slowing.

"Now you understand," the Seneschal said curtly.

"Yes," Zarifa managed.

She wondered what had happened to the others. If they'd made the same discovery.

Lucas Devereaux was an unknown. But how would it affect a man like Balthazar, with his dark appetites? His veneer of civilization was already thin as glass.

"You will be safe here," the Seneschal said, as if reading her thoughts. "The demon allows us to ward the buildings."

And if she didn't . . . you'd all be dead, Zarifa thought.

She shuddered and crawled into bed.

"Are you sure about this, my lord?"

Lucas had not been pleased to learn what Balthazar intended. In fact, he'd been furious. They were still arguing at the appointed hour early the next morning as they awaited Taj and his marids in one of the secluded courtyards of the Golden Flail.

"No," Balthazar admitted. "But if you'd seen the smug look on his face. . . . Someone needs to teach Taj a lesson in humility."

"I'm not sure you're the one to be giving such lessons," Lucas pointed out. "And I don't mean this gauntlet you've thrown down. I'm talking about the Trials."

Balthazar sighed. "We've been over this. At tedious length. I'm not changing my mind."

Lucas stared at him. "It doesn't trouble you that everyone who enters ends up dead? For the last *nine hundred years*?"

"Oh, it troubles me. But I see no other way out of this mess."

Lucas lowered his voice. "We could kill Taj. With adequate planning—"

"I'm sure no one's ever tried *that* before," Balthazar interrupted. "Yet here he is, alive and well. That should tell you something. I'd rather face a hundred of Fulad-zereh's creations than a single daēva."

"But—"

"Listen to me, Lucas." His voice grew hard. "Back in the day, their race was enslaved by men. I'm willing to bet this particular daēva used to be an Immortal. They were hellions in the field. You have no *idea*." He shook his head. "And that's when they had a human bonded controlling their power. Unleashed they're a thousand times worse. No, I'll take my chances."

"Then I'll enter the Trials as well. Better odds if we fight together."

"Absolutely not."

Lucas stared at him defiantly. "And how will you stop me?"

"I'll tell Taj to lock you up. I'm sure they have a dungeon around here somewhere." Lucas scowled and Balthazar dropped the sardonic tone. "Have faith in me," he said softly.

"Of course I do. It's just . . . this is a demon we're talking about. Even if you manage to win, do you actually believe she'll let you have the sword?"

"Don't worry, I've dealt with her kind before."

"No, you haven't. You're just blustering—"

"Look, you can't die, too. I'll need someone to write my biography." He gazed at Lucas solemnly. "Make it really smutty. Don't spare any of the sordid details."

Lucas turned as Taj appeared in the archway opposite with his three marids. "You've gone insane," he hissed. "I hope they whip you six ways to Sunday."

But Balthazar was already striding to meet them.

"How did you sleep?" Taj asked politely.

"Quite well, thank you." He eyed the marids. "Shall we begin?"

"By all means," Taj agreed. "Your choice of weapons."

"Katana," he replied without hesitation.

Taj nodded and stepped back. "To first blood, as before."

Balthazar and the marids moved to the center of the courtyard. They wore the shemaghs, but Balthazar knew them now. Yatha the Harmonious appeared serene, as always. Jabaar the Cruel glared. Qadir the Scented reeked of poppies.

All different, yet the same.

Everything had a weakness.

And Balthazar was a quick study.

The katanas materialized in the marids' hands, and a moment later, in his. He tested the balance, dubious that a jinn blade would be true to the original. But it seemed a perfect replica of the ones he and Lucas sparred with, forged by the old masters of Edo.

Light swords with a slight curve, single-edged. The steel

folded thousands of times to achieve an unrivaled degree of sharpness. And the point of balance lay farther up the blade than a European sword, making them ideal for quick slashes – and advantageous for a tall man with a long reach.

"Good morning! I hope I'm not interrupting?"

He turned with a frown to find Zarifa standing in the archway. She wore an innocent expression, but Balthazar felt sure she hadn't simply been passing by.

"As a matter of fact, you are," he said, just as Taj waved her over to his side.

Zarifa gave Balthazar a bland smile. "I heard a rumor there was an exhibition match in the courtyard. I thought I might watch."

"Isn't she supposed to be working?" he asked Taj.

The daēva shrugged. "The lady does have an interest in the outcome. I'll allow it, unless you have a strenuous objection."

"If my presence makes you nervous, I'm happy to leave," Zarifa said in a soothing tone. "I know how difficult it can be to perform in front of an audience—"

"Not in the least." He smiled. "Forgive me, I forgot your lineage. Of course you must enjoy blood sport."

That brought a slight flush to her cheeks.

The marids formed a semicircle. An intricate mosaic of diamond tiles covered the courtyard. Lacking proper shoes, Balthazar had opted to fight barefoot. The ankle that had worn the chain was still raw and weeping, so he'd bound it up with a length of cloth. He couldn't afford to start slipping around in his own blood.

"Begin," Taj said, his expression unreadable.

Balthazar immediately took the offensive, sweeping his blade around and forcing Yatha to parry. The katanas met with a soft *tink*. Balthazar twisted his grip and flung Yatha back a step.

A wave of bitter cold enveloped him. Jabaar, coming in

126

from the left. He spun, using momentum to deliver a vicious cross-cut. It forced Jabaar into an awkward parry that left him off-balance. Balthazar kicked his feet out, sending him sprawling, and flicked away Qadir's stabbing lunge.

A flurry of exchanges followed, but none drew blood. The marids' frustration grew palpable as he parried every blow. Offered not a single opening. Balthazar gave a contemptuous laugh, though he was pushed to his edge. The marids were fast, but not like daēvas, thank the gods. No, their advantage was different and he'd force them to use it.

Just wait . . . .

Jabaar vanished. Balthazar kept the other two at arm's length, panting hard. He gripped the katana in both hands as they slowly drove him back toward the archway. The music of the light, thin blades joining, a sound like wind chimes, echoed through the courtyard. He barely avoided a lethal thrust from Yatha, pivoting away to block Qadir's slash at his face.

Too close, that one, he thought shakily. A whisker away from losing an eye.

Then it came. A sudden blast of cold just behind.

He ducked an overhead cut from Yatha, spun, and drove the katana chest-height into thin air – the instant before Jabaar materialized around the blade. Blue eyes flew wide. Balthazar yanked it free and sliced Yatha's hand on the backswing. He heard Jabaar cursing, but kept his eyes on Qadir. Blue ice coated the katana where jinn blood froze to the steel.

One left.

With a wordless roar, Balthazar engaged the last marid, pouring every ounce of speed and skill into battering through Qadir's defenses. Blows rained down, relentless, lightning-fast. A flickering slash with the very tip . . . . And Qadir sank down, clutching his side, a look of pure astonishment in his eyes.

Taj leapt to his feet. His perfect face twisted into a mask of rage. "You're not human," he snarled. "What are you? A necromancer?"

"Just . . . a man," Balthazar gasped.

The blade vanished. He braced hands on knees, adrenaline still flooding his veins.

"I've never seen a *man* fight like that." Taj's took a step forward. "Tell me what you are or I'll stop your heart myself. Right now!"

Balthazar raised his palms and drew a deep breath. "Easy. I *was* an Antimagus, but I gave up the chains a long time ago."

Taj's eyes narrowed and he realized his mistake.

"*Antimagus*. Not a word one hears often these days." Taj's features went as still and focused as a stalking cheetah. "Exactly how old are you?" he asked softly.

"How old are you?" Balthazar countered.

Taj's gaze never left his face. "Still before *your* time."

"Maybe not."

They stared at each other in silence for a minute. Lucas shifted uneasily. The three marids watched with identically crossed arms, waiting for their master's next command. As Balthazar had guessed when he pulled the trick with Jabaar, the forms they wore were not truly corporeal. They'd bled, but the wounds had already healed.

"Let me guess," he said. "You were one of the Three Hundred Immortals."

Taj's expression didn't change, but his left hand curled into a fist. It was the hand that would have worn the gold cuff.

"And you were freed by Alexander the Great when he broke Artaxeros the Second's army at Persepolae," Balthazar continued. "It was quite a bloodbath when all those daēvas were released from their bonds, wasn't it?"

"You were there?" Taj demanded hoarsely.

"No." Balthazar looked away. "I was in the Dominion on other business at the time."

"Ah, the Dominion." Taj nodded to himself. "Was this business, by *any* chance, at the House-Behind-the-Veil?"

Balthazar nodded. There was no point in denying it.

Taj's pale eyebrows rose. "I see."

Zarifa looked at him in open amazement. "Are you speaking of Neblis? The Bactrian queen whose undead armies nearly overran Persia?"

"The same," Balthazar conceded.

Zarifa crossed herself. "By the Saints," she whispered. "That makes you—"

"Very old." He scowled. "When she died, I walked away from that life and never looked back."

"Of course," Zarifa replied evenly. "You no longer drain people with the chains. Instead you trick them into bed—"

Balthazar chuckled. "My lovers make the choice freely. And I never touch the same woman twice." His dark eyes flicked over her. "In your case I wish it had never been *once*."

"How selfless of you," she muttered.

"And is your own conscience unsullied?" The acid in his voice made her go pale. "Since we're all confessing our sins, be honest. You weren't merely Mortlake's offspring. You were his collaborator—"

"Enough," Taj growled. "You claim to have survived using the magic of the ouroboros, Balthazar, but your skills are razor sharp. Which means you've been killing *somebody*."

"Only necromancers," Balthazar said quickly. "That I swear to you. Hunting them is my way of making amends."

"Amends," Taj repeated flatly. "Or is it, perhaps, for sport?"

Balthazar shrugged. "I suppose I could collect ferns or play cricket in my spare time, but somehow they don't hold the same appeal."

Zarifa rolled her eyes.

"Well, there are worse things than hunting Antimagi," Taj conceded. "I wish you hadn't chosen one who happened to be useful to me, but that bridge is already ashes." He examined Balthazar like a biologist with a strange new species. "So you *are* a man, but something more." Taj rubbed his jaw. "That might be exactly what we need. Only mortals can enter the Trials, but you'd pass inspection."

Balthazar felt a surge of triumph. "Then we have a deal? The sword for the talisman?"

"Yes. With one small proviso."

He sighed. "What is it?"

"You must play the underdog. I don't want anyone realizing what you can do. Not until the second or third round."

"Greedy to the end, eh?"

"I haven't lied to you, Balthazar, not once, and I won't start now. So here's the unvarnished truth. I doubt you'll get the sword. All I ask is that you make it to the end." Taj spread his hands. "At least I'll turn a profit before you die."

"That's heartwarming. I'll do my best to increase your already obscene fortune."

"Thank you." Taj whispered something to Yatha. An instant later, the marid held a silver tray with cups of wine. Taj drank deeply and gestured at Yatha to serve the others. "The favorite this year is a brute named Akmal the Elephant. Try to keep him alive for a while, will you? It'll be boring otherwise."

Balthazar lifted a cup from the tray and sniffed it. "This deal is growing more tiresome by the minute. Let's be perfectly clear. I couldn't care less about *entertaining* you. All I care about is staying alive. Good luck and godspeed to the rest of them." He drained the cup. "And woe to anyone who comes within arm's reach."

"Fair enough," Taj said grudgingly. "I want you to succeed, of course."

"Do you?" Lucas wondered. He looked grim.

"Of course I do." The answer was smooth and offhand. "If there's anything you need, name it."

"Tell me about the arena."

"It's in the Empty Quarter of the desert, just beyond the

walls. The first Trial commences at sunrise tomorrow. You'll have the rest of the day to prepare."

Balthazar considered this. "How would you prepare?"

Taj laughed. "I'd make a will and bed whoever would have me." He glanced at Zarifa. "Pardon the crudity, Miss Everleigh." Again, the tone was contrite, but his face was a mask of indifference. Cold and calculating.

She waved a hand.

"How long will the Trial last?"

"It depends on what she sends and how fast you kill it," Taj replied. "But the first round is the easiest. Fulad-zereh likes to save a few contenders for the next." A thin smile. "Can't have everyone dead right away."

"Do I choose my own weapons?"

The daēva nodded.

"Real ones?"

"For the Trials, yes. Fulad-zereh's magic is too strong. It would overwhelm any working by my jinn. Besides which, she only permits weapons forged by mortals. No talismans, understood?"

"Understood."

Taj strode for the archway, then turned back. "Oh, and Balthazar?"

He looked up. "What?"

Taj eyed him with distaste. "You really need a new suit."

CHAPTER 11

Zarifa found Balthazar at the armory later that afternoon. A pair of jinn guarded the entrance, but they seemed to know who she was and allowed her to pass.

She'd worked in the Treasury for hours. The Seneschal was a hard taskmistress, but she finally relented when Zarifa burst into tears and claimed another throbbing headache. In truth, she wanted to check on her investment. Balthazar's duel with the three marids had earned her reluctant admiration, even if the man himself was vile. He moved with a fluid, lethal grace that was exhilarating to watch.

If she'd known what he was, how *old* he was, she would never have been so cavalier about crossing him. Mortlake had warned her. She should have listened.

But now they were allies of a sort – against Taj. She had to make him see that.

Shafts of sunlight spilled through narrow slits in the walls, casting vertical stripes across the stone floor. Balthazar stood in one of these golden squares, his back to her. He was examining something in his hands, dark head bent in concentration.

"What do you want?" he muttered without turning around.

"Only to wish you luck tomorrow," she said quietly.

"Really?" He half turned and she saw he held a crossbow. Balthazar returned it to the bracket. He faced her, leaning against the wall with his hands in his pockets. "I think you came to get a last eyeful. It's a shame. You'll never know what you missed."

Zarifa frowned. "I'm sorry, are you referring to a premature death?"

"I might have shaved off a month or so, but only at the very end." Balthazar gave her that infuriating smile. "I would have made it worth your while."

"You're a revolting parasite."

"And you're a mercenary hag."

She smiled back. "Now that we've disposed of the pleasantries, I want to know what your strategy is."

"My strategy?"

"For tomorrow. I have a strong interest in keeping you alive."

He strolled over to a brace of axes and ran a finger along the edge of a half-moon blade. "Well, let's see. If something tries to kill *me*, I'll kill *it*."

"Very sophisticated."

"If you have a better idea, now's the time to share it. Don't hold back." Balthazar hefted the axe in one hand and winced. "Christ, these things are heavy."

"Has Taj given you no more advice on what to expect?"

"Oh, I asked around. No one *knows* what to expect." Balthazar replaced the axe. "That's the genius of it. The last one was snakes the size of oak trees that shot venom. Before that, flesh-eating locusts. Um, something else with flaming eyes, I think. Captain Karatas was a little vague." He quickly surveyed a row of daggers, chose one and threw it in a sack. "So I'll be playing it by ear."

Zarifa strode up him. "Please say you don't intend to use the dagger for your off-hand," she said briskly. "That would be suicide."

He glanced at her, clearly amused. "What would you choose?"

"A greatsword," she replied without hesitation. "The katana made sense for the marids. It's fast and nimble and you had only to draw first blood. But lacking any foreknowledge of what you'll face, or how many there will be, you'll want to keep it simple. Lethality above convenience."

Balthazar gave a grudging nod. "Yes, that's what I thought, too."

"Something with reach and force." Zarifa walked over to the array of swords hanging from brackets at the far end. "If you were on horseback, it would have to be a one-handed blade. But for combat on the ground?" She turned to him. "I'd recommend heavy, long and utterly devastating."

Balthazar cleared his throat. "I can't argue with that," he murmured.

Zarifa laughed and reached past his shoulder. "This montante, for example." She touched a sword with a cruciform hilt and large quillions. "The perfect weapon for a lone man fighting multiple assailants."

Balthazar eased it from the bracket with both hands. The wide blade was nearly six feet from hilt to tip.

"No wonder these went out of fashion by the 1700s," he remarked. "It's monstrous."

"And effective." She waved a hand at the longswords. "They're all essentially the same. Choose a zweihander if you prefer."

He seemed about to reach for one of the German blades, then let his hand fall. "The montante has a certain flair. I think the old Iberian masters would approve."

He met her eye, the silence growing awkward as both

simultaneously realized this was their first civil exchange since the steamer. Balthazar cleared his throat, glancing at the door.

"Well," Zarifa said crisply. "I'm glad we got that sorted. Will you practice with it?"

"Practice?" He looked at her with a hint of scorn. "No, I'm familiar with greatswords." He frowned at the blade. "And I'd prefer to be able to lift my arms tomorrow. Do they expect me to walk back to the Golden Flail with this thing?"

"Certainly not, Noble Warrior," Qadir said, manifesting in a cloud of frankincense. "It shall be transported for you." He winked. "Better to be discreet. Most combatants keep their choice of weapon secret until the given day."

Balthazar nodded. He offered up the blade with a polite bow. Then he spun on his heel and left without another word.

Zarifa watched him go with a thoughtful expression.

"I didn't expect him to heed my counsel," she said softly. "He is a puzzling man."

The marid examined the blade. "This one belonged to the great fencing master Domingo Luis Godinho. It demands control and experience." Qadir's voice was dry. "I predict he will do well with it."

"What do *you* think of the Trials?" she asked, curious.

"We think what our master commands us to think."

Zarifa laughed. "You are intelligent beings. I am not asking to betray any allegiances. I suppose I just wonder if the outcome means anything to you. Are the jinn affected by the curse in the same way as mortals and daēvas?"

"Happily, no," he replied. "It would be chaos otherwise."

"Yes, I can only imagine."

"My master wants the sword. If I could give it to him I would, but it is beyond my power. If you are asking whether I hope Balthazar succeeds, the answer is yes, since that is what my master wishes."

Qadir gazed at her blandly, but she sensed hidden

currents. How could such a powerful creature be content only to serve?

Zarifa inhaled deeply and smiled at the marid. "Your company is most refreshing, O Great Jinn, but I can find my own way back to the Golden Flail."

Qadir seemed pleased at the compliment. "I can easily transport you—"

"I'd like the exercise."

"Then allow me to escort you to the door," he replied.

She inclined her head. "Of course."

As they passed the brackets of daggers, she stumbled over the hem of her robe, crashing into the wall.

"Are you hurt, mistress?" Qadir asked, steadying her with a frigid hand.

"I'm fine." She gave him an apologetic smile. "It's my boots. The soles are falling apart."

"I will see that you get a new pair at once."

"You're very kind." She gripped the twin daggers up her sleeve, recently liberated from their brackets. Chill air wafted from his skin, along with a heavy, cloying scent. "Is that lily of the valley? It's my favorite flower!"

The marid blinked. "Is it really?"

Zarifa much preferred earthier perfumes, but she shivered with pleasure. "Oh, yes. So sweet and delicate."

"No one ever notices," he murmured. "Thank you, mistress."

She beamed at him, quickening her pace as the daggers slowly slid through her sweat-slick hands. They left the armory and Qadir bowed.

"Enjoy your walk," he said. "Do not wander too far."

Zarifa managed a curtsy. "I shall. And . . . I won't!"

He vanished in a trail of smoke. She hurried around a corner and sagged against the wall of a garden. The daggers were quickly relocated to her boot.

As much as she enjoyed Al Miraj, it didn't seem like a wise place to go about unarmed.

Zarifa whistled a jaunty tune and set off for the Golden Flail.

———

THE ROOF OF THE BROTHEL HELD A SILKEN PAVILION THAT GAVE a view of both the city and the desert beyond the walls. Plush carpets covered the stone, but the sides were left open. Taj led Lucas to a table with stacks of paper. Lists of names, and columns for each of the three Trials. Only the first column had been filled in.

Lucas felt relieved to have a task he could grasp. Simple numbers. The logic of probabilities and odds. That the names were attached to human beings who would likely die tomorrow was not something he cared to dwell on. His only goal was to make Taj happy and avoid being pimped out like that poor Turkish captain Balthazar had gotten chummy with.

"I need to understand everything," he said briskly.

Taj inclined his head. "Of course, Mr. Devereaux."

"Let's start with the rankings. How are they determined?"

"I do that myself based on a number of factors, mainly experience and reputation. My marids have been recruiting for the last five years."

"How do you manage it without giving away the location of the city?"

"First, we only approach potential candidates in places where the story is known. Arabia, Egypt, North Africa. Not beyond. And those who agree must be guided here by jinn. Most have been in the city for some time now. We stage contests to further refine the rankings." He paused. "A few are mortals who found the city by accident and chose to enter. Under the law, any resident of Al Miraj has the right."

Lucas frowned. "So Balthazar could have demanded to enter?"

A small smile played across Taj's face. "He could have. But your master seemed so eager to prove himself, I could hardly say no."

"You wanted to see what he could do," Lucas said flatly.

"Better to know ahead of time. I meant it when I said I didn't want to sacrifice him pointlessly." He braced a hand on the table. Lucas saw the glint of a silver chain at his neck. The ouroboros? He tore his gaze away.

"Tell me the truth," Lucas said. "Please. What are his chances?"

Taj hesitated. "Better than the others. But I won't make empty promises. The Trials are brutal. Invariably."

Lucas drew a sharp breath and studied the long list of names. "It's incredible how many people are willing to commit suicide for the demon's entertainment," he muttered.

"Believe it or not, the marids turn down more candidates than they accept. It's invitation-only, but word gets out." He sounded weary. "I try to be selective. They must be physically fit and have experience with weapons. Preferably no wife or children. Most are mercenaries or tribal warriors."

"Why are some of the names crossed out?"

"They died."

"Here?"

Taj nodded. "There's always a few who ignore the curfew. Some make it back. Others don't."

Lucas studied the numbers. He wasn't a betting man himself, but Balthazar sometimes went to the races and asked his opinion on different horses. He held up the last sheet. "Who are these?"

It was a very short list, all with odds of a thousand to one — or more.

"Those are special cases," Taj said quietly, taking the sheet and returning it to the bottom of the stack. "Don't worry about them."

It went against Lucas's fastidious nature to let the matter go so easily. He frowned. "You can trust my discretion. But I can't help you when I don't understand—"

Taj's voice hardened a notch. "You don't need to understand. They'll die tomorrow, and that is their choice. Your concern is to evaluate the odds on the others and make sure I haven't made any costly errors. You'll find the cream of the crop at the top. Then the middle of the pack. As a last-minute entry, Balthazar will be placed at the bottom. For the moment, he's an unknown."

Taj pointed to another table, where jinn kept appearing to add scraps of parchment, and then disappearing just as abruptly. "Those are the bets. They're based on the latest rankings issued this afternoon. We need to review them all to determine the final rankings. Betting closes at midnight."

Lucas eyed the heaps of paper. "I'll begin straightaway." He cleared his throat. "I prefer to work in pencil. If possible, the Cumberland lead pencil by Waterlow & Sons. I'll need a dozen to start, and a decent sharpener. I would also like a rolltop desk and a chair with a swivel mechanism. Adjustable height, if it's not too much trouble."

Taj smiled. "Not at all, Mr. Devereaux. Is there anything else?"

"A cup of tea would be lovely."

"Milk and sugar?"

"Just milk, please."

Lucas watched Taj stroll over to the jinn and issue orders. The daēva moved like rippling silk. He wore a plain white tunic, his hair pulled back in a simple plait, as if he instinctively understood that anything more would be gilding the lily. Lucas sighed. In another time and place. . . . But Taj was a snake. He couldn't forget that.

Lucas began sorting through the scraps of paper, quickly

devising his own system. Balthazar would be livid if he learned that the bout this morning was merely for the daēva's personal assessment. Better not to tell him. Balthazar needed to stay focused. Avoid any unnecessary distractions—

Lucas flinched at the warm hand on his arm. "Your office is ready," Taj said with an amused smile, as though he knew exactly what Lucas had been thinking.

And there it was. A rolltop desk in polished walnut. A matching swivel chair, already set to his height. A dozen Cumberland pencils, sharpened to a fine point. And a steaming cup of tea.

"Do you require anything else?" Taj asked softly, his fingertips lingering.

"No," Lucas said quickly. "I'd best start." He glanced out at the desert. The sun was sinking over the dunes. He didn't want to be anywhere near Taj when it set and darkness came. The daēva claimed the pavilion was within the protective wards, but Lucas didn't care to test it.

"I should be done well before midnight. I'm sure you're busy. Er, you needn't stay."

"Thank you, Mr. Devereaux."

Taj retreated, but it was long minutes before the pressure of his touch faded.

Lucas reviewed every name, making small corrections as he deemed fit. Taj could approve it later.

At last, he reached the bottom of the list. The pencil froze, poised over the blank paper.

Then he wrote a single name.

Balthazar.

Lucas stared at the page. It felt like a betrayal. Like a bloody jinx. But Taj had insisted.

The pencil hovered for a long moment, then swiftly filled in the column for the first Trial.

Odds: Two hundred to one.

CHAPTER 12

The sun was swallowed by the dunes. The shadows lengthened. And within their hungry embrace, Balthazar watched Al Miraj change.

As the line of night crept across the city, stonework cracked and crumbled, sending the ubiquitous cats leaping away with low growls. Bronze statues turned green with verdigris. Marble fountains ran dry. Vines snaked through the ruins, their roots prying apart the lacy bridges. Deep silence descended, broken only by the occasional hair-raising howl.

The City of Gardens slumbered, and the City of Dogs and Thieves awoke.

From the safety of the fourth-floor terrace of the Golden Flail, Balthazar observed this transformation with reluctant awe. It was a clever curse. If she'd simply made the city a hellhole, everyone would have left by now, irritating mortals be damned. But half the time they were permitted to go about their business in paradise.

And the rest of the time? Well, no one would forget who was really in charge.

Balthazar sensed a presence behind him. He turned to find his drinking partner from the night before. The Turk wore a spotless white tunic that set off tanned skin and muscular calves. His wavy dark hair was combed, his beard neatly trimmed. There was no trace of a hangover. He looked ready to do brisk business, except for the sheepish look in his eye.

"Captain Karatas," Balthazar said dryly. "How are you faring this evening?"

Destan sighed. "I'm truly sorry. But my master's orders were clear."

"I don't blame you." Balthazar laughed. "Well, I did last night, but now I've moved on."

Destan looked relieved. "You seemed like the sort who could take care of himself. I'm glad you made it back."

"Let's hope you can say the same tomorrow," Balthazar replied. "I assume Taj sent you. What does he want?"

The Turk nodded. "The opening ceremonies are about to start."

Balthazar turned away from the ruins, leaning against the waist-high balustrade. "Really?" He looked up at the first stars, faint silver pinpricks in the darkening sky. "I thought I might just curl up for a bit and ponder the nature of existence. You know, while I still can."

Destan smiled. "It's tradition. Bad luck to refuse."

"I don't abide by superstition."

"I'm afraid the master insists."

Destan looked nervous and Balthazar took pity on him. "Very well, I'll put in an appearance. Where are we going?"

"The Hall of Heroes," Destan replied as they left the terrace through a wide archway and descended a flight of stairs. Fulad-zereh's spell did not extend inside the walls and Taj's domain was still pristine, if you fancied acres of burgundy silk and lewd tapestries.

"I hate the sound of it already."

"Then why are you doing this?" Destan asked frankly. "You seem smarter than the others."

"That's not saying much, is it? I have my reasons, Captain Karatas."

"I hope they're good ones."

"To me, they are. Chiefly, I don't care for your master. It's worth beating the odds just to see the look on his face."

Destan frowned. "So you actually believe you can take back the Shamshir-e Zomorrodnegar?"

Balthazar was silent for a long minute. "The gods punish hubris, Captain Karatas. I don't think I'll answer that question."

Destan laughed. "You claimed you weren't superstitious."

"I still don't care to tempt fate. She's capricious enough as it is."

"True," the Turk agreed. "Look at me. If my tentmate hadn't snored, I would never have woken in the night. And if I hadn't indulged in a third cup of wine, I would never have gone to take a piss. On such things do our lives hinge, my friend."

They passed into a wing Balthazar had never visited before, all chill marble and severe angles. He heard a distant hubbub of voices.

"The Hall of Heroes," his companion said, pushing open two wide bronze doors.

Long tables filled the chamber beyond, all laden with food and wine. Roughly a hundred contenders occupied the tables. Most wore the traditional robes and turbans of the local tribes, but the ranks included a contingent of Blue Men, who died their skin and clothes indigo, and a dozen tall warriors with painted faces who spoke in some Sahelian dialect. The Egyptian brothers from the caravan, Khai and Mosi, spotted Balthazar and gave friendly nods. He returned the gesture.

Taj held court on a raised dais in the middle of the hall. He wore his usual white tunic and his hair shone like beaten gold in the light of the talismanic globes suspended from the domed ceiling. He dined with two men and a woman, who were the source of appraising glances from the rest of the crowd.

A balcony circled the upper level. Daēvas looked down on the proceedings, occasionally whispering into the ears of black-clad jinn who vanished in puffs of smoke.

"They're still taking wagers," Destan said, following Balthazar's gaze. "The betting is open until midnight." He jerked his chin at the dais. "Those three are the favorites. The one on Taj's left is Akmal the Elephant."

"We passed him in the street," Balthazar said. "He was with a group of men."

Destan nodded. "Most have formed alliances. It's the traditional strategy to make it to the second round. Help each other – until it's time to kill each other."

Taj's gaze fixed on Balthazar for a brief instant. He gave no sign of recognition, returning to his conversation without missing a beat.

"The problem with alliances is that they tend to fall apart at inconvenient moments," Balthazar remarked. "Like when one's back is turned."

The Turk gave a feral grin. "Akmal's a monster, but I doubt he'll last long."

"Why?"

"Sheer size. The toe that sticks out gets the hammer."

Balthazar laughed.

"Now the thin one in the middle . . . He may not look like much, but he's a twelfth-degree blade master. I saw him spar. He moves like lightning."

"And the woman?" She wore a veil and long robes that covered her to the tips of her fingers.

"No one knows her name. They say she's an assassin. One of the guild's finest."

Balthazar took a step toward the dais and Destan laid a restraining hand on his arm. "Your seat is this way, my friend." He led Balthazar to the farthest corner of the hall. Judging by the smell, it was adjacent to the privies.

"Our master cannot appear to show you favor," Destan whispered, giving Balthazar a little push towards an empty seat. "If anyone asks, say you have a touch of the plague."

Balthazar frowned. "Wait—"

The Turk was gone.

He sighed and sank into the chair. There were three other men seated at the table. They all looked profoundly unwell.

"Welcome, brother!" the man at his left said with a smile. He sipped his wine with a trembling hand. "Don't be shy. The food is excellent. Might as well enjoy yourself, eh?" He winked.

"Are you . . .?" Balthazar cleared his throat. "Are you fighting in the arena tomorrow?"

"Of course." He raised his cup. "And may death come swiftly!" The others followed suit, toasting with grim cheer. He looked at Balthazar. "Will you not drink with us?"

"Of course. I'm just . . . So you actually *want* to die?"

The man stared at him. "Perhaps you were seated at the wrong table."

"No, no." Balthazar feigned a coughing fit and his companions relaxed. "I have a terrible case of . . . catarrh. My lungs are rotten with it."

The man nodded in sympathy. "Who knows?" he said in a kindly tone. "Maybe a miracle will occur and you'll make it through. Then your problems will be over. It is what we all hope for." He shrugged. "But we must also resign ourselves to the far more likely possibility that we will die."

He raised a scrap of cloth to his lips and spat. It came away red. When he smiled, his teeth were bloody. "None of us have much time left anyway. At least it will be quick, yes?"

Balthazar nodded. His chest felt tight. "You are brave men."

"Less so than the rest, I think. They have more to lose."

145

He passed Balthazar a platter of rosemary-spiced lamb. "But enough maudlin talk. We are here to enjoy our last night on this earth. It is for Allah to decide the rest."

The men at the other tables picked at their food and barely touched the wine. Balthazar watched in amusement as they sized each other up, trading cool stares and whispering to their allies. If the desert tribes were all represented, there would be more than one blood feud simmering beneath the surface. But his table of outcasts indulged with abandon, cracking jokes and polishing off an entire cask of rough red. Balthazar was glad he'd been banished. He much preferred the company of the dying.

On his raised dais, Taj laughed and bantered with the favorites. No doubt he had promised to heal anyone who made it through. And none of them would, Balthazar thought bitterly. A bargain the demon herself might have designed.

At last, Taj rose from his seat. The hall fell silent.

"Welcome to our fair city," he said, his voice carrying easily through the vast room. "You all know me. Most of you came at my personal invitation. Others proved themselves worthy and were offered a place in the roster. You have waited long, and patiently, as our guests. Tonight, it is my great privilege to officially inaugurate the Ninth Trials, three contests of skill and daring where the land's greatest warriors do battle with the most terrifying creatures magic can conjure!"

A few scattered cheers erupted, but most simply listened.

"The danger is great, but so are the rewards. A lifetime of ease and luxury. A king's ransom in gold. The eternal gratitude of the citizens of Al Miraj." He paused. "And the chance to become a legend. To slay the demon Fulad-zereh!"

Balthazar frowned. Slay the demon? What other *footnotes* to this contract had the daēva failed to mention? His fingers tightened to fists and Balthazar forced them open. Taj lied as naturally as drawing breath. *Let him underestimate me. He'll learn his mistake – after it's too late.*

"You are all courageous men." Taj inclined his head at the assassin. "And women. I must say, this is the most promising group ever assembled in this hall. You will all be given rooms at the Golden Flail tonight, with whatever last pleasures you desire. It is my gift." Taj winked. "Besides which, I'd hate to see you kill each other walking back to your lodgings tonight."

There was rough laughter at this.

Taj's speech continued, flattery mixed with more lies about his certainty that *this* would be the year Al Miraj finally produced a champion to take back the sword. It was no great stretch to imagine what he was really thinking.

Good luck, suckers.

Balthazar didn't wait for it to end. He bid his table companions goodnight and slipped out the back of the hall. The corridors leading to the Flail were mostly quiet, just a few bored-looking women with painted faces who made a desultory attempt to engage him in conversation. Everyone was obviously waiting for the ceremonies to conclude.

As he passed one of the interior courtyards, Balthazar saw Captain Karatas kissing someone in a dark alcove. He couldn't tell if it was a man or a woman – not that it mattered. He felt sorry for the Turk. For all of them.

He asked a servant where to find the room he sought. Unlike his own chamber, it had a proper door. Balthazar knocked. Zarifa opened it, her face growing wary when she saw him standing there.

"I'm sorry to bother you," Balthazar said. "It won't take long."

She didn't invite him inside. "What is it?"

"I just have a question. And as bizarre as it seems, you're the only one I trust to give me an honest answer."

She arched an eyebrow expectantly.

"Will Taj keep his word? Will he uphold our bargain?"

Zarifa sighed. "You know I can't answer that. I won't be responsible—"

"I'm not holding you responsible," he replied wearily. "I just want your opinion. You didn't know him, but your father did."

She gave a hesitant nod. "My impression is that he's ruthless, but not without honor. He never cheated Mortlake, not through all the years of their partnership. And his status among the other daēvas seems to be unquestioned. I don't think anyone would do business with Taj if he had a reputation for treachery."

"But the ouroboros . . . it would be tempting to just keep it—"

"He's a daēva. He doesn't need your talisman." She gave a rueful smile. "And now that I've seen his collection, I don't think a single object would mean very much to him. He already owns thousands, many of which are of equal or greater value."

"All right. Thank you." He turned to go.

"Balthazar?"

"What?"

She gave a playful grin. "I'd pray for your soul if you had one. As it is, I'll settle for this."

To his annoyed astonishment, she made the Sign of the Flame, touching fingers to forehead, lips and heart.

The old symbol of his faith.

"How dare you?" he said coldly.

Her smile faltered. "I was only joking about the soul part. I mean it sincerely—"

Balthazar strode away before she could finish. He did not look back.

THE DESERT ROSES HAD RUN RIOT, COVERING THE PATHS IN A matted tangle that looked black in the moonlight. Balthazar stood on the veranda, letting the night air cool his blood. He wished he could go for a walk, but didn't dare it – not even inside the garden walls. He could sense the subtle shift in atmosphere beyond the stone balustrade. A wild, baleful magic coursed through the city, just waiting to snare the unwary. He knew his own dark depths all too well – and didn't care to plumb them again.

The longsword waited on his bed, five and a half feet of naked steel, cruciform hilt resting on the pillow like a lover. Taj's little joke? Or was there simply nowhere else to leave the monstrous thing? Balthazar lay down next to it, one hand resting over the bare place on his chest where the ouroboros should be. He rarely thought of Neblis, but her face came to him now, the clever eyes and rosebud mouth. She'd been a harsh mistress, although she had loved him in her own demented way.

He was only sixteen when he fell under her spell, rising to become her lover and right hand. There was no crime he hadn't committed for her. But some shard of humanity had remained, buried deep inside. The Prophet Zarathustra had dug out that spark and blown new life into it. Had helped him remember who he used to be.

A magus.

The Prophet was long gone and so was Neblis. He was still here, no longer pure evil, but not precisely *good* either. Something else, balanced on a knife edge between the two. Balthazar smiled bleakly in the darkness. He'd done his best to walk that line, but the abyss to either side only grew deeper. Waiting for a single misstep to swallow him up.

Women had always been his downfall. *Always.*

Yet they'd saved him, too. All those hours spent in feather beds, pantries, garden alcoves, carriages and, on one memorable occasion, the Robing Room of the House of Lords, making his lovers as happy as he knew how. . . . It was the time he felt the most human.

And for all his cynicism, every so often he still fell hard.

Balthazar knew nothing could ever come of it. *Rake* didn't even begin to describe him. If he ceased his predations, he would die within weeks. But the alternative would be to drain the same woman over and over again – presumably one he cared for – until there was nothing left.

He never pursued the extraordinary ones, but it was oddly reassuring to know he could still feel deeply after so many centuries.

He scowled. Zarifa, though . . . What a reckless mistake.

If he died tomorrow and his life were laid out on a balance scale, would his good deeds outweigh his wicked ones? Balthazar pondered the question and finally decided it was too hard to answer. But there was a much simpler one.

Did it even matter?

He had worshipped at the fire altars of the magi before Neblis came along and bought his soul on the cheap. The promise of magic, some sensual delights, and a little power and he'd been happy to do almost anything she demanded of him. Rape was the only line he'd never crossed. Some might consider that a small accomplishment, but Balthazar thought it must be worth something.

For a long time, he'd feared the notion of Hell. If it existed, he would surely be going there. But now? He had little faith in anything except himself. And Lucas, of course.

Balthazar shuddered at how close he'd come to a brutal death in the desert. And the blood of the man he claimed to love as a son would have been squarely on Balthazar's hands. He'd been so preoccupied with getting the talisman back, he'd hardly spared Lucas a second thought.

I'm a selfish bastard. Why does he put up with me?

Another unanswerable question.

He finally drifted off. It seemed as if only minutes had passed before his eyes snapped open, some part of him attuned to the coming dawn.

"It's time, my lord."

Lucas stood on the terrace. With a yawn, Balthazar rose to join him. The sky was still dark, but a line of lighter blue softened the horizon. Birds chirped in the garden below. Lucas looked haggard, as though he hadn't slept at all. He gave Balthazar a tense smile.

"I brought you something."

He held a bundle in his arms. A new charcoal-grey suit, freshly ironed shirt, and pair of black leather shoes.

Balthazar smiled. "No cufflinks?"

Lucas held out his palm. "Right here."

They looked at each other for a long moment with that mixture of tenderness, amusement and perfect understanding that only comes from long friendship.

"Stay alive, will you?" Lucas said finally. "I don't care to be stuck here alone."

"Oh, I plan to." Balthazar felt the weave of the shirt between his fingers. "Not too shabby."

"I gave the seamstress explicit instructions. Can you believe she didn't know what a welt pocket is? Or a French cuff?" He shook his head in disbelief.

"They're savages," Balthazar agreed cheerfully. Despite his few hours of rest, he felt wide awake. Alert and ready for anything. "I'm just glad I don't have to wear a gladiator outfit. My legs aren't half as nice as yours."

Lucas colored faintly at the compliment, which seemed out of character. He was usually immune to such teasing. Balthazar chalked it up to nerves.

"Well, I'll let you get ready." Lucas paused at the curtain adjoining their rooms. "I'll be watching from the balconies."

"With Taj?"

He nodded.

"Excellent." Balthazar gave Lucas a feral grin. "Put a tack on his seat for me."

CHAPTER 13

The sky was beginning to blush a rosy pink as Balthazar joined the crowd milling in front of the city gates. The contenders wielded daggers and whips, spears and shields and maces. He saw the traditional hooked-pommel sword called the *saif anith*, forged from iron, and the *saif fulath*, forged from steel. The hopefuls were of every hue – including the indigo-dyed Blue Men – and ranged in dress from simple shawb*s* to cobbled-together bits of armor that might well date back to the Crusades.

Like the night before, attention centered on the favorites, who were first at the gates. Akmal the Elephant carried both sword and axe. Black-haired and hawk-nosed, he stood a head taller than everyone else and was practically pawing the ground in eagerness to reach the arena. The woman assassin was veiled and cloaked in a long flowing robe, only her hands and eyes visible. They met Balthazar's for an instant, cold and calculating. He inclined his head in polite acknowledgement – which was not returned.

The third favorite, a small, wiry man with a thin, pointed mustache, held only a light single-handed blade. He seemed dryly amused, a half-smile playing on his lips.

As for the rest . . . they sweated profusely, though the sun had not yet risen. The stench of stale wine and unwashed bodies was overpowering.

He nodded to the Egyptian brothers, Khai and Mosi (armed with matching scimitars), and the three men from the feast, who looked even frailer in daylight. The latter seemed to expect Balthazar to join them, but he took a position alone at the fringe, hardening himself against pity. They'd come to die. He couldn't save them. It would only dishonor their courage. And any weakness could end up costing his own life.

No friends. No allies.

No mercy.

Then Taj appeared in an archway leading from one of the guardhouses. He raised his hands for silence. Balthazar expected another flowery speech and felt a surge of impatience. But the daēva merely surveyed them all for a long moment, his face unreadable.

"Fight well or die well," he said quietly.

Jinn threw the gates wide and the contenders spilled out with a savage cheer, moving toward the Empty Quarter, a flat stretch of hard-packed sand before the dunes began. Taj's eyes briefly met Balthazar's as he passed, the greatsword braced point-up on one shoulder, and then he was through and following the pack to a large circle drawn in the sand.

Eight marids stood at cardinal points around the circle, which had a radius of about a quarter mile. The hopefuls entered the arena and spread into loose groupings, desert tribes and Blue Men; the Sahelian knights, tall and proud, in embroidered robes of crimson with hooked lances and plumed helmets; a few freelancers like himself. Balthazar turned to face the city, where daēvas packed the top of the wall and the terraces. He was close enough to hear the buzz of excitement, but couldn't make out the balcony where Lucas sat with Taj.

The men closest to the middle of the arena took hasty

steps back as a whirlwind of sand erupted. It resolved into a hulking creature with red skin and horns. Flames licked along its massive arms, which could have snapped Akmal's spine like kindling.

Ifrit. The most powerful of all the jinn. And a servant of the demon.

The contenders tensed, wondering if the Trial had already begun. But then a square frame materialized with a large bronze disk suspended by wires.

"The rules are simple," the ifrit bellowed. "When the gong sounds, the combat begins. When it sounds a second time, the round is over and you may leave the arena. If you try to leave before the second gong sounds, you will burn. None may enter the arena once the contest is underway or *they* will burn. I offer you a last chance. It will not come again. Who among you will leave?"

No one stepped forward.

The ifrit raised his arms. Taj's marids vanished from their posts. A wall of flames engulfed the perimeter of the circle just as the sun broke the rim of the eastern horizon. The ifrit raised its horned head to the sky. "All hail Fulad-zereh, Mistress of Shadows and Guardian of the Emerald-Studded Blade!"

A cloud appeared to the north, dark and ominous. It sped closer and assumed the shape of a dragon's head. Lightning flashed in its depths. Curls of steam trailed from the nostrils. The contenders murmured uneasily. When it was nearly on top of them, the jaws opened. Balthazar saw a tiny figure in shining armor perched between two of the fangs.

Sunlight reflected off her steel plate, making it impossible to see her face, though Balthazar judged her to be much smaller than the ifrit. Fulad-zereh raised a mailed hand.

"Let the first day of the Ninth Trials commence!" the ifrit roared. He struck the gong with a padded mallet. The sound reverberated against the high walls of Al Miraj, swelling in waves until it finally faded to silence. The ifrit vanished in a swirl of sand.

Necks craned to study the sky, then the ground, then each other. Something was coming, but from which direction? Would it stampede through the flames or erupt from the ground beneath their feet? Across the circle, men stepped back to give themselves room, or clumped tighter into their prearranged alliances. The audience on the walls watched in tense silence.

Blades rasped from their sheaths.

Arrows nocked to bowstrings.

Then a faint cry went up. On the eastern horizon, the sun darkened.

At first, Balthazar thought it was another cloud. When it reached a distance of perhaps five miles, the single mass separated into black specks. A minute later, it became clear that the specks were not driven by the wind but were flying under their own power. As they passed into the sunlight, he glimpsed snowy white breast feathers. Those along the neck and back were a vivid blue tapering to brown at the tips.

Their wings appeared to be beating very slowly, but this was only due to the creatures' stupendous size. Balthazar saw sharp beaks and muscular legs tipped with hooked talons, each the length of his forearm.

"Rocs!" someone yelled.

Balthazar turned to find Khai at his side, Mosi just behind. The birds opened their beaks and screamed, sharp, piercing cries he felt in his marrow.

"Join us," Khai urged, raising his scimitar. "We'll guard each other's backs."

"I fight alone," Balthazar replied evenly, though his heart raced. "But I wish you luck."

He didn't actually mean it. At the end of the Trials, there could be only one of them left standing and Balthazar meant for it to be himself.

The blade still rested over his right shoulder. He moved as far from the others as he could get, near the flaming perimeter. He counted nine Rocs against more than a hundred contenders.

Balthazar felt relieved. He'd expected much worse.

Then the Rocs swooped down on the circle, undaunted by the fire. Each plucked a human in its talons and flew off. In three seconds, Akmal the Elephant dwindled to the size of a squalling infant. Balthazar watched as the birds circled higher and higher, then opened their claws and dropped the unfortunates to the desert floor.

The survivors huddled together, quickly revising their plans. When the Rocs came again, they were met with a lethal volley of arrows, the barbed tips stained dark with poison. Balthazar allowed himself a moment of hope until the arrows bounced harmlessly off the birds and rained down on the people below. Nine more heroes took the fateful trip into the blue. Three others were struck by falling arrows and perished writhing in agony.

The nine Rocs circled above, drifting on the warm currents.

Balthazar took out his pocket watch. Seven minutes had elapsed since the gong sounded. A fifth of them were already dead.

He crouched at the edge of the flames. Like barracudas feeding on a school of fish, the Rocs focused their attacks on the largest groups where easy meat waited. So far they had overlooked him, but the ranks were thinning rapidly.

It was time to do something.

What exactly, though . . . that was the question.

Rocs were mythical creatures. Balthazar had a vague idea they were mentioned in the adventures of Sinbad the Sailor. If Lucas were here, he could probably recite the whole tale from memory. But knowing might not matter. He doubted Fulad-zereh would make it so easy.

The Rocs made a third pass, and a fourth. Balthazar waited, watching the attack pattern, knowing his turn would come.

Then a pair of yellow eyes fixed on him. Great wings beat and flexed in a dive. The Roc's black shadow fell across him and Balthazar knew the sudden terror of the rabbit caught in the open meadow. He forced himself to wait until the last second. Then he ducked under the clutching talons and hacked at one of the powerful rear legs.

The greatsword should have severed the limb. Instead, it whistled through *nothing*. The bird screeched and banked upward.

Balthazar shook sweat from his eyes. He scanned the sky.

So they *were* illusions. Just like the thieves in the alley. Flesh and blood, but only for the purpose of the test. In this case, to pick people up and hurl them back down like broken dolls.

He glanced up at the dragon cloud where Fulad-zereh observed the carnage from her lofty perch. Thin trails of smoke drifted aloft from the dragon's nostrils. She'd hooked one arm around a cloud-fang, her legs swinging like a restless child.

She wouldn't stage a simple slaughter. Not in the first round. Like Taj said, that would be boring. Which meant there had to be a way to destroy them. In his experience, monsters were generally vulnerable in two places – the head or the heart. Since he couldn't get anywhere near the creatures' heads, Balthazar decided to try for the heart.

He strode to the middle of the arena. Bodies littered the sand, bearing savage wounds from the claw-tipped talons. A few men still moaned, but a quick glance told him they were past saving. Beyond the flaming perimeter, dozens more lay scattered across the desert.

Khai limped towards him, bleeding from a deep scratch on his shoulder. His brother Mosi followed, head tipped back to watch the sky.

"Move aside," Balthazar said curtly. "Give me room!"

The Egyptian had the otherworldly calm that descends in the throes of battle. He glanced up as the dread shadows fell across the arena. "Here they come."

Balthazar watched with grim resignation as the Rocs dove out of the sun. There weren't many contenders left. The female assassin stood back-to-back with the blade master. A small knot of Blue Men fought together with iron lances and stretched-hide shields. The rest of the sorry bunch grouped by tribe. Less than two dozen altogether.

The birds chose their targets. Balthazar locked eyes with his own reaper. It was the largest one, with a wingspan close to two hundred feet.

The Roc circled, watching him. Once. Twice. Then it dove in utter silence.

In that moment, nothing else existed. He let go of conscious thought, trusting his own instincts. Wind ruffled the deep blue feathers as it plunged down. When it neared the ground, the Roc was forced to bank the angle of attack, rearing back to extend its powerful legs.

Balthazar heard distant screams as others were harvested, but it meant nothing to him.

He gripped the sword and leapt at the gap between the reaching talons. With unerring precision, he drove the six-foot blade up through the ribs beneath the left wing.

It was just a guess. If the heart was on the right side, he was done for.

The shock of steel slicing through bone and gristle shot straight through his wrist. The Roc screamed. It vanished in a puff of smoke. Balthazar staggered back. He was surprised to find blood running down his arm. A talon must have nicked him, though he didn't feel it happen.

He gave a ragged laugh.

Only eight more to go.

"The heart!" he shouted. "Pierce them through the heart!"

Ashen faces stared at him.

"It's on the left, you idiots!"

Then the Rocs were diving again and Balthazar turned his attention to staying alive. Again and again, the long reach of the montante saved him. He destroyed three more, sustaining another nasty slash along his left arm during the last encounter. The Blue Men rallied, using their spears to kill two others. The woman and the sword master took another two.

Leaving a lone Roc.

Balthazar watched it circle above. He had to admit they were majestic creations. Part of him was glad he hadn't killed anything real. It would have been a tragic waste.

Like the men who had died that day.

Khai knelt over the body of his brother, who lay in a pool of blood. The Egyptian's head was bowed. Tears streamed down his face. He'd taken a few wounds himself, but none appeared mortal.

Balthazar looked up at the armored figure of Fulad-zereh. She stood on the tip of the dragon's long snout, hands braced on her hips. The sun had shifted its position and her armor was no longer blinding. He had the impression of horns and a pair of folded wings that rose up on her back. Perhaps it was imagination, but Balthazar thought she was staring directly at him. He turned back to Khai.

"Leave him," Balthazar said wearily.

Khai didn't answer. He gazed at his brother with empty eyes.

"What did you expect?" Balthazar snapped. "Get on your feet or die!"

"I talked him into it," Khai whispered. "I said we'd get rich. I said . . . ." He trailed off.

A shadow fell over them. Balthazar spun around. The veiled assassin stood there, gazing at him with cold black eyes.

"Come join us," she said, indicating a small group that

included the blade master. "We'll dispose of the last Roc and see each other through until tomorrow."

"And then?"

She shrugged.

"No, thanks."

Her brows furrowed. "You throw your lot in with *him*? Look at him. He's useless."

"I throw my lot in with no one."

"Then you're a fool." She glanced at the sky. "It comes for him. What will you do?"

"Kill it," he growled. "That seems to be the only way to get them to sound the bloody gong."

Balthazar couldn't see her face, but he sensed she was smiling.

"I'll leave you to it then."

She strode away, lithe and light on her feet. He hoped he hadn't just made another enemy.

Never underestimate *women*.

Balthazar sighed and turned to face the plummeting Roc.

CHAPTER 14

The gong sounded, its harsh, deep reverberations echoing across the desert. The ifrit materialized in the center of the arena, shouting at the survivors. Zarifa conducted a swift head count. Out of a field of one hundred and twenty-two contenders, nineteen were left standing.

To her intense relief, Balthazar was one of them.

He laid his sword down. Then he leaned forward and hauled another man to his feet. She thought it might be the Egyptian from the caravan. The one who had shared his water. The man stumbled and Balthazar slid an arm beneath his shoulders. The two of them staggered through the wall of flames together, Balthazar taking most of the weight.

She wondered if the ifrit would object. But the Egyptian did walk out on his own feet. Apparently, that was adequate.

Balthazar returned for the sword, carrying it over his right shoulder. He was bloodied but didn't look seriously hurt.

Zarifa unclasped her hands, gazing blankly at the white half-moon marks of fingernails denting her palms. She'd joined Taj on his balcony in a mood of excitement and anticipation. But watching men die for entertainment was not something she planned to do again. Ever.

Her breakfast of bread and olives churned uneasily in her stomach. The daēvas on the other balconies had cheered for their champions, and booed or gasped when one died. Part of her understood. They had watched the Trials for nearly a millennium. Those who had no taste for such sport would have stayed at home. But it seemed that most of the city had turned out for the grisly spectacle. Did they truly not care? Or had they simply given up hope?

Either way, she felt soiled, sitting high and safe in the balcony while the Rocs spilled blood below.

"It's good he chose the montante," Taj said. "He might have died otherwise."

She glanced at him sharply, but the daēva showed no sign of gloating. In fact, he looked pale and subdued. Zarifa realized with surprise that for all his casual talk about odds and favorites, for all that he profited from the massacre, Taj took no pleasure from the Trials.

"I knew he'd make it," Lucas said in a shaky voice that belied his words.

Taj nodded. "I expected he would, too. A few always do. They're either very lucky or very skilled."

"Is the next round worse?"

"Yes." His voice was dry. "That's when you find out which is which."

The Egyptian had revived enough to make his own way to the gates. Balthazar stood alone, his back to the city walls, gazing out at the desert. One of the marids handed him a water skin. He tipped his head back and drank. Sunlight gleamed on the long blade over his shoulder. He should have looked silly in that bespoke suit, yet he carried it off. There was something timeless about the man, Zarifa thought. She could just as easily imagine him in a tunic and sandals — which, considering the era he was born in, wouldn't be far off the mark.

Zarifa saw they weren't the only ones watching. The daēvas on the walls had also seen him kill five of the Rocs.

"Who's that tall one?" a woman with dark skin and short, kinky curls called over from the next balcony.

Taj looked over, eyes hooded. "His name is Balthazar, I think."

"You *think*? Spare me, Taj. I'm willing to wager you had your gold on him."

Taj shrugged. The daēva laughed. "Where's he from?"

A slight pause. "Hungary."

She frowned. "Well, that's a first."

"Deadly poetry in motion, eh?" her companion remarked. "Put my money on that one for tomorrow."

Taj nodded. "Don't expect the same odds as today though." He looked over at Lucas. "What do you reckon?"

"Ten to one," Lucas replied tightly.

"Ten to one!" Taj called over. "Down from . . . I believe it was two hundred to one."

"Done!" the daēva shouted back. He chortled. "That's why I always choose the balcony next to yours, Taj. By tonight, you'll only be paying out four to one." He glanced at his companion. "The early bird gets the worm, eh, Kyra?"

"This feels so wrong," Lucas muttered.

Zarifa cast him a sympathetic glance. Lucas scowled at her. "Don't try to make nice to me now."

"I wouldn't dream of it," she said lightly. "But I for one won't be back tomorrow. I've had quite enough."

"The least you can do is watch," Lucas retorted. "Considering you're the one—"

"Now, now," Taj said with a thin smile. "Enough bickering. There's work to do."

Lucas clamped his mouth shut. Taj laid a hand on his arm. "Balthazar chose this," he said softly. "He clearly knows how to take care of himself. My advice is to let it go for now."

"Easy for you to say," Lucas mumbled.

"Come." Taj smiled. "Let's have some lunch."

"I've lost my appetite."

"Eat anyway. Then we must post the updated odds. There'll be a frenzy." He glanced at Zarifa. "And you're wanted in the storeroom," he said briskly. "The Seneschal is waiting."

She watched them leave with a frown. He'd been almost kind when he addressed Lucas Devereaux. If she didn't know better, she'd think . . . . Zarifa shook her head. No, it was impossible. Taj *had* no heart.

She turned back to the arena. Balthazar was gone. Carts rumbled toward the city, piled high with bodies. A small throng of weeping relatives gathered at the gates.

"What happens to the dead?" she asked the daēvas on the next balcony.

"They're given back to anyone who wants them," Kyra replied. "Those who go unclaimed are burned."

The arena sat empty and silent. Fulad-zereh had disappeared, though the dragon-cloud still floated in the sky.

"Does she stay until it's over?" Zarifa asked.

"Yes." Kyra rose with a sigh. "And let's hope she doesn't pop down for a visit. They rarely go well."

Zarifa shivered. Even as a tiny figure in the distance, the demon had been fearsome in her shining armor. She must be terrifying to behold up close. And she remembered what Taj had said about Fulad-zereh snatching mortals for her own nefarious purposes. Zarifa resolved to sleep in a windowless chamber that night.

She made her way down the winding stairs and walked the short distance to the Treasury, savoring the flower-scented air. Basking in the hot sun, Al Miraj was a marvel of beauty, its eclectic architectural styles united by the rose-colored sandstone and vibrant greenery. She saw no sign of the decay brought by the curse, but Zarifa still quickened her steps, conscious that she had already lost several hours of daylight.

The Seneschal sat at a long table making notations in the ledger. A talismanic lamp glowed at her elbow, casting soft white light on her face. She was quite lovely when she wasn't scowling.

"Did you watch the Trial?" the Seneschal asked without looking up.

"Yes." Zarifa sank into a wooden chair opposite. "It was horrible."

The woman glanced over with a level expression. "Did you really expect any different?"

"I don't know." Zarifa sighed. "I suppose I thought it would be more . . . heroic."

The Seneschal snorted. "I stopped going a long time ago. They gave me nightmares." She gestured at a pile of objects. "Start with that, Miss Everleigh. We're behind schedule already."

She identified a bottle of wine that made your voice as sweet as a songbird for one hour, a figurine that worked the weather, and a brass key that unlocked any door. Zarifa eyed the last one with intense longing, but the Seneschal placed it on her own ring to test it out later.

"I've never met anyone with your talent," she said, when they paused to share a pot of coffee. "You could have a permanent place here if you wanted it. Paid work. I'd be willing to speak to Taj—"

"It's tempting," Zarifa interrupted with a smile. "But I still hope to gain my freedom."

The woman eyed her curiously. "Where would you go?"

She'd grown to like the Seneschal, but she wasn't about to admit that Mortlake had a deposit box in London. Taj would just pilfer it himself.

"I don't know. But I'd be well-suited to continue my father's business." Her voice turned wry. "I think Taj would find me to be far more reliable. Do you think he might consider it?"

The Seneschal sipped her coffee. She must be aware of Mortlake's gambling addiction, but was too polite to mention it. "You'd have to ask him yourself."

"Can I ask *you* something?"

The woman nodded.

"You're not a daēva. How did you come to work for him?"

"My husband fought in the first Trials." She shrugged. "He died. I remained."

Zarifa blinked. "You've been here so long?"

"It doesn't seem so." She tilted her head. "Taj is a fair master, whatever you may think of him. I began as a scullery maid. But I served him with loyalty and diligence. I worked my way through the ranks to become his chief steward." She touched the streak of gray at her temple with a smile. "I am not immortal, but it took six hundred years before I showed the first signs of aging. Who knows? Maybe I will last for another six hundred."

"If the magic lasts, too," Zarida replied sadly.

"Yes. If the magic lasts."

They were quiet for a minute. Zarifa felt like she might have made a friend. Her first . . . . Well, pretty much ever. She didn't want to work too fast, it's true, but more than that, she wanted to share something. Give the Seneschal a gift.

"Would you like to hear a story?"

The Seneschal frowned. "It's getting late—"

"Just a short one. It's called *The Legend of the Specter Ship.*"

A brief hesitation. She glanced at the talismans. Then back at Zarifa's hopeful expression. Her face softened, the fine lines at the corners of her brown eyes deepening as she smiled. "All right. Just one."

Zarifa sat up straighter. She leaned forward, her voice lowering. "Once upon a time, there was a man who had a little shop in Balsora. He was neither rich nor poor, but one of those who do not like to risk anything, through fear of losing the little that they have . . . ."

Back at the Golden Flail, Taj and Lucas were holed up revising the odds over some very strong tea.

Destan Karatas entertained Kyra, who had put all her money on the Hungarian and felt she deserved to cut loose a little.

Jabaar the Cruel kicked a cat and was chastised by Yatha the Harmonious, who gave it a bowl of milk.

The survivors returned to the Hall of Heroes to drink and toast each other, except for the assassin, who retreated to her chamber to sharpen her knives.

And Balthazar lugged his montante up four flights of stairs to find a daēva waiting outside his room. She had short dark hair and a saucy grin.

"Taj sent me," she said, pushing off the wall with languid grace.

"For what?" he asked.

"For this." She seized his arm in a strong grip. He tried to pull away . . . and a shudder ran through him as icy power rippled through muscle and bone. A gasp tore from his throat. Balthazar yanked his arm free, livid.

"You could bloody ask first!" he snarled.

"Sorry." Her elfin head tilted as she studied him with open curiosity. She was small for a daēva, barely reaching his shoulder, but Balthazar had no illusions that she couldn't snap his neck in two seconds flat.

He pushed a sleeve up and examined his arm. The gouges from the Rocs' talons were gone.

"Thank you," he said in a calmer tone.

She nodded. "Taj would have come himself, but he's busy. He said you're free to do as you please for the rest of the day."

"How generous." Balthazar turned for the doorway. She reached for him again, then drew her hand back when he flinched. The daēva laughed.

"Care for some company?" she asked frankly.

Balthazar frowned. "Did he tell you to ask me that, too?"

"No." Her lips curled in a crooked grin. "But I don't think he'd mind."

Balthazar sighed. She was pretty.

And scary.

God only knew what her idea of foreplay would be.

"Did you see what just happened out there?" he asked, pointing vaguely in the direction of the city walls.

"Oh, I saw."

"Then you must realize I'm wobbly as a newborn fawn right now."

The wolfish grin widened. "I like fawns."

"Everyone likes fawns. But not in *that* way."

She reached up and patted him awkwardly on the shoulder. "In the city, they're calling you the Merciless Magyar. They say you will be our champion. But to me, you will be . . . The Elusive Unicorn!"

He watched her saunter off, shoulders quivering with silent laughter.

Back in his chamber, Balthazar yanked the heavy curtains shut. Then he fell into bed and slept.

Mercifully, he did not dream.

It was mid-afternoon when he finally surfaced with a dry mouth and aching head.

The sword only weighed four and a half pounds. But after a morning spent stabbing *giant fucking eagles*, the only thing he wanted to lift was a glass of Brugerolle.

He knew he shouldn't drink. However, knowing and acting responsibly on that knowledge were apparently two different things. His mind was a perfect blank as he retraced the route back to the dive in the upper city.

Just one, he told himself. To take the edge off.

Then he'd be a good boy and get some more rest before the next day's lunacy.

He kept his head down, avoiding the stares of recognition. The black-clad bouncer at the door wordlessly stepped aside at his approach. Balthazar's shoulders relaxed a fraction as he entered the dim cavern. All was as it had been. The dancing girls, the hypnotic strains of dutar and harp, the handful of patrons sprawled on cushions. He'd come here because it was easy, but he was still too tense to *lounge*.

"I wish there was a proper bar," he muttered.

"What's a proper bar?"

Balthazar looked up at the marid, who stood against the wall with arms crossed. "Oh, I don't know." He smiled. "Like the one at the Savoy."

"This?"

Balthazar blinked. A gleaming mahogany bar stretched between them. It had comfortable high-backed leather stools. He barely recognized himself in the long mirror beyond.

"I have blood all over me," he murmured, touching his stubbled cheek. A horrified laugh came out. "Christ. No wonder they were staring—"

The marid wiggled a finger. "Better?"

Balthazar let out a long breath. He wore immaculate white tie. His hair was perfect, parted just the way he liked it. His face looked freshly shaven. Only the shadows behind his eyes remained. It seemed even magic couldn't erase those.

"Yes. But please don't do that again. It's disturbing."

The marid slid a bottle of Brugerolle down the bar. "I'll add it to your account."

Balthazar poured himself a healthy measure. "How much was the valet service?"

The marid grinned. "On the house. You're eight to one now, Balthazar."

"How exciting."

"We're not allowed to bet. But if I could . . . I'd put my money on you tomorrow."

"That's very kind." He took a sip, savoring the cognac. It

was even better than he remembered. The screams of the dying faded. Balthazar closed his eyes.

A familiar scent wafted through the air. Lightly floral, but with an undertone of clean woman. The hair on his arms rose up. His eyes shot open.

Zarifa stood behind him. She wore a simple grey robe. Her black hair hung in loose waves around her shoulders. She looked even more beautiful than the night they'd spoken on the terrace of his hotel in Cairo.

He hated her for that.

"Is this seat taken?" she asked.

"Yes."

She gave a throaty laugh and sank onto the next barstool. "What are you drinking?"

Balthazar cradled the bottle in his arm. "It's delicious. And you can't have any."

"I didn't say I wanted any." A black cat slunk along the bar. Zarifa scratched it under the chin and the dumb creature purred in contentment. "No, I want something better."

"Champagne?" the marid asked.

She made a face. "No, I'll have a bottle of Moskovskaya," she said firmly. "Well-chilled, please."

The vodka appeared before her, coated with frost. Zarifa poured a shot. "Skol," she muttered, tossing it back.

"How'd you find me?"

"Destan."

He scowled. "Of course."

Zarifa poured a second shot, but let it sit on the bar. "How are you holding up?"

"Oh, swimmingly. Did you enjoy the show?"

"I expected to. But, no." She gazed at him with a serious expression. "Not at all."

Balthazar studied her in the mirror. She wore no jewelry except for the silver crucifix. It nestled in the hollow of her throat. He remembered how she'd crossed herself when they were speaking of Neblis. A quick, unconscious gesture.

"I've been wondering about something."

She arched a thick eyebrow.

"Are you a practicing Catholic?" he asked, taking a mouthful of cognac. "Because I could use a good laugh."

She sighed. "Partially lapsed."

"What does that even mean?"

"It's been a long time since I went to confession, but I still pray sometimes." Zarifa shrugged. "I was raised by nuns."

He turned, curious despite himself. "Were you really?"

"The Daughters of Charity of Saint Vincent de Paul. They ran a dispensary and orphanage in Alexandria."

Balthazar digested this. "Were they mean nuns or nice nuns?"

"A little of both. Strict, but mostly decent."

"And how does Mortlake figure into your deeply religious upbringing?"

"I didn't even know he existed until I was twelve. Only that I had an anonymous benefactor. He paid for my care but never visited."

"What about your mother?"

She smiled. "Just like I told you, English father, Egyptian mother."

"No, I mean what *was* she?" he asked with a slight frown. "A sorceress? Or perhaps a harpy?"

Zarifa turned to watch the dancers. "I never knew her. She died in childbirth."

She said it matter-of-factly, but Balthazar glimpsed an old pain in her eyes before she looked away. The woman was a consummate actress.

"Well, he did a good job keeping you secret." Balthazar eyed the cat, which had curled its tail around his Brugerolle. "Not even Lucas suspected and he's relentless at ferreting out secrets."

Zarifa gave a bitter laugh. "John Mortlake was *obsessive* about secrecy. And money. It's all he cared about."

The cat licked its paw and started grooming an ear.

"He wasn't very good at keeping it though, was he?" Balthazar said.

"Terrible. He was either flush or in the gutter. There was never any middle ground with Mortlake. Once he realized what I could do with talismans, he gave me the choice of helping him or becoming a nun."

"You poor thing," Balthazar said sympathetically. "Just like your *other* father gave you the choice of marrying Colonel Fitzwalter or becoming a nun?"

Zarifa cast him an amused look. "The best lies always have a kernel of truth. It makes them easier to remember. I was fifteen by then and dying to get out." She smiled wistfully. "I adored Alexandria. It's our most cosmopolitan city. But the convent was stifling. I knew I could never be a nun."

"Well, there's something we agree on," Balthazar said dryly. "How did he learn what you could do?"

She tossed back the shot like it was water. "I found his chains. Naturally, I was horrified."

"Naturally."

Zarifa rounded on him. "It's the truth! Who are you to judge me? I was just a girl, alone in the world, with a monster for a father. I did what I had to."

"Go on." Balthazar held out a placating hand. "I'm listening."

"Mortlake had taken me out for the day. He did that sometimes, when he was in the city on business. He would ask me questions about the tutors he sent." Her eyes narrowed. "I didn't realize it, but he was grooming me even then. My education went far beyond what the nuns could have offered. Classical Greek and Latin. Philosophy, mathematics, history.

"The sisters spoke French so that was my first language, but he made sure I learned English and Arabic, a bit of

German. Anyway, we went back to his hotel. He'd gone down to the lobby to send a cable. And I sensed something in the wardrobe. It . . . attracted me."

"Were you aware of your talent?"

Zarifa snorted. "I hadn't a clue. It's not as if the nuns left talismans lying about." She glanced at the marid, who was surveying the other patrons with a bland expression. "May I have a cigarette?"

"Sorry," he replied. "No fire allowed within the walls."

She sighed. "Just to hold then."

A pack of Players appeared. Her hand trembled slightly as she drew one from the pack and tapped it on the bar.

"When I touch a talisman, I get a flash of the last time it was used. The vision lasts anywhere from a few seconds to several minutes." She gazed at Balthazar. "The ouroboros, for example. I saw a red-haired woman, very fair with freckles. You were—"

"I know perfectly well what I was doing," Balthazar interrupted testily. "We were discussing Mortlake."

"Yes. When I touched the chains, I saw . . . . Let's just say yours was far more pleasant." A shudder ran through her. "I didn't fully understand it, but I knew what I had seen was real. When he came back, I confronted him."

"Weren't you afraid?"

"Terrified." She gave a grim smile. "But I wasn't good at playacting yet, Balthazar. I couldn't hide my shock and revulsion. At first, he was furious. I thought he would beat me – or worse. But then he grew quiet. Thoughtful. He swore he only used the chains on bad people."

"And you believed that?"

"I wanted to believe," she admitted. "Desperately. Later, I learned it was another lie. But by then I was fully in his power."

"Well, that's a good story," Balthazar said. "Am I supposed to feel sorry for you?"

"No." She didn't seem upset at his acid tone. "And I don't care if you believe me. I just wanted you to know that I didn't trick you for some notion of revenge. There's no question I'm better off without him." Her eyes flashed. "But I deserve *something* for all those years I put up with him. And it's not going to be whoring for Taj. That's all."

Balthazar eyed the bottle of Brugerolle. "Well, if it means anything, he didn't use the black lightning to defend himself. Unless he has other children stashed away somewhere, the only explanation is that he was afraid it might kill you. So perhaps Mortlake did care after all."

She stared at Balthazar in the mirror. Her face had gone very pale. "What are you talking about?"

"Don't you know? It's a necromancer's most devastating weapon. The ability to summon a bolt of lethal power." Thirst overrode good sense. He gently disentangled the cat's tail and poured another finger of cognac into his glass. "But there's a catch. One of the necromancer's own blood will die screaming. They can't know who it will be."

Balthazar raised the glass. "Family trees are convoluted things. When you're very old, they extend to hundreds of people, most of whom you've probably never heard of. The sacrifice needn't be a close relative." He tipped the amber liquid into his mouth and swallowed. "But it might be. Like I said, one can never be sure."

"You're wrong," Zarifa snapped. "He wouldn't have cared."

"You know him best. I'm just telling you, your father didn't use it." Balthazar set the glass down. "And because of that he died."

"Let me tell *you* something." Her voice was low and deadly. "Mortlake taught me to steal and fight and lie. To wear a thousand different disguises and play a thousand different roles. He used me to gull his marks, and then he'd rob them blind. He never once thanked me or uttered a kind word.

That's the sort of man he was. So don't tell me he gave a tinker's damn about my life. If you knew the sort of people he exposed me to . . . ." A flush crept across her cheeks and Balthazar felt his own blood stir.

It had to be the alcohol. He frowned at the bottle, shocked to find it was nearly empty. Speaking of which . . . . What the hell was he thinking, drinking with her? Was his short-term memory completely erased?

"I have no idea how I ended up in the position of *defending* John Mortlake," Balthazar announced, rising to his feet. "So let me reiterate that the man was scum. If he were alive, I'd kill him again." He was tipsy enough to automatically reach for a hat . . . and lo, there it sat. Black silk with a grosgrain band and cream lining. Balthazar turned it upside-down and read the label. Hart & Hobbs, which just happened to be his favorite London haberdasher.

"I think we really are in purgatory," he said with a note of wonder.

"Try a little farther south," Zarifa muttered. She raised her glass and turned to face him with a grim expression. "What toast shall I make? Oh, I know. To conquering heroes!"

The vodka slid smoothly down her throat. Zarifa banged the glass down. The cat arched its back with a hiss.

"If you happen to run across any," Balthazar replied, placing the hat on his head, "tell them there'll be loads of monsters waiting outside the gates at five a.m. sharp. In the meantime, I'll be sleeping it off."

He headed to the door with a steady gait but failed to notice the raised threshold and nearly fell on his face. Balthazar heard Zarifa say something to the marid. An instant later, the alley wavered like a mirage. He threw out a hand to steady himself . . . and found it braced against the stone wall of his own bedchamber.

Two days ago, such an abrupt transition would have been infuriating. Now he was merely grateful to be saved the walk.

A table waited with fruit, bread, meat and a dozen other savory dishes. Balthazar fell on the food like a starving jackal. When the last crumb was gone, the dirty dishes vanished and a jug of cold water appeared, beaded with condensation. He drank it down. The foggy dregs of the Brugerolle lifted.

As he undressed, Balthazar considered what Zarifa had told him in the cold light of sobriety. Another pack of lies, no doubt. Yet he sensed a hint of truth. The orphanage, for example. He couldn't imagine a man like Mortlake raising a young child himself. He lacked the patience. And Zarifa would have been a feral creature, not the polished woman who had wrapped him around her finger with almost no effort.

But wait until she was older and then exploit her for his own benefit, hiding her away when things grew too hot . . . . *That* was entirely plausible. And if it were true, Balthazar was forced to concede that she probably had little choice in the matter. If she'd run, Mortlake would have found her. Even if she had somehow managed to escape, what life awaited her?

Prostitution, and an early death.

One thing he knew for certain is that a woman like Zarifa would not accept that fate, under any circumstances. He wouldn't either, if he'd been in her shoes.

Balthazar rubbed his forehead. He *might* forego retribution when this was all over. Assuming he got his ouroboros back, of course.

"I was looking everywhere for you."

Balthazar turned to the door. Lucas stood there, a worried expression on his face.

"Where did you go?"

"Just having a drink." Balthazar waved him inside.

Lucas looked gaunt. His shirtsleeves were rolled to the elbows. Lead dust stained his fingers, though that was normal.

"Is it really wise to indulge in spirits?" he said cautiously.

"No, but I did it anyway. How's our illustrious master?"

"Pleased with you." Lucas scowled. "I despise helping these vultures wager on your life. I hope you realize that."

"Well, you have no choice." Balthazar smiled. "If I had any money, I'd put it on me, too."

"I wish I knew what she has planned for tomorrow."

"Don't we all?" Balthazar lay back on the pillows, head propped on his arms. "But never fear, I'll manage."

"I know you will." Lucas paused. "I wish I could go with you."

"Then I'd be distracted trying to keep you alive. This way I can be a total mercenary."

"You weren't today," Lucas pointed out. "I saw you help someone."

"Khai was a special case." Balthazar's voice hardened. "And he's on his own after this. I can't afford to have friends."

"Good. Trust no one, my lord."

"When do I ever? Except for you, of course." Balthazar looked at his pocket watch. "The hour grows late. I'd best get my beauty sleep." He covered a yawn. "None of the others have an ounce of style. I need to show them how it's done."

Lucas gave a quiet laugh.

"Oh, did you find any digestives? You have only to ask for some, you know."

"They're not real. I want the real ones."

"Don't tell me you're starving yourself." Balthazar patted his stomach. "I just ate enough to kill a mule."

"I had some rice before," Lucas conceded. "But I didn't like the pistachios. I picked them out." His nose twitched. "Were you petting a cat, by any chance?"

"Oh, God. Yes. They're everywhere. Don't go near my coat!"

Lucas gave a violent sneeze. He rubbed his eyes. "I'll be watching again tomorrow. I don't like it, but . . . it's . . . ." Another sneeze. "Better than not knowing."

"Of course," Balthazar said hastily. "See you in the morning, then!"

Lucas backed out, hand flapping before his red face. "'Night, my lord."

Balthazar drew the sheet to his chin. He felt oddly better.

Some things never changed.

CHAPTER 15

Balthazar stood in the arena, the longsword over his right shoulder, watching the sky lighten above the desert.

As before, the others waited in loose groupings. He gave a brief nod to Khai, who appeared to have forged an alliance with a few of the tribal warriors. The Egyptian looked better, though his eyes were reddened with grief. No one spoke. They all knew that whatever the demon sent, it would be worse than yesterday. And few would live to hear the gong sound a second time.

On the city walls, the balconies were packed with spectators. Jinn appeared to serve refreshments, vanishing just as quickly. The air of excitement was in sharp contrast to the mood in the arena, which was tight with tension.

Balthazar drew a deep breath. It was a fine morning, the air crystalline and still holding the cool of night. Every sensation felt heightened. The smoothness of the hilt against his palm. The quiet ticking of the watch in his pocket. The faint murmur of voices from the wall.

There had been no rousing speech from Taj this time. Not even *Fight well or die well*. The daēva merely watched from his balcony as they walked through the gates to the arena. Lucas sat next to him, though Balthazar saw no sign of Zarifa. He glanced up at the dragon cloud, where Fulad-zereh occupied her perch between two jagged fangs.

Then the first rays broke the horizon, striking her armored plate. She'd positioned herself perfectly to dazzle the audience. Balthazar smiled grimly. The demon had a certain panache. He looked forward to meeting her.

"You know the rules!" the ifrit bellowed, materializing in the center of the arena. Flames licked along his reddish skin as he hefted the mallet. "Try to leave before the final gong sounds and you burn!" Glowing eyes settled on each of them in turn. "Walk out alone or not at all!" The ifrit stared at Balthazar the longest, sending a pointed message. *No helping anyone today.*

Balthazar stared back, unflinching. Finally, the ifrit raised his mallet.

"Let the second day of the Ninth Trials commence!"

He pounded the gong. The sound vibrated outwards, then faded to silence. The flames leapt upward, sealing them inside.

The contenders eyed each other, all wondering the same thing.

Who would meet their deaths today?

And what form would it take?

The ifrit vanished. For endless minutes, nothing happened. The contenders grew restless. Some muttering began. Only Balthazar remained unruffled. He understood psychological warfare all too well. Fulad-zereh wanted them off-balance. She wanted to see them *squirm.*

He pulled an apple from his pocket and bit into it. When he was finished, Balthazar tossed the core away. He looked up at Fulad-zereh and gave her a little salute. He thought she gave a tiny nod back, but he couldn't be sure.

Balthazar settled in to wait. The sun climbed higher, painting the dunes a dusky rose. The landscape was eerily silent. Not a breath of wind stirred.

Like the Rocs, it came from the east.

The first sign was a dirty yellow smudge on the horizon. The smudge gradually spread into a wide band. It had the banked appearance of a cumulus cloud but hugged the earth, rolling in on itself from the crest downward.

Balthazar stripped off his coat. He wrapped the shirt around his head, leaving only a narrow slit for his eyes. Then he put the coat back on and buttoned it to the top, trying to protect as much bare skin as he could.

Most of the others already wore *keffiyeh* and they hastily followed suit, covering mouths and noses. They were desert dwellers and knew what was coming.

Haboob. The violent summer winds.

But all knew this would be no simple storm.

The wind picked up, whipping the top layer of sand into stinging sheets. Balthazar watched through narrowed eyes as the wall rolled towards them, billowing outward at the leading edge. When it covered the sun, the storm took on a hellish red glow as though great forges burned within its depths.

Balthazar's confidence wavered. He'd been engulfed by such storms before, though never one so large. They'd all be fighting virtually blind.

An almost imperceptible rumbling sound rose, like the roll of distant thunder. And beneath that drumbeat came another sound – a loud, steady hissing. The wall climbed higher. It filled the arch of the sky, tinged with swirling bands of purple and orange plumes of dust streaming off the crest.

The contenders crouched within the flaming circle. Their heads bowed against the wind, but every hand held a weapon.

Balthazar caught a last glimpse of the demon's shadowy silhouette before she was swallowed by the storm.

He filled his lungs. The next instant, all was choking darkness. Grit scoured every inch of exposed flesh. His shirt was a tight broadcloth weave, but sand still wormed its way inside.

The wind howled and hissed. He had no choice but to close his eyes against the onslaught.

A scream came from the left. Balthazar threw an arm across his face and cracked open one eye. He saw a flash of movement in the murk. His sword came up just as a huge barbed tail stabbed down at his face. Instinct sent him pivoting to the side, the blade slashing in a lateral cut. The severed tail flew away. But the creature attached to it kept coming. Through a stinging blur, he saw what looked like a huge wolf – if wolves had eight segmented legs and a pair of snapping claws.

Balthazar hacked in a frenzy until nothing remained but twitching pieces.

He knew the leading edge of the storm would likely be the worst. As it swept past, the wind abated slightly. He blinked rapidly but didn't touch his eyes. Rubbing them would be a fatal mistake. If he scratched a cornea, he'd be well and truly blind.

Balthazar barely had time to draw breath before the next monstrosity lunged out of the swirling sands. He had the impression of white teeth and a long snout. His blade drove into an eye socket, then added a vicious twist. The thing howled. A segmented forelimb whipped around, knocking him back. It didn't fall until he'd stabbed it a dozen more times.

From every direction, he heard the sounds of desperate battle. Screams of pain and terror, but also cries of triumph when one of the monsters was brought down. He spun away to evade snapping jaws . . . and an arrow whistled through the space he'd just occupied, burying itself in a shaggy throat.

He learned to watch for shadows within shadows. He learned to listen for the faint clicking of the armored legs. He learned to always take the barbed tail first. It was by far the most dangerous part.

Sometimes the sands parted and he saw the outline of a body, but the faces were all covered and he had no idea who had fallen. He swung the sword until his arms went numb. Still he fought on, praying the gong would sound.

He nearly killed Khai before he realized it was a man. The Egyptian emerged suddenly out of the storm, and Balthazar just managed to redirect the downstroke before it took his head off.

"They're endless!" Khai shouted, grabbing his arm. He pulled down his *keffiyeh*. His eyes were wide and panicked. "She won't stop until we're all dead!"

Balthazar laid a steadying hand on his shoulder, though his own eyes never stopped scanning the blowing sands around them. "Find your courage," he shouted, his voice muffled through the broadcloth. "It can't last much longer!"

Khai shook his head. "Can't you see? It's over!"

He started to back away.

"Wait!" Balthazar cried.

But Khai was gone, running headlong into the murk. Balthazar cursed and chased after him. In the dim light, he saw flames ahead. They were at the edge of the circle. He screamed another pointless warning. Khai never looked back. He ran across the perimeter and went up like a pitch-soaked torch. Balthazar saw him stumble and fall before a curtain of sand hid the grisly view.

Tears of rage filled his eyes. Then something slammed into him from behind. He hit the ground hard enough to see flashing lights. Teeth closed around his arm. The beast shook its massive head, worrying at the limb until it jerked from the socket with an audible pop. Balthazar heard bone snap, but felt no pain. A crushing weight pressed against his chest. The creature pinning him smelled like a fresh snowfall, cold and lifeless. His uninjured hand scrabbled blindly for the sword. His fingers closed on nothing but sand. The blade was lost.

A barbed tail rose above him, tipped with a venomous stinger. He'd seen what they did when they pierced flesh. A poison so virulent it burned away the skin on contact, dissolving its prey like acid. Fury filled him, to die this way. He screamed with his last breath. Screamed straight into the creature's pitiless face. The tail stabbed down. Mere inches before it impaled him, a scimitar flashed past his nose. A boot kicked the thing from his chest. The blade swept down again. And again. And yet again.

A slender hand seized him by the collar. It hauled him roughly to his feet. A wave of dizziness crashed over him. He would have fallen without that iron grip on his coat.

Someone unwound the shirt from his head. Balthazar sucked in deep lungfuls of air. His legs steadied a bit.

"You," he whispered in shock.

The assassin gazed back, onyx eyes amused above her veil.

"Why?" he managed.

Darkness was closing in again. He'd probably bleed out in the next five minutes. But she had saved him. Truly, wonders never ceased.

The assassin shrugged. "Like you said, Balthazar. It's the only way to get the bloody gong to sound."

The scorpion-wolf – or what was left of it – gave a final spasm. Right on cue, the howling sands vanished, leaving a clear blue sky in their wake. The ifrit swung the mallet. Its echoing reverberation raced outward across the arena.

"I'm afraid the charity ends here," she said crisply. "You'll have to leave on your own." She turned her back and strode away, black robes flowing behind her.

He was afraid to assess the damage, but did so anyway. Blood soaked his right side. Balthazar unbuttoned the coat just enough to see that his arm was dislocated and dangling by a thread of sinew. The pain was starting now, a dull, deep throb. His vision narrowed to a long, dark tunnel.

Balthazar forced himself to put one foot in front of the other. There were only the flames, and getting past the flames to the other side. Nothing else mattered.

Yet despite his best effort, they never seemed to get any

closer. The sun beat down. His steps dragged. Too much blood, he thought distantly. I've lost too much.

I'm still losing it.

He wanted to sit down and rest. Only for a little while. But he knew he'd never get back up.

And if it was the last thing he did, he planned to introduce himself to Fulad-zereh.

Alive and in person.

The darkness closed in. Seductive and devouring. He fought it with all he had.

He was the Merciless Magyar.

Who had said that?

The stink of death hung over the arena, clogging his throat. Blood ran in a steady stream from his shoulder. He focused on the pain, gripping it like a lifeline. It was all that kept him conscious. Another step. And another. A dim roar seemed to come from the city wall, cheers and shouts, but it might have just been the buzzing in his head. Another step.

Then the flames were *just there*. Right in front of him.

Balthazar walked through.

———

HE WOKE WITH A GASP IN TAJ'S SUNKEN POOL.

The water was stained crimson, edge to edge. Taj sat on the rim. His perfect face swam into focus. Aquamarine eyes studied Balthazar intently.

"Well," Taj murmured, his features relaxing. "That was a nasty one."

The familiar icy sensation of a healing receded from his limbs as Taj lifted his hand from Balthazar's bare chest.

Lucas knelt at his side. He looked deeply shaken, and deeply relieved. "My lord. We could hardly see anything . . . . What was in there with you?"

Balthazar drew his knees to his chest. They'd stripped him

naked. He ran a trembling hand down his right shoulder. It was unblemished, but he remembered that gaping wound all too well. The sickening crack of bone as teeth dug into his marrow.

"It doesn't matter," he said wearily. "How many others are alive?"

"Two," Taj replied. "One of the Blue Men and the hired killer from Jeddah."

"She saved my life," Balthazar said slowly.

Taj frowned. "Did she?"

"The woman is indestructible. I didn't see a scratch on her. What about the Blue Man?"

"Bloodied, but he staggered out. You were the last."

Balthazar's brows lowered. "You mean the Tuareg *beat* me?"

"His injuries paled in comparison if that makes you feel better."

"Did you heal him, too?" Balthazar demanded.

"You almost sound jealous," the daēva replied lazily. "No, I did not. He has his own patron."

Balthazar scanned the chamber. Only Taj and Lucas were there. He knew Zarifa didn't care if he lived or died, except to further her own ends. So why did he feel so angry?

Khai.

The sudden vivid memory of the Egyptian running into the flames made his stomach roll. He'd known the man would die – that all of them would likely die. But the sheer cruelty of his particular death made Balthazar loathe Fulad-zereh with new intensity. Not to mention Taj.

"I suppose you earned a fortune today," he said acidly. "You must be pleased."

"It's down to the three of you tomorrow," Taj replied. "I don't care about the odds anymore. I just want you to make it through. I want you to seek the sword. That's all."

Late morning sun streamed into the chamber, lighting his

hair in liquid gold. His features looked even more inscrutable and inhuman than usual. Like some aloof god moving pieces on a game board.

"Why not one of the others?" Balthazar demanded. "What does it matter to you?"

"Because I *know* they won't make it. They never do."

"Then why should I?"

"Because you're different."

His calm certainty was maddening.

"How?" Balthazar asked coldly.

A puzzled frown crossed Taj's face. "I don't know. You just are."

"Well, that's a rousing endorsement."

The daēva gave him an amused smile. "If there's anything you need, say the word."

Balthazar stared at the chain around his neck. His fists clenched. "Anything but what's rightfully mine, you mean."

"Anything but that," Taj agreed.

Several petty requests came to mind.

I want to see you shave those golden locks and don a hair shirt. A really itchy one.

I want you to get a shovel and bury each body yourself.

I want you to take that ifrit's mallet and shove it so far up your—

Balthazar stood, pink-tinged water streaming down his body. The daēva averted his gaze – as if he hadn't already gotten an eyeful when they stripped him down. Lucas tossed over a clean white tunic. Balthazar yanked it on with an expression of distaste.

He glanced at the bloody rags next to the pool. "Here's a thought. How about a new suit?"

"Of course."

"A real one. I don't want a garment that will vanish in a puff of smoke at an awkward moment."

"I've have my seamstress whip something up."

"I want some decent shoes, too. No *sandals*."

Balthazar retrieved his ruined coat. A generous quantity of sand poured out when he shook open the pocket, but his Vacheron watch was still ticking.

"God bless the Swiss," he murmured, looking for a place to put it.

That was the problem with bloody tunics.

"May I have some pants?" he asked the room at large.

Taj looked down at his trousers. "I'd let you borrow mine, but you're too tall. They'd look silly."

"Never mind." He thrust the watch at Lucas. "Hold this, please."

Taj smirked. "Maybe Mortlake's daughter would oblige—"

"Don't say it." Balthazar stared at him.

"But you have to admit, it was rather funny—"

"What's funny?"

Zarifa stood at the edge of the curtain. She barely glanced at Balthazar. His fingers tightened around the watch, anger bubbling back.

Taj cleared his throat. "Nothing. We were just discussing, er . . . ."

"What to do with your father's head," Balthazar said to Zarifa with a nasty smile. "Taj suggested a spike on the walls, but I thought for a lark we might put it on trial like they did with that pope. What was his name, Lucas?"

Lucas frowned. "Formosus," he muttered.

"That's the one," Balthazar said lightly. "The Synodus Horrenda. It was quite a spectacle even for the dark days of Rome. He'd been dead seven months, but why let such a minor detail stand in the way of justice? The new pope had him dragged out of his crypt and propped him on a throne for questioning." He sighed. "Too bad we only have Mortlake's head. But it might still be amusing. . . ."

He trailed off. Taj stared at Balthazar in appalled aston-ishment.

Zarifa had gone quite pale. "Do with it what you will," she said quietly.

Balthazar felt a rush of unaccustomed shame. "That was a crude jest," he said stiffly. "Please forgive me. I'm not in top form at the moment."

She seemed on the verge of a scathing reply when she noticed the bloody water. Zarifa swallowed. She gave him a level look. "Of course you aren't. I shouldn't have intruded." She hesitated at the threshold. "But I had an idea. The Seneschal mentioned an archive. I thought we might see if there's anything useful in there about Fulad-zereh."

Lucas perked up. "Research?" he asked hopefully.

"Exactly," Zarifa turned to Taj. "Surely you can spare us for a few hours."

"I suppose I could," Taj said slowly. "But what do you expect to find?"

"I don't know yet. But if Balthazar . . . . If he survives tomorrow, there's still the matter of finding the sword. Perhaps we can discover some clue about what she's done with it. Or a weakness."

The daēva shook his head. "I've already looked. Exhaustively."

"Maybe you missed something," Lucas said.

"None of the works are in English."

"I'm familiar with Latin and Greek. Some Persian."

"So am I," Zarifa added.

"The scrolls are very old." Taj looked reluctant. "Some would crumble at a touch. That's why I keep it all under lock and key."

"I've handled ancient texts before," Lucas said quickly. "Balthazar owns a large number of them himself. I promise we won't damage anything."

The daēva finally nodded. "I suppose a fresh set of eyes can't hurt. But I need Mr. Devereaux, in particular. Two hours only. I'll find you an escort."

He strode for the door. Balthazar glanced at his watch. The hands were barely past noon. The day stretched ahead, long and bleak. There was no real way to prepare for the last Trial other than dwelling on how bad it might be. If left to his own devices, he might end up back at the bar, which never ended well. Balthazar usually left the research to Lucas, much preferring action. But he found he didn't care to be alone. Dark thoughts were already crowding his mind. The stink of blood and burning flesh . . . .

"I suppose I might go with you," he said. "Provided someone gives me a pair of pants."

CHAPTER 16

The archives sat near the Summer Palace at the highest point of the city, surrounded by acres of parkland and the silver gleam of a lake in the distance.

Yatha the Harmonious led them up a wide flight of steps and unlocked the heavy double doors with a flick of his finger. Balthazar had expected some small, dusty chamber, but the main hall of the archives soared three levels high and several hundred paces deep.

Sunlight poured through skylights set into the vaulted ceiling. Vivid jewel-toned tiles formed a graceful geometric pattern underfoot. Long tables occupied the center of the hall, where scholars might sit and read. Tall ladders on sliding tracks gave access to the double-height ground floor shelving.

Balthazar gazed up at the tiers of balconies above, which enclosed more stacks beyond. There had to be several hundred thousand volumes and the same number of scrolls.

"Where did all this come from?" he asked softly, stunned by the sheer scope of it.

"Many places. The prince was a collector of knowledge, and my illustrious master continued the tradition."

"But the scrolls . . . I've never seen so many in one place."

"Perhaps you've heard of the Great Library at Alexandria?" Yatha asked.

"Naturally," Zarifa said. "But it was destroyed when Caesar burned the Egyptian fleet and the fire spread through the city."

"The worst disaster of the ancient world," Lucas agreed. "The contents were priceless." He looked at Yatha with incredulity. "You don't mean . . . this is it?"

The marid smiled.

"But how?"

"The library was founded by Alexander, of course. Rumor has it the prince was his lover once. When the prince learned what was happening, he sent the jinn to save what they could. We didn't rescue it all, but we managed to retrieve most of the scrolls before the library was reduced to ash. He ordered them brought here for safekeeping."

There was a moment of amazed silence.

"All that ancient knowledge," Lucas murmured. "Believed lost forever." His eyes roamed over the multiple tiers of shelving, stretching into gloom. "It's incredible."

"Who was this prince?" Balthazar asked. "Where did he come from?"

Yatha spread his hands in a helpless gesture. "I regret that the regent has forbidden his name to be spoken."

"Why?"

"It was his own hubris that caused this disaster – or at least the regent sees it that way. He should never have meddled with Fulad-zereh." The marid looked uneasy. "You'd best get started. My master gave you two hours and I must abide by his wishes."

They looked around at the endless stacks. It would take a lifetime just to catalogue the contents.

"Is there a system?" Lucas asked.

The marid nodded. "You have my master to thank for that. He gathered everything he deemed conceivably relevant into a section on the third level. I'll show you where it is."

"Excellent," Balthazar said, rubbing his hands.

He doubted they would find anything, not if Taj had already searched it. The daēva would have been thorough. But he welcomed any distraction at this point. And there was always a possibility they'd stumble over something of value. Lucas had a nose for such nuggets of gold. If it existed, Lucas would find it.

They ascended a winding staircase in the center of the hall and took it to the highest level. There were shelves of books bound in leather and cloth, along with the honeycombs where scrolls were kept. Everything was immaculately kept, the wood polished to a gleam. A table and chairs had been placed in an open space. For a moment, Balthazar imagined Taj sitting there, poring over the manuscripts. Hoping against hope that he would find a way to defeat the demon.

Or had he? Taj had done everything he could to discourage Balthazar from entering. He profited the most from the Trials. Wasn't it in his interest to see them continue? He could have been lying when he said he found nothing. He might have plundered the archives for the express purpose of *concealing* any useful information.

Trust no one, least of all Taj, Balthazar reminded himself. But we're already here. Might as well look.

"Where are the relevant manuscripts?" he asked.

The marid waved his arm. "Everything from here to there."

The gesture encompassed perhaps a thousand unmarked papyrus scrolls stuffed into a beehive of cubbyholes.

Lucas sighed. "I suppose that still narrows it down. Thank you."

"May I be of further assistance?"

"Is there a copy of the *Amir Arsalan*?"

"Of course. I will show you."

Yatha led him to one of the cubbies and withdrew a thick sheaf of paper. "The tale was composed by Mirza Mohammad Ali Naqib-al-mamalek, the chief storyteller of Naser-al-din Shah, but it was the Shah's daughter who wrote it down."

"How old is it?" Lucas asked.

The marid chortled. "Not very old at all. This century, in fact. My master did not find it useful. However, this manuscript being the original, I would ask that you treat it as gently as your firstborn child."

"I will," he promised, taking the stack with the utmost care and retreating to the table under the marid's watchful eye.

"May I join you, Mr. Devereaux?" Zarifa asked, tentatively. "I know the tale, but I would be interested to see the original text."

Lucas nodded at a chair and Zarifa sat down across from him. "I'm not sure what connection it might have. The genre is pure romantic adventure, similar to others of the time. I suspect he merely used the demon's name and spun the rest from imagination. Apparently, he didn't even get her gender right."

"True, but he notes that she wore steel armor. A telling detail—"

They were quietly debating the merits of the tale as Balthazar wandered into the recesses of the archives, perusing books and scrolls at random. The collection was hodgepodge, covering everything from histories to general demonology and prophecy. He found a few mentions of the sword, which didn't seem to possess any magical properties other than its ability to kill Fulad-zereh.

From what he gathered, the city itself was founded sometime around the birth of Christ. In his own youth, Balthazar had known Al Miraj as a large, arid region west of Babylon that stretched between the Red Sea and the Pars Sea. There was no city then, just an assortment of nomadic tribes. But someone – presumably the mysterious prince – had revived the name when he founded the daēva capital.

The City of Gardens. A place of unrivaled beauty, where his race could live in peace and seclusion from the mortal world that had persecuted them. Balthazar could hardly begrudge the dream. And he found himself pitying them, to have trusted Fulad-zereh and have her turn on them.

If I survive tomorrow, he thought, I will meet her myself. The idea was surreal, standing in the quiet hush of the archives, the only sound the rustle of paper and whispers of Lucas and Zarifa as they compared notes. Balthazar couldn't help but wonder what she would be like. The architect of the Trials, who watched men die for her pleasure. Who offered just enough hope to keep her victims waiting for salvation that never came.

Am I their salvation? Is it possible?

He knew his own skill. There were very few men Balthazar feared, and he'd already killed most of them. But he sensed that the demon's true power was greater than the monsters she conjured. The curse on the city – inflaming its denizens to bestial acts, showing them their darkest impulses night after night – revealed a degree of sophistication. Daēvas were proud. Haughty. It was her way of telling them, *You see? You are no better than I am.*

The Rocs. The sandstorm. They were a show for the audience. A grand spectacle designed to winnow the ranks, but also to impart a lesson. Illusion made flesh. *That* was the essence of the Trials. Taj said no one ever made it past the third. But why? What defeated them? If he could understand the reason, he might stand a chance.

Or will I end another discarded lump of flesh in the arena? Carrion for the vultures? Will my own pride and arrogance blind me to the truth – that the Trials are unwinnable?

He gritted his teeth in frustration.

What will she send?

He glanced at his watch. The two hours were nearly up. Balthazar shook off the pointless train of thought. He'd find out soon enough.

"Did you learn anything useful?" he called to Lucas, who had moved deeper into the stacks.

"Not from the *Amir Arsalan*, but take a look at this," Lucas answered.

Balthazar joined him at one of the cubbies. Lucas held a scroll in a language he'd never seen before. Jagged runes that made his eyes ache. A moment later, Zarifa joined them.

"That is the language of the jinn," she said.

"Can you read it?" Lucas asked.

She hesitated. "Mortlake taught me a little. I continued studying on my own, though such manuscripts are rare, more so the ones that give a translation. I'm far from fluent, but I can try."

They took the scroll to the table and unrolled it. Zarifa studied the runes for several long minutes. "It appears to be an account by a marid who was present the day Fulad-zereh stole the sword." She frowned. "This rune means *crowned one*. It must refer to the prince. It says he always wore the Shamshir-e Zomorrodnegar on his person, only taking it off when he . . . immersed himself . . . in the . . . I think this phrase means *royal waters.*"

"The lake by the Summer Palace?" Lucas guessed.

"That sounds likely." She resumed the halting translation. "He would leave his most . . . *something* daēvas to guard it. Trusted, perhaps."

"Go on."

"The prince sent Fulad-zereh out of the city to hunt a band of . . . not-living?" She paused in consternation.

"The Druj," Balthazar said. "They were Neblis's army. Wights, revenants, liches. When she was defeated, they scattered across what was then the Persian Empire. I hunted them myself."

196

She drew a soft breath, eyes narrowed in concentration. "Not all were . . . defeated. The prince tasked her with hunting down the . . . remnants, I think? And destroying them. But on . . . this day, she went not. Did not go. She hid until she saw him undress and enter the royal waters. She slipped into the waters and . . . in silence . . . dragged him down into the depths.

"He must have fought, but not having . . . without the sword, she was . . . she overpowered him. Then she . . . I think it says *cloaked herself* and swam back to shore . . . or the prince swam back to shore?"

"Illusion," Balthazar murmured. "She cloaked herself in illusion and returned in his guise."

Zarifa met his eye, her face excited. "Yes, I think so." She laid a finger on the scroll, finding her place again. "The daēva standing guard was . . . fooled. He gave her the sword."

"Who was it? Does it say?"

Zarifa stared at the runes. "I'm not certain—"

"It was my illustrious master."

They all turned as Yatha materialized at the head of the table. He gazed at them with his usual serenity.

"Taj handed the demon the Shamshir-e Zomorrodnegar?" Lucas said slowly.

"All know the tale." The marid sounded a touch defensive. "It is no great secret."

"Funny," Balthazar said with a mirthless smile. "He must have forgot to mention that part."

The marid's blue eyes darkened. "Are you calling my master a liar?"

"Of course not," Zarifa said, shooting Balthazar a look. "But since you joined us, perhaps you can translate the rest. My vocabulary is quite limited."

Yatha glanced at the scroll. "There's no need to translate. I can tell you the end myself. Fulad-zereh laughed in my master's face. She cursed the city and its inhabitants. They

KAT ROSS

would henceforth wear two faces, as befit their treacherous nature. Then she dived down to the bottom of the lake and surfaced with the prince in her claws. My master watched them fly away and that is the last time anyone saw him."

Balthazar absorbed this. "Who appointed the regent?"

"When news spread of what had happened, the Guardians of the Watchtowers arrived. They were very angry. They argued about what to do. The four of them together could have taken the sword back and slain her."

"So why didn't they?" Zarifa asked.

"Mikal argued that the prince brought it upon himself by forcing her to do his bidding. Azrael took his side. The other two would not act without a consensus. Then Fulad-zereh sent an ifrit with a message. She offered the daēvas a chance to win back the sword. This was deemed acceptable and Mikal agreed to remain as regent."

The marid sighed. "He issued new laws, but the lords of the city constantly broke them. Mortals came, some by accident, others for the Trials. The city became more and more corrupt. And Mikal grew to despise us. He does not want to be here, but remains out of obligation. Over time, he ceded the responsibility of enforcing his own edicts to my master."

"The regent trusted Taj after what he did?" Balthazar asked in surprise.

"It was not his fault. The demon deceived him. I think my master has done the best he could under the circumstances."

"These Guardians," Balthazar said. "Are they really archangels? As in, *soldiers of God?*"

Yatha looked uneasy. "I cannot say what that means to mortals. I am an elemental. We jinn have no God. I know only that we were made to serve the Guardians and we rebelled, so they cast us down to serve the daēvas."

"Archangels exist in all major religions," Lucas said thoughtfully. "In the Christian tradition, they are Michael, Gabriel, Uriel and Raphael. In Islam, the names are slightly different. Mikal, Jibrail, Azrael and Israfil. The Hebrews describe them as Malakhi Elohim. Angels of the Lord. Though they are not mentioned often or by name."

"The magi called them Amesha Spentas," Balthazar said. "Divine beings who occupy the physical plane as protectors of humanity." His lips curled in a sardonic smile. "I've known men who claim divine mandate, but they're not angels. Not in a literal sense."

Zarifa idly tapped the scroll with one finger. "In Pagan traditions, they rule over the elemental plane. Each Guardian represents a Watchtower that corresponds with one of the four cardinal directions. Air in the east quarter, Fire in the south quarter, Water in the west, Earth in the north. All beings, mortal and magical, are said to be comprised of those elements."

Lucas nodded, eyeing her with new respect. "The Watchtowers. Yes, I believe the phrase derives from the Enochian magic system developed by—"

"John Dee in the sixteenth century," Zarifa finished with a smile of delight. "Did you know that the famous Voynich manuscript was actually written in jinn—"

"That's all very fascinating," Balthazar interrupted. "But I'm more interested in the one who's living in the palace next door." He turned to Yatha. "What's he like?"

The marid spread his hands. "I only met the regent on a handful of occasions, all long ago. They say he is the angel of mercy, but I have not seen him display this quality. According to the ancient legends, Mikal was so shocked by the sight of Hell he never laughed again. It could be true. He is stern and unyielding. Do not expect him to intervene. He blames us for the predicament."

"So there's nothing in the archives about what comes after the Trials?" Lucas asked, carefully rolling up the scroll and returning it to the cubbyhole.

"The champion will enter Fulad-Zereh's realm and hunt

the sword." Yatha paused. "No weapons are permitted. That is all I know. And now your time is up."

"But we haven't found anything!" Lucas objected.

"Because there is nothing to find."

Taj stepped from the shadows. He looked aloof and elegant, as always. Balthazar wondered how long he'd been listening.

"I told you it was a waste of time," Taj said. "And there's real work to do." He flicked a finger at the marid, who bowed deeply and vanished — though Balthazar thought he saw a wary look cross the jinn's face in the instant before he turned to smoke.

Balthazar studied Taj with new insight. He might not have learned much about the demon, but he understood the daēva better. And he couldn't help but wonder if the "theft" of the sword had in fact been orchestrated. With the prince gone and the regent cloistered away to sulk in the Summer Palace, Taj had free rein to do as he pleased. The Turk had told him as much his first day here. *He's the unofficial mayor.*

Taj's gaze swept across the three of them. It held a hint of challenge, as if daring anyone to comment on his role in the debacle. His stony expression made it clear he knew what they'd found.

Balthazar rose to his feet. "You were right," he said mildly. "A colossal waste of time."

Zarifa and Lucas quickly stood, avoiding looking at anyone.

"It'll be dark soon," Taj said. "I'll escort you all back."

They trailed him down the circular staircase to the first floor. Long shadows fell across the stacks. Balthazar looked around at the hoard of knowledge. Homeric poems, works of mathematics and geography, medical texts, philosophical treatises — a priceless collection, staggering in its breadth and antiquity. And here it sat, just another dusty jewel in Taj's treasure pile. He reminded Balthazar of a dragon, endlessly acquisitive but valuing nothing.

He probably never set foot in the archives unless it was to organize an orgy on the tables—

Balthazar halted in a weak shaft of sunlight, his eye caught by furtive movement above. An instant later, a dark blur whizzed past his face. On the second-floor balcony, a hooded figure was spinning away. Strong hands shoved him aside, a knife flashed through the air, but the assassin had vanished into the gloom. Zarifa muttered a curse, a second knife already poised to throw.

"Crossbow!" Lucas pointed to the bolt that lay on the floor, its point shattered by the stone wall. His hand groped for a sword that wasn't there as Taj ran for the spiral staircase.

"Stay back!" he called over his shoulder.

Lucas followed, and so did Balthazar, who had no intention of following orders. Taj quickly pulled ahead, his expression a mask of rage. They found him a minute later prowling the stacks. He noted Balthazar's presence with a flicker of irritation, but said only, "You search that way." A finger stabbed to the right. "I'll check this side. He must be here somewhere."

"And if it was a jinn?" Balthazar demanded.

"It wasn't," Taj snapped. "I would have sensed it materialize."

Balthazar gave a curt nod, though he wouldn't take anything Taj said at face value. He and Lucas searched for long minutes, moving cautiously as a pair. Even a medieval crossbow could be reloaded in about ninety seconds. They found several doors, all locked, but no sign of the assailant. They finally met Taj back at the staircase.

He looked grim. "They must have fled down one of the back staircases."

Balthazar watched him closely. Could Taj have ordered it himself? Being present at the time would throw off suspicion.

Yet the daēva could have killed him in a dozen easy, unde-
tectable ways. Why a clumsy attempt with a crossbow? None
of it made sense.

"Only the Seneschal has the keys," Taj said. "I'll question
her as soon as we return."

"Do you trust her?" Lucas asked.

"With my life," he replied without hesitation.

"A daēva could have opened the tumblers with Earth and
Air," Balthazar pointed out.

"Yes," Taj admitted. "It's a distinct possibility."

"Someone doesn't want him to contest the third round,"
Lucas said. "You must have an idea who it could be."

Taj snorted. "If you're implying it's a backer of one of the
other two, that still leaves dozens of suspects. Balthazar left the
arena last today. That counted against him. Most of the
wagers are on the woman now."

"I'll see who has the most money riding on her," Lucas
said. "And the Blue Man, too. It would have to be a large bet
to warrant such an obvious attack."

"Or," Balthazar said in a chilly tone, "it has nothing to do
with the betting at all."

Taj's inscrutable gaze settled on him. "What are you
saying?"

"That it's someone who doesn't want the sword back.
Someone who prefers the status quo."

"Like who?"

"I've no idea," Balthazar said. "But we have to consider
everything."

"And they're certain you'll get it before the third round? I
find that doubtful." Taj inclined his head. "But I won't rule
out anything. I'll get to the bottom of this. If you wish, I'll
assign some jinn as bodyguards—"

Balthazar stared back, anger and frustration mounting.
He'd wasted the day with nothing to show for it. And now

someone was so eager to see him dead they couldn't even wait until the morning.

"No. I won't be shadowed everywhere I go."

Taj's lips thinned. "I think that's unwise."

"Perhaps you should listen to him," Lucas ventured. "If it's a daēva—"

"They've already tried and failed. I doubt they'll make another attempt so soon."

"You don't know that—"

"Leave it, Lucas," he snarled. "I want to be alone."

He pushed past them and strode down the stairs. Zarifa waited at the bottom. She noted his glower and stepped back, the dagger still in her hand.

"No one came this way," she said. "I made sure of it."

He drew a deep breath. "Thank you. And for . . . pushing me aside. You have fast reflexes."

She looked at him seriously. "Watch your back, Balthazar. It's getting late."

He nodded and strode past, eager to leave the stuffy confines of the archives. The heavy quiet felt like a tomb. Once through the doors, he took a path around the lake. The surface was dark and still, reflecting the willows that grew at its edge.

She slipped into the waters and . . . in silence . . . dragged him down into the depths.

Mysteries wrapped in mysteries. And now he had another to contend with.

Who wants me dead?

A ragged laugh escaped him as he considered the implications. Perhaps he should rephrase the question.

Who *doesn't* want me dead?

Lucas. That he could say with utter certainty. And – far more reluctantly – Balthazar added Zarifa to the list. She only stood to gain if he succeeded in the Trials. And she'd held his life in her hands before.

So: two people he could rule out.

As for the rest of them . . . .

He crossed a simple wooden bridge over the lake's inlet and entered a park with acres of neatly tended lawns and sparse clumps of trees. The itchy feeling between his shoulders receded. No cover for an assassin — and they couldn't have known he'd come this way. The fading light gilded the great dome of the Summer Palace, an airy confection with slender spires and large arched windows framed by stone carvings. Half the lower walls were not even solid, but elaborate grill-work. A building that placed aesthetics over defense. The prince had not feared invasion by foreign enemies — or even a civil uprising. Only a man who was utterly confident in his own authority would build such a keep.

Not a glimmer of light showed through the windows, nor any sign the place was occupied. If the regent was still there, he must be deep inside, doing . . . whatever archangels did when they were angry and bored.

Mikal had not come out to watch the Trials. Did he care about the sword anymore? Or was he secretly gratified to watch his charges slowly turn feral? Maybe he was just waiting to smite them all.

The sun sank lower and Balthazar sought a path leading back down to the first tier of the city. He had only to survive the night; and then the next day; and then one more night; and then the final contest with the demon. Simple, really.

A snapping twig made him spin, adrenaline pumping, but it was just a child. Ten or eleven, with solemn eyes and a mop of unruly dark hair. A moment later, two others stepped out from behind a tree. A girl and a boy.

Balthazar scowled. "Scat."

They stared at him, whispering together. Then the first one approached. He was dirty and unkempt, just the sort of young scoundrel Lucas would give candy to and then discover his billfold had been lifted.

"Shoo," Balthazar snapped. "Go on. Beat it."

"My mother says you will be our champion," the child said, giving him a bold appraisal.

"Your mother lied. Parents do it all the time. You can tell her I said so."

The child hesitated. He laid a palm on the bole of a huge oak. His friends watched with wide eyes. The hair on Balthazar's arms rose up as the child worked elemental power. When he took his hand away, it gripped a tall staff. Before Balthazar could react, the child scampered forward and pressed it against his chest.

"For you," he said reverently. "Fight well tomorrow, Magyar."

The child darted away, his friends dashing behind. Balthazar watched until they were lost to the lengthening shadows. He looked at the staff with annoyance.

I am nobody's champion.

Balthazar cast it to the ground and strode off.

CHAPTER 17

With the onset of evening, Yatha transported the rolltop desk to a spacious chamber on the top floor that was protected by the wards. Lucas glanced up from his paperwork as Taj entered.

"Where have you been?" he demanded. "I need your approval on the final odds."

"Making inquiries into the attempted murder of your friend," Taj replied dryly.

"And?"

"The Seneschal insists no one touched her keys. A crossbow is missing from the armory, but the guards didn't see anyone enter or leave." He sounded frustrated. "I cannot say if the culprit was mortal, djinn or daēva, though the last seems most likely." He paced over to the desk. "Balthazar was unhappy about it, but I set guards outside his room. They will watch over him tonight. He is there now, brooding and disagreeable."

This was true. Lucas had tried to see him twice and been rebuffed. Balthazar refused to even open the door.

"So, what do you have for me?"

Lucas quickly ran through the day's numbers. Balthazar

and the assassin were the favorites, though most of the money was on her. The Blue Man came in a distant third.

"Where are your markers?" Lucas asked. "I'll need them before midnight."

"I'm not betting on this round," Taj said.

Lucas looked up at him in surprise. "Really?"

"Really."

"So *now* you find it distasteful?" he asked acidly.

"I always found it distasteful. But this time is different. I told you, I don't care about the money. I just want the sword."

Taj stared at the twilit city beyond the terrace. The streets had emptied. Cracks wound their way up the tallest towers, followed by the choking vines. In the deepest shadows, hungry things began to stir.

"It still breaks my heart," Taj murmured. "Every single night."

"At least the city returns to normal at dawn," Lucas said. "Half of the time, Al Miraj belongs to you."

Taj gave a bitter laugh. "Yes, but it's the wrong half."

"What do you mean?"

"We daēvas are nocturnal. Before the curse, we slept in the daytime and conducted our business at night." He shook his head. "Not just business. Our *lives*. Why do you think we made the rooftop gardens? They were the meeting places, under the moon and stars, in the coolness. We danced and sang, told stories, shared meals." He glanced at Lucas. "You might have noticed how unbearable the sun is during the day. It keeps us isolated inside our walls. *That* is what Fulad-zereh has taken from us."

"Can't the marids do something?"

"They are creatures of ice. They keep the gardens alive, but to shift entire weather patterns? Not even we can do that." Taj rose and paced to the window. "Al Miraj was the culmination of a centuries-long dream. A homeland that belonged to *us*." His voice had an edge of deep bitterness.

"And our sanctuary has been turned into just another prison."

"You could leave."

"And go where?" A blond brow arched. "London? New York?"

Lucas shrugged. "Why not? You'd pass for human."

"They are places of men." Taj's hands clenched into fists. "I would rather die than be forced to hide who I am!" He turned back to the city, shoulders relaxing. "*That* is why I want the sword, Mr. Devereaux. I want to walk in the moonlight again. To smell the night flowers. To live as I was meant to."

Lucas, who longed for home himself, understood the sentiment. "I suppose the demon knows all that?"

"Of course she does." Taj came over and leaned on the edge of the desk, uncomfortably close. "May I ask you something?"

"Go ahead," Lucas replied warily.

His gaze moved to Lucas's mouth. "How did you get that scar?"

"Why do you want to know?" Lucas laid the pencil down. "Is it a *marketable* asset?"

"No," Taj said quietly. "Because I think it means something to you."

Lucas leaned back in his chair, a bit nonplussed. "A necromancer."

"Ah. Mortlake?"

"No. I was only a child." He looked at Taj challengingly. "I owe my life to Balthazar. I know what you think of him. But he's a better man than anyone realizes."

"What happened?"

"The necromancer . . ." Lucas drew a breath. He hated telling the story, but something about the daēva's tone, brisk and matter-of-fact, invited confidence. Easier to get it over with. "He slaughtered my family. It was over a talisman."

Taj's eyebrows rose a fraction.

"Not the ouroboros. A different one Balthazar had given my father for safekeeping. He blamed himself. When he found me afterwards, hiding under a bed upstairs, he took me in and raised me as his own." Lucas's brown eyes flashed when Taj said nothing. "He didn't have to do that. Most men in his position wouldn't have troubled themselves over a crying brat. I'm telling you this so you understand what . . . ." Lucas broke off and turned away. It was a long minute before he could speak again. "What he is to me."

Taj only nodded. "What happened to this necromancer?"

"I killed him. It took a long time, but we finally found him."

"*You* killed him?"

"Are you so surprised?"

Taj smiled. "Not really. I suspected there was more to you than met the eye."

Lucas's cheeks warmed under his intense gaze. He frowned. "What are you after, Taj? You always want something."

Taj sighed. "I think you judge me unfairly, Mr. Devereaux."

"Unfairly? Balthazar nearly died today—"

"I begged him not to enter the Trials. You know that. In fact, I refused him. He insisted."

"Perhaps, but only because you're holding his talisman hostage!"

Taj's eyes sparked with anger, but he quickly mastered himself. "See it from my point of view for a moment. Balthazar killed a man who owed me a great deal of money. Then he tried to prevent my marids from bringing the man's daughter here to answer for the debt. If word spread that I'd shown lenience, all would expect it. And the only thing that keeps them from turning on each other is their fear of *me*."

The daēva's gaze was luminous and unsettling. "Yatha tells me you learned the whole story today. So you know the regent has abdicated his responsibilities and left them resting entirely on my shoulders. If I didn't keep my own brand of order in this city, it would have devolved into anarchy centuries ago."

"But still . . . ."

Taj waited patiently.

Lucas stared at him. "You were the one who handed her the sword."

"I was," Taj agreed. "She has powers of enchantment we were all ignorant of. Anyone would have done the same. If there is blame to be meted out, let us begin with the prince and the Guardians who abandoned us in our time of need. I'm merely doing what I can to sweep up the mess."

"And what of the mortals who had nothing to do with any of it, yet still serve in your brothel?"

"Like Destan Karatas, you mean? No one forced him to run up an enormous bill he had no means of paying. That was his choice. If he hadn't come here, he would be long dead. Forgotten. Don't feel too sorry for him."

"You must despise us," Lucas muttered.

Taj laughed aloud. "What, humans? I'll admit, it was no treat to be enslaved by your kind. But that was a very long time ago. My bitterness has faded. I know you're not all evil and cruel. Nor are we."

Lucas felt a surge of relief as Taj rose and moved away to pour two cups of wine.

"I don't drink," Lucas said firmly.

"I'm sorry, of course you don't." Taj set them aside untouched. "I should have guessed."

"What does that mean?" He hated the defensive note in his voice. Taj had a way of knocking him off kilter without seeming to try.

"Nothing at all." Taj tilted his head. "Only that you are different from Balthazar. You have a quiet soul, Mr. Devereaux." He glided back to the desk. "I find the quiet types to be far more interesting when you get to know them."

Lucas swallowed. The room was growing very warm. He reached for a sheaf of parchment.

"I need your seal on these—" he began hastily.

Taj laid a hand over his. The sleeve of his tunic rode up, revealing a bronzed, muscular forearm. "Can't they wait a little while?" he purred.

Lucas gazed up at him in helpless fascination. "This is all wrong," he managed.

"How?" Taj looked baffled.

"Because Balthazar hates you. And rightfully so."

"Do you hate me?" The thumb traced a lazy circle on his wrist.

"I . . . I'm not sure," Lucas admitted.

He had a few discreet lovers back in London. But Taj was . . . Lucas could find no other word except *spectacular*. It seemed his own personal Trial had arrived.

And he was on the verge of failing it miserably.

"Lucas," Taj murmured, drawing him closer by the wrist.

"Hmmm?" It was hard to focus. All the blood in his brain seemed to be rushing toward his nether regions.

"Whatever happens between us . . . ." Taj paused to tenderly kiss the scar. "Stays between us." Lucas felt the scrape of a beard against his cheek. "You have my word," Taj whispered.

No doubt there would be hell to pay tomorrow, but Lucas found he didn't care. He'd been existing in a state of unremitting stress and anxiety since Cairo. No, since *London*. He didn't like the food, or the heat, or the strange smells. That morning he'd found a spider in his shoe. A large, black, hairy one. He had shaken it out into the garden, not wanting to harm the hideous creature, but now he cringed every time he put his socks on. Balthazar, who had brought the whole colossal load of shit crashing down on them both, was being snappish and petty. He'd lost weight and the lack of digestive biscuits was wreaking havoc on his constitution. Lucas knew he looked like death warmed over.

Yet here was a *god* of a man who apparently found him attractive.

Not even the sight of the ouroboros lying against Taj's smooth chest was enough to pull him back from the brink.

"I won't use it on you," the daēva said in an amused tone, following his eyes. "I don't need it."

Lucas tore off his tie. "I know you don't."

Papers scattered. Inkpots spilled. He laughed with reckless abandon. Who needed digestives when there was *this*?

BALTHAZAR SLEPT POORLY, PLAGUED BY DREAMS OF A BLACK-haired witch on a broomstick who chased him across a pitted wasteland. He woke in a cold sweat before dawn.

The sword was propped in the corner. Balthazar stared at it for a long moment.

It had served him well for the first two Trials. But now a wave of superstitious dread washed over him – precisely the thing he had claimed to Destan that he was immune to. He thought of the child. The gift. How the gods despised hubris.

My mother says you will be our champion.

He had treated the boy in a rotten fashion. Not uttered a word of thanks.

And there had been runes on the staff. Not carved, but daēva-worked.

Did he dare reject it in such a cavalier way?

Did he dare *accept* it?

Balthazar dressed quickly and went to Lucas's chamber, where he lay in a deep slumber, a soft smile curling the edges of his mouth. Balthazar touched his arm. Lucas sat up, wide-eyed.

"My lord!" He ran a hand through his hair. "What time is it?"

"About four, I think." Balthazar's eyes narrowed. "You smell like . . . ."

Lucas drew back. He laughed. "Pardon?"

Balthazar studied the bright eyes, the excessively cheerful demeanor . . . the obvious love bite on his neck. "Sex," he concluded.

Lucas laughed again. "I don't know what—"

"Captain Karatas?" Balthazar hazarded.

Lucas seemed to find this even funnier. "The Turk? Er, no."

A short list of alternatives flitted through Balthazar's mind, but there was only one that made any sense.

"Oh," he said softly. "My God."

They stared at each other for a long minute.

"You could at least look sorry about it!" Balthazar finally erupted.

"Well, I'm not." Lucas crossed his arms defiantly. "It was very nice."

"Very nice is a cup of Darjeeling at your favorite tea shop." Balthazar gave a mirthless laugh. "I'd bet Taj was more than very nice."

"All right." Lucas pretended to think. "Do you prefer magnificent? Glorious? Heaven-sent?"

Balthazar paced the carpet. He halted and stabbed a finger into the air. "I know! It was the curse. That bastard took advantage of you—"

"We were within the wards at the time."

Balthazar glowered. "You did this to punish me, didn't you? I'll admit I was rude yesterday—"

Lucas threw his hands up. "It might be inconceivable, but not everything has to do with you." He leapt out of bed and paced to the balcony in his smallclothes. "Assuming you haven't been struck blind, you'll have noticed how diabolically attractive he is. You might prefer women, but if you were stranded on a desert island with him, I don't see you holding out for very long."

"That's not the point!" Balthazar blustered. "It's a matter of self-control—"

Lucas rounded on him. "Are you seriously going to talk about self-control?" he asked slowly. "To me?"

"Well, I . . . ."

"If you had any ability whatsoever to keep your trousers buttoned, we wouldn't be here in the first place!"

Balthazar frowned. "Now, listen—"

"No, you listen." Lucas's voice was neither loud nor accusing, but Balthazar had the cringing sensation it was about to get much worse. "I've watched you stumble home reeking of sex since I was ten. I have inadvertently walked in you *having sex* in nearly every room of the Mayfair house, not to mention your various other residences. I have procured prostitutes for you on dozens of occasions. I've listened to women weep and throw tantrums at your callous treatment. I've swept up broken crockery, paid off footmen, lied about your whereabouts literally thousands of times, and – when all else failed – faked your accidental death."

"You can stop now," Balthazar said tonelessly.

But Lucas was not to be stopped. He drew a deep breath. "I've fended off enraged husbands, lovers, sons, brothers and uncles. Do you recall the time in Kandahar when they came for you with torches and we had to ride through the mountains in a blizzard to escape an impromptu hanging? On donkeys?"

"I hoped you'd forgotten," Balthazar muttered, his gaze fixed on the date palms beyond the terrace.

"Well, I haven't. And I would point out that I have never, not once, chastised you for any of it."

"That's true."

"Yes, it is. So if I choose to have a fling with Taj, or really

214

anyone at all, you will refrain from expressing an opinion on the matter."

Balthazar was silent for a minute. He heaved a gusty sigh. "Am I so despicable?"

"Yes." Lucas's face softened. "And no. You've performed acts of great generosity on occasion." He smiled. "I keep your books. You think I don't know?"

"Blood money," Balthazar mumbled.

"Call it what you will. I also know you care for each of them in your own way. You're cruel so they go away, but you don't enjoy it. You do it to protect them. Just as I protect you." His jaw set. "Because I . . . I love you no matter what you do."

Balthazar didn't answer. He suddenly felt every second of his age. All those long centuries pressing down. And for what purpose?

In the end, what was his life truly worth?

"It's time," Lucas said in a gentler tone.

The sky was lightening in the east. Balthazar joined him on the terrace. "If I don't come back, it all goes to you. The documents are in the safe."

Lucas scowled. "I don't want your money."

"You'll get it anyway." Balthazar laid a hand on his arm. "But don't worry. I plan to come back." His mouth curved in a wicked grin. "Where's your golden-haired lover?"

Lucas shot him a quick, suspicious glance. "Why?"

"I just want a quick word with him. Not about you, don't worry."

"Probably on his balcony."

Balthazar started for the door and turned back. "I need you to do something for me."

He told Lucas what he wanted, giving as precise a description as he could. The oak tree was the largest in the park. It wouldn't be hard to find. Lucas frowned but nodded. "I'll try."

Yatha and Jabaar stood guard outside his chamber. Balthazar asked the jinn to help Lucas with his task. Then he made his way to the city gates and followed the stairs up to the balconies. He found Taj alone, sipping a cup of black coffee. The daēva watched him approach with wary eyes.

"It's none of my business," Balthazar said. "But I do have one thing to say to you."

Taj waited, preternaturally still. In the early morning light, he looked like some Greek statue – and with as much emotion.

"Lucas Devereaux is the most decent man I've ever known. If you break his heart, I *will* come for you. Even if it's as a revenant."

Balthazar expected some sardonic reply, but Taj merely looked thoughtful. "Lucas is not a child. He understands the nature of the relationship. That said, I never make promises I can't keep, Balthazar."

"Fine." His lips thinned. "But here's one you'll make to me right now. If I die, you will let him go. With an escort, so he isn't wandering the bloody desert."

"Done," Taj replied immediately. "Lucas owes me nothing. He is only here because of his loyalty to you. But he deserves the choice of staying if he wishes."

"Fair enough," Balthazar agreed. "I have your word?"

"You have my word."

"Thank you."

The balconies around them were starting to fill up with spectators. The marids stood at their cardinal points around the circle. But no crowd waited at the gates. They were all dead, save for three.

"You'd best get down there," Taj said. "The gong will sound any minute. Where's your sword?"

"I'm not carrying it today."

Taj's brows drew together, but he nodded. "I trust you know what you're doing, Balthazar. Good luck. I'll see you after."

Balthazar dashed down the stairs two at a time. If Lucas hadn't found it . . . . He had a knife strapped to his calf, but no other weapon. A group of daēvas passed him on their way up to the balconies. They were forced to flatten themselves against the wall as he thundered past. The stairs led straight down to the gates. He saw with relief that Lucas waited for him there.

Balthazar's hand trembled as it closed around the oak staff. Words in a flowing script ran down the shaft, either the language of the jinn or something even older, for he couldn't read it.

"Hurry, my lord," Lucas urged. Sweat beaded his pale brow. "You're late!"

Fulad-zereh stood in the jaws of the dragon-cloud. She stared at them with a posture of impatience, hands on hips, head jutting forward like a hawk about to launch itself towards prey.

Lucas's final words were lost to the rush of blood in his ears as Balthazar ran for the arena.

CHAPTER 18

The veiled assassin and the Blue Man were already waiting inside the circle. The instant Balthazar crossed the line, a wall of flames erupted. He hurried to a place equidistant from the others, who stood well apart from each other.

No allies today. It would be every man and woman for themselves.

The Tuareg stared straight ahead, the butt of his spear propped in the sand. The assassin gave Balthazar a brief nod, noting his staff with a minuscule twitch of one eyebrow. Her hands were empty, but she was surely armed to the teeth beneath her black robes.

The ifrit glowered at Balthazar as he raised the mallet.

"Let the third round of the Ninth Trials commence!" he bellowed without preamble.

They all knew the rules by now.

The gong sounded.

There was no wait this time. In a single disorienting instant, Balthazar found himself in the thick of battle.

Acrid black smoke filled the arena. The smell of burning flesh took him straight back to the Druj wars – that, and the

Antimagi who strode through the circle with human captives linked by collars and chains to the necromancers' wrists. They were fighting Immortals, bonded pairs of human and daēva who served the Persian king.

Black lightning lanced down, scorching the sand to sheets of obsidian glass. He heard the clash of iron swords. The roar of revenants when a necromancer fell. The screams of the Immortals when the daēva of the pair drew too much power and incinerated them both. The Persians wore tunics of scarlet and robin's egg blue with a roaring griffin emblazoned in gold on the chest.

Balthazar looked down at himself. His eyes narrowed. He wore the close-fitting leathers of an Antimagus, fashioned from human skin. Even back in the day when he was as pitiless as the rest of them, he had scorned that uniform, preferring simple cotton tunics.

An illusion, he reminded himself firmly. *All of it.*

Through the haze of smoke, he watched one of the Antimagi approach. He was even taller than Balthazar, with yellow hair and a razor slash for a mouth. His four captives had the blank eyes of dolls. Skin hung in loose, shrunken folds on their emaciated bodies. A yank of the chains brought them stumbling forward.

"Brother!" the necromancer exclaimed, a mad light dancing in his eyes.

"Molon," Balthazar replied grimly.

Molon was nearly as thin as his captives, but Balthazar knew he was much stronger than he looked. He carried a black blade that seemed to absorb the light.

"I've waited a long time for this," the necromancer said softly. "A very long time indeed."

Balthazar wondered if he'd made a fatal error leaving his own sword behind. He gripped the staff in both hands. It was barely as thick as his thumb.

Molon discarded the bracelet linking him to his captives.

They knelt on the ground, staring at nothing. He stepped forward and paused. Deep-set eyes flicked across the staff.

"What's that toy you've brought?" Scornful laughter. "Let's cut it in twain, shall we?"

Molon suddenly pivoted and brought the sword down in a crushing overhead blow aimed at Balthazar's head. He parried, expecting it to cleave through his defense with ease. But when sword met staff, the runes flashed blue fire. The slender oak held. Before Molon could lower his guard, Balthazar delivered a stinging crack to his ribs. Molon staggered back. His eyes widened.

They circled each other.

"Filthy traitor," Molon spat. "You were never truly one of us."

"Which is why I'm alive and you're two thousand years dead," Balthazar replied calmly. "*Brother.*"

Again and again, his staff parried the black sword. Distant screams cut the air, including the enraged howl of a woman he felt sure was the assassin. Each must be facing their own Trial. Who knew what nightmares the others were seeing?

Balthazar spun the staff, muscles loosening as they remembered their training. That was one advantage of a long life. Time to master every form of combat. The sword was his first love, but he would have been remiss to neglect other weapons. And staffs were underrated. They had reach not even a longsword could equal.

In three brutal moves, he cracked Molon on the knee, wrist and skull. The necromancer crumpled. Balthazar drove the butt end of the staff into the hollow of his throat. Molon bared yellow teeth. He jerked and writhed. His captives fell over in boneless heaps. Balthazar reached for the black blade, thinking he'd better take the head to be certain. It vanished before he could touch it. So did Molon and the captives.

Yet the scene did not change. He leaned on the staff, panting. His skin felt clammy where the leathers touched him. The oily stink of burning flesh filled his nose.

Not real.

Another necromancer strode from the smoke. This time it was Vashi. Black-haired and broad-shouldered, with a pointy beard he took inordinate pride in. Also one of their very best with a sword.

"I've waited a long time for this," the necromancer said softly. "A very long time indeed."

He raised his blade.

Balthazar lost track of time after that. He killed Vashi, and six more. By the end, he didn't bother waiting for them to speak. His assaults were savage and relentless. Batter down the defenses and crush the windpipe. One after another, they fell to his staff.

But the scene never changed. The gong didn't sound. He had no idea if the other contenders were alive or dead.

He wondered if he would have to destroy every single one of his brethren.

At the peak of the war, they numbered in the hundreds. He didn't even know all of their names.

A wave of exhaustion rolled over him. But he would do what he had to.

He would not lose.

They came in pairs. Then three at once. Thought ceased. Balthazar bent all his attention to keeping those black swords from slicing his flesh. Every few seconds, blue fire flickered along the staff as oak met Bactrian-forged iron. Perhaps a little of the power leaked into him, because he fought long past the point where stamina should have given out.

Finally, they stopped coming.

He stared into the smoke, as blank-faced as the captives, waiting. For what, he wasn't sure.

But he knew it wasn't over. Not yet.

A figure emerged from the murk. Tall and straight, with a

long grey beard. White robes dragged though the sand at his feet. He, too, carried a staff, though he used it to lean on.

Not real.

Balthazar's heart sped up as the figure slowly approached.

"My son," Zarathustra said. "I am truly sorry to see you in this place."

He spoke in old Avestan. Hearing his learned, kindly voice brought vivid memories rushing back. The tide nearly swept Balthazar off his feet.

"I'm not your son," he said hoarsely.

The magus stroked his long beard. It was a gesture Balthazar knew well.

"Not by blood. But I loved you as one."

Balthazar retreated a step. "Get away from me."

"I have not come to harm you," Zarathustra replied. "Only to give you a piece of advice."

"You're dead," Balthazar whispered. "I watched you cross the Cold Sea."

The magus moved closer, spidery fingers gripping the staff. He lifted shaggy white brows. The eyes beneath were sharp and bright. "Do you remember when I told you there is always a choice?"

Against his will, Balthazar nodded.

"This war you fight is futile. Come with me now." His voice grew gentle. "It is your time."

"No!"

His weathered face assumed a sorrowful look. "Do you not know, Balthazar? Your soul has already been parted from your body."

Suddenly, he realized that the arena had fallen silent. Empty. There was only that acrid, swirling smoke.

"This is an abomination," Balthazar growled. "Go, before I destroy you!"

Zarathustra gazed at him serenely. "Look in your heart. You know I speak the truth."

In answer, Balthazar swept his staff at the old man's head. The magus parried. Then they were trading blows, lightning-fast. Balthazar felt a rib crack. When his daēva staff met the other, the runes blazed, but with a sickly, dying light. The old man had his own power.

Balthazar took another hard whack on the shoulder. In desperation, he feinted left. The magus took the bait, leaving an opening. Balthazar reversed his strike in midair. The staff flew from gnarled hands.

Their eyes met. Zarathustra's voice sank low. "Please. Don't—"

The words turned to a blood-choked gasp. Balthazar yanked the staff back, tears filling his eyes.

He watched the magus die clutching his ruined throat.

"Fulad-zereh!" he howled at the sky. "Where are you? Come down and fight me!"

No answer came.

Only another conjuration in the guise of the man he revered above all others.

The one he had betrayed to Neblis. And would now betray again.

Balthazar hardened his heart. He readied the staff.

"How many times will you kill me, Balthazar?" the Prophet asked.

"As many times as it takes," he snarled.

"Have you forgotten who absolved you of your sins?" Zarathustra asked quietly.

"I've forgotten nothing. But you *are not him*."

The magus gazed at him steadily. "Your soul was a with-ered, blackened husk when I found you. You barely deserved to be called a man. But there was still a part of you, deep down inside—"

Balthazar launched a frenzied attack, driving the magus back. Shame and hatred burned in him. The staff was a deadly blur. With each shattering blow, he felt himself slide nearer to the abyss. When the old man finally crumbled under the onslaught, Balthazar sank to his knees. He seized Zarathustra's trembling hand and pressed it to his lips. He felt warm, living flesh the instant before it vanished. The coppery taste of blood lingered on his mouth.

The next one appeared unarmed, until he drew a dagger from his sleeve and tried to plunge it into Balthazar's chest. The one after sought to engage him in a philosophical debate, as they used to do in the magus's chambers when Balthazar was still a novice. The third incarnation came weeping in chains, screaming at him to help, please, for the love of the Holy Father, they're coming to lock me away in a dark cell. . . .

Each ultimately tried to kill him, and was killed in turn.

Balthazar bowed his head, clinging to the staff for support.

Not *this*. He'd rather be whipped and flayed. Given to the revenants for sport. *Anything.*

The gong would never sound. He understood that now. It would just go on and on. Death without end. Pain without hope of mercy.

He knelt there, silent tears streaming down his cheeks, until he heard a soft footfall behind.

He turned and forced himself to stand.

"You're not real," he said brokenly.

The magus smiled. "When we parted on the shore of the Cold Sea, do you recall what I said to you, Balthazar?"

He licked parched, bloody lips. "That I must never return to the Dominion."

Zarathustra's eyes narrowed. "And have you kept that promise?"

Balthazar hesitated. He knew there was no point in engaging with this thing, but at least it would postpone the inevitable violence. "Partly."

The magus laughed. "Ever the equivocator. I know where you've been and what you've done." He frowned. "I know why you're still alive. But none of that matters. You have another choice now. The most important choice you'll ever make. Come peacefully with me or remain in this arena until you perish from exhaustion. What will it be?"

"I will fight you," Balthazar replied wearily.

The magus nodded. "So be it."

His gaze flicked over Balthazar's shoulder.

Balthazar started to turn, but he reacted an instant too late. The black blade pierced him straight through, catching on the broken rib before it erupted from his side. He screamed.

He fell.

A second magus stood over him, this one clad in pale leathers, a dripping sword in his hand. Zarathustra made the sign of the flame, fingers brushing forehead, lips and heart. He bent down and closed Balthazar's eyes.

Balthazar saw himself in the robes of a novice, praying at the fire altar in Karnopolis. He saw himself enter a cistern, sinking down and down. He saw Neblis as she first appeared to him, young and beautiful and full of promises she never quite kept.

He saw himself, pinned by her hand beneath chill waters, the very last time they saw each other. The iron grip around his throat. The smile playing on her rosebud lips.

A voice came from the green murk. Zarathustra.

"Get up!"

Balthazar scrabbled in the sand, but Neblis just shoved him deeper.

"Get up, Balthazar! Get on your feet, you—"

"—BASTARD! GET UP!"

Balthazar's eyes fluttered open.

The last reverberations of the gong were fading.

His side throbbed as though it held a live coal. Through a

sheet of flame, he saw Lucas. Just beyond the edge of the circle.

Lucas shouted and cursed. He tried to reach across the perimeter and was driven back, blisters rising on his arm. But Balthazar, who lay within inches of the flames, felt no heat.

Only the contenders can pass through the flames, he recalled vaguely.

"Get up!" Lucas screamed again. "Damn you, Balthazar! Use the staff!"

He tried to speak, but his mouth was full of blood.

"The staff!"

Warm sand brushed his groping hand. Numb fingers closed around the slender oak shaft. But the thought of further movement seemed ridiculous. Death stood at his shoulder. Balthazar was ready to welcome it. Why didn't they just let him go?

He turned his head a fraction and saw Taj. The daēva met his eyes. He looked resigned. It was a look that said, *Oh, well. You gave it your best shot. And you weren't quite good enough, were you? Don't feel bad about it. I understand. We'll give you a hero's sendoff. And I'll keep Lucas as my pet, until I tire of him, of course . . . .*

Balthazar summoned the last of his reserves. At the least, he wouldn't die inside this bloody circle. Half-fainting, he levered himself to sitting. Gore stained the sand around him. He grasped the staff in both hands and gritted his teeth. When he pushed to his feet, he felt things tear loose inside. Breath whistled through the hole in his chest. A knee buckled. He forced it straight.

A deep, sonorous tolling enveloped him. It sounded like a death knell. With a scream of agony, Balthazar stepped through the flames.

CHAPTER 19

Zarifa watched in horror as Lucas cradled Balthazar in his arms. A steady flow leaked from the wound in his side. It was bright red heart's blood.

A very bad sign.

She pressed a hand to her mouth, sick with regret. She'd vowed not to watch the Trials, and she hadn't — not until the very end. She'd come out to the balcony just in time to see him fall to the blade of an invisible assailant. Taj had been unable to stop Lucas from running down to the arena and Zarifa had followed, fearing the worst.

I should have let him go. Walked away from the bazaar and never looked back.

Balthazar's face was ashen. Lucas tore open the coat and shirt and grimaced. He'd been stabbed clean through a lung. Through the blood, Zarifa saw the white gleam of bone. His ribcage was shattered.

"Heal him!" Lucas screamed.

Taj knelt down, but he didn't even try to touch Balthazar. "I'm so sorry," he said quietly. "That wound . . . it's beyond my skill."

"Try anyway!"

"The shock would kill him for certain."

Lucas seized a fistful of Taj's tunic. His eyes were wild. "Then who can?"

Taj held his gaze. "The regent. Perhaps. But he despises me. And he hasn't spoken in more than a century—"

"I don't give a toss!" Lucas tried to lift Balthazar in his arms, staggering beneath the weight. Zarifa hurried forward. "Let me help."

They each took an arm. Balthazar's feet dragged in the dirt. His head hung limp against his chest.

Taj rose and clapped his hands. Yatha materialized, his hands pressed together.

"Yes, master?"

"To the throne room," Taj snapped. "All of us. Now!"

The ground wavered. Zarifa shared a quick look with Lucas and tightened her grip on Balthazar. She drew a breath. When she exhaled, two huge bronze doors stood before them. Taj didn't knock. He just pushed them open and strode inside.

Zarifa and Lucas followed, Balthazar a dead weight between them. A marble hall with a double row of huge pillars stretched ahead. Each column was covered with an intricate motif of interlocking flowers and geometrical designs, but the hall itself was long and gloomy, the walls naked stone. The place felt cold and sterile. Devoid of life.

"This way," Taj said. He slowed his pace to match theirs, which was as fast as they could manage considering Balthazar's size. Blood soaked Zarifa's robe, a terrifying quantity of it. Balthazar's head rested against her shoulder. She couldn't tell if he was still breathing.

Hang on, damn you, she thought furiously.

"Couldn't you have taken us straight to the regent?" Lucas panted.

"Jinn are not permitted within the throne room," Taj replied tightly. "Not anymore."

Their footsteps echoed in the cavernous chamber, but it was otherwise silent.

"Are you sure he's still here?" Zarifa whispered.

"Oh, he's here," Taj said in a dry voice. "Honor would not allow him to leave without telling me. And Mikal has *honor* – if nothing else."

They did not speak after that, only hurried onward to the far end where a golden throne sat on a dais. Light filtered through a round stained glass window set far above, but the throne was cloaked in shadow. She glanced at Taj. His expression was unreadable. *What if he's wrong?* Zarifa thought, near panic now. *What if—*

At the sound of their approach, the shadows stirred. Some primal instinct urged her to drop her burden and run, but her feet kept going. She owed Balthazar that much.

He was unlike anyone she'd ever known. A bundle of contradictions; jaded and self-absorbed on the surface, but she'd caught glimmers of a different man beneath. One who'd had lived through two millennia without losing his sense of humor. Who had witnessed the rise and fall of empires, seen places and things she could only imagine, yet still cared enough about a perfect stranger to offer his help – even if his motives were tangled up in seduction.

Balthazar was one of a kind. It couldn't end here, in this barren, dismal hall.

It couldn't.

As they drew closer, Zarifa saw that the throne was not empty.

The regent lifted his head. Her breath froze in her throat.

Mikal had blue-black skin and wings of iridescent ebony feathers that gleamed like metal. He wore a golden breastplate that she had mistaken for the throne itself. His eyes were the same burnished gold. They flared in anger.

"What is this?" The voice roared like thunder in her ears.

The archangel rose to his full height. Black wings flared. "You dare enter my sanctuary without permission?"

Zarifa clung to Balthazar, who did not stir. She wanted to fall to her knees. To beg forgiveness. Lucas whispered fervently in French. It sounded like the Lord's Prayer.

Only Taj was unmoved by the archangel's wrath.

"The champion is dying," he said simply.

Mikal's eyes moved to Balthazar. Zarifa saw not an ounce of pity in that stern gaze.

"Your champion is not dying," the regent said.

"What? Can you not see—"

"He is already dead."

There was a terrible silence. The color drained from Taj's face.

"No," he mumbled. "It cannot be. . . ."

Lucas pressed his fingers to the pulse point at Balthazar's neck. His hand trembled slightly. A long minute passed. Lucas made not a sound, but his fingers finally released and clenched the bloody shirt collar.

Zarifa sank down to the marble floor, easing Balthazar's head into her lap. His features had relaxed, the mouth soft. At least there would be no more pain. Tears spilled down her cheeks. She smoothed the dark hair from his brow. Lucas knelt next to her. His gaze was unfocused, lost.

"Go," the angel said, settling back on the throne. "You have come too late. Now leave me."

Taj's hands balled into fists. He took a step forward.

"You can still bring him back."

Lucas's head shot up, the sudden hope in his eyes painful to behold.

"That is not my purpose here," Mikal replied.

Zarifa stole a quick glance. He was beautiful, with high cheekbones and a shaved skull, but his face was terrifying in its utter aloofness.

"I know how much you despise us," Taj said. "How much

you regret accepting this regency. Well, this is your chance to get out! Restore his soul. Let him take back the sword. Then you can leave this place forever."

Mikal gripped the arms of the throne. A trickle of dust filtered down as the stone cracked. "It's against the rules," he growled.

"I disagree. He walked out of the arena alone and unaided at the end of the third round."

Mikal said nothing.

"No one else has ever achieved that!" Taj persisted. "Healing is permitted. Why not resurrection? It's not explicitly forbidden."

The angel glowered. "I know the contract. Better than you do."

"Then you know it says only that the champion must leave the arena alive."

"No." Mikal's voice rang with contempt. "You are like a cunning little eel, seeking to wriggle out of the net. But I will not allow it! In the spirit of fairness—"

"Fairness?" Taj demanded, his voice rising. "There is nothing *fair* about the Trials! He was in there for hours. The gong did not sound until he'd taken a fatal wound! Having watched nine of them in succession, I can assure you that it never sounds until all hope is lost. Can you not see that *this* is the last Trial, regent? The only way out of the arena is to die! That is the true pact Fulad-zereh has offered us and if you deem it *fair*, you have lost all sense of honor." Taj filled his next words with scorn. "Perhaps not even you are beyond her corrupting influence."

Zarifa had been quietly cheering him on, but now she feared he had gone too far. The angel towered above them from the dais. Those mighty wings extended to their full reach with a metallic crack. Power gathered in the chamber, a subtle displacement of the air that made her skin itch.

Zarifa wasn't sure if it came from the angel or the daēva. Both, perhaps.

Taj went lethally still. His lips pressed together, his head lowered like a bull about to charge. She had never seen a daēva in battle, but she knew the stories.

They were all about to die.

She flinched as Mikal suddenly strode down the three steps, ignoring Taj completely. His gaze fixed on Balthazar.

"If he's gone to the boats, it's too late. Even I cannot bring a soul back once the crossing is underway."

"Then there's no time to waste," Taj said, his posture relaxing slightly.

The archangel stared at Zarifa and Lucas, who still huddled over the body.

"Get out of my way," he said.

She gently lifted Balthazar's head from her skirts and laid it on the stone floor. Then she scrambled back with unashamed haste. Lucas did the same.

Mikal bent one knee. His huge wings folded down, embracing them both until Balthazar's body was hidden from view. To Zarifa's surprise, Lucas reached for her hand and held it tight. She gave him a brief reassuring nod.

"Shield your eyes," the angel commanded.

HE STOOD ALONE ON A LONG, DESOLATE SHORE.

Water like milky glass stretched to the horizon. His hair stirred in a chill wind that didn't touch the surface. No sun or stars or moon illuminated the sky above. All was cloaked in the eternal twilight of the Dominion.

A boat with reefed black sails drifted a short distance out. Small enough for a lone man.

He couldn't remember how he came here. One moment

the world was blind agony. Then the stench of his wound had faded. He'd smelled a fresh salt breeze.

The Cold Sea.

I fought to my last breath, he thought, wonder and sadness mingling. To the last ounce of blood. There is nothing more to sacrifice. Nothing more to give.

The final debt has been paid.

He gazed out at the water.

Balthazar had feared this moment for as long as he could remember. The Great Reckoning. But all was still and quiet, the boat drifting gently. He did not know what lay on the other side of the Cold Sea, but this mystery held no terror anymore.

A strange relief filled him. He was just a man after all.

Two thousand years ago, he had nearly died on this shore. But he had been saved.

Reborn.

Now it would end where it began.

He waded out, aware that he now wore a simple white tunic. He himself had named it the Cold Sea, and the water *was* cold, but the sensation felt distant. A small swell lifted the boat. It broke against the sand, soaking the hem of his tunic where it met his thighs.

Balthazar felt a twinge of unease. He had brought Zarathustra here long ago. The sea had been smooth as a pond. He took another step. A wave curled and exploded into foam, shoving him back.

The black-sailed boat began drifting further away.

Along the shore, he saw four dark shapes running at full speed.

Old, instinctive fear gripped him.

They could only be Shepherds, the massive hounds that guided the dead across the Cold Sea.

They despised necromancers above all things.

But he wasn't that, was he? Not anymore.

I must reach the boat, he thought desperately. Before they pull me down.

The dogs caught his scent. The one in the lead howled. They angled towards him, heavy hindquarters bunching and lengthening. He knew they could never be outrun. Not once they had his scent.

Frantic baying erupted as he threw himself into the turbulent waters. A wave seized him and tumbled him into its frigid undertow. He broke the surface, arms thrashing. The dogs stood in a line on the shore. Saliva flew from massive jaws as they snarled and snapped.

But they feared the waves. The largest ventured forward . . . and retreated with a whimper as water surged up the beach.

He found his feet and dove beneath the next wave. He could still see the boat, though a current was dragging it away. He started stroking for it, long arms slicing the water in an easy rhythm. When he'd passed the line of combers, he turned back and made a rude gesture at the Shepherds. They sat on their haunches, panting. Oddly enough, they seemed to be *grinning*.

A shadow fell across him.

Balthazar turned in time to see the largest wave yet towering above. A solid mountain of water that was just cresting white at the summit. His eyes widened. Then he was lifted like a doll and hurled with shocking speed upon the shore. He'd barely gained hands and knees before they were upon him. Teeth gripped his tunic, dragging him through the wet sand.

But that wasn't the worst of it.

Something *else* was coming.

A figure that blazed so fiercely he could only throw an arm across his face, though it did him little good. He felt his eyes boil in the sockets, his hair sizzle to ash. The dogs howled. The light grew brighter, brighter, a thousand stars exploding in unison.

Then he was falling through blessed darkness.

Falling being a relative term. He wasn't sure what could be left of him.

I think I've just been judged, he thought.

And Balthazar started to laugh.

CHAPTER 20

"*Why do you fight?*"

The voice was deep and relentless.

Balthazar rolled over and spat blood. He drew a ragged breath.

The question came again, this time with a sharp note of impatience.

"Why do you fight?"

Vision returned in hazy fragments. He lay on a stone floor. A large chamber, for its recesses faded to shadow.

"Give him a minute, won't you?"

The second voice, dry and faintly condescending, sounded like Taj. Balthazar frowned. He saw a hand in front of his face. The fingers flexed.

My hand.

I have a hand.

Someone crouched next to him. They lifted him up.

"My lord?"

Lucas's anxious face peered at him.

"Where are we?" Balthazar managed. His own voice sounded surprisingly strong.

"The throne room of the Summer Palace."

He blinked. "The Palace?"

"You were . . . healed."

Even in his befuddled state, Balthazar caught the slight hesitation.

"By whom?"

Lucas swallowed. "By *him*." He turned Balthazar's shoulders.

"Ahhhh." The word came out more as a lengthy sigh of amazement.

The regent sat upon a marble throne shot through with veins of crystal. His polished gold breastplate looked dull against the gleaming metal of his dark feathers, the burnished ebony of his skin. An aura of vast, ancient power surrounded him. There was no hint of welcome on that stern visage. He leaned forward, gaze intent.

"Why do you fight?"

Taj watched them both with loosely folded arms. He'd struck a casual pose, but he radiated tension. To Balthazar's surprise, Zarifa was there, too. She gave him a tentative smile.

"Pardon?" he asked.

"Is the question so difficult to comprehend?" the regent snapped. "Why do you contest the Trials? What is your motive to endure such hardship?"

The chamber fell silent. He felt Taj staring, but he wasn't about to lie to a bloody *archangel*.

"A bargain," Balthazar said.

"Bargain?" The angel's brows lowered. "What *bargain*?"

"The sword for a talisman. It was stolen from me. Taj has it, and he said—"

Mikal's rage was a thing to behold. Incandescent barely described it. He rounded on Taj. "You tricked me!"

The daēva was all wide-eyed innocence. "In what way, regent?"

"This mortal was compelled to fight. It is an outrage. An

abomination!" He slammed a fist down, shearing off the arm of the throne. "Where is this plundered relic?"

Taj hastily lifted the ouroboros from around his neck.

"Return it at once," Mikal roared. "I didn't believe your race could sink any lower, but it seems I was wrong. You have broken every law, trampled every edict. But this!" His voice sank to a deadly hiss. "You are worse than the demon herself. At least she respects free will."

"I warned him not to enter," Taj protested. "I offered him reasonable alternatives. He insisted—"

The angel cut him off with a glare. "What satisfaction do you demand?" he asked Balthazar. "Hand? Nose? Both?"

Balthazar let Taj twist in the wind for a minute, pretending to mull it over. He rose creakily to his feet. Balthazar slipped a hand into his pocket, palm closing around the gold watch. He held it often, fancying he could detect its ticking pulse. Now it felt strangely lifeless.

"No," he said at last. "Taj is not the one who stole it. Not directly." He glanced at Zarifa, who had gone a sickly green. "Having my property returned is adequate."

"Do it," Mikal growled.

Taj strode forward, his expression unreadable. He thrust the ouroboros at Balthazar without a word.

Balthazar gazed at the talisman in his fist. His eyes misted. He hung it around his own neck, a familiar comforting weight.

How swiftly the tables turn, he thought with satisfaction. Balthazar decided that he liked this regent, even if his bedside manner was a touch abrupt. He only wished he'd come here *before* being repeatedly skewered.

"Well," he said briskly. "Good luck to you all. Come, Lucas. We'll be on our way now."

Taj seized his arm. Balthazar scowled at him. "Let go of me."

"You were dead," Taj grated. "He brought you back to

find the sword for us. You are the champion! And you would walk away?"

The niggling doubt that had entered his mind when Lucas claimed he was healed now returned, though it wasn't *niggling* anymore. He'd assumed it was all a fever dream.

"What did you just say?" Balthazar asked softly.

"That you *owe* us—"

"No. I mean the first part."

"Don't you know? You were dead." Taj pointed to the trail of blood leading the length of the long hall. The trail that Balthazar had avoided looking at too closely. "It happened somewhere along there, I suppose." Taj shrugged. "But you had a heartbeat when you left the arena. Technically, you're still the champion."

Balthazar digested this in silence for a long minute.

"So the Shepherds—"

"I sent them," Mikal said. "Had you reached the boat, you would have crossed."

A chill swept over him as he remembered how hard he'd fought to escape.

Lucas laid a hand on his shoulder. "You were only gone for a few minutes, but . . . ."

"I was actually *dead*?"

"Yes."

"Not at death's door?" Balthazar asked hopefully.

"No. Well, you were when we first arrived. But then . . . you passed the threshold."

Balthazar pulled out his watch with an unsteady hand. The hands were frozen at 11:57. He stared into space, the ouroboros forgotten.

It was real.

I nearly crossed the Cold Sea.

Emotions warred within him, too many to absorb at once. But the greatest was relief.

He didn't know what waited on the other side – no one

did, not even the Prophet – but he had not been thrown into one of the lower levels of the Dominion. He knew the creatures that dwelt there. Things of shadow and flame and bottomless hatred. All had once walked beneath the sun. They were too corrupted to make the crossing. Now they existed in a miserable limbo, feeding on whatever scraps they could glean from the living.

But a boat had awaited him. His soul was pure enough for that at least.

Just a man after all.

He released a long breath.

"The Trials are not finished," Taj said. "There is still the matter of the sword."

Balthazar turned to him. "Still the matter of the sword," he repeated slowly. "Are you *fucking joking*?"

"Not in the least."

"Then I suggest you go collect it yourself."

Taj scowled. "Believe me, if the demon permitted it, I would go without hesitation. I would have fought in the Trials! Given my own life a thousand times over. But she forbids it!" He clenched a fist. "It *has* to be you."

"And what's in it for me, eh?" Balthazar wondered. "Besides another quick trip to the Dominion."

The regent watched them both with an expression of distaste.

"So this is your best hope?" He sighed. "Let him go, Taj. The champion must be pure of heart or he will fail."

Balthazar laughed. "You see? I'm afraid I'm disqualified."

"You're condemning us to death!" Taj seethed. "If the balance is not restored, the protective magic will collapse. Already it wavers! We will be exposed to the world. The Turks will come and the British will come and Al Miraj will be no more. They'll either destroy it with cannons or sell tickets to tourists!"

"You have jinn," Balthazar said. "Fight them off."

"It doesn't matter how many we kill. You *know* that. They'll just keep coming. And there's an endless supply of them."

"Not my problem."

The daēva looked away, but not before Balthazar saw the mask slip. His perfect composure was finally cracking under a tide of emotion. "I haven't dared to nurture hope in nine centuries," he said in a low voice. "I accepted our inevitable fate. But you . . . . You gave me hope. And now you snatch it back."

"I thought you didn't believe in me," Balthazar snapped.

Taj turned to face him. "I might have exaggerated."

The truth hit. He felt a perfect fool. "Oh, you bastard."

"If I'd asked you to contest, what would you have said, Balthazar? But if you thought you were doing it to spite me. Well . . . ." He licked his lips. "What does it really matter? You've come this far." A hint of the old taunting entered his voice. "Are you afraid to finish it?"

Balthazar smiled. "Call me a coward, I honestly don't care. This is not my war."

Taj's face hardened. "I won't let you leave."

"You *will*," Mikal grated. "I've allowed you far too much autonomy. That fault is mine. But I will not permit this." He turned to Balthazar, his voice ringing with command. "By direct order of the appointed regent, Watchtower of the East, the Divine Messenger and Sword Hand of the Creator, you are free to leave Al Miraj at the time of your choosing." He glared at the daēva. "With all limbs and senses intact!"

Taj spun on his heel and stormed away, his swift steps echoing through the hall. Balthazar gave the regent a deep bow.

"Thank you," he said. "You've restored my faith in . . . whatever, er, deity you . . . represent."

The archangel stared down at him, sudden weariness dimming his gold eyes. He flicked a listless finger.

"Just go. All of you."
Balthazar didn't wait to be told twice.

No jinn appeared with magic carpets so they walked
back to the Golden Flail.

Eyes followed Balthazar's passage from every window.
Lucas and Zarifa trailed along behind, but they seemed to
realize he was in no mood for conversation and left him a
wide berth.

Balthazar kept his own gaze straight ahead. The resurrection had left his body in perfect condition. His mental state
was another matter. He wanted to put Al Miraj as far behind
him as he could. To lose himself in the teeming masses of
London. He craved the belch of factories and rattle of
carriage wheels; street lamps and rude cab drivers and gentleman's clubs where the butler didn't wear a shemagh. He
wanted to forget what he had done, and what had been done
to him.

Given enough time and alcohol, he might just manage it.

Back at the brothel, Balthazar went in search of Taj,
determined to make him fulfill his promise on the instant. Not
surprisingly, the daēva was nowhere to be found. Zarifa left
them while Lucas rooted out Jabaar, who claimed ignorance.

"The regent said—"

"It's all very well what the regent said," Jabaar interrupted
with an evil smile. "But Taj is my master. It is his orders I
follow, and his only."

Captain Karatas expressed relief and surprise to see Balthazar alive, and promised to keep an eye out. He was with the
Seneschal, who in turn had been searching for Zarifa. Lucas
quietly informed her of the morning's events and she agreed
to "let the girl off the hook" until the next day.

"He can't hide from me forever," Balthazar snarled, once he and Lucas returned to their chambers.

"I'm sure he'll appear. At least you got the talisman back."

"No thanks to Taj!"

Lucas sighed. "You weren't there . . . ." He paused. "Well, you were there, but not *there*, if you know what I mean."

"What's your point?"

"That you would be dead if not for Taj. The regent refused to bring you back. He said it was against the rules. Taj made a forceful argument. Baited him. *Fought* for your soul. I didn't even suspect it was possible."

Balthazar gave him a level look. "You do realize he only did that because he needed a champion?"

"Who cares? I thought Mikal would kill him. Hate Taj if you must, but he's apparently the only person in this city willing to stand up to the regent."

"You're just besotted," Balthazar grumbled.

"Give me a little more credit. Taj will keep his word. He has no choice."

"Then you go find him," Balthazar snapped. "Or I'll return to the palace and inform the Sword Hand of the Creator that I changed my mind and want Taj's nose after all. And maybe some other bits, too!"

Lucas left. Balthazar paced the chamber in his blood-spattered shirtsleeves. He felt no relief at being alive. No joy at regaining the ouroboros. Only a bitter disappointment whose source he couldn't quite pinpoint.

All for nothing. I could have gone to the regent on the first day here. Taj must have known, the lying bastard.

But that was only part of it. He had his talisman, but there was something he wanted almost as much. Something he'd never really *stopped* wanting.

And he couldn't have it. He could never have it.

The skin on his neck prickled. Balthazar spun around,

hoping it might be Taj. Instead, Zarifa stood at the curtained doorway.

"May I come in?"

When he didn't refuse her, she slipped inside.

"Why are you here?" he asked warily.

Zarifa drew a deep breath. "First, to say I'm sorry. I never meant for any of this to happen. I only wanted to sell you back the talisman. To have something to start a new life with. That's all."

A dozen sharp retorts sprang to mind, but he simply nodded. "What's the second?"

She paused, her face solemn. "To ask you to reconsider."

Fury filled him, sudden and searing. "Taj sent you."

"No! I'm here of my own accord."

"Of course." He nodded slowly. "Without the sword or the talisman, you're stuck here. Well, my advice is to appeal to the regent—"

"The Seneschal already told me I'm free to go."

"Then why do you hound me?"

She twisted the sleeve of her robe. "Just listen—"

"I'll say this once, Zarifa. I'm leaving this place. Tonight!"

"I don't blame you," she said quickly. "No one has any right to ask more. But—"

"Ask *more*?" He strode up to her. "You don't even know what I've already endured. You haven't a clue."

She recoiled at the expression on his face. The raw misery in his eyes.

"I'm not talking about dying. That was a bloody cakewalk! I'm talking about the arena. What she made me do. It will haunt me for the rest of my days. I can't even begin to imagine what the demon has in store for me next." He gave a wild laugh. "What could possibly be left? I've lived my worst nightmare, over and over. And yet I'm sure, by some *fucking miracle*, she'll devise something even worse!"

"Balthazar." She laid a hand on his arm. Her touch burned. He angrily shook it off.

"Don't you dare say my name like that."

Her thick brows furrowed. "Like what?"

"Like you give a damn!" he exclaimed.

"I *do* give a damn," she said patiently. "And I know that if you do this, you'll always regret it."

He stepped back, his breath coming hard. "Why? Why would you think that?"

"Because I saw your face when we first came here. When you first saw the city." She smiled. "You were enchanted."

His eyes narrowed. "What do you care anyway? Taj would have sold you to the highest bidder!"

She stared at him. "This isn't about Taj. It's about *magic*."

Balthazar felt his pulse skip beneath the cool weight of the talisman.

"We both know how little there is of that left in the world. But this place . . ." A wistful expression stole over her lovely face. "The old ways are not dead here. Not yet. You could make it as it once was."

Balthazar shook his head. "You've read too many fairy-tales, Zarifa. I lived in that world. It was brutal and ugly."

"Some of it, perhaps. But not all."

"How would you know?"

"I can see it in your eyes. Just as I knew you wouldn't torture me to get your talisman back."

"This is ridiculous," he muttered.

"You pretend to be so cynical," she continued relentlessly. "But I don't believe it. I think you do care."

"Well, you're wrong."

Zarifa nodded. "All right. Tell me one thing. Why did you become a necromancer?"

The question caught him off guard. "How is that your bloody business?" he spluttered.

"You're not a cruel man. Not like the rest of them. Not

like my father. So I doubt you took pleasure from killing. Which means you had other reasons." She leaned closer. "Sex and power are perennial favorites, of course. But I think you did it for the *magic*."

The final word was a mere whisper. He stared at her in shock.

How did this woman, who had known him barely a week, cut straight to the marrow?

He was still searching for a response when she smiled. A crooked, knowing smile.

"I might have done it for the magic, too, if I were you. You see, we are the same. And that is how I know I'm right." Zarifa sighed. "The regent issued a pronouncement. He is leaving the city tomorrow. He said his time here is done. When that happens, the last remnants of the spell will fade."

She bit her lower lip, then reached up and touched his cheek. "I thought you should know."

He wanted to lean into that hand. To cover it with his own. To drown himself in her.

"Get out," Balthazar growled.

Zarifa's face hardened. She spun away. He heard the door slam behind her.

He stalked out to the terrace, shaking with resentment and confusion.

He'd carefully walled away the memories, but they crashed over him now. Zarathustra, broken and pleading. The sound of bones snapping. Blood. So much blood.

If the old man was here right now, Balthazar knew exactly what he would say. Some platitude about loyalty and selflessness, no doubt. And he'd believe every word.

Magic.

What a seductive little shell game *that* was.

How many times could he learn the same painful lesson?

The fairytales were just nightmares in disguise. The only creatures with real power were parasites like Taj or slaves like the jinn. Would the world truly be a worse place without them?

And yet . . . .

And yet.

Taj was right. Not even the daēvas' elemental power would save them when the spell failed. There would be a bloodbath. In the end they would lose, just as they had before.

His gaze fell on the staff propped in the corner. What would become of the child who made it?

Balthazar had been around the same age the first time he met a daēva. He remembered snow falling from a bleached summer sky. How the daēva formed it into fantastic shapes simply for the amusement of a mortal boy. Balthazar had been starving and desperate, on the verge of selling himself for a crust of bread. But for a few precious minutes, he had laughed in unbridled delight.

When the daēva went away, his belly was still empty, but something in him was forever changed. And he had chased that childish dream straight down the road to perdition.

Balthazar sighed. Lucas had forgotten his request to remove the sword and staff. He walked to the corner and hefted the staff in one hand. The runes briefly sparked electric blue, as though it remembered his touch.

He wouldn't be allowed to carry it into the demon's lair.

No weapons.

I'd be insane to even consider it, he thought.

And yet. . . .

And yet.

Fucking magic.

CHAPTER 21

Balthazar returned to the Summer Palace, walking straight up to the main doors. They were not locked. He had no recollection of going there before. No recollection of anything after the arena, until he woke up on the floor with a mouthful of blood and an archangel interrogating him.

Now he looked around for a way up to the throne room. It had been on one of the upper levels, but he'd been too stunned to pay much attention when the three of them left. Balthazar wandered through chamber after chamber, all grand and empty and full of dust – the first place he'd seen that wasn't pristinely kept. There were no interior doors, just graceful archways in the Byzantine style. Tiles of aquamarine, azure and gold formed intricate foliage patterns. Once it must have been beautiful, but now it felt like a sad monument to some bygone era.

He entered a long gallery. Stripes of sunlight fell on a series of mosaics depicting different scenes, the colors faded but still legible. A clan of daēvas wandering the desert. The founding of the city. Feast and celebrations, but also battles, necromancers and Druj falling to the spears of flaming ifrit. He paused before a figure in shining armor. Her face was turned away, but he could make out a pair of small horns rising from her brow. She held a sword, but it was a simple blade.

Not *the* sword.

Balthazar knew this for certain because the next mosaic showed a man standing with his boot on a slain Antimagus and a jeweled blade in his hand. Balthazar stared at it in fascination. Despite the passage of centuries, the Shamshir-e Zomorrodnegar seemed to shine with a dark luster. The man must be the prince. He wore a long dark cloak, but cracks marred his face and Balthazar couldn't say if he recognized the features.

He turned left at the end of the gallery and finally found the bronze doors leading to the throne room. Balthazar pushed them open and strode the length of the long hall, a peculiar and rather unpleasant feeling coming over him. The blood was still there. His blood. As he passed one particular column, a shudder swept through him, though it was no different from any of the others.

I think I just stepped over my own grave.

Then Balthazar heard raised voices. He slowed to listen. Taj was arguing with the regent, loud enough that they hadn't yet noticed him.

". . . can't just leave us! At least send one of the other Watchtowers to take your place. We'll abide by the law, I swear it."

"And why would they come here? There is nothing to save."

Taj was silent for a long moment. When he spoke, his voice was barely audible. Humbled and desperate. "I'm begging you, regent."

"Even if I could find him, Azrael would never agree. As for the others, they're even less inclined—"

Balthazar cleared his throat.

Two heads, one golden, the other a gleaming ebony, swiveled towards him.

Taj scowled. "Can you not wait a few minutes more, Balthazar? I will honor the edict. But I must speak with the regent alone—"

"I've reconsidered the situation."

Taj stared at him. "You mean . . ."

"I will do my best to bring you the Shamshir-e Zomorrodnegar."

"Why?" the regent demanded.

"My reasons are my own. But they have nothing to do with personal gain or revenge. Is that good enough for you?"

Mikal gave him a penetrating look. "This change of heart is unexpected. But I will not reject it." He looked at Taj, who still appeared stunned. "It seems you have your champion."

The daēva broke into a grin. "I won't ask why, either. But. . . . Thank you, Balthazar."

He drew a breath. "What does the next part entail?"

"Not the arena," Taj replied quickly. "You will ascend to Fulad-zereh's realm. She will guide you to the final task. The hunt for the sword."

"Are you certain she'll keep her word? Will she truly allow me to leave with it?"

"She *will*," Mikal said firmly. "Or the demon will answer to me."

They all looked up as a raven winged through the columns. It alit on the ruined arm of the throne and gave a dry croak. Mikal tilted his head. "She does?" he murmured.

The bird emitted another harsh cry.

"I see." The regent shared a meaningful look with Taj.

"She wants to speak with you," Mikal said to Balthazar.

He frowned. "Fulad-zereh?"

"No," Taj replied with a worried look. "Her mother."

THE WITCH LIVED ON AN ISLAND IN THE MIDDLE OF THE LAKE. Taj escorted him to the shore, where a small boat was tied up in the reeds. Mist hung over the water, but Balthazar could make out a thatched hut with smoke trailing from the chimney.

"You permit her to have a fire?" he asked.

"Permit?" Taj gave him a level look. "Beletsunnu does as she pleases."

"Scared of her, are you?"

"You would be, too, if you had any sense!" Taj mastered himself, adopting a conciliatory tone. "Just be respectful. I have no idea what she wants, but she's a very powerful witch."

"Has she always lived here?"

"Since the founding."

Balthazar studied him with narrowed eyes. "And yet you neglected to mention that fact before."

"It was irrelevant. She keeps to herself."

Balthazar gazed at the house. "Did she help Fulad-zereh steal the sword?"

"She says not. I went to see her several times after it happened. I begged her to intervene with her daughter. She laughed in my face."

This was growing less appealing by the moment. "How do you know she won't kill me?"

"I don't," Taj admitted. "But she issued her invitation in the presence of the regent. If she wished to dispose of you, it would be foolish to announce it. And I suspect it would make Fulad-zereh very angry if she murdered you in cold blood. It would break the rules, such as they are."

"What else, Taj? I can see you're holding back."

He looked away, pretending to study the clouds. "The demon is already anticipating your arrival tomorrow."

"You're unbelievable!"

"I merely took the precaution of informing her we have a champion. You are expected at daybreak." He smiled weakly.

"I hoped there was a small chance you might change your mind. I wanted to see if she'd quibble about your miraculous recovery, but my messenger said she appeared pleased at the news."

"And her mother knew what I intended two minutes after I spoke the words."

"I told you, she's powerful."

Balthazar studied the house. It looked innocent enough – which was exactly what those stupid children thought before they ended up in the oven.

"What if I refuse her summons?"

"That's your choice. But perhaps she will break her silence and help you."

"Why would she do that? It's her own daughter I'm facing."

Taj thought for a moment. "Beletsunnu is . . . complicated. She shuns us, but I have seen her skulking about at night sometimes, after the curse comes. She feeds the dogs and heals all manner of wild creatures. There is kindness in her heart."

"So she feeds a few strays, yet she also allows men to go to their deaths—"

Taj looked uneasy. "She could be listening right now."

Balthazar looked around. A flock of small yellow birds stared at him from the branches of a tree. They exploded into flight.

"Well, I'm sure she's a fine, reasonable woman," he said loudly. "I look forward to meeting her."

He clambered into the boat and pushed off with a pole. The crossing was swift and uneventful. Balthazar tied up the boat at the opposite shore. The trees on the island were thick firs and twisted cypress that blocked out the sun, leaving it in a perpetual state of gloom. He followed a path to the front door of the ramshackle dwelling.

It was opened by a woman in her middle years, with dark

hair and the kind of beauty that only ripens with time. Strong cheekbones, full lips with a curl of mischief at the edges. She wore a stout wool dress. There was nothing very witchy about her, although the house smelled weird. Like an apothecary shop inside a zoo.

"Balthazar." She smiled. "Come in."

He ducked beneath the low threshold. Bats clung to the underside of the thatched roof. A snowy owl peered at him unblinking from its perch on a cupboard. Mice skittered through the straw scattered on the floor. A few ancient mongrels lounged before the hearth.

"Please, sit down."

He looked around. The only chair was occupied by the most morbidly obese cat he'd ever laid eyes on. Its girth filled the seat and overlapped the edges in a shapeless mound of tatty orange fur. The cat gave him a challenging look.

"I don't mind standing," he said.

"Don't be silly." Beletsunnu removed a bright green lizard from a stool and tucked it in her pocket. "Will that do?"

He sat. The spindly legs creaked under his weight.

"The angel brought you back," she said. "How nice of him."

Balthazar wasn't sure how to reply. He simply nodded.

"Well, I do hope you enjoy your borrowed time. Make the most of it, dear. Have some fun at the Flail tonight." She smiled. "Because it won't last long."

"Pardon?"

She gave him a pitying look. "What have they told you?"

"Can you be more specific?" he hedged.

She lifted a bundle of dried herbs from a hook and crumbled the leaves over a bubbling pot. "About the final test."

"Very little," he admitted. "Perhaps you can explain it to me better."

"Oh, I'm happy to." She stirred the pot with a long wooden spoon. "I imagine you're hoping I'll bestow sage advice on you now. Something to give you a little *edge* when you head up to the cloud. I might even reveal a deep, dark secret about my daughter that will help you return in a blaze of glory, the sword in your hand. Am I right, Balthazar?"

He gave her his most charming smile. "That would be lovely, madam."

She laughed, a rich, hearty chuckle. "Wouldn't it though?"

"But that's not what you're about to say."

Her laughter died. Sharp eyes speared him to the stool. "No."

He sighed. "Just get it over with then."

She sniffed the pot and added a dash of murky liquid from one of the bottles lined up on the counter.

"Here is my advice." She tasted the brew and winced. "Go back to London."

He waited for another minute, watching her putter around the room, gathering a dram of this and a pinch of that. The owl stared at him with predatory intensity. A foul odor wafted over. At first he thought it was the stew, but then he realized it was one of the ancient dogs breaking wind.

"That's it?"

"That's it."

"You could have saved me a trip," he muttered.

"I know you're disappointed," she said sweetly. "But disappointed is better than hopelessly insane, isn't it?"

Balthazar laughed. "She hasn't driven me mad yet and she's given it her best."

It was the witch's turn to guffaw. "Do you truly believe that?"

He didn't, but Balthazar wasn't about to admit it. "Madam, I have more restless ghosts than the Dominion itself." He assumed a cavalier tone. "Let her conjure up my dead sister. Or perhaps my parents, risen from the plague pits?" He stroked his chin. "Wait, I have it! The first poor souls I drained with the chains. They can point accusing fingers at me. How awful!"

She gave him a sardonic look. "I know what you were, Balthazar."

"Then you know that I have lived with them all for an eternity already. And I'm not a complete idiot. In fact, she tipped her hand in the arena. Fulad-zereh relies on her powers of enchantment, so I will trust nothing and no one."

"It seems you have it all figured out." She paused. "Except for one thing."

He couldn't resist taking the bait. "And what's that?"

"My daughter is smarter than you. She is more ruthless than you. I have already seen the outcome of this futile quest." She sprinkled something that looked like claws into the pot. "It isn't pretty."

"I don't believe you can see the future. That's just . . . carnival mumbo-jumbo! It isn't written yet—"

"Stark raving mad," she said sadly. "Trapped in the twisted labyrinth of your own mind. Trembling, drooling. That handsome face all . . ." And here Beletsunnu bugged out her eyes and did an impression of a lunatic, complete with incoherent gibbering noises.

"Stop that," he snapped.

Her features instantly returned to normal. She stirred the pot.

"Taj is a liar, but you know that already. The regent loathes us all, including you." She cackled. "*Especially* you. He's still annoyed that he wasted a resurrection on a former Antimagus who spends his time sucking women's *zi* out of their vaginas."

The witch used an old Sumerian word meaning "life's breath."

"Well, that's a crude way of putting it," Balthazar muttered.

"As the demon's mother, it's my duty to tell you the truth. It's hopeless."

"So there's no chance that the sword can ever be taken back?"

"I didn't say that." She stirred the mess bubbling on the stove. "I said *you* can't."

"Why not?"

"You did well in the arena, which doesn't surprise me." She glanced at him. "You reek of death, Balthazar, and I don't mean your own. Violence is second nature to you."

He smiled. "It's not my only quality."

"Perhaps not." She scrounged through the cupboard and took out a vial of black powder. "But I fear it is your dominant trait. You tell yourself that you are doing this to help the daēvas, but in truth you only want revenge for what she did to you."

Balthazar went cold. "It was all an illusion. I knew that. *She* is the monster here." He stood abruptly, startling the owl, which flapped its wings and then settled on the roost again. "I think you're trying to trick me. To frighten me off."

"Don't be a fool. You're hardly so pliable. You'll go regardless of what I say."

"Then why bother?"

"You deserve to be warned." She picked up a shaker of salt and tasted the brew again. This time she nodded in satisfaction. "Want some soup?"

"No."

She shrugged. "Suit yourself."

She ladled out bowls for the dogs and set them by the hearth. Balthazar listened to the curs slurp in mounting irritation.

"What does your daughter want?" he demanded. "I mean, what is it, really?"

The witch cast him a thoughtful look. "That's not a bad question. Perhaps you're getting warmer."

He ground his teeth. "Which means?"

"Whatever you make of it."

"I have no idea! Why don't you just tell me instead of speaking in riddles?"

She braced her hands on her hips. "Are you truly so dense? It couldn't be any clearer!" She turned her back. "My advice stands. Leave while you can."

"And if I don't?"

She shrugged again. "Then be just, Balthazar."

The cat rose and stretched, arching its back. It settled its massive bulk with great care, tail lashing.

"*Be just.* Thanks ever so much. That's truly enlightening."

She didn't reply.

Balthazar strode to the door and turned back. "Who was her father?"

The witch smiled coldly. "No one you know."

He nodded with a slight frown. "I'm just wondering if it wasn't one of the Watchtowers. It explains why they're protecting her."

The witch bared her teeth. "I look forward to seeing what remains of you tomorrow. Now get out, necromancer!"

Balthazar gave her a low bow, which was fortuitous since she chose that moment to hurl a bowl of soup at his head. "Good day, madam."

The cat hissed, but was too fat to reach him before he fled.

Balthazar scampered back to the boat, hauling on the oars like he was in a race down the Thames.

Bloody women.

CHAPTER 22

T aj waited anxiously on the far shore.

"Well, that was pointless," Balthazar muttered as he climbed out of the boat.

Taj searched his face. "What did Beletsunnu tell you?"

"She tried to frighten me off."

"What did she say exactly?" he persisted. "She must have had a reason to summon you."

Balthazar sighed. "She said the sword could be won back, but not by me. That I should return to London. That I was no match for her daughter." He waved a hand. "Et cetera."

"Did she elaborate on *why* you couldn't get it?"

"Not really. But she implied it had something to do with what Fulad-zereh wants. Why she stages the Trials to begin with." He gave Taj a level look. "You must have known her."

"Not well, but yes. I served under her command during the campaigns."

"What was she like?"

They started walking back to the Golden Flail. The late afternoon sun trailed long shadows behind them, reflecting on stained glass windows and gilded minarets. Balthazar heard the gentle murmur of fountains in cloistered gardens.

Peacocks wandered along the grassy verge. Jasmine scented the air. A light breeze stirred the palms. It was another idyllic day in Al Miraj.

And soon the curse would unravel all that perfection and bring its own dark magic. Would this be the last night the citizens hid behind their walls?

Hubris to believe otherwise. Yet he had to – or else there was no reason to try.

"A brilliant general and strategist," Taj replied. "She led us to victory after victory against the Druj. Decisive. Fearless. Smart. Merciless when following orders."

"And she did? Follow orders, I mean?"

"Yes. She had no choice." He smiled grimly. "But I suspect she's like a binge drinker. Stay sober for days, months, even years. Then fall off the proverbial wagon hard. Her nature is chaos. That is Fulad-zereh's predominant demonic quality."

"Will she expect me to fight her personally?"

Taj considered the question. "I don't think so. She would have something more elaborate planned."

"There's one thing I can't understand. It's rather fundamental, so I'm hoping you can explain it." He paused. "Why on earth would she allow me to take the sword?"

Taj's jaw tightened. It was clearly a question he'd been dreading. He turned to Balthazar, his gaze intense. *Burning.* "You have no idea how much I'd like to lie to you right now. Tell you she can be trusted. But I can't. You had the decency to stay. You deserve better." He drew a deep breath. "The truth is I don't know why she would keep her word. There's no guarantee."

Balthazar swallowed. "The regent said—"

"I have no idea if she even fears the regent. I told you, she's unpredictable." His voice hardened. "Which is why you have to kill her at the first opportunity."

Balthazar glanced at him. They were crossing one of the bridges. "That wasn't part of the deal."

"What deal?" Taj shook his head in frustration. "Don't you understand? You're the first and last champion we'll ever have. This is it! One chance. When it comes, I hope you'll take it."

"You may be right," Balthazar conceded. "In fact, you're probably right. What about the no-weapons rule? I don't care for that one. There must be a way around it."

Taj nodded. He looked relieved at Balthazar's agreement. "I've considered it, of course. It'll be tricky. If she suspects you've broken the rules, she might disqualify you at the outset, which would be a disaster. But the contract only says you can't bring your *own*. At worst, you may simply have to disarm an ifrit."

"Of course," Balthazar said dryly. "Piece of cake."

"There might be other options. We can discuss them in my chamber." He gave a thin smile. "Along with a thousand other details."

They passed through the garden gate. It was nearly sunset. Suddenly, Balthazar craved a few minutes to himself. Once he holed up in a strategy session with Taj, he wouldn't escape until daybreak.

"I'll meet you in a few minutes," he said, stopping in the courtyard.

Taj frowned. He looked worried that his prize stallion might bolt. "Where are you going?"

"A short walk. To clear my head." Balthazar stared at him. "It's been a long day."

Taj hesitated. "I still don't know who tried to kill you—"

"I'm going for a walk. Alone. I will find you shortly."

The struggle on Taj's face was a delight to behold. How he wanted to argue! But he also feared pushing his new champion too far.

"Of course," Taj said smoothly. "Just stay within the walls."

Balthazar gave a brusque nod and turned down one of the paths leading into the gardens.

ZARIFA SAW A TALL FIGURE DISAPPEAR INTO THE DATE PALMS AS Taj made for the front doors. Balthazar looked stone-faced, but Taj . . . he almost seemed *happy*. She hurried down the stairs and caught him as he entered.

"What happened?" she asked.

"We have a champion," he said, unable to suppress a grin. "Balthazar just informed the regent that he will seek the sword tomorrow."

Her eyebrows rose. "He did?"

"I must admit, I didn't expect it. But I must spread the news." He exhaled. "There will be a great celebration tonight."

"Where has he gone?"

Taj studied her. "He wanted to be alone. I'd leave him be."

"Right." She smiled. "I'll speak to him later then. Don't let me keep you."

Taj frowned slightly, but he strode inside. She waited until he disappeared and hurried into the gardens, following the path Balthazar had chosen. She was glad he'd taken her words to heart, but she was also afraid of what the next day might bring. It was unlikely she'd get another chance to speak to him alone.

The heavy scent of desert roses filled the air as she followed the gently curving path. She found him sitting on a stone bench next to a pool with lotus blossoms drifting on the surface. He looked up as she approached. His expression was not welcoming, but she forged ahead.

"Please, Zarifa," Balthazar said wearily. "Not now."

"I won't stay," she said. "I only wanted to thank you."

"Thank me?"

"For following your heart."

He gave her a cold look. "It's rarely been a wise course, has it?"

She frowned.

"You of all people should know that." His voice was cutting. "So let's just say I'm following my conscience, which might be equally dubious but at least remains in working order!"

The last rays of the sun sank beyond the vine-draped wall. A slight chill raised goosebumps on her bare arms.

"I hope you're not implying that you followed your *heart* when you pursued me," she said. "No, that was another organ entirely—"

He shot to his feet. "At first, yes. When you paraded yourself through the dining room. But when I came to know you, I . . . ." Balthazar cut off with a frown. "Never mind. You got what you wanted. I'll play the puppet again, dangling from your bloody strings—"

"Don't be an ass!" She suddenly itched to slap him. "You are the most selfish, self-absorbed creature I've ever run across, and I've moved in some very low circles. I could have just slit your throat and been done with it, but I spared you!"

His pupils dilated, turning the irises solid black. "What a saint you are, Zarifa. They ought to make *you* regent when Mikal leaves. I'm sure you'd do a fabulous job of torturing everyone with your—"

She was dimly aware of the roses darkening to a deep, bruised purple. The dry crackle of vines snaking across the grass. The darkness falling over them both like a cloak. But her gaze was fixed on his mouth, the lips curled in anger but sensuous nonetheless.

"I hate you," she whispered.

He closed the distance between them in one swift step. "Not as much as I fucking hate *you*," Balthazar snarled.

And then his lips were on her neck. Hands grasped her

waist and jerked her hard against him. Animal heat consumed her.

"So much," he whispered between frenzied kisses. "Holy Father—"

She let her head fall back, let him devour her. His breath was hot against the tender skin of her collarbone. The voluptuous scent of the flowers made it hard to draw air. Her own breath came fast and shallow. One hand was pinioned against his chest. She forced it inside his shirt, seeking the skin beneath . . . and her fingers met gold. She snatched her hand away.

Yet even that cold reminder of what he was failed to douse the flames.

The robe had slipped from one shoulder. Balthazar yanked it down, a hand sliding up to cup her breast. She bit her lip hard enough to taste blood. If she didn't stop him now, she never would. Zarifa shoved him away with all her strength.

He staggered back, panting. His eyes were black as midnight.

She heard a sound like the sudden loud drone of a wasp. A crossbow bolt whizzed between them and buried itself in the trunk of a date palm.

Balthazar blinked like a man awakening from a dream. Or a nightmare. His face went perfectly blank.

"Get down," he growled, pushing her to the ground.

Zarifa twisted around. She saw a quick flash of movement at one of the windows.

"Up there!" she cried, pointing. "The third floor!"

Balthazar glanced at her. "Forgive me," he said in a curt tone.

She shook her head. "Please, there's nothing—"

But he was already gone. She watched him run for the doors. An assassin inside The Golden Flail. Someone willing to risk Taj's wrath to get rid of Balthazar. And *she* was the one who'd convinced him to stay.

Zarifa stood and adjusted her robe, belting it tightly again. The gardens were dark and shadowed. Beyond the wall, a dog howled.

"The curse made us lose our heads," she told herself firmly.

She knew it was a lie. Oh, it wouldn't have happened otherwise. But the desire was there to begin with. It always had been. In truth, she'd never quite forgotten that drugged kiss.

Or how glad she'd been when he drew a first shuddering breath in the Summer Palace.

We're both fools, she thought sadly. And the sooner we part ways, the better.

BALTHAZAR TOOK THE STAIRS TWO AT A TIME, SHOVING AWAY the memory of what he'd done. But he could still taste her on his lips and it did little to improve his mood as he stormed up to the third floor. Curtains lined the corridor facing the gardens.

He yanked the first aside. A small bedchamber lay beyond. There was no one on the adjoining terrace.

Balthazar strode to the next curtain.

An identical chamber, also empty.

He yanked the third curtain aside.

"What the hell?" a deep voice demanded.

Three naked people stared at him in annoyance.

"Sorry," Balthazar muttered, drawing the curtain closed.

He turned to leave and saw the tip of a black robe disappearing around the end of the corridor. Balthazar broke into a run. He was panting when he reached the end, but whoever it was had vanished. He swore under his breath.

"Are you lost, Champion?"

Balthazar spun around. Jabaar stood behind him.

"Where did *you* come from?" Balthazar asked suspiciously.

"My master sent me to look for you." The marid's eyes glittered with malice. "Darkness is falling. It is not safe to be outside."

Balthazar barked a mirthless laugh. "No, it isn't. Did you see anyone pass this way?"

"Not a soul." He gave a mocking bow. "If you are done harassing the paying clientele, my master awaits."

Balthazar stared at him for a long moment. "I can find my own way."

"As you wish." Jabaar turned into a streamer of smoke and disappeared into a crevice.

Balthazar went to Taj's chambers, where the daēva sat cross-legged on the carpet studying a thick sheaf of papers.

"Someone just tried to kill me," he announced. "*Again.*"

Taj leapt to his feet. "What?"

"Right in the gardens. Another crossbow bolt. It nearly parted my hair."

Cold rage settled over Taj's face like a shell of ice.

"Did you send Jabaar to find me? He was lurking in one of the corridors."

"Yes," Taj snapped. "I know his demeanor can be rough, but he is loyal. He has no choice in the matter."

"But—"

"It cannot be the marids, Balthazar. They are *bound*." His expression darkened. "And they know what I would do to them if they fail me. No, this assassin is of flesh and blood. And I *will* find them!"

Taj clapped his hands. When the three marids appeared, he ordered them to assemble everyone in the courtyard and search the Golden Flail, chamber by chamber.

"You'll handle the questioning," he snapped at Jabaar.

"No torture, but use your powers of persuasion. I want results."

Jabaar bowed and vanished without a word.

"As for you two, make the announcement that a curfew is in effect, starting this instant. Anyone found in the streets will be presumed guilty and locked in the cells."

"Yes, O Terrible Master."

"Fetch Mr. Devereaux. And I want guards outside this room. No jinn. Daēvas only. Now go!"

Twin streams of smoke snaked beneath the edge of the curtain.

Taj stood for a moment, his brow lowered. Then he retrieved the papers and handed them to Balthazar. "This is the contract with Fulad-zereh. I've been looking for a loophole. Do you want a drink?"

"Gods, yes."

Taj poured two cups and handed one to Balthazar.

"Someone doesn't want the curse lifted," Balthazar said. "Surely you have an idea of who that could be."

"If I did, they'd already be in chains before the regent. But I examined the first bolt, the one from the archives. There was a substance on the tip."

"Poison?"

"That's the odd thing. It was a drug to induce temporary paralysis, but not in a fatal dose. The attacker wanted you out of the Trials but not dead."

Balthazar frowned. "The wound—"

"I could have healed it. Whoever it was knew that." He sighed. "Purging your system of the drug would have been far trickier. If it had hit you, there's a fair chance you would have slept through the second round."

"And that's all they wanted?"

"It would seem so. But you will not leave my sight until the matter is resolved."

Balthazar didn't argue the point. He set his wine aside,

untouched. "Lucas doesn't know about my decision yet," he said with a twinge of guilt. "I should have found him and talked to him—"

"Yes, you should have."

Balthazar's head turned as Lucas entered the room, Zarifa behind him. She avoided Balthazar's eyes.

"I just heard that you intend to stay. May we speak privately, my lord?"

Lucas looked composed, but Balthazar sensed simmering anger. Understandably.

"Of course," he said, following Lucas out to the veranda.

"He can hear us, you know," Balthazar said, glancing back at Taj.

"I don't care." Lucas gripped the stone balustrade. "I just want to know what the *hell* is going on. Two hours ago, you were in a frenzy to return to London."

"I changed my mind."

"Obviously. Why?"

"Zarifa didn't tell you?"

Lucas looked confused. "How would she know?" He stared at Balthazar. "Are you saying *Mortlake's daughter* had something to do with this? Oh, my God—"

"Not in the way you think," Balthazar said hastily. "I mean, whatever it is you're thinking. But she made a persuasive argument that Al Miraj was worth saving."

"I don't dispute that. I merely question whether it's possible."

He sighed. "So do I. But I'll never know if I don't try."

"If you fail—"

"There's no one else, Lucas. It's the only homeland the daēvas have."

Lucas studied him in consternation. "Why do you care?"

"Because it's a chance to make amends." Balthazar looked away. "When I was a necromancer, I didn't only kill mortals."

"You were at war."

"And I fought on the wrong side. I owe them this much."

"And what about me?" Lucas asked bitterly.

"I told you, you'll get everything—"

"That's not what I'm bloody talking about and you know it!"

"We risk our lives every time we hunt an Antimagus. This is no different."

"How can you say that? Those are targeted assassinations. Carefully calculated risks."

"And look how the last one turned out," Balthazar said dryly.

Lucas rubbed his forehead. "I suppose you have a point. But you'll be completely in the demon's power. Pardon me if I'm not thrilled about it."

"I spoke to the regent again. He promised to enforce the bargain."

"What happens next?"

"I meet Fulad-zereh tomorrow. She sets me the final challenge."

Lucas was quiet for a long minute. "I'll help in any way I can. But you already know that."

"Thank you."

Balthazar looked at Zarifa. She sat on the edge of the pool, bare feet in the water, a distant expression on her face. It was that same aura of sadness he'd noticed the night at the party. Or not sadness exactly. More like someone utterly alone in the world.

"What did she say to you?" Lucas asked.

"Only what needed to be said."

So she hadn't spoken of what passed between them. Balthazar was relieved, but he wished she hadn't come. It was . . . distracting. He despised himself for losing his self-control in the garden. She clearly did, too. She'd shoved him away like a live coal. Deservedly so.

"I think we're wanted," Lucas murmured.

Taj was staring at them both with impatience.

"We're reviewing the contract," he said as they came back back inside. "I won't send him up to the cloud empty-handed, not if I can help it. But the ban on weapons is clear. No wiggle room there."

"I've been thinking," Zarifa ventured. "The first three Trials were all armed combat. Would she repeat herself for the final round? Or would it be something more cunning?"

Taj nodded slowly. "The language of the contract refers to a quest, and later a hunt."

"When I saw the demon standing on her cloud in the shining armor, her wings spread, the sunlight hitting her just so . . . . It reminded me of a famous story. I couldn't think which one, but then it came to me." Zarifa paused. "Icarus."

"The boy who flew too close to the sun in wings of wax?" Lucas asked. "I don't see—"

"Who was his father?" she prompted quietly.

Lucas stared at her. "Daedalus, of course."

Zarifa smiled. "The architect of the great labyrinth at Knossos. Think about it. Icarus is the prince! By ensnaring her with the sword, he dared rise above his station and was cast down for it."

"I don't know," Taj muttered dubiously. "It's a stretch."

"But what if I'm right?" Zarifa persisted. "If she's been giving you a clue. That Balthazar will face a maze—"

"They're not the same," Balthazar interrupted quietly. "A maze has many possible solutions, a labyrinth only one." He turned to Taj. "But the witch used the word as well. She said I would be trapped in a labyrinth of my own mind. Now I wonder if she didn't mean it literally."

He recalled his chance meeting with Flinders Petrie, who had just unearthed the remains of another labyrinth at Hawara. Balthazar suddenly felt the web of fate tightening around him. He swallowed the last of his wine.

"Let me search the storeroom," Zarifa said. "Not for a weapon, but a talisman."

"It can't be anything that could be construed as threatening or dangerous," Taj warned. "Or anything she'll even recognize as a magical object."

"Of course. We can rule out the larger talismans right away, including weapons. It has to be something small. Jewelry or clothing. Something that won't arouse suspicion. But that still leaves hundreds of objects. I'll need some help sorting them while I determine the uses."

"I'll go," Lucas said immediately.

"You'll both be accompanied by the Seneschal," Taj said. "I appreciate the effort, Miss Everleigh, but you *are* a thief."

She frowned. "Fine. Although I would never——"

"Of course you wouldn't," he replied dryly. "I'm just not in an especially trusting mood, given recent events." Taj walked over to Lucas. He laid a hand on his arm and whispered something in his ear. Lucas nodded. "Tell the guards outside you need an escort. They'll find the Seneschal."

Balthazar watched Zarifa leave, black hair rippling like silk down her back. He could still feel it between his fingers. When he looked back at Taj, the daēva was staring at him with open amusement.

"What?" Balthazar demanded.

"Nothing," Taj said innocently. "I was just thinking that hatred is often a sign of some underlying passion——"

He nimbly dodged away as Balthazar hurled the contract at his head.

CHAPTER 23

Lucas gave a low whistle as they entered Taj's Treasury. "You weren't joking," he muttered, looking around the vast, cluttered space. "These are all talismans?"

"Each and every one," Zarifa agreed.

"How many remain unidentified?"

"Hundreds," the Seneschal replied. "I would suggest starting with those." She pointed at the stacked wooden crates against the far wall. "None are in the form of weapons and most are small."

Destan Karatas had been recruited to help with the sorting. He and Lucas lifted one of the crates down and pried it open with a metal bar. It was filled with objects wrapped in yellowing linen.

"Bring it over to the table," the Seneschal said. "I will keep a record as Miss Everleigh works."

Lucas was curious to see Zarifa's talents in action. He watched as she sat down and the Seneschal opened a large ledger. The first object to be unwrapped was a moonstone necklace. Zarifa lifted it in her hands. Her eyes grew distant. "It is a healing charm," she said after a few moments.

"That could be useful," Lucas said.

"If Balthazar suffered from swelling of the joints, yes," she said dryly. "But it is quite specific."

The Seneschal made a note, the necklace was rewrapped, and the next parcel opened. A woven silver belt.

"This one induces a deep, dreamless sleep," Zarifa said, after a brief touch. "Not what he has in mind, I think."

Piece by piece, they catalogued the contents of the crate. Nothing seemed helpful except for a ring that gave its wearer the power to stop hearts at a touch, which was too openly against the rules.

"Let's try the next one," Zarifa said.

The first crate was pushed aside as Lucas and Destan hauled over another, this one filled with a hodgepodge of items. Zarifa found several love charms, a slender black wand to cure baldness, a nasty little teapot that caused anyone who drank from it to speak gibberish, and a mirror that permitted communication with its match, which was missing.

"Do you need a break?" the Seneschal asked, eyeing Zarifa with concern. "Your head . . . ."

"I can continue for a while," she replied, looking oddly guilty.

The third held more love charms – clearly a popular item – and a beaten gold bracelet that let its user speak to birds. Lucas unwrapped the last item, a crude clay disk covered with arcane symbols.

"Can you read those?" Zarifa asked the Seneschal.

The woman shook her head. "It's not jinn or daēva. I don't think I've ever seen runes like that before."

Zarifa lifted it with a frown. Her eyes widened. She shuddered and dropped the disk. It landed with a thud that shook the table – far too heavy for a clay object, Lucas thought uneasily.

"What is it?" the Seneschal asked, her voice sharp.

"I . . . I don't know. I saw a portal open." Zarifa stared at the disk with dismay. "To a place of utter darkness. And I . . .

." She swallowed. "I thought I heard voices, crying out. *Coaxing*." She turned to the Seneschal, her face pale. "Wrap it up and hide it away. That disk should never, ever be used. It's dangerous."

The Seneschal carefully lifted it with the linen wrapping and set it aside. "I will make sure of it," she said firmly.

"I think I will take you up on that offer of a break now," Zarifa said wearily. "Just for a few minutes."

She stood and knuckled her back. The Seneschal moved away to speak quietly with Destan. They seemed close, but Lucas supposed it made sense. The few humans in Al Miraj would share a bond of kinship, and both of them were indentured to Taj. He could only imagine how long they'd been here.

"Are you all right?" Lucas asked. Zarifa looked tired and drawn.

"I'm fine." She looked at the opened crates and sighed. "None of these would be of help to him. But we have many more to go. I'm sure we'll find something."

At some point along the line, Lucas's hatred had waned. He'd assumed she would be like her father, but Zarifa had decency Mortlake lacked. In truth, there was plenty of blame to share for their predicament.

"Thank you for doing this," he said quietly.

She seemed surprised. "Why wouldn't I?"

"Balthazar did kill your father."

She snorted. "The only thing Mortlake had a surplus of was enemies, Mr. Devereaux. Someone would have done it eventually. You two just got there first."

Lucas raised an eyebrow. "That's a rather abrupt turnabout."

"Not really. I never hated Balthazar. Nor you."

"I don't understand. Why punish him then?"

Zarifa looked away. "I only wanted enough money to pay the debt. I figured he owed me that much." Her face darkened. "John Mortlake owed me that much. But he was dead. Balthazar was obviously rich. And I'll remind you that he approached me, not the other way around." A small smile played on her lips. "It was too tempting."

"He does like women, you know," Lucas said loyally. "Not just as a . . . a parasite. I mean he really *likes* them."

"I know."

"He's been good to me."

"You're lucky, Mr. Devereaux. To have someone who cares." She sounded wistful.

"Was your childhood very hard?" he asked. "I suppose that's a stupid question."

She hesitated. "It got worse when my father entered the picture. He was not a warm person, to say the least."

Lucas remembered those first terrible months after he lost his birth parents. At first, Balthazar had seemed distant and frightening, a tall, somber man who obviously had no experience with small children. He'd hired a series of nursemaids, but they weren't mama, and Lucas was so difficult none lasted more than a few weeks before quitting. Most of it was a miserable blur, but he had one clear memory. The latest nurse had just packed her bags and left. He was in his bedroom, howling, when the door opened. His new guardian entered and sat on the edge of the bed, which creaked alarmingly under his weight. Lucas burrowed deeper under the covers.

He expected a stern lecture for driving off another nurse, but Balthazar simply sat there until Lucas stopped crying.

"Listen," he'd said calmly. "I won't pretend I wanted you, but we're stuck together now and I won't ever leave you. Not ever, do you hear?"

Lucas had been unsure how to respond, but he sensed honesty, which was a balm after the false cheeriness of the nursemaids.

"I will help you find and kill the man who destroyed your family," Balthazar continued. "But that will probably take a long time. You must be a grown man before we attempt it. Do you understand?"

Lucas pushed the covers away and sat up. Balthazar handed him a handkerchief. Lucas wiped his red, tear-streaked face. "Yes, my lord."

"Good." Balthazar did not smile, which Lucas also appreciated. They gazed at each other with perfect serious-ness. "Then we are in agreement. And I am willing to show you some things now, if you like. Have you ever lifted a sword?"

Lucas shook his head.

"Do you want to try?"

Lucas nodded.

Balthazar did smile then, a fleeting smile that was not amusement at the child's expense, but more an expression of mutual complicity. He took Lucas's hand and led him upstairs to a hidden room filled with weapons of every shape and description.

"Since you don't seem to like any of the other toys I've bought for you, this will be the new playroom," Balthazar said. "But you are never to come here without me present."

Lucas nodded solemnly, his eyes wide. "Do I have to have another nursemaid?"

Balthazar peered down at him. "Can you be trusted not to drown in a bath? Because I draw the line at washing you."

"I know how to wash!" he replied indignantly. "I'm not a baby."

"Then you shall be liberated from nursemaids, although you *will* go to school when the time comes. I mean for you to receive the finest education. You will need it, young master Devereaux, if you hope to outwit your enemies."

Although it scared him, Lucas *liked* the idea of having enemies. It gave focus to his rage and despair – as did the promise of retribution. At that moment, he felt clarity for the first time since the awful night when the men came.

"We will begin with drawing and sheathing the blade only," Balthazar said. "No poking."

Thus commenced his first lesson in swordsmanship at the tender age of five. As promised, there were no more nurse-maids. In the evenings, Balthazar would read to him, and it seemed perfectly natural when he would lean over and press a tender kiss to the boy's forehead before blowing out the candle.

Boarding schools followed, starting at the age of ten, but Lucas always came home for holidays and summer vacations. And Balthazar was always waiting there to greet him. The years passed. Lucas grew up, but Balthazar never looked a day older. . . .

"When did you learn the truth?" he blurted to Zarifa. "About Mortlake?"

"I found his chains." She stared at Lucas with a mixture of pity and understanding. "And you?"

"He told me himself when I was sixteen. All of it."

Lucas had been taken aback at the particulars, but he was so passionately devoted to his guardian at that point, he didn't care. He'd always known there was more to it. Things Balthazar wasn't telling him. All in all, he'd been relieved it wasn't worse.

"And you choose to stay with him?" Zarifa asked, sounding more curious than condemning.

"Yes," Lucas replied simply.

She smiled suddenly. "Well, he does have his charms. I wouldn't be helping him if I thought he was a monster."

"You helped—" Lucas bit off the words, but it was too late.

"Mortlake? That was not a choice, Mr. Devereaux," she said crisply. "My father made it quite clear what would happen to me if I didn't." She strode back to the table and sat down. "Fetch another crate, please."

The hours passed. Dozens of talismans were examined

and catalogued. Still they found nothing. Lucas could see the strain on her face. As unhappy as it made him, he thought it might be time to concede defeat.

"You look ill, Miss Everleigh," Destan Karatas said gently. "Perhaps you should stop."

The Turk looked almost as exhausted. His eyes were bloodshot, his face thinner, the cheekbones prominent against hollowed cheeks. The strain of the Trials was wearing on all of them, Lucas reflected.

"I can continue," Zarifa said stubbornly. "What time is it?"

"After four," Lucas replied, rubbing his eyes. "The sun rises in an hour."

They were down to the last two crates. No doubt it would be more of the same. Love charms and things that healed gout but nothing else, and things that turned pigeons into swans, or swans into swine. All of it useless.

"Looks like clothing," Destan announced as he cracked the lid.

"Bring it here," the Seneschal said. She had tucked the streak of white hair behind one ear; it made her look girlish, though her tone had the ring of a woman used to being obeyed without question.

The first item was a pair of shoes that allowed the wearer to leap like a cat. They had potential, but they were sized for a woman. Balthazar would never be able to get his feet into them – and the demon would no doubt wonder why he wore pink silk slippers.

Next came a tunic with gold embroidery at the hem. Zarifa held it for a long minute, a puzzled expression on her face.

"What did you see?" Lucas asked when she finally set it down.

"I'm not sure." She frowned. "It has never been used. I saw only the making."

"And?"

"A woman creeping through stone corridors, following a golden thread. She held a spindle. As she walked, she wound up the thread." Zarifa lifted the tunic in her hands again, her gaze unfocused. "Now she works a loom. She is making the tunic and hemming it with the thread."

"May I see it?" the Seneschal said. She lifted the garment and examined it closely. Her eyes widened at a complex symbol stitched into the inner seam, just beneath the left arm. "That is the mark of Beletsunnu. Fulad-zereh's mother!"

Lucas leaned over, his exhaustion vanished in a rush of excitement. "What could it mean?"

The Seneschal shook her head. "I don't know." She turned back to Zarifa. "You cannot determine what it does?"

"I told you, I only see the last time the talisman was used. This has never been used for its true purpose."

"Describe the place you saw," Lucas said. "Stone corridors?"

"Yes. Very dark, except for the thread, which had a faint glow. They twisted and turned like a—"

"Labyrinth," Lucas whispered. "What if it is Ariadne's Thread?"

Zarifa inhaled sharply.

"Who do you speak of?" Destan asked.

"Ariadne was the daughter of King Minos," Lucas explained. "He placed her in charge of his labyrinth, which was guarded by a fearsome beast. Minos had conquered Athens and every nine years, he demanded a sacrifice of seven young men and women. After a while, the Athenians grew tired of this bargain. They sent the great warrior Theseus to slay the beast. Ariadne fell in love with him. She gave him a sword and magic thread so that he could find his way out."

"What happened?"

"Theseus killed the beast and escaped using her thread. The two of them ran away together, but their love would not

last. According to the stories, she eventually married Diony-
sius. I have never heard what became of the thread." He
gazed at the tunic with wonder. "It's all just an ancient
myth."

"Where did the tunic come from?" Zarifa asked.

"Let me look." The Seneschal opened her ledger and
leafed through the pages. At last she stopped and ran a finger
down the entries. Her face froze. She looked up at Zarifa.
"Mortlake sold it to Taj nearly two hundred years ago. Provenance unknown."

"My father?" Zarifa echoed in astonishment.

"It all circles around, doesn't it?" Lucas said softly. "Beletsunnu's mark. Mortlake. The labyrinth."

"As if we were meant to find it," she agreed, rubbing her
arms from a sudden chill. "Hold it up, if you would. I do not
wish to touch it again."

Lucas shook out the tunic. The fit looked perfect for a
large man.

"It cannot be construed as a weapon," he said. "Unless the
demon recognizes it, there is no reason she would be
suspicious."

"Go fetch our master, but say nothing of what we have
found," the Seneschal told Destan.

The Turk tore his gaze from the tunic. He looked stunned.

"Hurry!" she urged with a slight frown.

He visibly pulled himself together and ran for the door.

"Is it safe to pass through the streets at night?" Zarifa
wondered.

The Seneschal smiled. "Destan Karatas knows how to
move unnoticed. Those of us who have been here for
centuries are not so affected by the curse anymore. He will
deliver the message."

"I wonder where Mortlake found it," Zarifa mused. "We'll
probably never know."

They were all silent, thinking of the long and winding

path the talisman must have taken to end up in this storeroom on the eve of the final Trial.

"Do you believe in fate?" Lucas asked.

"I didn't before," Zarifa replied. "And I don't like to imagine that our entire lives are predestined." Her mouth twisted wryly. "But I cannot deny that something seems to be at work here."

"Could Beletsunnu have known what its ultimate purpose would be?" Lucas persisted. "Does the witch see the future?"

"That I cannot say," the Seneschal replied. "But she was old when the world was still young." Her voice lowered. "Taj is an infant in comparison. If she has taken a hand in arranging matters, I for one would not interfere."

"But she wants Balthazar to succeed?" Lucas dearly hoped it was the case.

"I do not know her mind and nor do you," the Seneschal replied. "This may be of use, or it may not." She studied the cloth with a critical eye. "But Beletsunnu does weave very fine work, I must say."

Destan must have run like the wind, for it was only a few more minutes before he returned with Taj and Balthazar, who wore a dapper new suit.

"It's nearly time," Balthazar said curtly. "I'd given up on you." His gaze fell on the white garment spread across the table. His lips tightened. "This is what you found? I'm not wearing a bloody *tunic*."

"Trust me," Zarifa said with satisfaction. "You'll wear this one."

<hr>

THE SKY WAS STILL DARK WHEN BALTHAZAR ENTERED THE plaza before the Summer Palace. A sliver of moon shimmered in the still waters of the lake. On the island, a figure stood before the thatched hut. Beletsunnu's face was a pale smudge in the distance, but he felt the heat of her gaze.

"Approach the palace and wait until the regent summons you," Taj whispered. He was dressed in embroidered silks and a deep purple sash. The long plait hung over one shoulder.

"Do I have to do this?" Balthazar scowled. "Can't I go straight to the gates—"

"Just do as I say for once!" Taj hissed.

He melted into the crowd ringing the plaza. Every daēva, jinn and mortal in Al Miraj had assembled, but there were no cheers at Balthazar's appearance. They simply watched in silence as he walked to the foot of the steps.

A long minute passed. Then the doors swung wide and Mikal strode through, his face an unforgiving mask. He paused at the top of the steps to survey his flock. None seemed willing to meet his eyes. When he spoke, his voice was wintry.

"As regent, I have done my utmost to stave off the moral decay of this city, a task that has proven both thankless and futile. It seems your last hope rests on the shoulders of this mortal champion." Mikal lowered his voice to a barely audible mutter. "Who is apparently the best you sorry savages could come up with."

Balthazar sighed.

"The Watchtowers maintain a neutral position in this dispute. Yet I cannot deny that it has gone on far too long. If there is even a small chance the balance can be restored, I will pledge my support to the endeavor."

Taj whispered something to the Seneschal. They both looked deeply relieved.

"Let him come forward!" the regent declared.

Balthazar climbed the steps. He bent a knee before the angel, who laid a hand on his head.

"May you remember in the dark what you learned in the light," Mikal said loudly. "May your feet keep to the true path."

A cold shiver went through Balthazar as if he'd just taken the Water Blessing of the magi. The exhaustion of a long, sleepless night vanished. He felt hale and strong. The fear remained, but he could manage that.

He raised his head and met eyes of burnished gold.

"I brought you back, Balthazar," the archangel said quietly. "Don't make me regret it."

The unspoken words *more than I already do* hung in the air.

Mikal released him and stalked back into the Summer Palace. The doors slammed shut with a resounding boom. His departure punctured the subdued atmosphere and a cheer went up among the daēvas. Taj hurried over as Balthazar got to his feet.

"That went better than expected," Taj remarked. "I feared Mikal might deny you his blessing."

"You call that a blessing?" Balthazar muttered. "I've seen exorcisms with more warmth."

The daēva shrugged. "Take what you can get. Come, I'll walk you to the gates."

Lucas and Zarifa joined in as they started down the wide avenue leading from the Summer Palace. The people of Al Miraj lined the way, two and three deep, their faces solemn again. As Balthazar neared the gates, a child ran up. It was the one who'd given him the staff. He looked cleaner today, his long dark hair combed and plaited, yet he still had an air of mischief about him.

"I said you would be our champion, Magyar," he announced cheerfully.

Balthazar sighed. "I don't have the sword yet, boy."

The child gazed at him with innocent confidence. "You will."

Balthazar simply stared for a long moment, at a loss for words. "Thank you," he said finally.

The boy bobbed his head and ran off, joining a group of laughing friends.

Balthazar had never experienced the carefree joys of childhood – or if he had, he didn't remember them. It was the hardships that lodged in one's memory, like splinters of glass. The gnawing hunger. The fights over a dry patch of ground to sleep. The certain knowledge that however bad things seemed, they could always get worse.

He'd tried to do better with Lucas, but somehow all his good intentions had failed to produce any semblance of a normal life. Part of that was due to the circumstances that brought the boy into his custody. Lucas had needed revenge. Balthazar promised to give it to him. The deed was finally done, the necromancer who murdered his family dead, but Lucas was still here. Loyal to the end. Balthazar had no clue what he'd done to earn it, but at least Lucas seemed to think he was doing the right thing.

The sky lightened as they made their way through the winding streets. Jinn stood in clusters, sealing the cracked stonework and restoring the gardens to their manicured glory.

"So what are my odds?" Balthazar asked Taj in a light tone. "A thousand to one? Two thousand?"

"The regent has forbidden betting on the final outcome."

"That puritanical bastard."

Taj nodded agreement, oblivious to the sarcasm. "I know." His voice lowered. "But he can't stop us from making unofficial side wagers. I have an exceedingly large sum riding on you. If you don't come back, I'm out a fortune."

Balthazar glanced over. "Is that your sleazy way of saying good luck?"

Taj laughed, but it was laced with tension. "I doubt luck will have much to do with it."

Ever since the Seneschal had explained the curious history of the tunic and how it came into his hands via John Mortlake, Taj seemed gripped by superstitious dread. He was pale and distracted, his gaze restlessly roaming across the rooftops as though seeking an invisible assassin. Had there been time,

Balthazar felt sure he would have leapt into the boat and rowed over to Beletsunnu's house to demand answers.

He'd gone over the witch's words in his own mind a hundred times. He couldn't recall a single cryptic hint meant to help him. Quite the opposite. If the tunic was a trap, he'd walked straight into it. But the alternative – going to the cloud empty-handed – was even less appealing.

"Balthazar!"

He turned as Captain Karatas came running up. He was breathing hard, as if he'd sprinted all the way from The Golden Flail.

"I . . . . " He swallowed hard. "I just wanted to say it has been a pleasure knowing you."

"Well, don't dig my grave just yet," Balthazar replied dryly. "We might see each other again."

Destan flushed. "Of course. I didn't mean it that way. Only that I . . . I'm sorry for that first night."

Balthazar waved a hand. "It's forgotten."

"Thank you." He gave a formal bow. "Goodbye, then."

Balthazar frowned as Destan Karatas melted back into the crowds lining the street. Did he know something? Taj gazed after his servant with an unreadable expression, but the city gates loomed before them and there was no time to pursue the matter.

"Do what you must," Taj growled at Balthazar with a pointed look. "Forget the so-called bargain. Once you have the sword, make good use of it."

"I plan to." Balthazar stepped away before the daēva could harangue him further. "I need a word with Lucas. Would you excuse us?"

"Of course."

Taj moved to stand with Zarifa. Balthazar felt her watching as he lifted the chain from his neck and pressed it into Lucas's hand. "Don't lose that. I'm going to need it."

"Of course you are," Lucas said with feeling.

"Could you do me one last favor?" Balthazar gazed at him earnestly. "It would . . . ." He swallowed. "It would mean a great deal."

Lucas gave a feverish nod. "Anything, my lord."

"Use it on Taj, will you?"

Lucas gave an exasperated laugh. The gates opened. Balthazar squared his shoulders.

"I'll want a bottle of that Brugerolle when I return." He glanced down at the leather sandals. "And some decent shoes."

With those words, he departed for the final reckoning with the Mistress of Shadows.

CHAPTER 24

Balthazar crossed the Empty Quarter with a brisk but relaxed stride. The wind had scoured away any trace of the arena. He saw no sign of Fulad-zereh in the dragon's jaws, although the ominous cloud hovered just beyond the walls, occasional forks of lightning illuminating its black depths.

As usual, jinn and daēvas filled the balconies behind him. Balthazar did not look back. He might be going to meet his doom, but it somehow seemed fitting. As much as he loathed Fulad-zereh, he felt grudging respect for her. Like him, she had hunted the Druj. She was unfathomably old and powerful. A formidable adversary − unlike the John Mortlakes of the world who hardly deserved to be called necromancers.

Balthazar had never expected to die in an armchair by the fire. In truth, he'd never expected to live this long at all.

He stopped as a whirlwind of sand erupted ahead. The pillar resolved into a red-skinned ifrit with a brutish, scowling face and ridged horns jutting from its thick forehead. He couldn't tell if it was the same one that had overseen the Trials in the arena.

"Do you carry any weapons?" the ifrit demanded in a deep, growling voice.

Balthazar held up open palms. "I come to your mistress unarmed and defenseless."

The ifrit gave him a hard look. It stepped forward, bringing the searing heat of a blacksmith's forge, and searched him with ungentle hands. Since he wore open-toed shoes and what was essentially a knee-length dress, this process was mercifully brief.

"You may pass," the ifrit growled.

It waved a hand and a staircase descended from the cloud. It looked like grey mist, yet the narrow steps felt firm beneath Balthazar's feet as he started on either side. He kept his eyes straight ahead, ascending higher and higher, the steps behind him vanishing the instant his feet moved onward.

When he reached the top, he stood in the dragon's jaws, where Fulad-zereh had watched the first three Trials. The head was immense, each fang as long as his arm and tapered to a sharp point. From the high perch, he saw Al Miraj laid out before him, the daēvas crowding the balconies as tiny as grains of rice. Balthazar waited for a minute, but no ifrit appeared to guide him further.

He walked deeper into the dragon's mouth, passing the rear fangs and entering the serpentine throat. The mist thickened. It soaked his hair and trailed clammy fingers across his skin. The light dimmed almost to pitch darkness. He listened intently, but the heavy cloud dampened any sound save for his soft footfalls. Balthazar continued forward, testing each step in the treacherous fog.

Had the Trial already begun? The demon obviously enjoyed playing games. Would she thrust him into the quest without a word of explanation? Or was this Fulad-zereh's idea of foreplay? Let him sweat a little before she made her grand appearance? Either way, Balthazar found himself despising her with renewed intensity.

It seemed he walked through the impenetrable fog for a long time, though it might have been minutes. At last, he turned a corner and the scene abruptly altered. The mist dispersed. Rocky cliffs rose to a great height on either side. Directly before him was a soaring temple-like structure with a rectangular doorway at least a hundred paces high, but only wide enough for a single man to pass through. The slanting angle of the sun left whatever lay beyond the doorway in perfect darkness.

Balthazar drew a deep breath and entered a large redstone cavern. In the dim light, he saw ifrit lining the walls, each twice the size of a marid, with gold bands circling their massive arms and heavy half-moon blades slung at their hips. Torches burned in brackets on the walls. The air was smoky and stifling.

Fulad-zereh sat on the floor with a pile of black stones, wisps of cloud floating around her.

She wore close-fitting armor of bright steel. She had the same broad nose and full mouth as Beletsunnu, but her chin was pointier and her skin had a bluish cast. Her eyes were the most alien feature, topaz set against pure black. Small horns jutted from her hairless scalp.

Balthazar gave a respectful bow.

Fulad-zereh looked him over. Her eyes narrowed.

"Where is the handsome suit you always wear?"

She had small, sharp teeth.

"I chose simpler attire today," Balthazar replied.

"Why?" Her voice held an edge of distrust.

He smiled. "Why do you wear armor when there is only one thing on earth that can do you harm and you have it securely in your possession?"

"It makes it easier to see me from the arena and the balconies." The demon's voice was raspy, with a breathless, sibilant quality.

"So you don't wear it all the time."

"No," she admitted.

"It's just the two of us now. We have no need to impress anyone."

He feared she would pursue the matter, but Fulad-zereh only frowned. "That is true."

She seized a handful of cloud and shook it out. Vapor solidified to a fine cotton weave. Fulad-zereh snapped her fingers and an ifrit rushed over to unbuckle the breastplate. Piece by piece, a surprisingly slender body was revealed. The demon pulled the tunic over her head. There was the sound of ripping cloth as her leathery wings popped through.

"Is it cold where you come from?" she asked.

"Sometimes."

"I would not like that." Her gaze was measuring. "The staff came as a surprise. Contenders rarely change weapons when the first has proven effective. They fear it will bring bad luck."

She returned to her cross-legged position and began arranging the black stones in a line. They were flat and all exactly the same size and shape.

"It was a gift," Balthazar said.

"I know. I still didn't expect you to use it." She started a second row at right angles to the first. "You made a wise choice. The runes served you well."

He felt a rush of curiosity. "What do they say?"

She looked up at him. "You do not know?"

He shook his head.

"It is old daēva binding magic. Every blow from an enemy's hand makes the wood stronger. It can only be done with oak or ash." The stones began to form a pattern beneath her fingers. "There is a price, of course. The maker's name is one of the runes. He or she will be bound to that particular tree for life. If it is cut down or burned . . . ." She shrugged.

Balthazar felt cold. "A young boy gave it to me."

"Then his fate is bound to the tree."

"Can you not . . ." He paused, his throat tight. "If I fail, can you strengthen the spell to hide the city?"

Her hands moved faster now, expanding the pattern. "No."

"What will you do for entertainment when they are no longer there to torment?" he asked bitterly.

"I am not refusing you. But that kind of magic is not my kind of magic. It's too . . . coherent." She eyed him with a puzzled expression. "I see this saddens you. I find that peculiar. But I have never encountered an Antimagus who forsook the chains and turned on his own kind. I think you are the only one."

"There's another," he replied without thinking. "He calls himself Gabriel D'Ange."

"I will remember that name." She stared at him unblinking for an uncomfortably long time. "I used to enjoy hunting Druj. The liches, in particular. They gave good sport. But I have not seen any lately."

Balthazar wondered how she perceived the passage of time. *Lately* could mean last week, last year – or a thousand years ago.

"Perhaps you killed them all," he said.

"Would that make you happy?"

He didn't hesitate. "Yes."

She tilted her head. "Why?"

"Because they're evil."

Fulad-zereh returned to her task, face intent. "The ifrit were the first jinn. They are more ancient than both our lifespans multiplied together, Balthazar. Yet they serve me by choice. Why do you think that is?"

"I don't know," he admitted.

"Because I am a fair mistress. I favor no race above another. I hunted the liches because it amused me, but I never hated them. Not as you do."

"You're not vengeful at all." Balthazar knew he skated on

thin ice, but her superior tone annoyed him. "You've only punished an entire city for nine hundred years."

"That is not punishment."

"What do you call it?"

"The spell lowers inhibition. It has no power to compel." She gazed at him with those unsettling eyes. "Whatever you have done, it already lay in your heart."

"I wasn't talking about myself," he said quickly. Balthazar cleared his throat. "The observation was purely theoretical."

She flashed pointy teeth. "Of course. But why do you think the regent is so angry with them? He believes they could resist, if they were only as pure as he is."

"That's an impossible standard."

"I agree. Mikal is rigid and overzealous. Still, he has more compassion than his brothers. It could be much worse."

The pattern covered several square feet now. It dizzied him to look at it.

"Your father, you mean?" he said quietly. "Azrael."

Balthazar took satisfaction from the surprise on her face.

"Who told you?" Fulad-zereh demanded.

"No one. I figured it out on my own."

She leaned back, a stone in her hand. "No doubt you are wondering how I turned out the way I did. You think me cruel after what I subjected you to in the arena."

He remained silent.

"The first two tests I devised myself. But even I did not know what the last would be. Everything you saw and did came from your own mind, down to the last detail."

"Is that supposed to make me feel better or worse?"

"Neither. But you entered the circle freely. I merely held a mirror to your conscience. I find it to be the most interesting round. The truth always comes out."

"And is your own conscience so light?" he asked dryly.

"Yes," she replied without hesitation.

"That must be the angelic half." Balthazar knew his

tongue was too sharp, but he no longer cared. "A penchant for self-righteousness."

"I simply don't see things the way you do. I am not concerned with blame or guilt. Right or wrong. You hate the liches because they feed on your race, and therefore they must be evil. But I find them beautiful to look upon."

Balthazar frowned. Beautiful? They were tattered shreds of shadow and smoke. One touch from a lich brought instant death.

"You just said you hunted them for your own amuse-ment," he reminded her.

"And they hunt you for theirs. And you hunt necro-mancers for yours. Do you see the great circle?" Her lips twitched. "Like a snake biting its own tail."

Balthazar bristled. "I don't do it for *amusement*—"

"Of course you do," she interrupted. "We both know it to be so." She crawled behind him to continue the pattern and he was forced to spin around to keep her in view.

"Just tell me what I must do to find the sword," he said, weary of her banter.

"I'm getting to that. I merely wanted to make my position clear. You may enter the Labyrinth. If you prove yourself worthy, you will leave with the Emerald-Studded Blade."

"Ah," he said softly, sensing another of this crafty crea-ture's loopholes. "And who decides if I am worthy?"

"You do, of course." Fulad-zereh laid the last stone in place. "There. It is done."

Balthazar realized he stood at the edge of a diabolically complex circle with innumerable branching passages. He tried to memorize the design, eyes darting from one dead end to the next. The solution was right in front of him if he could only see it.

"The sword waits in the center," she said. "Find it if you can."

"Just wait a moment—" he began desperately.

The miniature suddenly grew and spread before his eyes. It was no longer laid out on the cavern floor, but in a chasm far below. With a sickening lurch, the stone beneath his feet tilted and rent open. He tumbled into empty space. Wind tore at his tunic. His arms wheeled, terror slamming his heart against his ribcage. The labyrinth grew bigger, an endless panorama of interlocked pathways spiraling towards a dark heart. It raced up to meet him.

An instant before he hit, everything went dark. There was a sensation of weightlessness, like drifting at the bottom of the sea. Then he felt solid ground beneath his feet again. Balthazar blinked, swallowing a wave of nausea. He stood in a hardwood forest so dense almost no daylight penetrated the canopy. A hedge ten paces high stretched into the gloom on either side. The only breach was a stone archway with a carving of a double-bladed axe at the top.

The *labrys*, an ancient Lydian word.

And so it begins, he thought, steeling himself. She is old and clever. But so am I.

Trust no one and nothing.

Balthazar stepped through the arch.

Tall hedges rose on every side. He immediately faced a choice of continuing straight ahead, or turning to the left or right. He tried to reconstruct his glimpse of the labyrinth from above, but saw only a mass of spiraling lines. If he'd been given hours to study it . . . but that was Fulad-zereh's signature brand of torment. Offer a shred of hope and snatch it away.

The path was made from jointed stone slabs, so there would be no trace of his own tracks. But she hadn't reckoned on him coming prepared. Balthazar picked at the embroidery on the hem of his tunic until a single thread came loose. It shone faintly in his hand. He examined the hedge more closely. It had glossy serrated leaves and vicious-looking thorns the length of his thumb. He tied the thread to a thorn and turned right. It unfurled smoothly behind him as if from a spool.

He followed the path around the corner to a dead end and doubled back. There was just enough light to see the glowing thread, although the sky overhead was lost to gloom. He wondered where he truly was. Another cavern? Atop the dragon cloud? The thought that he might be thousands of feet above the ground was disquieting and Balthazar pushed it away.

He had only to reach the center and whatever waited there — which would surely be more than the sword. But one step at a time.

He returned to the starting point and chose the leftward path, snapping the thread and starting a new one. This time, the way continued through several more turnings before ending at a wall of thorns. He retraced his steps to the previous juncture and tried a different route. Again and again, he met blind cul-de-sacs. But the thread kept him from turning the wrong way twice. And it never ran out.

In this painstaking manner, he gradually moved deeper into the labyrinth. When he encountered an island with multiple outlets, he always tried the right-hand turning first. But there seemed no rhyme or reason to the design. Sometimes the right side petered out almost immediately. Other times, it led to further branchings. Progress was agonizingly slow. But as the hours passed, the ways grew narrower and more sharply curved. Balthazar hoped this meant he was nearing the heart.

If he had not viewed the entire labyrinth from above, he might have thought she intended to let him wander forever. But he *had* seen it — if only for an instant. And he knew there was a way to the center, if he could only find it.

Left and right, forward and backward. Dead ends and turnings. Sometimes he caught sight of threads he had left behind, shining in the darkness of a distant path. Balthazar shuddered to imagine what it would be like to walk through this place with no certainty that he hadn't passed the very same spot before. Perhaps that was the insanity Beletsunnu spoke of.

He laughed softly, though it sounded too loud in the perfect silence. "I'm not mad yet, witch. Not yet."

Still, the sheer tedium of the exercise was numbing. He lost all sense of how long he had been inside. His fingers bled from careless pricks by those diabolical thorns. He trudged onward, mechanically tying and untying threads. It seemed that nothing would ever change.

Until he heard something on the other side of the hedge.

Balthazar froze and cocked his head, straining to listen.

It had sounded like the breathing of a large animal.

The foliage was too dense to make out what lay on the other side. There were no gaps that he could see, unless it found a way to circle around behind him. He retreated, moving silently on the balls of his feet, and found another turning in the opposite direction. The way remained clear until he reached an island with multiple outlets. He thought he'd left the creature behind. But then he heard the soft pad of hooves on stone somewhere nearby.

He was being hunted.

He snapped off the thread. He couldn't risk using it anymore. The shining filaments would be a beacon leading straight to him – if it was intelligent enough to follow his trail, which he had to assume it was. Balthazar quickened his pace.

He moved blindly now, choosing turnings at random, backtracking when he reached a dead end. He saw no evidence of old threads, so at least he wasn't heading back out again. Sweat trickled down his back. Could it smell him?

Probably.

Balthazar turned a corner and saw an island ahead with three branchings. Some instinct made him pause and watch, hardly daring to breathe.

In the dim light, he saw the shadows shift.

He turned and ran in the opposite direction, blundering through the labyrinth as fast as he could go. The thing pursued. Sometimes it sounded close behind. Then all would go quiet again. He couldn't tell if he'd lost it, or if it was silently stalking him. At every intersection, he paused and peeked around the hedge before continuing. Once, he saw a dark shape in the distance disappearing down another path. He drew back, pulse racing, and waited until he was sure it was gone to take a route in the opposite direction.

Balthazar knew he was lost. He didn't dare use Ariadne's thread. But he had to find the center before the creature found him.

The dead ends were the worst. Every time he met a blank wall of thorns, he expected to turn and find it slinking towards him. He moved swiftly and silently in the half-light, pausing only to snap off a branch to mark paths he had already explored.

He knew it was all a grand illusion, but he had to believe in the possibility, however remote, that the sword was here somewhere and that it could be found. If he stopped believing that, he might as well just sit down and wait to get eaten or impaled or whatever grim fate awaited.

He turned right, then left, passing a blind alley he'd already marked with a broken branch, and left again. He felt a surge of excitement. This pathway was longer than any he had taken before. It ran straight towards a wide gap in the hedge. Something shone in the gloom beyond.

His heart sped up as he ran down the path and burst into a clearing filled with columns of clear glass that rose to head height. Within the glass, suspended with its jeweled hilt facing down, was the Shamshir e-Zomorrodnegar.

Not just one. Dozens.

He had reached the heart of the labyrinth.

CHAPTER 25

"Beletsunnu requests your presence, master."

Taj looked up as Yatha materialized inside the pavilion on the roof of The Golden Flail. Since Balthazar entered the jaws of the dragon, the daēva had been staring moodily into an untouched goblet of wine, his face expressionless.

Lucas, who paced up and down along the fringe of carpet, looked over with alarm. "Has something happened?" he demanded.

Yatha spread his hands. "I do not know."

The tent blocked the sun, but it was still brutally hot. Taj had shrugged off his ceremonial robes and wore only his usual short white tunic. The taut muscles in his legs flexed as he rose to his feet, but Lucas barely noticed. He stared at the cloud. There was no sign of movement.

"What's going on?" Zarifa asked groggily. The heat combined with a sleepless night had finally overtaken her, although she'd refused Taj's entreaties to go lie down. Instead, she'd dozed off on a cushion. Now she pushed up to sitting, fully alert. "Is there news?"

"I'd better go find out," Taj replied, his jaw tight. "I'll

summon you if I have need," he told Yatha, striding away.

Lucas watched him disappear in an agony of uncertainty. Balthazar had been gone for hours. The sun was already descending in the sky, and Lucas instinctively knew that if he did not return before it set, he would not return at all.

"The witch said nothing else?" he demanded.

Yatha's ice-blue eyes gazed at him with a grave expression. "I never spoke to her. My message was a pretext."

Lucas frowned.

"There is no time to spare. Hear me out before he returns." Yatha's voice lowered. "My master has betrayed you."

"Betrayed?" Zarifa exclaimed. "What on earth do you mean?"

"I cannot refuse Taj's direct orders, but he neglected to bind me to silence. The tunic Balthazar wears is a fake."

Lucas and Zarifa exchanged a puzzled look. They had both seen Balthazar take it from the table. He had changed in a dim corner of the Treasury. Then they'd all gone straight to the plaza of the Summer Palace, where Balthazar received the blessing.

"How is that possible—" Lucas began.

"I switched them," Yatha said.

"You *what?*"

"Taj commanded me to."

Lucas's mind reeled. *It couldn't be.* Taj wanted more than anything for the sword to be found.

"No." Lucas shook his head. "What possible advantage could he gain?"

"For the last year, he has gone in secret to the archives to peruse old books of magic. I believe he has found a way to revive the protective spell that conceals the city."

"But the curse—"

"Who profits from the chaos more than my master?" Yatha asked quietly. "It was he who arranged the attempts on

Balthazar's life. Jabaar held the crossbow, but it was Taj who commanded it."

"Where is your proof?" Lucas demanded.

Yatha glanced at the stairs with a flicker of unease. "The true Thread of Ariadne is hidden in his chambers."

Lucas stared at the marid, his pulse racing. It was all *conceivable* – except for one thing. "Why would you betray Taj? You yourself admitted that you're bound to his will!"

"That is true," Yatha conceded. "But only in part. Before Taj, I served the prince. He is my real master. If there is any chance he lives, it is my duty to see him freed." Yatha hung his head. "I feel shame for what I have done. If Balthazar does return, I fear Taj plans to kill him. To kill all of you."

Lucas swore under his breath. He didn't want it to be true, but there was no denying Taj's mercenary tendencies. He was fully capable of sacrificing Balthazar if it served his own interests. Lucas wasn't convinced the daēva would really murder them all in cold blood, but that was scant reassurance. He hardly knew Taj – or he knew only what the daēva allowed him to know. And the facts were rather damning. He'd done business with Mortlake for years. His marids recruited fodder for the Trials – men Taj knew would die. And he ran his little empire with an iron hand. It didn't stretch one's imagination to think he might want to claim power for himself.

"Here is my offer," the marid said to Lucas. "I can take you to the cloud without the demon knowing. Find Balthazar. Free the prince, if he lives. Let him find the sword. But we must hurry, before Taj discovers I sent him on a fool's errand." He turned to Zarifa. "There is a talisman of Traveling in the storehouse. You can all use it to escape. Meet me there and I will aid you in getting inside."

"Wait," Lucas said, fresh doubts arising. This all happening too fast. "Why didn't Taj simply allow Balthazar to die after the Third Trial?"

"I wondered the same," Yatha said. "I think he wished to

ensure the regent would leave. Mikal has done all he could. If the effort fails, he has no obligation to remain. There will be no more Trials. And my master will become the new prince."

It made a twisted kind of sense. Yatha could be lying, but what would his reason be? Lucas felt torn in half, but he couldn't take the chance that Balthazar had been abandoned to the demon's lair with no means of escape.

"Show me the Thread of Ariadne," he said.

They all hurried down the stairs, Zarifa continuing onward to the Treasury while Lucas and Yatha went to Taj's chambers.

"Don't worry," the marid said softly. "It will be some time before my master returns. He must cross the lake there and back."

They entered the curtained chamber with the sunken pool. Shafts of light spilled through the repeating arabesque scrolls on the far wall, creating a dappled pattern on the water. Taj had healed Balthazar in that same pool. Dragged him back from the brink. Was it all a ruse to keep him intact for the final sacrifice?

Such a plot seemed excessively elaborate, but Lucas's heart was heavy with dread as Yatha led him to a square chest against the wall. Lucas tore the lid open. Stacks of linen towels filled the space. He dug down and brushed a gold-embroidered hem. Lucas withdrew the tunic. It was identical to the one Balthazar had worn. More importantly, he could sense its talismanic power.

He felt the fine weave between his fingers, rage building at Taj's betrayal.

"I should never have allowed him to go alone," Lucas muttered.

"You had no choice," Yatha replied reasonably. "Those are the rules."

Lucas turned hollow eyes on the marid. "Do you have any idea if he is still alive?"

"I'm sorry, I cannot say." The marid gazed at him shrewdly. "You are loyal to your master."

"To my dying breath."

"Why?" He spread his hands. "If you don't mind my asking."

Lucas looked away, his face grim. "I owe him a great deal."

"That's all? Because you owe him?"

"No," Lucas muttered. "Because he is a good man. Not in every way, but in all the ways that matter."

"I see. You are fortunate to have such devotion." The marid looked thoughtful. "The prince was a good master, too, despite his faults. It was no great burden to serve him. But Taj is cut from different cloth. He cares only for himself."

The words echoed Lucas's own thoughts. "I must go after Balthazar myself."

Yatha nodded. "He has already embarked on the quest, but with luck, it is not yet too late."

"I'll need a sword."

The marid hesitated. "If Fulad-zereh finds you with a weapon, she will kill you."

"Then I'll make sure I'm not found," Lucas replied tersely.

Yatha conjured a curved blade and scabbard. Lucas belted it on. He rolled up the tunic and placed it in a small satchel he strapped across his back.

"How will we find the prince?" he asked.

"That is up to you." The marid's face hardened. "But I will not bring you back until he is freed."

"And if he is dead?"

"Then you are, too."

Before Lucas could reply, the marid laid a chill hand on his arm. The desert shimmered and blurred. An instant later, they stood in a dark wood, the branches twining overhead.

"Follow the path," Yatha whispered, his eyes darting

around. "It will lead you to the labyrinth. If you hurry, you will catch up with him before he has gone too deep."

Lucas stepped back. "You have set an impossible task," he hissed. "I might be able to find Balthazar, but the prince could be anywhere. Or nowhere!"

Yatha bowed. "I have faith in your abilities."

Lucas opened his mouth to argue, but Yatha was already gone.

"Bloody hell," he muttered.

The forest was silent and gloomy. It had an ancient, primeval feel, with massive trunks and almost no under-growth. He wondered if he were somewhere inside the cloud, or if Fulad-zereh's realm was farther away. Dead leaves carpeted the ground in thick drifts. There was no birdsong or chirp of insects, only a low wind that rustled the intertwined branches far above.

But Lucas could make out a faint trail. He set off, one hand resting lightly on the hilt of the sword. Huge roots thrust out of the earth like writhing serpents. He moved with caution, scanning the murk on either side while trying not to trip over the roots. After a few minutes, Lucas heard a low, deep voice. He hurried off the path and pressed himself behind one of the thick trunks.

A minute later, two ifrit came striding along the path. He felt the heat of their passage, like a hot gust from the desert. Lucas held his breath, his heart hammering. He gripped the sword, but didn't dare to draw it unless he had no choice.

One of the ifrit growled something in a guttural language. And then he heard them continue onward, their heavy foot-falls fading into the distance.

Lucas waited another ten minutes until he was certain they were gone. Then he followed, crossing a stream and following the path on a gentle downward slope. The decid-uous forest gave way to towering spruce and pine. After a while, he encountered a tall hedge. He followed it, half his attention focused on the ground ahead, the other half lost in dark ruminations.

I can't believe I slept with him, Lucas thought glumly.

He recalled the conversation when Taj described what Al Miraj used to be like before the curse. The pain in his face had seemed so genuine. Perhaps that was part of the sport for Taj – to toy with his emotions. The daēva denied hating mortals, but that could be another lie. It stung Lucas's pride, but his only concern was to find Balthazar and get them both out before they were discovered.

How he would manage that without Yatha, Lucas had no idea.

In his twenty-nine years, Lucas had wiggled out of plenty of precarious situations. This was easily the worst. He sighed. If they did live through their latest misadventure, he would insist on a holiday. Brighton, perhaps. Or the Isle of Wight. There was a spa with bathing machines that he had heard were most salutary—

He rounded a curve and saw a tall figure some distance ahead. Lucas froze, then hurried silently to catch up. He drew nearer, creeping like a shadow from tree to tree. The figure paused before an arched breach in the hedge. Lucas knew the determined set of those broad shoulders. The curling dark hair at the nape of his neck. Balthazar had not yet entered the labyrinth!

"My lord," he breathed, rushing heedlessly forward. "Thank God."

The figure half turned. Lucas gazed into a pair of alien eyes. He drew up short, hand scrabbling for the sword buckled at his hip – now gone.

He felt an instant of profound regret before his limbs turned to stone. Lucas could only watch, helpless, as the features blurred into someone else entirely.

"It seems a little gnat has flown into my web," the demon hissed, her thin lips curling into a smile.

CHAPTER 26

Balthazar approached the nearest glass pillar and pressed his palm against it. There was no seam or joint. He gave the pillar an experimental kick with the sole of his sandal. The glass felt solid all the way through. He moved through the columns, testing each one. They might have been stone.

So the problem was twofold. Determining which was the real sword, and getting to it.

The blades revolved slowly within the glass columns. They looked identical in every way. The emeralds embedded in their hilts gathered the faint light like cat's eyes.

There must be a solution. He had defeated the labyrinth. Surely that was the hardest part—

Balthazar spun at the sharp click of hooves striking stone.

The creature snorted and pawed the ground when it saw him. He felt no surprise to learn it was half-man, half-bull like the fabled Minotaur. Sleek black hide covered its torso and legs, which were tipped with pointed hooves. It stood erect, towering on powerful haunches. The chest and arms were hairless, but its head was bestial, with thick curling horns and a muzzle.

Should all this prove insufficient to dry the spit from his

mouth, Fulad-zereh had added her own special touch. An enormous double-bladed axe in one hand.

Balthazar absorbed these details in the split second before it thundered towards him. The creature blocked the exit, leaving no choice but to run deeper into the pillars. He glanced over his shoulder just as a rock caught his left sandal. He fell, landing hard on one side. Breath rasped as he rolled away. The half-moon blade whistled past his head and sank into the earth. He gained his feet as the Minotaur tore it free with an enraged bellow.

For the next minute, he led the beast on a merry chase, feinting and dodging between the columns. It finally retreated a short distance, hooves pawing deep furrows in the earth.

If he could somehow get the axe . . .

The Minotaur charged. He ducked under the curved blade, but a blow from one of the massive arms sent him flying headfirst into the hedge at the far side of the clearing. Thorns raked his skin. The tips curved like fishhooks, holding his tunic fast as he struggled to break free. The Minotaur strode towards him, axe whickering in figure eights.

The harder he fought, the worse he was ensnared. He heard the tunic rip along one seam. Branches cracked, whipping across his face. He managed to yank an arm out, but he was engulfed to the waist. Even his hair was hopelessly tangled. The Minotaur gave an ear-splitting roar behind him.

And then Balthazar saw a greenish shimmer inside the hedge, so faint he feared he'd imagined it. He shook sweat from his eyes. Even that tiny movement drove the thorns deeper. But there was something . . . . He dug his heels in, biting back a scream as he forced himself deeper into the hedge. He had only seconds before the Minotaur was upon him. But he could see the jewel-studded hilt now, inches from his fingertips. With a final thrust that flayed half the skin from his arm, Balthazar gripped the sword.

He felt its talismanic power instantly. A torrent of magic dedicated to a single purpose.

It sliced through the brambles like dry stalks of wheat. He got the blade up just in time to parry the downward slice of the axe. Sparks jumped from the contact. The Minotaur bellowed and swung the axe back.

Balthazar wrenched himself free of the hedge. Blood soaked his arm. His skin was aflame in a hundred places. Several dozen three-inch-long thorns were still embedded in his body. The tunic hung in shredded rags. But none of that mattered.

He had a sword.

No, he had *the* sword.

The blade was single-edged and perfectly balanced.

Balthazar struck, aiming for the thick wooden haft blurring toward his face. The Minotaur snorted as the Shamshir-e Zomorrodnegar cleaved it in half. Small yellow eyes fixed on him, full of desperate cunning. It parried his overhead stroke with the head of the axe. Then it pivoted on its hooves, faster than Balthazar could believe, and cracked the severed haft against his left temple.

He'd dodged at the last moment so the blow was glancing, but the force of it still stunned him. He stumbled back, vision blurring. The Minotaur charged. It wielded the axe like a hatchet, long arms compensating for the shortened reach.

Balthazar blocked a flurry of frenzied blows, retreating on wobbly legs. Something hard pressed against his back. One of the glass pillars.

The beast snorted, carving the half-moon blade in tight arcs. Balthazar ducked as the Minotaur swung for his head. The blade sank into the glass column and wedged there. As it struggled to free the axe, he drove the sword through its shaggy belly. The eyes dimmed. It gave a weak grunt. Balthazar shoved it back and pulled out the dripping sword. His next swing took the Minotaur's head from its shoulders. It toppled and lay still. Dark blood pulsed from the severed neck, soaking into the bare earth.

He stood over the fallen beast, panting. One by one, the false swords inside the glass columns faded away.

But the labyrinth remained.

Balthazar gave a grim smile. Let the demon play her little games. He'd find his way out eventually. If she thought to stop him, he was no longer unarmed. No longer at her mercy. In fact, nothing would give him greater pleasure—

The ground shook violently beneath his feet. Cracks zigzagged up the columns. With a shatter of glass, they exploded. He threw an arm across his face, trying to keep his feet. A terrible shrieking filled the air. And a wind, cold and laden with the smell of the sea—

The labyrinth vanished. Balthazar stood on a bare rock beaten by waves. An angry sea stretched out in all directions, slate grey and whipped to frothing whitecaps. In the middle of the rock, a naked man lay spread-eagled in chains. He had a cap of dark hair, matted with sweat. His belly was torn open. Gulls squabbled over the entrails, their beaks smeared crimson. Balthazar thought he was dead until the ashen face weakly turned his way. The eyes opened.

Not a man. A daēva. Balthazar knew him.

His name was Lysandros. One of the oldest. He'd vanished after the war.

They had been enemies then. Balthazar could hardly remember his face, but he remembered those extraordinary violet eyes.

The gulls paid him no attention, stabbing their sharp beaks into the gaping wound. When they paused to swallow a morsel, the wounds healed, only to be torn open again seconds later. Balthazar swallowed a wave of nausea. He raised the sword and brought it down against the rock, severing the iron links. The birds scattered with angry screeches.

Lysandros lay unmoving for a long minute, his face still contorted in agony. Then he lifted a trembling hand. He pressed it against his belly. Balthazar watched the flesh knit together. The daēva rolled to his side. He curled there, knees tight against his chest, shivering in the cold spray of the waves.

Balthazar looked around. He knew the scene couldn't be real, yet like all the demon's illusions it was entirely convincing. The choppy swells, the salt tang of the open ocean, the gore-stained rock. Had she brought him here to free Lysandros? It made no sense.

What does she want? What is she really after?

The only thing he felt certain of was the blade in his hand. He could sense its power.

"How did you come here, Antimagus?"

The voice was hoarse and decidedly unfriendly. He glanced at Lysandros, who had pulled himself up to sitting.

Balthazar didn't bother disputing the title. He was too tired.

"I'll explain later. After we find a way off this rock."

Lysandros hunched over, clutching his stomach. "Nine hundred years, necromancer," he grated. "That's how long I've been her prisoner. Carrion for the gulls!" With a groan, he slid his hand away. The flesh beneath was raw and pink. "Waiting for a rescue party that never came—"

"They thought you were dead," Balthazar said.

"Death would have been preferable!" He stared at the sword, a sudden hungry light in his eyes. "How did you come by that?"

"I took it. And it brought me to you."

Or someone did.

"You took it," Lysandros repeated flatly. A mirthless laugh escaped his lips. "No. I think you are not real. Just another torment. Another of her tricks—"

"I'm real enough." Balthazar held up a mangled arm. The bleeding had stopped, but he looked like he'd lost a wrestling match with a wildcat. "And my prize didn't come cheap, daēva. Can you touch the power?"

That earned a withering glare. "Obviously not. She's blocked me."

"How?"

"I've no idea! But I cannot sense the Nexus. This is *her* realm. *Her* rules. And neither of us will leave without permission."

Another wave crashed against the rock, soaking them both. The water seemed to be rising.

"She told me that if I was worthy, I could find the sword and bring it out. I've done all she required!" Balthazar clenched his jaw in frustration. "She made a pact with your people. Taj warned me not to trust her—"

"You've seen Taj?" Lysandros's face went very still. "He lives?"

"Oh, he's running things. And I doubt you'd approve of his management style."

"We have to get off this rock," the prince snapped.

"How do you propose to do that?"

"I'll swim if I have to!"

The next wave submerged the rock in an inch of water before receding.

"We may have no other choice," Balthazar muttered. Hot rage was rising in him. There was always one more task. One more obstacle. The quest would go on and on—

Lysandros stood. He pointed. Balthazar saw a smudge on the horizon. It was the dragon cloud, speeding towards them. Fulad-zereh stood in the jaws. She had donned her armor again. An army of ifrit stood behind her.

"Give me the sword," Lysandros growled, his face setting into lines of implacable hatred as he gazed at the demon.

Balthazar took a step back. He tightened his grip on the hilt.

The dragon filled the sky overhead. It had scales of dull

silver that shone with each flicker of lightning. The demon held a long blade in her hand, perhaps the same he had seen in the mosaic at the Summer Palace.

Lysandros turned to face him. "Only I can finish this, Balthazar. We both know it."

"Oh, really?" He arched a brow. "I don't recall you coming out on top last time, *Your Highness*."

The prince scowled. "She only overpowered me because I'd left the sword behind. You've never seen Fulad-zereh fight. She'll make mincemeat of you."

"I have the Shamshir-e Zomorrodnegar."

Lysandros gave him a level look. "You still have to get through her guard before she kills you and that is no small feat. Even for you, Balthazar."

"I'll take my chances."

The dragon's head lowered toward the rock, its huge wings extended in a dive. Fulad-zereh crouched in the jaws, ready to leap down. The horde of ifrit at her back unsheathed their flaming swords.

"You cannot defeat her, necromancer! The blade was always meant for me—"

Lysandros cut off as the point pressed against his throat. His eyes narrowed.

Trust nothing and no one.

"Show yourself," Balthazar said. "Or I'll finish you."

Lysandros gritted his teeth. "You're making a terrible mistake—"

Balthazar pressed the point deeper, to the edge of drawing blood. "I'm curious how this works," he said in a conversational tone. "Do I have to behead you? Or will a mere scratch with the Emerald-Studded Blade do the trick? Two more seconds and we'll find out."

The prince's lean, handsome face shimmered like a mirage. The brown skin assumed a blue tint. Horns sprouted from his forehead. An instant later, a pair of topaz eyes stared at Balthazar.

"Very clever," Fulad-zereh hissed.

The rock vanished. They stood in the heart of the labyrinth amid the shattered glass columns. She meant to throw him off balance, but this time Balthazar was ready. He knew two things for certain. The sword in his hand was real. The demon was real. The rest didn't matter. She tensed as if to run, but he held the blade steady at her throat.

"How did you know?" she demanded.

"It was obvious."

She frowned.

"If Lysandros truly believed I was a necromancer, he would have asked where my chains were. And he would have known I'd be nearly as fast as a daēva. But he treated me like a regular man. Then there was the remark, *Even you, Balthazar.* We barely knew each other. I was a fair swordsman back then, but not half the one I am now. *Two thousand years later.* He couldn't have known that."

The demon laughed. "I thought I had you. A pity."

"What is this game you play?" he snapped. "If you had no intention of honoring the bargain, you could have just kept the sword!"

She bared her small, pointy teeth. "I cannot wield it unless it is given freely. But it matters not. Go on, kill me, stupid creature! It's your only way out. I will never let you leave with it!"

Hatred boiled in his veins. He thought of all the things she had done to him. All the men she had slaughtered. Fulad-zereh was the incarnation of chaos. If he didn't kill her now, she would invent some new Trial for him. She would send punishment after punishment until he was finally broken.

One flick of his wrist and it would be over.

Is that what the demon wanted in the end? To goad him into killing her?

He studied her face, so like her mother's, and thought of the witch's words.

Of Fulad-zereh's own words.

And who decides if I am worthy? he had asked.

You do, she'd replied.

The final test.

"No." Balthazar lowered the blade, his heart pounding.

Her eyes narrowed in distrust. "Why would you spare me?"

"Because it is just."

She tilted her head. "How so?"

"Until this moment, you have kept your word." He swallowed, praying to any god who might listen that he had chosen right. "The bargain was a harsh one, yet it was still better than they had any right to expect. I believe you will honor your promise and let me go."

She fell silent for a long minute. "Do you not think me evil? Like the liches?"

He considered the question before answering. Balthazar was on intimate terms with evil. He'd been its friend and enemy both – occasionally at the same time. Evil had shaped him, but it had never defined him. The truth was more complicated. He suspected it was for her, as well.

"No," he said at last. "They are pure darkness."

"I have darkness in me," she growled. "More than you know. How else could I have devised such tortures?"

"We all have darkness." Balthazar smiled. "Some of us more than others, it's true." He held her gaze. "We are more alike than you realize. And it is my choice, is it not? My *right*."

She regarded him with a peculiar expression. Her eyes darkened. A scar bisected her lip. Balthazar backed away, the sword raised again.

"What the hell is this?" he snapped.

The horns shrank. Bare blue scalp sprouted hair of a glossy chestnut brown, parted sharply on the side. Armor turned to a shirt and trousers. Lucas Devereaux stood before him. His face was a livid white.

"Sweet Jesus," Lucas gasped, pressing a hand to his forehead. "I thought you were going to kill me." His expression softened with relief. "Thank God you're alive—"

Balthazar took another step back. "No." He gave his head a vehement shake. "No! Enough!" He glanced around, keeping the avatar of Lucas in view in case it decided to turn nasty. "Where are you, Mistress of Shadows? Come out and show yourself!"

"My lord—"

"Get away from me," Balthazar snarled. "Whatever you are."

A look of hurt crossed Lucas's face. "I told you, she cloaked me with illusion." He drew an unsteady breath. "She spoke *through* me, like I was a bloody puppet."

Balthazar felt like he'd stumbled into a house of mirrors that stretched to infinity. Beneath every mask was another, and another, and another . . . .

"So you just happened to turn up here," he said acidly. "How convenient. At least the last one was somewhat plausible—"

"He came to rescue you," said a figure in shining armor, striding through the only gap in the high hedges.

Balthazar stared at this new incarnation of Fulad-zereh. "I'm leaving," he announced. "No more games. Try to stop me if you will, but I'm finished here."

The demon nodded. "Yes, you are. The Trials are over. You may keep the Shamshir-e Zomorrodnegar. I will escort you out myself."

Balthazar frowned.

"Take your friend with you. I did not harm him."

Lucas made a huffy noise. "I respectfully disagree. The experience was very unpleasant. Particularly the part where you egged him on to kill me!"

Balthazar stared at Lucas, then at the demon. He knew she could produce nearly perfect facsimiles from his own memories. Zarathustra, for example. The voice and mannerisms were faultless, yet the eyes had a dead quality. Lucas looked bewildered and angry, but not *empty*. A sick feeling stole over him. "That is actually him?"

"Yes." She looked amused.

"How?" he demanded.

"I visited The Golden Flail in the form of one of Taj's marids. I told Lucas the daēva had betrayed you." She smiled. "You think I did not know about the tunic? I allowed you to keep it, Balthazar. It was not explicitly against the rules. And I was curious to see what lay in your heart if you managed to pass the Minotaur and get the sword. My mother thought you would fail. Not to kill, but to show mercy. I disagreed. You helped a man in the arena." She studied him. "But I also knew you were clever. You would expect some ruse. Thus I showed you Lysandros first, chained to the rock, which you saw through. And I presented you with a choice."

"So if I had chosen otherwise . . ."

"You would have slit his throat."

Balthazar absorbed this in horrified silence. He wanted to believe it was just another subterfuge, but her words had the ring of truth. It was exactly the sort of ruthless test that fit with what he knew of her character. Now he understood what Beletsunnu meant when she said he would be driven mad. Lucas was the one person in the world he loved without reservation. It would have destroyed him.

"But how did you know . . . . " He swallowed. "How did you know who was most dear to me?"

"He followed you into the desert. He stood by you during the Trials. And he came to my realm without hesitation, knowing it would likely mean his own death. I did give him a choice, at the end."

"If he had refused?"

"I would not have forced him." She glanced at Lucas with faint puzzlement. "I cannot pretend to understand mortal emotions, but I assumed his loyalty would be returned."

Her cold detachment was infuriating. Fulad-zereh sighed at Balthazar's expression. "Come, do you really think I would submit myself to you without knowing first?"

"Knowing what?" he snapped. "That I am a complete and utter fool?"

"That you could be trusted with it."

Balthazar was silent for a long minute. The larger truth was beginning to dawn and he didn't like it one bit, though he should have foreseen this earlier. "When you say *trusted* . . . . What do you mean, exactly?"

Her stare was fierce. "I think you know."

He chose his words with care. "This is a great burden you place upon me. What if I don't want it?"

"Then you may leave. But I will keep the sword." She scowled. "And I will not lift the curse until a new champion comes along who is willing to safeguard it."

Which would likely be never.

"The daēvas won't like this," he warned.

"Their feelings on the matter do not concern me." Her wings tensed. "I will not see it returned to Lysandros."

That came as a shock. "So he *is* alive?"

She nodded.

Another piece of bad news. Balthazar bore no particular ill will towards Lysandros, but it complicated matters.

I should leave with the sword before she changes her mind. Rescue is not part of the contract.

But he kept seeing the rock. The chains. The expression of agony.

The scene had been conjured. Yet Balthazar knew how realistic her illusions could be. She called him Lysandros, so that much had been true. He thought of the Rocs. The Minotaur. She could easily devise a torment that would seem painfully real to her victim.

"What have you done with him?"

Fulad-zereh's expression went flat. "Why do you care?"

"His people want him back."

"Lysandros hungers for revenge. If I let him go, he will take the sword from you and try to kill me. You cannot prevent it." A tiny smile hovered at the edges of her mouth. "*Even you*, Balthazar."

She was right, of course. But to simply leave him here . . . .

"What if the regent promised to enforce a new bargain?" he asked. "I keep the sword. You release Lysandros and lift the curse. I promise to hide it away where he'll never find it. If he makes any attempt to do so, he will be returned to your custody."

"Why should I?"

"Because it is just."

She tilted her head.

"He has served a sentence of nine hundred years. Is that not sufficient punishment?"

She considered it. "I am willing to send a message to Mikal. But I will not let Lysandros go until I get word from the regent."

"Fair enough." Balthazar paused. "Where is he?"

"With my mother."

"Beletsunnu?" he asked in surprise.

"It is she who leashed his power so he cannot escape."

Balthazar stared at Fulad-zereh suspiciously. "If she can do that, why didn't she help you before? When Lysandros forced you to serve him?"

The demon looked away. Something in the hunched set of her shoulders struck him as sheepish. "She doesn't think I should have the sword. She says it upsets the balance of things. We argued over this many times."

"Yet she aids you now."

"Yes." The demon did not elaborate. "I will take you to him. He might as well know what has transpired." She lifted her pointy chin with a look of satisfaction. "And I look forward to seeing my mother's face when she learns that she was wrong and I was right."

CHAPTER 27

Fulad-zereh strode through the labyrinth, Balthazar and Lucas walking behind. The direct path turned out to be ridiculously short. Within ten minutes, they reached the stone arch and passed through it, taking a narrow trail into the woods.

Balthazar girded himself for any number of horrors, but the trail ended at a stone cottage with white shutters and a neat vegetable garden on one side. He exchanged a wary look with Lucas as they all entered. The room was comfortably furnished and lit by talismanic globes. Lysandros lounged in an armchair playing Go with Fulad-zereh's mother, who perched on a footstool. The witch looked up at Balthazar with a slight frown.

"Well," she said grudgingly. "You took my advice." Belet-sunnu glanced at her daughter. "He is not as shallow and heartless as I thought."

Lysandros's reaction was different. First, he registered the sword. Then he recognized Balthazar. His handsome face drained of color. His mouth twisted in rage.

"You!" He turned to Fulad-zereh with a desperate look. "You cannot let him have it. He is—"

"A just man," she interrupted. "More than you are, Lysandros."

"I don't know what lies he's told you but—"

Balthazar stepped forward. "Do you have any idea how much time has passed since last we saw each other?" he asked mildly.

Lysandros stared at him with loathing. "A few centuries, I suppose. What does that matter, Antimagus?"

"A little longer than that," Balthazar replied dryly. "People change."

Lysandros barked a mirthless laugh. "*You?* I don't think so."

"Let me bring you up to date," Balthazar said, his voice colder. "I answer to myself now. Why I'm still alive is not your concern. But I've come to help you, so it's your choice if you return to Al Miraj or remain here forever." He eyed the black and white stones scattered across the board. "And it looks like you're about to forfeit anyway."

Lysandros leapt to his feet, the spring of a panther. For a tense moment, it seemed he would lunge at Balthazar. Lucas bravely stepped between them with a grim expression.

"He won the blade through stamina and cunning," Fulad-zereh warned in her soft, hissing voice. "And he will keep it. Do you object, prince? Speak now."

Beletsunnu leaned forward and touched Lysandros's coat sleeve. A light touch, but he jerked as if burned.

"Sit down," she said sternly.

A look passed between the two of them. Lysandros finally obeyed, although his full mouth tightened into a grimace of distaste. He drew a deep breath, violet eyes regarding them each in turn. He seemed to realize he was outmatched – for the moment – although Balthazar did not trust him a whit.

"This man is your champion?" he asked in a calmer tone.

"Yes," Fulad-zereh said. "He could have left with the

sword, but he argued for your freedom. I do not know why. You clearly despise each other."

Lysandros seemed surprised at this. "Then I am grateful," he said smoothly.

"You should be," Beletsunnu said, moving to a small stove where she began to brew a pot of tea. "He saved you from losing to me yet again."

Watching the daēva, who sat in his armchair like a coiled snake, Balthazar hoped he hadn't made a mistake. If he'd known the sentence was served hoeing vegetables and playing Go, he wouldn't have been so quick to intervene. But it was too late now. The main thing was to stay on Fulad-zereh's good side and get out as soon as possible – before Lysandros did something stupid.

"Mistress of Shadows?" Balthazar said politely. "Would you send a messenger to the regent? Ask him if the Watchtowers will enforce the arrangement. I'll wait for an answer."

She nodded. "It will be done."

Fulad-zereh left. Beletsunnu handed out vile-smelling tea. Balthazar dragged another stool to the door and sat with the Shamshir-e Zomorrodnegar between his legs, one hand resting on the emerald-studded hilt. Lucas stood next to him. They waited in brittle silence.

"What will you do with it?" Lysandros asked, eyeing the sword.

"None of your business," Balthazar replied.

Lysandros picked up a stone from the board, turning it over with long, elegant fingers. "How did you come here? I thought you were long dead."

"I thought the same of you."

"That's no answer."

"It's the only one you'll get."

Beletsunnu laughed. "Look at you two. Old acquaintances, I gather."

"Very old," Balthazar muttered.

Lysandros stared at Balthazar's tunic and sandals with puzzlement. "What year is it?" he asked.

"1890." Balthazar gave a thin smile. "Anno domini. That means *after* the birth of the Christian messiah, in case you're muddled."

The daēva seemed stunned. "Has it been so long? It did not seem so."

"Where did you go after the war?" Balthazar asked. "The last I heard you were in Alexander's camp."

"Freeing my brothers and sisters. Some still wore the cuffs of the Immortals, though their masters were dead. When I had gathered all I could find, I brought them here." Lysandros sighed. "I wanted to build a homeland free from the feuds and clan politics that destroyed us in the first place. The Watchtowers sent the jinn to help build the city. One of them brought me the Shamshir-e Zomorrodnegar."

"To guard," Beletsunnu said with a scowl. "Not to blackmail my daughter with!"

Lysandros gave a careless shrug. It was clearly an old argument between them. "There were still Druj to hunt. It seemed a waste not to employ her talents. She was a very fine general. I thought she was content."

Balthazar arched an eyebrow. "Apparently not."

"My people must hate me," Lysandros muttered.

"Taj doesn't," Lucas said quietly. It was the first time he'd spoken, and Lysandros looked over with a touch of surprise, as though he'd forgotten Lucas was there. "He has done what he could to hold them together, but I think he tires of the burden. I suspect he would welcome your return."

"Taj." There was no bitterness in Lysandros's voice, only a kind of rough affection. "I would like to see him again."

Balthazar glanced at Beletsunnu and decided not to mention Taj's fervent desire that he kill the demon. "I'm sure you can make amends," he said quickly. "I plan to leave with Lucas straightaway." He gave Lysandros a pointed look.

"There is no reason our paths need to cross again. The Druj are dead."

"And what of the Antimagi?" Lysandros asked, quiet menace in his voice.

"Leave them to me."

The prince frowned.

"We've already killed dozens," Lucas said earnestly. "Their numbers are fewer each year."

Lysandros stared at him. "Who *are* you?"

"My adopted son," Balthazar said, sudden emotion tightening his chest. "The one I almost killed getting this bloody sword. I think I've earned it."

Lysandros absorbed his words in silence for a minute. "Then perhaps we've both been saved," he said finally.

They all looked up as Fulad-zereh appeared in the doorway.

"What did the regent say?" Balthazar asked, rising.

"Nothing." Her face set in a grim expression. "He is gone."

"Gone?" Balthazar echoed in dismay.

"We have been used," Fulad-zereh hissed. "This new bargain was all a ruse to buy time." She looked at her mother with fury. "The daēvas come to murder us all!"

Lysandros jumped up, his face pale. "No—"

"I should have killed you long ago," Fulad-zereh spat at the prince. "Perhaps it is time I rectify that error."

CHAPTER 28

ONE HOUR EARLIER...

*Z*arifa hurried through the city, the hood of her cloak raised to cover her face.

The late afternoon heat clutched Al Miraj like the claws of a fire drake. A few cats dozed on shaded windowsills, but everyone was sweating it out on the balconies waiting for their champion's return and she saw not a single soul until she reached the Treasury.

Two jinn stood guard at the doors. Zarifa pulled back before they saw her and crept around to the rear of the long, rectangular building. It faced a stretch of open parkland, with the archives and part of the Summer Palace visible in the distance. Zarifa found a grove of tamarinds and settled in to wait for Yatha under the spreading branches.

In truth, she'd never trusted Taj. John Mortlake taught her to suspect everyone of potential treachery, and he was often right. If her father were here, he would take the talisman of Traveling for himself and get out, to hell with the others.

But she was not her father.

Oh, he'd tried his best to fashion her in his image. And who knows how she might have turned out had Mortlake raised her from infancy? Just the thought sent a shudder down her spine.

But he had come too late. By the time Mortlake took her from the nuns, she was nearly a woman grown. She knew right from wrong, even if she couldn't always obey her conscience. Zarifa had guarded this kernel of humanity all through the long years that came after, praying that someday she would be rid of him.

Now her heart was clear on the matter. She had induced Balthazar to hunt for the sword, and she would not abandon him.

Taj, on the other hand . . . . The thought that she had spent all night searching for a way to help only to have her efforts thrown away made her furious. When he returned and found her and Lucas gone, he would no doubt be suspicious. She would have to find a way to delay him long enough for them to return. There were several nasty talismans in the collection that would do the trick, if she could figure out how to use them herself.

Zarifa waited with mounting impatience as the sun sank and the shadows lengthened. Yatha did not appear. Perhaps Taj had summoned him. Well, she would just have to find a way inside on her own.

She studied the windowless building. The night she stayed late with the Seneschal they had taken a different route from the upper level, which led to the network of bridges. She had seen the Seneschal lock the door behind her with one of the keys from her ring.

Zarifa drew a deep breath and circled outward, seeking one of the entrances to the bridges. After a few false turns, she found the slender span leading back to the Treasury. She crawled across it on her belly, hoping no jinn servants chanced to look down from any of the windows of adjacent houses.

Once she reached the door, she took a pin from her hair. Zarifa had yet to encounter a lock she couldn't get through, and this one proved to be simple. She gently probed for the tumblers, exhaling as they slid into place. The door swung open. With a sigh of relief, she entered and closed it behind her.

She stood on a high walkway just below the gorgeous *muqarna*, a vaulted ceiling dome with a honeycomb motif decorated in red and blue mosaic tiles. The storehouse below was dark and empty. She hurried down a flight of stairs and went straight to the glass cabinets, searching for the distinctive spiral shape of a Talisman of Traveling. Mortlake said they were shells from the shore of the nameless sea in the Dominion. She did not know if this were true, but she had seen one once. It bent the eye in a peculiar way—

"What are you doing here?"

Zarifa spun around, her heart in her throat. Taj stood a few paces away. His ability to cross the entire storehouse floor without making a single sound was deeply unnerving, but she tried not to show it.

"I hoped to distract myself by doing some work this afternoon," she said with an easy smile.

"Without the Seneschal present?"

His face was unreadable in the dim light.

"I couldn't find her."

"That's odd." He took a step closer. "She told me she was looking for you."

"We must have just missed each other."

Taj stared at her without speaking for a long minute. "If you're working, why aren't you sorting through the unidentified talismans?"

"I just arrived."

"And yet the guards didn't see you come in." He glanced up at the walkway. "How *did* you get in, Miss Everleigh?"

"I . . ."

He had her and they both knew it.

"Here's what I think," Taj said in the same toneless voice. "I think you came to steal from me."

Zarifa wordlessly shook her head.

"Why else would you be here?" He studied her intently. "What are you looking for?"

"Nothing!" she choked. "I . . . ." Zarifa hung her head. "Yes, all right. I was looking for a talisman. Just something small to sell when I leave. Something you wouldn't even notice was gone." Tears brimmed over her lashes. "I'm sorry. Truly I am."

Zarifa peeked up at him. It was clear that her tragic female act had no effect. She'd always found him achingly handsome, but now there was a menacing quality to his chiseled features that sent a spear of ice down her spine. No one knew where she had gone – and it wouldn't matter if they did. He was like a king here. She was just some mortal who owed him a debt. Anonymous and dispensible. For the first time since coming to Al Miraj, Zarifa felt deeply afraid.

"You know the penalty for theft." Taj's eyes gleamed like shards of glacial ice. "Which hand will it be?"

"Please . . . ." She took a step back, knowing it was hopeless. He'd catch her in three strides. And she had a feeling he suspected. That her punishment would be far worse than a hand—

Taj's lips curled in disgust. "Come. We're going to the regent. Let him deal with you."

That caught her off guard. "The regent?"

"Since he seems to be out of retirement, I'll allow him to enforce his own edict. Must I drag you, or will you go willingly?"

Zarifa's thoughts raced. Why would he take her to the regent and risk his treachery being discovered? Unless he was innocent. Which meant . . . . Oh no, she thought, feeling like a complete idiot. *Lucas.*

"Yatha claimed you betrayed Balthazar," Zarifa said in a

rush. "That you hid the real Thread of Ariadne and gave him a fake. He said you were behind the attempts on Balthazar's life."

Taj stared at her like she'd gone insane. "*What?*" He clapped his hands.

The marid appeared with a low bow. "Master?"

"What in nine hells is going on?" Taj demanded. "Did you speak to Mr. Devereaux?"

Yatha quailed. "No, master. I did as you bade me and waited on the balcony to observe the cloud in case your champion emerged."

Taj gripped the marid's throat, lifting him a foot from the ground. "If you're lying to me, I will send you back to the elemental plane in pieces!"

"I speak the truth, master," Yatha gasped. "I have not moved since the champion passed through the gates. Ask anyone!"

Taj loosed his servant. "It is Fulad-zereh," he snarled. "She has gone too far this time. Where is Lucas?"

"He went after Balthazar," Zarifa said quietly. "Whoever it was promised to take him to the cloud."

Taj's jaw worked. "How long ago?"

"An hour, perhaps."

His eyes darkened to a shade that made her think of the deepest, coldest part of the North Sea. "She's killed them both," Taj said in a voice so soft she strained to hear him. "It's time to face the truth. She never intended to honor the bargain."

Zarifa felt a wave of despair. I've read too many stories, she thought bitterly. The hero always triumphs in the end. But not this time.

"What will you do?" she asked.

Taj didn't reply. He simply stood there, so still and expressionless it made the hair on Zarifa's neck stand up. As in the throne room, she sensed power gathering around him. Her ears popped at a sudden change in air pressure. The doors to the Treasury blew wide, tearing from their hinges with a screech of ruptured metal. Glass exploded along the cabinets. The table she'd worked at hurtled against one wall, smashing into splinters. Jagged cracks sliced the stone floor.

Zarifa dropped to a crouch, covering her head with her arms. A hellish wind rattled the axes and swords in their brackets, but it did not touch the daēva. He stood at the center of the whirlwind, livid red spots cresting his high cheekbones like war paint. The cultured, pleasure-loving Taj was gone; an avenging demon had taken his place. Zarifa had heard wild stories about the destruction daēvas were capable of. Cities leveled, mountains uprooted, seas turned to cracked salt plains. At that moment, she believed them all.

"Gather my brothers and sisters to the Flail," Taj snapped at Yatha. "Every one, save for the children under twelve."

The marid gave a bow that nearly scraped the floor. He was trembling all over. "Right away, O Dire Master!"

Taj turned his wintry gaze on Zarifa. "If you had come to me first, Balthazar and Lucas might have stood a chance."

"I'm sorry," she stammered. "The demon was . . . very convincing."

And you made the same mistake once.

She wisely did not voice this thought, although Taj's eyes narrowed to slits. His initial burst of frenzied rage had cooled to smoldering embers, though she sensed any wrong word could set it alight again. He tensed and Zarifa feared he would kill her, but after a long moment, Taj simply strode away. The wind died. She picked her way over the shards of glass and shattered wood.

All she could think of was to find the Seneschal. Taj trusted her. Maybe she could talk some sense into him. If Balthazar and Lucas were alive, they wouldn't be helped by Taj unleashing his temper against Fulad-zereh. A frontal attack would just provoke her to kill them.

Zarifa lifted her skirts and ran, but by the time she reached the courtyard outside the Golden Flail, it was already packed with daēvas. They listened with hard faces as Taj told them of Fulad-zereh's betrayal.

"I just came from the palace. The regent is gone!" he shouted, standing on the rim of the fountain to address the anxious-looking crowd. "Our champion has been deceived and most likely killed." He looked around. "She has taken our freedom. She has taken our dignity. Now she would take our home!"

Angry muttering erupted and he held up a hand. "Many of us remember the time before, when we wandered in the wilderness. Persecuted and hounded." His voice lowered and the crowd fell silent, leaning forward to hear his words. "I would rather die than return to that life. There is only one safe place for us and the time has come to defend it. Will you join me?"

They roared with approval. Taj gave a hard, decisive nod.

"Arm yourselves!" he shouted. "We march on the demon's realm at sunset!"

He leapt down from the fountain and strode inside the Flail. Zarifa watched the mob fan out across the city, presumably to raid their own personal armories. Within minutes, the courtyard was empty, the flowerbeds trampled. What could she do to stop this madness? The answer was nothing.

"He shouldn't have gone."

She spun around. It was Destan Karatas. He had a strange expression on his face.

"I agree," she said wearily. "It will not end well."

"I don't mean Taj." Dark circles ringed his eyes. He looked ill.

Zarifa studied him with growing disquiet. "You're speaking of Balthazar," she said.

"I tried to stop him." The Turk gave a hollow laugh. "I wish I had managed it. He would still be alive."

"It was you!" she exclaimed. "The crossbow—"

"Was meant only to disable, not kill," he replied with a note of shame. "I convinced myself it would be better for both of us. He wouldn't have to face the arena and I would make my escape once the spell dissolved." He sank down to the edge of the fountain. "But I failed, where Balthazar did not."

Zarifa felt both pity and anger. "Why are you telling me this?"

Destan shrugged. "It doesn't matter now." A bleak smile twisted his mouth. "My timing is truly cursed."

"What are you talking about?" she demanded.

"Had I but waited a few more minutes, I might have learned what Taj plans. If he fails to return . . . . Well, then I would be free. But now it is too late."

Zarifa frowned. "Too late?"

"Destan!" The Seneschal came running out. "What have you done?" Her voice was stricken. Zarifa thought she meant his reckless attempts on Balthazar, but then she saw a flask in the woman's hand. Destan clutched his stomach with a groan. The Seneschal rushed to his side.

"You fool," she whispered tenderly, tears glinting in her eyes.

Zarifa realized with a shock that they must be lovers.

"I'm so sorry . . . ." He half fell into her arms. His face was a chalky white now, his lips tinged blue.

"What did you take?" she demanded, holding up the flask.

"The same thing I put on the crossbow bolts," he managed. "But in much greater quantity." Destan winced. "I don't know what it is. I bought it from a jinn."

"How long ago did you drink it?"

His eyes slid shut and she gave him a hard shake. Destan's eyes fluttered open.

"How long?"

"Half an hour . . . ."

The Seneschal shook her head. "All the healers have gone

to wage war." Her tone was brisk efficiency, but Zarifa saw the terror in her eyes. "We must purge the drug from your system." She looked at Zarifa, a plea on her face. "Help me get him up."

Zarifa hesitated, but only for a moment. She had liked Captain Karatas before his confession, and she believed him when he said he didn't mean to harm Balthazar. This was all Taj's fault. He treated people like chattel.

They quickly carried him inside and down a corridor to a small room on the ground floor that must be the Seneschal's. Zarifa helped lay Destan out on the bed, while she rooted through a cabinet and took out several packets of crushed powder.

"What is that?" Zarifa asked.

"Bayberry, mustard seed and mandrake," the Seneschal said, stirring pinches from each packet into a cup of water. "They are powerful emetics." She threw an arm around Destan and forced him to sit. "You must drink it all," she snapped. "The results will be unpleasant, but that is your punishment."

He sputtered and made weak protests, but together they managed to pour most of the cup into his mouth.

"Fetch that chamber pot," the Seneschal told Zarifa.

She hurried to do so. Destan was covered in sweat, his face grimaced with pain. With a gasp, he began retching. The Seneschal held him steady. Zarifa wrinkled her nose, but managed to catch most of it in the chamber pot. When he had emptied his stomach, the Seneschal eased him back on the bed and covered him with a sheet. "Let us hope that suffices," she said softly, wiping his face with a damp cloth.

The lines of pain on his face smoothed out. He seemed to be sleeping.

"How did you happen to have all this handy?" Zarifa asked, glancing at the store of powdered herbs.

"I get them from the witch on the island," the Seneschal

said absently, still watching Destan. "Sometimes the customers drink themselves near to death. Or the indentured have unwanted pregnancies. They know they can come to me for help." She looked up at Zarifa. Her strong, handsome features were resigned. "Will you tell?"

"Taj?" She glanced at Destan's limp form. "Not right now." Zarifa rose. "I must go see what is happening. Perhaps there is still a chance to avert disaster."

The Seneschal nodded. "Go. And . . . thank you."

Zarifa ran full tilt for the gates. The sun was lowering, bathing the city in pale golden light. She feared the worst, but still held out hope that Balthazar might live. He had already accomplished the impossible merely by surviving the first three Trials. She still didn't understand why Fulad-zereh would take Lucas Devereaux, but who knew the convoluted mind of a demon?

It's all my fault, she thought furiously. If Taj hadn't caught me at the storehouse, he would still be waiting for Balthazar's return. I must stop this somehow.

The lower streets were deserted, but as she topped a rise, she saw the column of daēvas. They carried swords and quivers bristling with arrows, though their main weapon would be elemental power. Hair flying from its last few pins, Zarifa sprinted down the wide avenue leading to the gates. She caught up with Taj just as he passed through. The daēvas next to him cast her unfriendly looks, but she ignored them.

"Don't do this," she pleaded between gasps for breath.

He regarded her with blazing eyes, though his tone was calm. "Why not?"

"Because you could be wrong. And if you are, you'll get everyone killed!"

"I'm not wrong."

He held a figurine in his hand, a squatting man with an eerie reptilian face. With a shock of recognition, she realized it was the same one she had identified that worked the weather.

"But—"

"Go back, mortal," he snapped. "You don't belong here."

Zarifa scowled and moved away, but she kept pace with the daēvas as they marched for the staircase. A wind rose, driving sheets of sand across the Empty Quarter of the desert. Lightning streaked down. It was answered by jagged blue bolts rising from the cloud. The skies darkened.

When the daēvas of Al Miraj were halfway across, ifrits poured forth from the dragon's jaws. Flames licked along their skin, glowing orange in the twilight. With a shattering toll of thunder, the skies above opened. Rain gusted down in a deluge. The parched, hard-packed soil turned swiftly to a shallow lake. The daēvas broke into a run. The ifrits rushed down the stairs to meet them.

Power crackled between the two armies, rending the earth. The wind rose to a tortured scream. Brief flashes of lightning illumined faces set in lines of implacable hatred. Zarifa realized with a sinking heart that nine hundred years of pent-up frustration had boiled over at last. They would obliterate each other.

An arrow arced through the air, piercing the throat of the first ifrit to reach the ground. Its brothers flowed over the fallen body without pausing. They carried double-bladed axes that whistled in deadly arcs. She caught a glimpse of Taj in the vanguard. He raised a hand and the ifrits flew back as if thrown by a giant. But there seemed an endless number of them. And they wielded fire.

A gout of flame shot forth. Zarifa's breath caught as it streaked at the daēvas and was doused in a wall of water. I must be mad, she thought dimly. Taj was right. I don't belong here. Yet she stubbornly slogged forward through the mud, thinking that if she could just reach him before the bodies began to pile up, before they passed the point of no return—

Without warning, the rain ceased. A hole opened in the heavy black clouds, whirling like a vortex. Four dots sped down from the patch of blue sky. Two were fair, two dark, but all wore gleaming gold breastplates. As they neared the earth, she was forced to cover her eyes against a fierce, blinding light. When she opened them again, the four archangels stood in a line between the two armies, their great wings flaring.

"*STOP!*"

The voice shook the city walls. A spire cracked and tumbled slowly to the ground. Stunned, Zarifa touched her ear. A drop of crimson blood stained her fingertip.

Her head was still ringing as Taj walked forward, his voice slicing the buzz like a whip crack. "Let us pass," he shouted. "She has betrayed the pact!"

There was a stir in the jaws of the dragon. Fulad-zereh's silver armor pushed through the mass of ifrits. "He is the traitor!" she cried. "He attacks with no reason—"

"Silence!" One of the Watchtowers strode forward. His skin was milky white, his long hair a deep shade of blue. "Where is the sword?"

There was a long pause. "Their champion has it," Fulad-zereh snarled.

It took a moment for Zarifa to absorb her words. She sagged with relief.

"Bring him out!"

Fulad-zereh hesitated, but the angel simply waited, his face a thunderhead. Finally, she turned and issued an order. There was a muttering among the daēvas. Then Balthazar appeared at her side. He held a blade in his hand. Even from the desert below, Zarifa could make out the gleam of emeralds on the hilt.

"This foolishness will cease at once!" One of the ebony-skinned angels stepped forward, stabbing an accusing finger at the dragon-cloud – and then at the daēvas for good measure. Zarifa smiled. There was no mistaking the imperious, disapproving voice of Mikal. For once, she agreed with him. "The bargain has been satisfied. Let your hostages go!"

"Tell them to disarm first!" Fulad-zereh shouted back with a note of defiance.

Mikal faced the daēvas. "Do it," he grated.

They hesitated – until Taj gave a brief nod. Weapons were thrown to the muddy ground.

"There is a new bargain regarding the Emerald-Studded Blade," she announced. "Will you pledge to enforce it?"

"What are the terms?" Mikal demanded.

"They are fair. That I swear on my honor." She lifted her pointy chin. "Give me your word!"

The angels conferred for a moment. "If we deem it fair, we will enforce it," Mikal declared.

Fulad-zereh leaned in to whisper something to Balthazar, who nodded. She stepped aside. Lucas appeared, and beside him a dark-haired man, not quite as tall as Balthazar but with a lithe, slender grace. At the sight of him, the daēvas fell still. Zarifa glanced quickly at Taj. He looked too shocked to speak.

The daēva – he must be, from the panther-like way he moved – descended the staircase. He gave a low bow to each of the regents. They spoke in voices too soft for her to make out. Mikal gave a hard nod. The black-haired man approached Taj. He had dusky skin and eyes of an arresting shade, darker than Taj's but equally vivid. They faced each other for a long moment. It was so quiet, Zarifa could hear the faint rush of water along the city walls.

Then Taj sank to his knees, tears dampening his cheeks. "My prince," he said hoarsely. "I never dared to hope—"

The prince reached out a hand and hauled Taj to his feet. They embraced tightly.

A joyful cheer went up among the daēvas.

"Lysandros is returned!" Taj shouted. His voice took on a challenging tone as he surveyed his brothers and sisters. "Do any of you dispute his right to the throne? If so, you may pass through *me*."

No one took him up on the offer.

"I was treated well," Lysandros said loudly. "I do not hold a grudge against the Mistress of Shadows, and nor shall you." He grinned. "Gods, it's good to see you all."

The daēvas crowded around their prince as Balthazar and Lucas trotted down the stairs. Taj turned to watch them. It was not Balthazar he fixed on, but Lucas. His smile widened.

Forgotten by all, Zarifa crept closer to eavesdrop as Balthazar approached the Watchtowers. She'd grown accustomed to seeing him covered in blood, but this time he looked like he'd been clawed by cats. His face held a trace of uneasiness, though his stride was confident as ever. He caught her eye for only an instant before bowing to the archangels. She suppressed a grin. The gesture was formal and performed with grace, but not so low as to be groveling. He was already establishing his authority with them.

"Guardians of the Watchtowers," he intoned. "I am Balthazar, the mortal champion of the daēvas of Al Miraj."

"We know who you are," Mikal snapped. "What is this new bargain?"

"I promised to keep the Shamshir-e Zomorrodnegar." He held the sword with the flat of the blade resting on his palms. "Will you accept the arrangement?"

Mikal frowned and opened his mouth, but the blue-haired angel cut him off. "It must be taken far away, that much is certain." He gazed up at the cloud. "Fulad-zereh! Come down here!"

She crossed her arms and didn't budge.

"Now, daughter!" the archangel bellowed.

With hunched shoulders, the demon spread her wings and circled down to land among them.

"Azrael," she said stiffly. Her skin was the precise shade of his hair. She turned to Mikal. "Regent."

"Do you not greet your uncles?" Azrael demanded.

She pressed a fist to her heart. "Jibrail," she murmured to

the other dark-skinned angel. Like the regent, his scalp was shaved, but his eyes were burnished silver. "Israfil."

The last had long black hair and razor-sharp cheekbones. He turned to Taj and Lysandros, summoning them with a perfunctory flick of his hand.

"Why do you accuse her of treachery?" Israfil demanded.

Lysandros spoke first. "It was a mistake. Was it not?" He shot Taj a pointed look.

"Yes," Taj said flatly. "A mistake."

Azrael nodded. "Daughter, do you agree they won the sword fairly?"

She bared her teeth. "No."

There was a fraught silence. The Watchtowers exchanged weary looks.

"*They* didn't," she added. "He did." She pointed a black-nailed finger at Balthazar. "He is a just man. I am content for him to vouchsafe my doom."

"And does Lysandros agree to this?"

"I do," the prince agreed, if with a touch of ill humor.

Azrael regarded Fulad-zereh with irritation, though it was tempered by fondness. "Then I am relieved this impasse has been resolved to the satisfaction of all parties concerned. The entire matter was childish."

Fulad-zereh managed to hold his penetrating gaze for a full ten seconds before lowering her eyes, which Zarifa found impressive. She'd always wondered what Fulad-zereh looked like up close. The demon was neither beautiful nor ugly, but something in between that was far more interesting.

"Azrael." A woman in her middle years strode forward. Full lips curled in an enigmatic smile. Her dark eyes held infinite knowledge and patience and cunning. Zarifa knew instantly that this must be the fabled witch who lived on the island. The weaver of Ariadne's Thread. "You look well," she purred, eyeing him up and down.

"As do you, Beletsunnu." The angel returned her appraising look.

Fulad-zereh rolled her eyes. She turned to Balthazar. "I never gave you the scabbard."

He blinked as a finely worked leather sheath appeared, belted around his waist.

"Thank you," he said, sliding the blade in. "So this is goodbye, Mistress of Shadows."

"For now," she agreed. "I very much enjoyed watching you."

He arched an eyebrow. "Bleed?"

"Fight."

Balthazar's mouth curved at some private joke. "Was I as much fun as the liches?"

"More. They are not so clever." She gave him a tiny smile. "And they do not look half as pretty in a suit."

He gave her that lazy, seductive grin Zarifa both adored and despised. "Be good, Fulad-zereh."

The demon made a wheezing sound she interpreted as laughter. "Perhaps you should heed your own advice, Balthazar."

"Oh, I can't claim it's mine. A friend told me that a long time ago." His smile died. "I've rarely achieved it, but I never stopped trying."

"A friend?" She looked at him shrewdly. "The old man with the staff."

"That one," he agreed.

"He was a wise man?"

"Very wise."

"I care for *good* as little as I do for *evil*," she replied thoughtfully. "But I will keep it in mind."

"Daughter!"

Fulad-zereh turned to face her father. She had to crane her neck to look up at him, but she gave not an inch.

"I must speak to you alone. There are matters to discuss."

The angel spread his wings and soared up to the cloud. Fulad-zereh gave Balthazar a final nod and obediently followed.

Zarifa gathered her courage and walked over to him. "I think she likes you."

"Some women do," he murmured, still watching Fulad-zereh as she alit in the dragon's jaws.

Zarifa felt a perplexing stab of jealousy. "What happened up there?"

"Why do you care?"

"Don't be difficult."

He lifted his chin. "If you must know . . . I lost a battle with a hedge."

She burst out laughing. And then they were swept up in the flow of the mob, now disarmed and singing, as the daēvas carried Lysandros on their shoulders to the city gates.

CHAPTER 29

T he sun set.
        Across Al Miraj, daēvas gathered on the rooftops to watch the coming of night. Children who had never been outside beyond the first hint of twilight clutched their parents' hands, wide-eyed and excited. Cats prowled restlessly along the stone balustrades, feline senses attuned to a subtle change in the atmosphere.

A cool breeze swept in from the desert. As the last sliver of molten gold sank beyond the horizon, the city held its collective breath.

For the first time in nine hundred years, all remained the same. Pristine marble fountains gleamed in the moonlight, flowers obediently stayed within their beds . . . and beneath the dark, star-strewn mantle of sky, spontaneous celebrations erupted atop the palaces, with groups moving to and fro to visit across the bridges.

The four Watchtowers accompanied the prince to the Summer Palace, keeping their pledge to remain in the city until the sword was safely taken away.

Zarifa made her way to the Seneschal's chambers, where she found Destan awake. His face was hollow and gaunt beneath his beard. He stared at the wall, not acknowledging her gentle greeting.

"Has he recovered?" she asked the Seneschal quietly.

The woman nodded. "I told him what happened. That the wards will stand." She clasped her fingers tightly together. "I'll admit I suspected. It's why I made him help us at the Treasury when you found the Thread of Ariadne. To keep him out of trouble." Her anxious gaze searched Zarifa's face. "But I swear I didn't know for certain. Please forgive me. I should have spoken up, but—"

Zarifa took her hands and gave them a brief squeeze. "You have nothing to fear from me. There is no reason for anyone to know the truth."

The Seneschal let out a long sigh of relief.

"He did a foolish, reckless thing, but he was desperate," Zarifa said. "I think he's suffered enough." She glanced at the keys around the Seneschal's neck. "So he took the key to the archives from you."

"Not to the archives. Taj questioned me right after it happened and I showed him the key. But do you remember the talisman you found?"

"The key to open any lock." She shook her head, feeling foolish. "I should have thought of that before."

"I'd mentioned it to Destan. He must have returned it later, before I noticed it was gone."

They looked at each other, a faint flush creeping across the Seneschal's cheeks. Zarifa had never seen her without the ring of keys securely around her neck. She obviously took care with them. If Destan had access . . . .

The Seneschal's spine straightened. "I never paid him. We care for each other." A tear slid down her cheek. "He had it much harder than I did. I knew he was unhappy, but I didn't realize . . . ."

Zarifa moved to the bed and sat down. Destan finally looked at her.

"You must despise me," he said.

"No." She gazed at him frankly. "I know what it is to have no control over your own destiny. There have been times when I considered doing just what you did." Her mouth tightened. "Taking the quick way out."

He frowned. "What stopped you?"

"I was raised Catholic. Suicide is a mortal sin."

"That's the only reason?"

"No." She smiled grimly. "I refused to let my father win."

He sighed. "You have more courage than I do."

"I think it takes a good deal of courage to put up with Taj for as long as you have." Zarifa paused. "If you were free from your debt, could you be happy here?"

Destan's face went blank again. "There is no chance of that."

"But if there were?" Zarifa persisted.

Destan looked at the Seneschal. "I would stay for her," he replied softly. "Making whatever life we can, if she will have me. But Taj holds my debt for hundreds more years—"

"Leave that to me," Zarifa said rising.

"What will you do?" the Seneschal asked. She looked worried.

"Taj should be in a good mood right now," Zarifa said dryly. "I will speak to him."

"But why would he listen—"

"I think he owes me a favor." She shrugged. "It cannot hurt to try."

A MILLION STARS SHONE OVERHEAD AS ZARIFA STEPPED OUT onto the roof of The Golden Flail.

After much pleading and cajoling, Yatha had finally told her where his master might be found. She'd expected him to be celebrating with the others, but Taj lay on his back beyond the edge of the pavilion, one knee bent and a cup of wine near his outstretched hand.

The sounds of laughter and music drifted over from adjacent rooftops. He propped himself up on an elbow as she approached. In the moonlight, his golden hair looked silver, the clean lines of his face watchful – and a touch annoyed.

"I thought you'd be with your prince," she said.

"Lysandros is meeting privately with the Watchtowers," he replied. "And I wanted to savor this moment." He glanced up at her pointedly. "*Alone.*"

"I won't stay long."

"Then you must come down here," he said, patting the tiles next to him with a faint grin. "They're nice and cool."

Zarifa lay down next to him. They each rolled to their sides to face each other. It was oddly intimate and she felt her face warm. He really was a gorgeous specimen – and he knew it full well. She decided she'd better launch into her speech before things got out of hand.

"I sorted a large number of talismans for you," Zarifa said. "In return, I would like to ask a favor."

He arched an inquiring brow.

"That you free Destan of his debt."

"Karatas?" Taj frowned. "Why?"

"Your Seneschal loves him. And he loves her."

Taj rolled to his back and gazed up at the stars. "I hadn't noticed."

"Well, it's quite obvious to anyone paying attention. At least you could give him a better position in your household."

"Such as?"

"He was a soldier. Let him guard something."

"Like the Treasury?" He barked a laugh. "I'll admit, I'm not pleased with the jinn who were on duty when *you* broke in."

"Then it's settled," she said firmly.

He glanced over. "And you care because . . .?"

"Because I like and respect her."

"Are you implying I don't?" The tone was neutral, but she sensed dangerous ground.

"Of course not. Only that you're preoccupied with more important matters at the moment. But it would mean a great deal to both of them." She studied the softly parted lips. "And I think you're secretly a romantic, Taj."

He laughed and clasped his hands behind his head. "Fine. But Destan was one of my most popular employees. I hope you appreciate the sacrifice I'm making."

"My heart bleeds for you," she said lightly.

He rolled back to his side. "Are we done? I have a party to plan." His eyes moved over her like a caress. "Or maybe you'd like to stay a while. I can tell you about the constellations."

It was Zarifa's turn to laugh. "Don't tempt me."

"Why not?" His tone was playful, but with an undercurrent of heat.

Zarifa drew a deep breath. Why not indeed?

There was no one around. She'd be leaving in a few hours. And if his reputation was only half true, it would doubtless be a memorable experience.

But in the end, it wasn't his touch she longed for.

"Because I'd hoped our relationship might be a bit more than a fling."

Taj looked alarmed, and she laughed softly. "I don't mean that." She hesitated. "If I brought you talismans, would you buy them?"

He pretended to mull it over, but she saw a gleam of avarice in his eye. "Possibly. Thinking of carrying on the family business?"

She fell to her back again. After a moment, Taj did the same. The moment passed, and although she hadn't really wanted it, Zarifa couldn't help but feel a pang of regret.

"Possibly."

"I'll miss your father. He was vile, but his network was unrivaled."

"If you did business with me, you'd know exactly what sort of talismans you were getting."

"That *is* an advantage," he conceded.

"And I don't gamble."

Taj studied her. "Yes, you do. Just not at the card table."

"I mean I know the consequences of crossing you. So I wouldn't."

I might cross *other* people, Zarifa added silently, but not you, Taj. Never, ever again.

"Well, you know where to find me," he murmured, which she took as agreement.

"Thank you," she said, sitting up. "I think I'll go now."

"I told Jabaar to leave suitable attire in your chamber." He gazed up at her. "You're a formidable woman, Miss Everleigh. I'm glad you're free of that bastard."

"So am I. But would you . . ." The words came out in a rush. "Just give his head a decent burial."

"I already did."

Zarifa nodded. There seemed nothing more to say so she strode for the stairs. She met Lucas Devereaux on his way up.

"Is he . . . ?" Lucas asked, eyeing the door to the roof.

"Yes," she said. "Star-gazing."

"I need to, er, ask him something." He eyed her warily. "Were you . . . ."

"We just had a brief conversation about my father's business." She smothered a laugh, feeling very relieved she'd declined Taj's offer. She sensed he was about to get another one. "I'll see you shortly."

Lucas gave her a weak smile and hurried past.

Zarifa stopped to tell the Seneschal and Destan what had transpired. Both were elated at the news.

"He gave his word," Zarifa said. "And I mean to see he keeps it."

The Seneschal smiled. "Taj has his faults, but he never lies outright. I believe he will." She glanced at Destan. "So you will guard his warehouse. I'll have to make sure you don't get too bored."

He scrubbed a hand through his beard, a boyish grin erasing the hollows beneath his eyes. For the first time, Zarifa saw genuine happiness in his face. "With all the years ahead of us, Claudia, you'll have your work cut out for you."

They shared a hug and Zarifa promised to visit when she returned. Then she went to her chamber and changed into a proper dress. She felt both excited and nervous to be returning to London. Every decision in her adult life had been dictated by Mortlake. But she was her own woman now.

As for Balthazar, her feelings for him were a muddle. He had surprised her in many ways, but the essence of who he was remained unchanged. A man who fed on the lives of others. He was clearly keeping his distance from her. She would do the same. And once they reached London, she would walk away and never look back.

Zarifa stayed in her room until midnight, which was the appointed hour for their departure. Then she squared her shoulders and set off for the Summer Palace.

***

"I still can't believe they're giving it to you," Taj said with an incredulous laugh.

He stood with Balthazar in the throne room, where jinn were in a tizzy of redecorating. Lysandros directed the hanging of tapestries on the bare stone walls and inspected the newly repaired throne. He still wore the plain wool coat Balthazar had found him in, but a silver crown perched in his dark curls. He had not looked at the sword once since they reached the palace – likely because the regent watched stone-faced from the shadow of one of the great columns.

"Who else would they give it to?" Balthazar wondered. "Not *you*, obviously. You're even less trustworthy than Lysandros."

"Perhaps. But let's not forget you're only here because you managed to lose your most precious possession. Not what I'd call sterling credentials." Taj covered a yawn. "You'd better not misplace the sword. I'd put the odds on you surviving Mikal's retribution at . . . oh, let's say ten thousand to one."

"That's generous of you," Balthazar replied.

"I think so, too. If it was Azrael, the odds would be much, much worse." He glanced over with a slight frown. "Lysandros said Fulad-zereh nearly killed him and you managed to talk her out of it. What did you say?"

Balthazar smiled. "Only that you had a terrible crush on my secretary and took it the wrong way when she snatched him from your tender embrace. A *crime passionnel*—"

"Yes, thank you," Taj interrupted, clearing his throat. "That was quick thinking."

"Would you have come after *me* with a whole army, I wonder?" Balthazar continued. "Honestly, all you lacked was a white steed . . . ."

"Don't be an ass," Taj muttered savagely – a little too savagely, Balthazar thought with amusement.

They both looked over at Lucas, who stood talking with Zarifa. It had been decided that the three of them would share a Talisman of Traveling to London. Zarifa had never used one before, and Taj didn't want to part with two such talismans in any case as they were very rare.

"Well, I think it's time we left," Balthazar said. "I'd thank you for your hospitality, but I only lie credibly when I'm drunk."

"That reminds me." Taj paused. "There is one last thing."

"Oh?"

"The matter of your bar tab."

Balthazar stared at him in disbelief. "Christ. I thought you'd forget about that, considering."

"I'm afraid not." Taj produced a slip of paper.

"How much is it?" Balthazar demanded, craning his neck to read the numbers.

"Eight hundred and twenty pounds, six shillings."

"*What?*"

Taj's blue eyes twinkled. "Brugerolle doesn't come cheap. Especially the 1795. It's a rare vintage."

"But your jinn conjured it!" Balthazar spluttered.

"I go by the fair market value." Taj made a sad face. "Still short on cash?"

"I don't have a bloody copper to my name." Balthazar turned out his pockets to illustrate the point. "As you well know."

Taj pressed his palms together. "Tell you what. I'll let you work it off—" He burst into laughter at his companion's murderous expression.

"I assume you're joking," Balthazar said stiffly.

It took a long moment before Taj could speak. Balthazar waited impatiently for the hilarity to subside.

"You still owe me the money." Taj winked. "But I'll bend my rules and wait to collect."

"I don't much care for owing you a debt of any sort."

Taj shrugged. "Your choice."

"What would the terms be?" Balthazar asked. "A few centuries on my back?"

Taj squinted into the middle distance. "Roughly. I happen to have a position coming available—"

"A debt is acceptable," Balthazar said with a tight smile. "And I do intend to pay it."

"Of course. But be aware the interest compounds annually—" He broke off as Lysandros approached.

"Guard that, Balthazar," the prince growled, stabbing a finger at the sword.

"From you? Yes, I plan to."

"From Fulad-zereh! If she ever gets it back, that's on *your* head."

"I know," he replied wearily. "It's all on my head. I've half a mind to sink it to the bottom of the English Channel."

"Do not jest," Mikal growled sternly from the shadows. "This is a sacred burden you bear. And I will check on you periodically to make sure you are fulfilling it!"

Wonderful.

"Your oversight would be most welcome, regent," Balthazar said smoothly. "I don't suppose I need to give you my address in Mayfair?"

"That is not necessary." Mikal stared at him. "I know how to find you."

Balthazar closed his eyes. *Of course you do.*

When he opened them, Zarifa was gazing at him with amusement. She wore a long-sleeved silk dress with lace at the neck that would be suitable for London, but she'd foregone a corset and the thin material clung to the natural curves of her body. Balthazar looked away. He had to be rid of her at the first opportunity. The moment they reached London.

Taj was needling him when he mentioned the ouroboros, but it was all true. He had made the worst mistake of his life when he pursued her. Well, maybe not the worst . . . but a very bad one. His pride still stung. And he absolutely despised the fact that he still wanted her. After everything.

Out of sight, out of mind. That was the ticket.

Lysandros laughed. "Come visit. I promise your stay will be more pleasant next time."

"Yes, do," Taj said, looking at Lucas, whose cheeks warmed.

"Will this work?" Lucas asked, holding up the talisman. "Or do the wards prevent it?"

"Now that you've been here once," Lysandros said, "it can be used to come again." His tone hardened. "Which is why you must guard it as closely as the sword. We don't want to be found."

The three marids stepped forward and bowed.

"You may Travel from the courtyard," said Yatha the Harmonious, smiling serenely.

"We will escort you," offered Qadir the Scented, who reeked of garlic.

"And be quick about it!" snapped Jabaar the Cruel.

Voices and life filled the once-dreary palace as they followed the jinn outside, where a dark, still pool awaited. Zarifa visibly steeled herself and Lucas spoke softly in her ear. Whatever he said seemed to reassure her. She caught Balthazar's eye. "I'm ready," she said.

"You won't drown," he replied. "But hold tight to Mr. Devereaux. It's easy to get lost in the gloom."

Lucas took her hand and gave a firm nod.

They entered the pool single file with Balthazar in the lead. He tensed as the water closed around him, fearing some last bid by Lysandros to take back the sword, but it didn't come. And then they were moving through the undersea realm that bordered the Dominion, a strange place of twilight and unseen watchers. Balthazar fixed his destination in mind, holding the image firm. They walked through tall grey reeds, swaying in an invisible current. Shadows pressed close on all sides, drawn by the power of the sword, and Balthazar felt their hunger not just for the talisman but for the three living souls who dared encroach on this place of the dead.

Yet they seemed to fear him just enough to hold their greed in check. The soft ground underfoot began to rise again. With a gasp, Balthazar stepped out of another pool halfway around the world, one he reserved for just this purpose. A moment later, Lucas and Zarifa emerged behind him. Their garments remained dry, but the air came as a frigid shock.

Zarifa looked around in wonder at the dank cellar, illuminated only by a shaft of moonlight spilling through a tiny barred window. "That was . . . very interesting."

Lucas laughed softly. "Home," he whispered. "*Thank God*."

Zarifa shivered, exhaling a plume of white. The points of her breasts were clearly visible beneath the thin silk.

"I need a drink," Balthazar muttered, striding for a narrow staircase leading to the upper floors of the townhouse.

CHAPTER 30

R ain lashed the windows of the drawing room, a torrential downpour with all the chill of mid-January. Zarifa rubbed her arms as Lucas lit a fire in the hearth. Somewhere deep in the house, a clock chimed two o'clock.

"Where exactly are we?" she asked.

"Mayfair," Lucas replied.

Balthazar stood at the tall windows overlooking the garden. He was acutely aware of her presence in his sanctuary and didn't like it in the least.

"Don't let us keep you, Miss Everleigh," he said without turning around.

"Yes," she agreed. "I should be going."

"Where?" Lucas asked.

"I . . . I have friends in London."

"Oh, really?" Lucas remarked, as Balthazar silently cursed him. "I thought your father kept you hidden away."

"He did . . . but . . . ." She cleared her throat. "I'll manage."

"I'm happy to pay for a hotel," Balthazar said, finally glancing over his shoulder.

"I don't want your money," she said.

"Oh, *now* you don't want it?"

"No." Her tone was firm. "We're even."

"Happier words were never spoken," Balthazar muttered. "If you'll excuse me, I need to lock this sword away before some new disaster occurs. Lucas can summon a cab."

He strode through the drawing room and took the stairs to his bedroom on the second floor, where he kept a wall safe. Balthazar secured the Shamshir-e Zomorrodnegar and was pouring himself a brandy when Lucas appeared.

"There are six guest bedrooms," he pointed out. "It would be gentlemanly of you to offer one of them."

Balthazar took a slow swallow. "When have I ever been a gentleman?"

Lucas stared at him. "It's raining cats and dogs. The banks are closed. Do you truly expect her to sleep in the streets?"

"She's not my responsibility."

"No, but I think she's redeemed herself enough to deserve some charity."

Balthazar downed another mouthful of brandy and set the glass down. "Fine. I'm going out anyway."

"In this weather?"

"That's why the Chinese invented umbrellas."

"I won't ask where," Lucas muttered. "Do you want the carriage?"

"No, I'll walk."

It was late, but he knew places where they'd open the door to him at any hour. He decided to visit Honey's in Covent Garden. Balthazar had very few ironclad rules, but one was that he never patronized establishments that sold children – which ruled out most of the brothels in London. The women at Honey's were paid well and treated well. The owner was a shrewd but big-hearted woman who didn't tolerate misbehavior. Her reputation attracted the loveliest, most skilled girls, in turn making her house exceedingly profitable. He knew she wouldn't bat an eyelash if he turned up in the middle of the night.

Lucas nodded. "I'll tell Miss Everleigh she can have the teal room."

"I doubt she'll accept," Balthazar remarked. "She seems perfectly self-sufficient to me."

Lucas shook his head and left. Balthazar drew a bath. He took his time shaving and dressing. When he went back downstairs, the drawing room was empty, with only a single lamp left burning. With luck, Zarifa was gone. If not, the banks would be opening by the time he returned and she'd have no reason to linger.

His top hat waited on a table next to the front door. Balthazar put it on, grabbed an umbrella from the stand, and set off into the stormy darkness.

COUNTESS KATYA VON JÜRGENSBURG WAS DOZING BY THE fire when she heard a brisk knock at the front door. She startled awake, managing by long experience not to spill the half-drunk glass of sherry in her hand. Business had been slow since the turn of the year, and on this filthy Sunday night, it was non-existent. Most of the customers came and went before eleven o'clock. It was now past three. If the sherry hadn't made her drowsy, she would have been up to bed hours ago.

The knocker sounded again, more insistent this time.

"Will someone *please* answer the door?" she cried imperiously.

"Sorry, my lady," a breathless voice called down the stairs. It sounded like Charlotte.

The countess had been born Gertrude Acker of Blackpool, where her father operated a fish and chips stand on the promenade. She began her career as a fortune-teller, but quickly realized there was far more money entertaining the gentlemen who took the train down from London to sample the delights of the seaside resort. She already went by Katya for business purposes – no one wanted their fortune told by Gertrude Acker – and it was a simple matter to append the title of countess. She adopted a vaguely European accent and air of tragic mystery, which doubled her profits.

Unlike the other girls, who spent their earnings on stockings and French perfume, she lived modestly at home (still claiming to her parents that she read tarot cards) until she had saved enough to rent a house in London.

Upon arrival, the countess had sensibly made friends of several other well-established madams, learning which policemen to bribe and how much, who could be trusted to hire as security, and a hundred other details. The countess had once been beaten so badly she was bedridden for two months. It was long before and the scars had faded, but the experience was not forgotten. She politely but firmly made it clear to new clients that her girls were valuable and any complaints would bar the offender from returning. Some men balked at that, but there was no shortage of disorderly houses catering to every taste. And those who broke the rules would find themselves tossed out by a pair of giants named Thom and Billy, both of whom had brothers on the Metropolitan force.

In short, trouble was a rare event at Honey's. So rare that she had given Thom and Billy the night off. Now she felt a twinge of unease. Who could be calling at such an hour? Perhaps she shouldn't have told Charlotte to open the door after all.

She rose as the girl entered, her cheeks flushed.

"It's him!" Charlotte hissed. "The Hungarian!"

The countess let out a sigh of relief. "Well, don't keep him waiting in the hall! Bring him in at once."

She unconsciously patted her hair into place and thrust her bosom out, smoothing the dark silk dress around her

KAT ROSS

ample hips. The Hungarian was her favorite client, and she generally felt indifference toward her patrons, if not outright dislike. He was handsome as sin, a generous tipper, and had impeccable manners. She also found it amusing that he was an actual count. He had to know her own title was a charade, but he never let on.

"Countess von Jürgensburg, I must apologize for the ungodly hour of my visit," he said with a slight accent, bending over to kiss her hand.

"My lord," she said smoothly, also in a foreign accent, though hers was more decidedly Slavic. "Don't be silly. I'm always delighted to see you. As are my young ladies."

"You look radiant this evening." He smiled. "I'm afraid they'll pale in comparison."

The countess laughed. "I have several new girls since last you visited. I'm sure one will be to your liking. Do sit down." She frowned at his bedraggled coat. "Did you *walk*, my lord?"

"I've just returned from a long journey. I wanted to stretch my legs."

"Ah. By sea?" She knew he was a collector of some kind – the countess kept tabs on all her clients – but not even the most avid gossips seemed to have a clue where his money came from.

"A tour of the Orient," he said, offering nothing else.

The countess took the hint. "Would you care for a drink?"

He often took brandy, but now he shook his head. "Thank you, no."

"Then if you'll excuse me, my lord, I'll fetch the young ladies."

He was staring into the fire with a distracted look.

"Do you have any special requests?" she prodded delicately.

Unlike most men, the Hungarian wasn't fixated on a particular type. His whims were capricious. She'd seen him pass over raving beauties for girls that were just shy of plain. But she always asked anyway.

"What?" He looked up. "Yes, as a matter of fact. . . . Are any of the young ladies blond? And petite."

"I have just the one," she said.

The girls were eavesdropping at the top of the stairs. At the countess's approach, they prodded one of their number forward with amused smirks.

"I suppose you heard everything," the countess said, her accent pure Blackpool again. "Mary, you're up."

She was a lovely girl, pale and ethereal, with light golden hair and the sort of fragile, doll-like features that brought out either the best or the worst in the male species. Some would take pleasure in destroying her beauty, and the countess was glad she'd found the girl before it happened.

Mary peeked down the stairs. "Is he as handsome as they say?"

"Come see for yourself," the countess replied tartly. "I don't care to keep him waiting."

"Oh, no!" The girl pinched her cheeks to put some color in them. "Of course not."

She glided prettily down the stairs in her linen shift, which was trimmed with lace. Count Koháry rose to his feet when he saw her. His expression didn't alter and the countess feared he was displeased, but then he seemed to visibly take hold of himself. It was quite peculiar, she thought. Almost the way one might down a stiff drink in preparation for some odious task. The flush in Mary cheeks faded. She looked uncertain. Then his face softened into a smile.

"What's your name?" he asked.

"Mary, my lord," she said, giving a curtsy.

"Enchanted." The count kissed her hand quite elegantly and Mary blushed. She took his arm and led him up the stairs.

The countess sighed and poured a fresh sherry. Sometimes

the Hungarian was quick, but other times he lingered for hours. There was no telling how long it would be before she could go to bed. She stretched her feet toward the fire, listening to the rain hiss outside. It really was a dreadful night. She'd have to summon a cab. Surely he'd be too worn out to walk home.

She was just dozing off again when she heard the front door slam. She set her glass aside and hurried upstairs. Mary sat on the bed in her room, crying softly. She was wrapped in a sheet. Anne and Charlotte sat on either side, stroking her hair.

"Did he hurt you?" the countess asked, quite taken aback. Nothing like this had ever occurred before – not with the count, at least.

Mary shook her head.

"Did he *pay* you?"

This earned a sullen nod. The countess spotted a wad of bills on the dresser. She quickly counted it. The amount was more than enough for three girls at once, plus an obscenely large tip.

"Then what are you wailing about?" she demanded.

"He didn't even touch me!" Mary exclaimed. "Just sort of collapsed on the bed. I undressed and sat in his lap. I kissed him. And . . . ." Her lip quivered.

"There, there. What did he do?"

"Nothing!" She gulped. "He just sat there, staring into space like a bleeding statue. He couldn't . . . . "

Charlotte suddenly giggled and Mary glared at her. "You see? I'll be a laughingstock!"

Her friends shared a quizzical look. "Did you show him your tits?" Lucy asked.

"Yes, and he just rubbed his forehead like the sight of 'em gave him a headache!"

"That *is* odd," Charlotte ventured with a frown. "I heard he really fancies tits. All shapes and sizes—"

"That's enough of that," the countess said firmly. "I'm sure it's nothing to do with you, Mary. Men are mercurial creatures. You should be grateful he saved you the trouble."

"That's one way of looking at," Lucy agreed. "I had him once. He kept his clothes on, hardly let me touch him. But the things he did . . ." She sighed. "When he left, I told milord I ought to pay *him*."

Mary burst into a fresh round of sobs.

THE RELENTLESS DRIZZLE SOAKED HIM TO THE SKIN AS Balthazar stalked back to Mayfair. In his eagerness to escape, he'd left both hat and umbrella in the foyer, but that was the least of his worries.

It wasn't the inability to perform. He had no particular urge to feed. He felt as young and strong as the day he'd left London. Besides which, intercourse was overrated. He often found that giving a woman pleasure was enough to satisfy him.

No, it was the complete lack of desire.

That was something new. And hugely problematic.

Because Balthazar *was* aroused. Painfully so.

Just not for the girl at Honey's.

He considered walking the streets until dawn. It wouldn't be the first time. But it was raining hard, and he was damned if he'd be exiled from his own house.

A few more hours and she'd be gone from his life forever.

He took the front steps two at a time and burst through the door. He'd have another brandy in the study. Maybe three or four. The instant the sun rose, he'd make Lucas rouse her from the guest room—

Balthazar halted his charge toward the stairs. Candlelight flickered at the end of the hall. It was coming from the kitchen. He paced down the hall and stopped in the doorway.

"What do you think you're doing?" he demanded.

Zarifa turned around. She had a plate in her hand. "I'm hungry."

"That's my cake." He scowled. "And my shirt."

She stuffed a huge forkful of cake in her mouth. He watched her chew and swallow.

"I'll give it back tomorrow." Zarifa looked him over. "You're dripping wet, Balthazar." She helped herself to more cake. "Would you like a piece? Speak now. I might finish it if you don't."

"You've done something to me," he snarled. "I don't know what it is. But I want it to *stop*."

"You're only fixated on me because I turned you down," she scoffed.

His eyes flashed with outrage. "You didn't turn me down. You drugged and robbed me!"

"What's your point?" She stuck another forkful of cake in her mouth.

"My *point* is that I've been turned down before." He laughed. "Do you honestly believe no woman has ever refused me? In two millennia?" Balthazar raked a hand through his hair. "Not many, it's true, but you're hardly the first!"

Zarifa set her plate aside and reached into the icebox for the milk Lucas took in his tea. The housekeeper had strict instructions to keep the larder stocked at all times, even when they were away.

"I didn't put a hex on you, if that's what you're implying," she said in an amused tone. She looked around at the multitude of cupboards. "Where are the glasses?"

"I'm not telling you."

Zarifa shrugged. Balthazar seethed as she tipped her head back and drank straight from the bottle. It was deplorable manners, he thought sourly. Not to mention indescribably erotic.

"Maybe not a hex. But you've done *something*," he grated. "I don't know. Some kind of talisman . . . ."

Zarifa returned the empty milk bottle to the icebox. Lucas would pitch a fit when he woke up.

"You'll get over it," she said over her shoulder, bending lower to rummage for something else to devour.

"I won't. I've tried." He exhaled as the shirt rode up, unable to tear his gaze from those strong thighs. "You've no idea how much I despise myself right now."

Zarifa turned. She smiled sweetly. "If it's any consolation, you aren't the only one."

Something snapped. Balthazar stepped forward, looming over her. "I want you out of my house," he said coldly.

"It's the middle of the night!" She rose to her full height and seemed to realize how close they were, mere inches away, for she bit her lip in the most adorable fashion.

"I told you, I'll pay for a hotel. But this entire situation is intolerable."

They stood there for a moment, Balthazar's hands braced against the icebox on either side of her waist.

He knew he had no excuse this time. He was behaving like a pig. But he was beyond caring.

Zarifa laid a palm on his shirtfront. His heart sped up.

"I happen to agree," she said evenly. "What shall we do about it?"

He leaned closer, his mouth hovering just above her ear. "Are you offering yourself to me?" Balthazar asked softly.

She raised her own lips so they brushed the line of his jaw. "No," she whispered.

He pulled back, clinging to self-control by a thread. Maybe *this* was the madness the witch prophesied for him. To be raked over the coals again and again—

"I might, though. If you beg," she said with a wicked smile. "On your knees, Balthazar."

He went very still. Zarifa's breath caught. He saw her wonder if she'd pushed him too far.

Apparently, there was no such thing.

Balthazar gave a low laugh. "I thought you'd never ask."

He sank down and curled warm fingers around her bare knee. He could spend hours just on that knee. Balthazar gazed up at her with a solemn expression. "Please let me ravish you, Miss Everleigh."

His hand slid higher, thumb caressing her thigh just below the hem of his shirt. "Pretty . . . pretty . . . pretty . . . please."

With each *pretty*, he bent his head and kissed her. Zarifa knotted her fingers in his damp hair.

She cleared her throat, her voice ragged. "Well, since you asked so politely——"

She gasped as he suddenly stood, lifting her in his arms. Balthazar took the stairs two at a time. One swift kick to his bedroom door and they were inside. He set her on her feet, his heart thumping in his chest. Zarifa's black eyes speared him.

"I have another condition," she said.

He let out a long breath. "Name it."

"You have to take that off." She stared at the ouroboros. "I won't be drained by you, Balthazar."

"I wouldn't dream of it," he murmured with a frown. "What do you take me for?"

"Exactly what you are," Zarifa replied with a fond laugh.

He lifted the talisman from around his neck. "Turn around," he said playfully.

She did. Balthazar locked it in his wall safe, glancing over his shoulder to make sure she hadn't cheated. When it was safely stowed away with the sword, he watched her for a moment. No woman had ever worn his shirt quite like Zarifa Everleigh.

He removed his wet coat and tossed it to the floor. The rest of his clothes followed.

"It's safe," he declared.

She spun and looked him up and down with a lazy regard that set his blood pumping. "I don't think it is."

Balthazar closed the space between them. He took her hand and pressed it against his heart. Looking into her dark, almond-shaped eyes, the warmth of her body seeping through the thin layer of broadcloth between them, Balthazar knew he would happily endure the Trials ten times over as long as it ended with this woman in his bed.

"You see?" she murmured, her palm pressed against his bare chest. "I told you it wasn't broken."

"It was a little bit," he said softly, kissing the hollow beneath her ear.

"That's worrisome. Perhaps we'd better made sure everything else is in working order." Her breath caught as he pressed more firmly against her. "On second thought, I think I can vouch for that already."

He slid a hand under the shirt to caress the velvety skin of her back.

"Zarifa?"

"Yes?" she managed, arching against him in a way that was extremely dangerous.

"No more talking." His hand slid lower, finding her round bottom. "Just for a little while."

Their lips met, a feather-light brush. Zarifa twined her arms around his neck. Balthazar deepened the kiss, the sweet taste of her shattering the last shreds of his self-control. He held her against him with one palm braced in the center of her back, his fingers tugging at the laces of her knickers. Zarifa drew a sharp breath as he lifted one leg and pinioned it against his hip.

"But . . ." Her lower lip caught between her teeth. "Oh!"

A SQUARE OF LIGHT CREPT SLOWLY UP THE BED, WHICH HAD moved several feet from its starting point and now sat directly in the path of the sun. When it hit Balthazar's face, he woke. Not with a groggy, painful start as was often the case in the mornings, but with a pleasantly languid return to consciousness.

He reached across the bed, eyes still closed, seeking her warm, naked body. He wasn't half done with her. In fact, he'd only stopped the night before out of mercy to them both. But his desire for her wasn't even remotely quenched . . . . His fingers groped further, finding nothing but rumpled sheets.

Balthazar sat up, his hair wild. The bed was empty.

And the safe door hung slightly ajar.

He sprang to his feet and raced over, heart in his mouth.

The sword was there.

The ouroboros was there.

Everything else was gone.

He squinted. Or not quite . . . Something glimmered in the very back.

A silver crucifix. Folded inside a brief note.

I think you need this more than I do, sweetling.

Balthazar stared at the note for a long moment. Then he burst out laughing.

He threw on a dressing gown and galloped down the stairs, where Lucas was sitting at the kitchen table reading the newspaper. He looked cleaned and pressed, his mustache waxed into little points.

"The cook came by," Lucas said. "There's coffee and all the unhealthy things you like. I had porridge." He frowned. "You look happy this morning."

"I've been robbed again," Balthazar announced, pouncing on his eggs and toast.

There was a dire silence. Lucas stared at him. "By Miss Everleigh, I presume?"

"None other." Balthazar bit into a piece of bacon and chewed. Gods, he was starving.

"What did she take this time?" Lucas asked in a neutral tone.

"Oh, a few baubles." He smiled.

"Not the sword?"

"No."

"Nor the ouroboros?"

Balthazar shook his head, still grinning idiotically.

"Thank God for that."

"Hmmm. Is there more bacon?" He rose and plundered the sideboard for a second helping.

"Still," Lucas mused. "She's not very nice, is she?"

Balthazar chuckled over his shoulder. "Why do you think I like her?"

"So you're not angry?"

"Angry? Not at all. I think she's rather wonderful."

He sat down and finished his breakfast. Lucas returned to the paper.

"We should go to the house on Lake Baikal tonight," Balthazar said. "I'll keep the sword there."

"That's wise," Lucas murmured. "Since she seems to have no trouble cracking your safe." He paused. "Do you think we'll ever see her again?"

The question evoked a complicated tangle of feelings Balthazar couldn't even begin to address. Nor did he care to try. It cut too deeply to the bone.

"I doubt it," he replied wistfully. He patted the crucifix, which now rested next to the ouroboros. "But it was lovely while it lasted, wasn't it?"

ZARIFA WAS WAITING OUTSIDE DRUMMOND'S BANK WHEN A clerk unlocked the doors at nine o'clock sharp. She showed him the key and explained which box she wanted. The clerk led her to a small room and retrieved the box in question, then retreated to give her privacy.

Zarifa drew a deep breath and opened the box. As Mortlake said, it held only a few hundred pounds, though that would be enough to get back on her feet. The contents were mainly loose papers – receipts, invoices, sketches – and a small, fat diary bound in red leather. When she saw the book, Zarifa felt a rush of relief. It was Mortlake's Bible, containing meticulous records of all his clients, including notes indicating which ones he'd betrayed and which remained in good standing.

There were dozens of names, with addresses throughout Europe and the Ottoman East; even a few in America. Her eyebrows rose at some of the titles. Dukes and padishahs, prime ministers and captains of industry. All fabulously wealthy collectors of occult and magical objects.

Zarifa felt confident she could gain introductions as Mortlake's daughter. As for the ones who had blacklisted him . . . well, she would invent a new identity for herself. She'd make a start with the talismans from Balthazar's safe, though that wasn't the reason she'd stolen from him.

It had been a way to irrevocably sever all ties between them. If she were ever tempted to seek him out again, she need only remind herself that such a reunion would be extremely awkward.

In truth, she liked him rather a lot. And if she allowed the relationship to go any further . . . well, there was no future with such a man, so why go through the inevitable suffering?

Zarifa doubted he'd bother coming after her. She'd taken only minor talismans – except the one for Traveling, which was too valuable to cede. If Balthazar did try to pursue, he would find no trail to follow.

She was organizing the papers in her satchel (also borrowed) when she noticed a folded sheet of foolscap at the bottom of the box. It had her name penned in Mortlake's hurried scrawl.

Dearest daughter,
If you are reading this, I am dead. And there are things I must share that I never dared to tell you while I was alive.

Zarifa frowned, a knot forming in her stomach.

I know I was a poor father. I treated you with callous disregard. I abandoned you for long periods without a word. But it was only because I cared for you deeply and did not want you to suffer the pain of loving a monster. I saw what it did to your mother. It was better for you to despise me. But please know that your welfare and happiness was always uppermost in my thoughts. I hope you can forgive me.
John Mortlake

Zarifa set the paper down with dry eyes. She locked the empty box.

"Self-serving to the end," she muttered. "Now that he is gone, he wants to be remembered as someone else. To have his cake and eat it too. Well, to hell with that!"

She crumpled the letter and dropped it to the floor. Then she strode to the door, where the clerk awaited her.

"You may close the deposit box," she said. "I won't need it anymore."

Zarifa stepped into the street. Crowds rushed along the sidewalks. They'd been washed clean by the rain and the air was uncommonly fresh for grimy, coal-blackened London. She decided to go buy a hat. A large fancy one with feathers.

This marks the first chapter of a new tale, she thought, strolling down Charing Cross in search of a haberdasher. The story of a girl from Alexandria who became the greatest thief the world ever saw.

She considered the little red diary, her imagination taking flight.

And it begins thus . . . .

THE MAHARAJA OF BHURTPORE WAS A MAN OF REFINED TASTE and good judgment, as all his wives and courtesans could attest to. His collection of rare objects was the envy of all the other nobles, for the Maharaja was not only rich, but well-connected. None knew the source of his talismans and this secret he guarded most jealously.

Until one day when the Maharaja was taking his usual luncheon of stewed chickens fed exclusively on a special diet of saffron. His hazir-bashi approached with a bow.

"You have a visitor, O Great King," he said.

"Who is it?" The Maharaja wiped his mouth with a silken sleeve, a bit annoyed to be interrupted during his repast. He preferred his meals in silence, which his court physician advised was conducive to digestion in the heat of the day.

The hazir-bashi uttered a name. The Maharaja arched a thin brow. He made a small gesture with one bejeweled finger.

It was a woman, modestly clothed and veiled, but of a shape that pleased the Maharaja's discriminating eye. For he was a man of refined taste and good judgment, as all his servants and retainers could attest to.

"I have a gift for you," she said, kneeling in a humble manner that befit both their ranks.

In her hands was a satchel, and in the satchel were many wondrous things.

The Maharaja smiled.

AFTERWORD

We've reached the end — but not *The End*. Rest assured there will be many more Gaslamp Gothic books to come, particularly since the cast seems to keep growing. In the meantime, I'm finishing up my Lingua Magika trilogy, which is quite different but equally entertaining, I hope.

If you're curious about Balthazar's past as a necromancer serving under Queen Neblis and haven't read the Fourth Element series, Book #1, The Midnight Sea, is free to download at all online booksellers.

And take a moment to sign up for my newsletter at www.katrossbooks.com so you don't miss any new releases!

ACKNOWLEDGMENTS

Huge thanks (as always) to Laura Pilli, who loves these characters as much as I do and can be relied upon to forcefully yank me back from the precipice when needed. To Leonie Henderson, for her wit and wisdom. And to Jennifer Wu, for kindly agreeing to read and critique, not to mention sharing her sourdough secrets.

Last but never least, for all the wonderful folks at Acorn publishing for their talent and support.

ABOUT THE AUTHOR

Kat Ross worked as a journalist at the United Nations for ten years before happily falling back into what she likes best: making stuff up. She's the author of the Fourth Element and Fourth Talisman fantasy series, the Gaslamp Gothic adventures, and the new Lingua Magika trilogy. She loves myths, monsters and doomsday scenarios.

www.katrossbooks.com
kat@katrossbooks.com

facebook.com/KatRossAuthor

instagram.com/katross2014

bookbub.com/authors/kat-ross

pinterest.com/katrosswriter

ALSO BY KAT ROSS